Ready Or Not?

Grace Wynne-Jones

Published by Accent Press 2007

Copyright © 2003 Grace Wynne-Jones

ISBN 1905170653/9781905170654

Cover design by Joëlle Brindley

Grace Wynne-Jones was born and brought up in Ireland and has also lived in Africa, the US and England. She has a deep interest in psychology, spirituality and healing and she also loves to celebrate the strangeness and wonders of ordinary life and love. She has frequently been praised for the warm belly-laugh humour and tender poignancy in her writing and has been described as 'a novelist who tells the truth about the human heart'.

Her feature articles have appeared in many magazines and national papers in Ireland and in England and her radio play *Ebb Tide* was broadcast on RTE 1. Her short stories have been published in magazines in Ireland, England and Australia, and have also been broadcast on RTE and BBC Radio 4. She is the author of four critically acclaimed novels: *Ordinary Miracles*, *Wise Follies*, *Ready Or Not?* and *The Truth Club*. She has written and broadcast a number of talks for RTE's 'Living Word' and 'Sunday Miscellany' and has been included in the book 'Sunday Miscellany A Selection From 2004 - 2006' (New Island). She also contributed to the travel book 'Travelling Light' (Tivoli).

Please visit her website for more information:

www.gracewynnejones.com

For my dear brother Patrick Wynne-Jones

ACKNOWLEDGMENTS

A huge thank you goes to my agent, Lisa Eveleigh, for all her hard work and savvy and support. Heartfelt thanks also go to Hazel Cushion of the wonderful Accent Press for being such a dedicated, dynamic and creative publisher. I am also extremely grateful to Joëlle Brindley for the wonderful jacket artwork. And Alison Walsh gave me enormous help and encouragement with this book. She really cared about the characters and her input was invaluable. Thanks also go to Tana French for her well honed skills and support. I'd also like to thank: all my friends, both at home and abroad, my lovely neighbours in Bray, the very wise Jonathan Hutson, Gilly Smith, John O'Donohue, Maura Egan, Nicola Warwick, Joe Griffin, Joe Keveny, Noirin Callanan, Peadar Nolan, Anne Doody and Denise Walker of the Ulster Bank, Philip Casey for his support and friendship, Gran and dearest Mum and Dad, computer expert Tim Wynne-Jones, the Writers' and Translators' Centre of Rhodes, everyone at the Heyokah Retreat Center in beautiful New Mexico, cat lover extraordinaire Jane Carr and darling Puddy. And I want to say a really enormous 'thank you' to my brother Pat who gave me a lot of support with this book when I was sharing a house with him in Horsham, West Sussex. He was a real pal and supplier of biscuits and much more. Gratitude also goes to various pals in wonderfully 'alternative' Totnes in Devon, including Colin and Helen Moore, Philomena Wynne and Julie

Turner. A big printed bunch of pink roses to all the lovely readers who wrote to me about my other novels. I really treasure their letters. And of course love and light is sent to my various 'helpers' and to the characters in this novel who let me into their lives and shared their hearts' longings...and who taught me so much about the meaning of love.

PRAISE FOR *READY OR NOT?*

'The story, at times poignant, at times embarrassingly funny, keeps you interested right to the end…This is the perfect summer read.' Woman's Way

'…this is one of the best Irish novels this year…The trip to Greece is steeped in olives and jasmine, cicadas and sunshine…readers will love the local gigolo, Dimitri. Grace writes with great humour…On a more serious note, her portrayal of friendship, commitment and the complexity of relationships is very real and most enjoyable.' Valerie Cox, Evening Herald, 2003

'Love, remarks Grace Wynne-Jones in her latest tilt at romance….is like the Tour de France; heightened expectations and then the riders sweep by in seconds. The romantic progress in and out of bed…is chartered with wit and style by Grace Wynne-Jones through the age of McDonalds, nightclub encounters, Continental train propositions, angst-ridden parental relationships, turbulence on land and in the air and the restorative powers of bridge.' Mayo News

'At times poignant and hilarious…' Mourne Observer & County Down News

'Thought-provoking, original and hugely enjoyable.' Katie Fforde

'One summer; four people on the cusp of change in a Dublin that's throwing them up choices they never knew they had. Gorgeous Caddy and her secret, smart but lonely Roz, Tom who's always settled for less, movie-star Dan who's sizing up Caddy's restlessness like a barometer. Paths cross, dreams stretch and pop: all seasoned with zest…' RTE Guide

'A lively story woven round the lives of four creative Dubliners and the tangled mess they have made of their love lives…the humour leaps off the page and ping-pongs like rapid fire between the characters. When they're not jibbing with each other, they're tearing each other's clothes off!' U Magazine

PRAISE FOR *ORDINARY MIRACLES*

'Wynne-Jones's sense of humour and the self-mockery of her heroine makes it both funny and touching.' Times Literary Supplement

'Funny, heartwarming and special.' Marian Keyes

'Wonderfully dry…I really enjoyed it.' Catherine Alliott

'Beautiful, tender and funny, written with great perception…a remarkable novel.' Katie Fforde

'The belly-laugh being a rare enough commodity on this planet, this promises to be one of my favourite novels of the year…very very funny.' In Dublin

'Grace Wynne-Jones writes up a storm of wit in her first novel…a fine new writer.' RTE Guide

'*Ordinary Miracles* has that rare combination of depth, honesty and wit…and all of this backed by a deliciously soft, gentle and loving humour…If you try one new author, try Grace Wynne-Jones.' OK Magazine

'She has an assured style and a wonderful insight into the separated lady's lot…I couldn't put it down. I literally read it from cover to cover.' Muriel Bolger, 'No Jacket Required' RTE Radio One

'A delight of love, laughs and starting again…which is very far from ordinary.' Yvonne Roberts

'*Ordinary Miracles* is about relationships and love and sex and a little bit of guilt. Jasmine is a worried and witty heroine…an engagingly high-spirited and perceptive debut.' The Irish Independent

'I really enjoyed it.' Shakti Gawain, bestselling author of 'Creative Visualisation'

Ordinary Miracles – ISBN 9781905170647   £6.99

PRAISE FOR *WISE FOLLIES*

'Grace Wynne-Jones has a wicked sense of humour which enlivens every page...Alice and her friends, and her hilarious magazine assignments, at times leave the reader rocking with laughter.' The Irish Times

'*Wise Follies* is a smooth refreshing read...Bring tissues and a paper bag to laugh into when you read this book outside the privacy of your home.' Irish Tatler

'This fresh new voice will appeal to women of all ages.' Publishing News

'A quirky, hilarious novel.' What's On

'Sharp, funny and moving.' Woman & Home

'When you think Alice, think Bridget Fonda chasing Matt Dillon in 'Singles', think Kirsty MacColl singing, 'I put you on a pedestal/You put me on the pill'...this is a novel about finding yourself, and we can't but cheer for Alice's gradual emancipation.' Irish Examiner

'A superior romance full of wit, honesty and perception.' RTE Guide

'A gently amusing account of finding love in the nineties, an enjoyable read written with an observant wit.' Books Magazine.

'This may sound like Bridget Jones territory but Alice is less spikey, certainly drinks less and makes more effort to make a life for herself...The writing is full of quirky wit and energy.' 'Book of the Week' The Express

'....hilarious and touching.' She

Wise Follies – ISBN 9781905170630   £6.99

AVAILABLE AUGUST 2007

Also by Grace Wynne-Jones

The Truth Club – ISBN 9781905170661   £6.99

Prologue

THERE WERE MANY MYSTERIES that summer. One of them was why four people who had so much to share had seldom felt so alone. They were all ready for love, but they wanted it to happen in a certain way, and so they didn't notice its tender though enigmatic entreaties. They were also unwilling to admit that what they believed they wanted might have altered, that life was guiding them towards deeper and more enduring affections. Certainly Tom Armstrong's thoughts on love had radically altered since he took the photograph. And yet, when he looked at that young girl running towards her lover, the memories came flooding back to him, fresh and bright and new.

Looking back, it seems like I was waiting for her outside the National College of Art and Design, though I couldn't have known she would appear. When she ran towards him I lifted my camera and – click – the image was captured. My hands were steady but my heart was pounding, just like hers must have been. I hadn't known the force of love until that moment – how it can change and free you, set you alight with its wonderful, crazy conviction. I hadn't known that it can make a pretty face beautiful. And she is beautiful, the woman in my photograph.

I'd seen her around college, but we'd never met. She usually sat with a group of friends in the canteen. Sometimes they were serious, and sometimes they laughed so hard they almost fell off their chairs. They looked so wild and confident I wouldn't have dared to approach them. I could have spoken to her if she was alone, but she never was.

I was a photography student, and Dublin still felt new but was becoming familiar. Even the aroma of freshly ground coffee in Grafton Street no longer seemed so exotic. Capital cities creep up on you. When you first arrive, you might as well be in Marrakech; and then one day you belong, and it's

1

the place you've left that seems strange.

I somehow feel the woman in my photograph would understand that. There's something about her – a freshness, an innocence – that seems to come from another place. I felt this about her even when she was spluttering at some joke with her friends over coffee. I sensed that she had left somewhere so that she might know the secret longings of her heart. And she found them. You can see it in her eyes, her smile, the blur of her feet on the pavement.

The minute she stepped out of the college that evening, she started looking. Her face was tight with anxiety. Would he be there? Had they missed each other? Her cotton dress was light yellow and covered in tiny pink flowers. I'd only seen her in jeans before. She stood on tiptoe, trying to see over the crowds. She bit her lower lip and peered down the busy street. Then she started to fiddle with a silver bracelet on her arm, as if embarrassed. She lowered her head in disappointment. And then she looked up and saw him.

He was tall and still and standing at the other side of the street. Her face lit up. I didn't know a face could just light up like that, grow so luminous and certain. He must have smiled, because she smiled back and waved. Her feet danced with impatience as she waited to cross the street. He was hungry for her. You could see it in the way he stood. Then the sun burst out from behind the clouds and they were both ablaze with waiting.

She walked at first, slowly and steadily. Her eyes grew bright and excited as she began to run, headlong and sure, without a second's hesitation. Her dress billowed around her legs and her long hair flew wildly in the breeze. And suddenly there was this smile on her lips. The smile of an unexpected and huge happiness.

I knew the moment. Sensed it as the shutter clicked.

It was just before she reached him.

Chapter One

WHITE THINGS WERE FLOATING around Caddy Lavelle's bedroom. In her half-asleep state she thought they might be angels, or snow. Of course, snow didn't normally fall in one's bedroom in June. Perhaps it was just one of those things that happened when you moved house... She turned over and ignored the miracle. When you were half or fully asleep these things happened all the time. She had spent the previous hour chatting with Matisse about his collages and was keen to resume the conversation.

'Atishoo!' One of the white things was tickling her nose. She looked at it. It was a feather – and it came from her pillow. Feck it, anyway. That was what came of not bothering to put on a pillowcase. They must have been leaking all night, and now the breeze from the open window was hurling them around the room.

Caddy rubbed her eyes sleepily. Waking was never particularly easy for her. It would have helped her to know that lots of people feel like this; but, like lots of people, she believed her feelings were so odd they must surely be unique. There was a terrible and unnecessary loneliness to this belief, since it was so often completely inaccurate. For who does not feel incomplete and not quite prepared for life's mysteries?

And who is not wary of love, once they have known its wounds?

'Feathers,' she muttered to herself. 'And they'll be all over the place now. I must get new pillows.'

She had fallen onto her futon the night before after drinking far too much wine with a friend called Roz. Their excuse for this overindulgence had been swimming. Roz had recently spent a small fortune joining a leisure centre and now felt deluged with guilt because she hardly ever went to it. So the obvious solution was to get drunk.

'We're lost causes,' Roz had declared happily.

3

'Not completely lost,' Caddy had corrected. 'After all, we've only had three and a half packets of crisps.'

Caddy did not wake with much of a hangover, because she'd drunk plenty of water before she went to bed. One cannot reach forty without gathering a certain amount of knowledge. For example, she also knew that she must never carry bananas in her handbag, or fall in love with anyone until she'd worked out why she was so bad at it and therefore would not repeat the same mistakes.

That was why meeting Dan MacIntyre had not caused her to jump in the air and shout, 'Yippee!' In fact, she had felt more like clutching her stomach. He was gorgeous, there was no denying that, but he had behaved like a freak. First of all, he didn't seem to think there was anything particularly wrong with her, which meant he must be spectacularly unobservant. How disappointed he would be when he found out the truth! Also, he had pursued her far too rigorously, which was unnatural. Men were the ones who were supposed to dither infuriatingly, which gave women time to make up their minds and feel a bit hurt and rejected. This was all good preparation for the inevitable imperfections of a relationship. And it was also a wonderful excuse not to have one. Caddy had been using it for ages.

Of course, some women seemed to sail through life meeting suitable men and fitting them neatly into lives that were already fulfilling. But for others, such as herself and Roz – and, frankly, nearly all her close friends – the whole man-woman thing was crazily unsatisfactory. They had tried so bloody hard. It wasn't as if they hadn't made the effort. But it was still like Mills & Boon meets that film where everyone gets chased by giant worms.

Actually, the giant-worm film had been quite fun to watch. Caddy and her teenaged daughter Jemma had chomped corn crisps and hidden behind cushions during the entire thing. They had even screamed. It was wonderful rubbish. Watching stupid television together was one of their many pleasures. But now Jemma was staying with cousins in Arizona for the

4

summer... new house... absent daughter... feathers... it just didn't feel quite right.

At times like this Caddy was very glad she was a parallel woman. This meant that she could have two parallel trains of thought in her head at the same time. So, even when life seemed too odd, mysterious or just plain lonely, she could still summon the resolve to floss her teeth and shave her legs. It was this part of her that had moved house, and now it wanted her to get up and unpack the boxes. It was also making her dimly aware that life can open or close you and that she was at some sort of crossroads. But, as is so often the case, it was not clearly marked. And of course there was always the possibility that some eejit might have come along and moved the signpost in the middle of the night.

'I am a wonderfully wise and balanced person... and I am going to have an adventurous summer.'

It suddenly seemed a good time to say a positive affirmation. Her cocker spaniel Chump, who adored his gentle mistress, clearly agreed with her: he licked her face in encouragement. She patted his belly in gratitude. A good dog was a great comfort.

'I am not going to hide away and watch too much telly and think everyone is better than I am,' she continued. 'And I am going to appreciate myself, and I am also not going to be bossed around by my mother.'

She immediately felt a bit better, and Chump went, 'Woof'.

'I have worked very hard at moving house, and now I am going to pace myself. I am not going to try to do everything at once.' It was wonderful how sane and wise one could sound even if one didn't feel it!

Caddy happily lay back on her leaky pillow. 'I will have firmer thighs, and I will not spend hours wondering how on earth I have ended up like I am and feeling that it was all supposed to be more straightforward.' Her large blue eyes shone with determination. She would get better at being happy and feeling less burdened and dutiful. Now that she'd finished marking exam papers, she was a free woman. Thank God for the summer holidays!

Caddy had wanted to be an artist, but everyone had said that being something else would be far more sensible. So she had become an art history teacher. A good one. She cared about her pupils and drew things out of them – not just details about Chagall or Rembrandt, but their own stories, needs and dreams. She gave this gift passionately because it was the gift she most needed to receive. Like many people, she had reached forty without anyone ever asking her who she was and what she wanted. And now she hardly dared to ask these things herself.

It is unpleasant but not at all uncommon to reach this stage of timidity. And with it comes a terrible impatience, because one knows there is a part of oneself that isn't timid at all. It can love fully and dance to its own music and make peace with sorrow and life's multitudinous imperfections. But how do you reach it? Sometimes it seems so distant it might as well be in Outer Mongolia, even when it is stored carefully in your heart.

Caddy didn't like to think of hearts in the romantic sense because hers had been broken so purposefully. She had loved the young man who had become Jemma's father so fully and madly that she had almost been destroyed. She hadn't even known that love can almost obliterate you, so that had been an added shock. She had run towards it with a nice sense of annihilation, a wonderful sense of losing herself to something and someone. How much she had wanted to be bigger and brighter and something else! Even the memory made her frown.

Men liked Caddy's frown, though she assumed it was exactly the sort of thing that would put them off. It was fierce and innocent and unexpected. She was a passionate woman, and, though she had ceased to believe in passion, her features couldn't lie. She had an oval face and smooth olive skin that tanned easily, apart from the backs of her legs. And – this would have surprised her – sometimes she looked calm and peaceful and a deep gentleness shone from her eyes.

'You should be an actress,' one boyfriend had said. But another had believed that she was 'very like a cat'. This was somewhat confusing, because they were surely entirely different vocations.

Dan MacIntyre... the name floated back into her head. Why on earth had that happened? She scratched her elbow and wondered if he would be forever jumping in and out of her brain at the oddest of moments. She glared at the ceiling, then sighed deeply and dramatically. Of course: it was the 'You should be an actress' comment that had sent him scurrying back into her consciousness.

Dan was an actor. She'd had very little contact with actors before; it seemed an impossibly glamorous and distant profession, rather like being an Amazon explorer or a fashion designer. But any time that word 'actor' was used, or even thought, she'd think of him and get this same tight, sad feeling in her stomach. She would see his steady, deep brown eyes staring at her tenderly. And she would miss him, even though he'd said she 'analysed things too much' and had 'a sad closed heart'. That was such a terrible thing to say to someone! No wonder she had a sad closed heart if people like him went round saying it.

Life was difficult. Buddha himself had said it. Expecting things to be easy all the time made people dreadfully unhappy. She tried to tell this to her art history pupils and to Jemma, but they never listened. Falling in love, in particular, was arduous and strange – but it was like giving birth: so many people wanted you to do it that they glossed over its difficulties.

She reached up and gingerly touched the scars Jemma's father had punched onto her forehead. Alain had said he loved her. He had cried and wanted her to cradle him each time his fury subsided. What on earth had he meant by it? What was this love that he spoke of with such passion? And how could she have let him do these things to her? That was the worst question, the one that haunted her. How could she ever trust herself not to let that happen again?

The phone rang and broke the trance. It was a trance,

7

though Caddy was unaware of it. There is a black-and-white part of the brain, and she had wandered into it. It made her feel that love was all or nothing; one either lost oneself to it or built a big barricade and tried to keep it out.

The caller was one of Jemma's friends, who wanted her address in Arizona. She and Caddy had a nice chat and agreed that they missed Jemma far more than was reasonable. Jemma inspired affection. Any time she walked into a room it felt brighter and better. She could drive you mad with her stubbornness, but you had to admire her for it. Even when she was five she had been her own person and would have nothing to do with Barbie. Somehow she had been born knowing who she was and what she wanted – the very things her mother was often so unclear about.

However, on the morning on which we meet her, Caddy was absolutely clear about two things at least: she needed new pillows and pillowcases. The feather situation was getting out of hand.

An hour and a half later she was on South Anne Street in central Dublin. Pillows and pillowcases…and she also needed dusters and a new floor mop and bin-liners and… goodness, there were so many things. Why hadn't she made a list? Still, it was nice to be out of the house and not thinking about anything complicated. People who didn't think about complicated things were so much happier. If only she could be more like that colleague who devoted her whole year to getting ready for the Dublin marathon! She pounded through life so happily and was always having to take showers and change out of drenched T-shirts.

I'm just going to think about really practical things all morning, Caddy decided. *My brain needs a rest. Perhaps I should cross O'Connell Bridge and find all sorts of bargains in those little side-street shops. It will make me feel really rugged and virtuous.* Life suddenly seemed supremely simple.

And then she saw him.

He was sitting outside a café, reading. A white cup lay on

8

the round chrome table. As he reached for it, she turned away and almost pressed her nose against the glass of a shop window. He would surely look up at any moment and sense she was there. With her back turned to him, she edged away in the direction of Grafton Street. Pedestrians pushed past her hurriedly. How could so many people be in a rush? Where were they all going, and why? Suddenly Caddy felt like screaming, 'Stop! Please just freeze this moment like a photograph so I can look at him without him seeing me. So that I can study his face and look into his eyes.'

She paused at another shop window and pretended to study the display. Surely the distance would shield her. She turned round and saw that he had just looked up and was now recommencing his reading.

Dear God, he seemed so alone and still in all this rush and busyness. Was he happy or sad? She could hardly bear not knowing. His high broad forehead looked so solemn as he bent his head. What thoughts were in there? She had only once seen tears in his eyes: when he was talking about his mother, who had passed away last year. An almost unbearable tenderness assailed her as she saw he still had the same small rip just under the right knee of his jeans.

He was looking up again. Caddy looked away quickly, hurried on to Grafton Street and began to walk, in a daze, towards St Stephen's Green. She needed time to think. She ducked into Laura Ashley and stared blankly at a row of scarves. She would go over to him. She would say, 'Hi, Dan!' and tell him about her new house. The air would feel gentle between them and there would be that old wild sweetness, even if he was aloof and unwelcoming. Her heart would pound and her eyes would shine and she would just be glad that he existed.

That was what she always felt about Dan MacIntyre, even though he didn't understand her and was so impatient. She was glad that he existed and that she had met him.

She took a deep breath and was just about to leave the shop and face him when a voice shrieked, 'Caddy!' from behind a curtain of floral skirts. It was a colleague from college, Nancy. 'Caddy!' she exclaimed again. 'How are you? What have you been doing?'

Caddy felt as though she had been hit by a hurricane. She learned all about Nancy's caravanning holiday by Brittas Bay with the kids, and how her husband had come for the weekend, and how little Brian had got stung by a jellyfish, and how little Fiona had got sunstroke in the only three hours of pristine sunshine, and how Sam, who was fourteen, had got at the beer when no one was looking and vomited over the sun-lounger, but it had still been 'absolutely great'. 'Why don't you join us sometime?' Nancy asked, but Caddy was gazing out into the street. 'Caddy, are you all right?'

'What?'

'You seemed very far away.'

'Did I?'

'Yes.'

'Oh, sorry…I…I have to buy some pillowcases. For my new house.'

'Of course!' Nancy exclaimed. 'Moving is so much work, isn't it? Pop by any time you want a break. If you need any curtains altered, I know this great woman who…'

'Thank you.' Caddy was already moving away.

She almost ran back towards the café. He would still be there – he had to be… But he wasn't. Only a few minutes had passed, but the chair was empty. A waitress was removing the white cup and the tip that Dan had left. Caddy looked up and down the street. Why was she feeling such dismay? Hadn't she already resigned herself to this? But seeing him brought back so many feelings. It hadn't ended properly. They cared too much about each other to part with such disappointment. They could be friends; she knew they could, once he got used to the idea.

She started to walk in a daze towards a large department store. Bargain-hunting was the last thing on her mind now. She would purchase the pillows and pillowcases and go home.

And then she would write him a letter.

Chapter Two

DEAR DAN...

Caddy bent intently over her task.

I thought I'd drop you a line to let you know I've moved to a villa – which sounds very posh, doesn't it? Only it isn't a villa, it's just called that – it's semi-detached, like myself. I think you'd like it. It's got floral plasterwork on the ceilings and a big bay window at the front.

Would you like to come round to lunch one day? I'd cook you that bread-and-butter pudding you like. I can't believe I haven't seen you for so many months. During term-time I'm not very sociable. Teaching art history makes me feel like one of Picasso's later portraits! But friendship is so important, isn't it? Chump misses you...

She frowned and took a deep breath before adding, '*and I do too*'. She paused, wondering whether she should write 'best wishes' or 'very best wishes'.

Best wishes, Caddy

It was amazing how quickly you could do something when you felt ready.

Ten minutes later, she popped the letter into the post-box without a moment's hesitation. The deed was done, and it felt good. She let Chump run through the park and threw sticks for him, then bought a bar of chocolate on the way home and ate it before she reached the front door. How pretty her new pink house looked in the summer sunshine! Suddenly the afternoon felt full of energy and conviction. She would mow the front lawn immediately. Hopefully her new neighbour would not be waiting behind his hedge for a conversational pounce. Cecil was in his seventies and pleasant, but his obsession with battleships strained Caddy's patience.

'Really? It's amazing what they can do with steel.' Ten minutes later, Caddy was desperately trying to extricate herself from a conversation about huge guns and why they were so important. Cecil was pruning his roses and keen to tell her about a documentary that had contained extraordinary and previously *unseen footage* – there had been an excessive number of television documentaries on the subject recently, along with the usual ones about the origins of man, warfare and celebrities. Cecil was virtually delirious with enthusiasm.

'Well, much though I'd like to…you know…' Caddy couldn't bring herself to say 'discuss warfare further', so she left the sentence hanging. She glanced ostentatiously at her watch.

'Oh, dear, how time flies! I'd better get on with the mowing.'

'I videoed it.'

'Oh. That's nice.' Dear God, maybe he was going to ask her to *watch* it.

Cecil's wife Shelagh joined them. 'Don't you find this weather strange?'

'Oh, absolutely,' Caddy agreed. Shelagh was forever commenting on the weather and how it did things to her: when it changed from cold to hot too quickly, she almost jumped out of her skin, and she hated it when it rained or was muggy. Luckily, she was normally content with a quick corroboration that the climate had gone mad.

Twenty minutes later, the lawn was cut and Caddy was in the sitting-room, unpacking boxes. Van Morrison was serenading her and the maple floor felt cool and comforting under her bare feet. She'd always wanted a maple floor. And how she had longed for more space!

She had moved because her dear old home had been so small and cramped, though it was in an area that had suddenly become 'desirable'. She had actually made a profit when she'd sold it to a couple of young Celtic Tigers. They were involved in software and had that new way of speaking in firm, no-nonsense tones even when they didn't know what they were talking about. That was the thing about the new way of speaking: if you didn't know what you were talking about, you spoke with even more conviction – especially when you were trying to sell people daft shiny things they didn't need. Caddy hoped Jemma's early years as an aspiring eco-warrior might make her less prone to this fraudulence, though it had been really worrying that time she chained herself to a tree. She still had a radical side to her, though it had softened.

'Well, Mum, this seems more like our kind of place,' she had announced when she saw their new 'villa'.

'Why?' Caddy smiled.

'Because it's kind of weird.' This was obviously a compliment, so Caddy didn't question it. Certainly the neighbourhood had no aspirations towards gentility. People pottered around and walked their dogs in the park, and sometimes they just stood in their gardens and stared into space – which Jemma and Caddy regarded as highly desirable behaviour, because dreaming was, after all, a form of art. The woman in the small newsagent's loved Barry Manilow and had once thrown her knickers at Tom Jones during a concert. She had also once followed a showband called 'Big Tom and the Mainliners'. 'Ah, youth!' she exclaimed philosophically. 'Ah, youth!'

'Yes, indeed – ah, youth!' Caddy replied. Ah, youth what? It was not something one could ask.

She continued her unpacking. As she tore thick brown tape off yet another box, she was suddenly assailed by how much bloody work this was. It had been going on for months, too – packing, moving, unpacking… Were her belongings breeding? On more than one occasion she'd had an urge to fling most of them into a skip. But she'd done this before. She had to remember that every time it felt never-ending. Eighteen years before, she had walked out another door with her baby daughter, not knowing where she would go.

Something in her eased at this memory. Of course, that was why she felt so strange and vulnerable: moving house reminded her of that other time when she'd had no choice but to leave. She had gone to stay at that women's refuge, full of shame that she needed to. Then she had moved to a grimy bed-sit, then to a small flat, until, eventually, she had found a house of her own – the dear, poky sanctuary that she had just left. And people had been kind, though she had felt her life was over.

'Have you ever felt your life is over?' She had asked Dan that once when they were sitting in a café. The question had surprised her: she usually made sure they didn't stray onto topics that were too personal or serious. Why had she shown him this small window in her heart?

'No,' he'd answered, too quickly. 'No. Not really. It's too much like giving up, and I don't give up. Or at least I try very hard not to.' He had smiled and added softly, 'No guts, no glory. I could never be an actor if I got dispirited at every failure.'

She had tried to hide her disappointment, but in that moment she had known he would never truly understand her. Deep underneath his gentleness must be the innocent callousness of someone who had never scraped the depths of defeat. People like that were astonished by desperation and said things like, 'Oh, well, you'll feel better after you've had your hair done.' It was the worst kind of loneliness, being with someone like that. If your heart was breaking, they kept going on about how at least you weren't living in the Third World. Dan hadn't seemed to be like that, but every so often he said things like, 'Life is not a rehearsal,' which had a hint of that kind of thing about them. It was a clever expression, but the fact was that he was an actor so lots of his life *was* a rehearsal. She should have pointed it out to him.

Caddy felt the memory of their parting swimming towards her like a large and lugubrious creature in an aquarium. Sometimes her head really felt like an aquarium. There was all sorts of stuff floating around in there.

'Why do you laugh when your eyes are sad?' That was what he had asked on their last evening together. 'Why do you close your lips when I kiss you?'

She hadn't replied.

'I want to know you.'

So you can leave me. She had thought it automatically.

14

Once you know me, you won't want me. I know it may be unreasonable to believe this, but I do – and it's happened to me before. I wouldn't be feeling this if I were ready.

She didn't say any of this to him, because he wouldn't understand.

'I want it to work between us, but I'm not sure it can this way, Caddy. I...I feel like you're surrounded by a brick wall or something. I can't get through to you.'

It was obvious he was just about to dump her, but in a way that was going to make her feel guilty. *I've disappointed him,* she thought. *I have disappointed him terribly and I hate it. But I would have disappointed him anyway, even if I'd done all the things he wanted. It was just a matter of time.*

He had become angry because he thought she wasn't listening to him. For an awful moment she had thought he might reach across the table and thump her, which was clearly ridiculous. Instead he deepened his gaze and straightened the spoon in the bowl of sugar. They were sitting in a café. It didn't seem right that all around them people were chatting and joking. 'Oh, Caddy...' He suddenly looked so solemn. 'Oh, Caddy, how can I reach you when your heart is so closed and sad?'

She let his words land silently, as though onto snow. She didn't want to flinch or show her pain. She didn't want to beg him to take the words back, to say it wasn't true. Outside, on Wicklow Street, it was nearly Christmas and raining. Shoppers were bustling past the café with bulging bags and the season's usual mixture of cheer and desperation.

'I'm sorry you feel that way.' Her voice felt faraway and small. 'Maybe we should just leave it then.'

'What?'

'Us.'

He grew still. 'Is that what you want?'

'Yes.' She stared out the window at a woman who was trying to tie together the broken plastic handles of a shopping bag.

'All right, then.' He grabbed his leather jacket and rose

15

sharply from the table. He seemed about to leave when he turned and faced her. 'I'll leave you alone, Caddy,' he said, 'but I'll never understand it.'

'What?' She tried to harden her gaze and prepare herself for the insult.

'Why you didn't want something that could have been so beautiful.'

Dear God, just thinking about it made her want to cry.

She was about to take a swig from a bottle of Rescue Remedy when the phone rang. It was Harriet, a former neighbour, wondering if Caddy needed a large fake fish that talked to you when you walked past it. She also desperately needed to get rid of five aromatherapy burners because she had ten of them ('people keep giving them to me').

'Thank you, Harriet, but I'm actually trying to cut down on…you know…things I don't absolutely need,' Caddy said carefully. Harriet was clearly in the throes of a feng shui clutter-clearout – she had them regularly. Any minute she would mention the huge vase with the painting of the naked man on it. He was hung like a horse; when he had been purchased in Greece, the price tag had hidden his outstanding genitalia.

'Phew!' Caddy exclaimed as she put down the phone. Harriet was persuasive.

She sat down on her newly covered sofa. The fabric was called 'Tropical Lagoon' and was a delicious Caribbean blue. White sand, swaying palm trees, sun and cocktails – that was what she needed. A comfortable little beach hut without a box or a man in sight.

She lay back and let her arm dangle over the side of the sofa as though she were in a boat. Her hand touched something that felt old and familiar. It was a book, and it was on top of one of the boxes she had just opened. She gazed over the side of the sofa as though into warm blue water.

A diary. It was her diary. Dear God, she must have been eighteen when she wrote it.

She opened a page at random. '*I have just met someone*

16

absolutely amazing.'

Oh, dear.

'*He's a brilliant sculptor and he plays the guitar too. Not just three bad chords, like me – real ones. I don't know how he does that with his fingers. I must learn more about jazz. He knows piles about it. I'm meeting him tonight and I only met him this afternoon in St Stephen's Green! We got talking because I was trying to get the ducks to eat my cheese sandwich. He went "Quack!" behind me and I jumped, and then I laughed. He made me a daisy bracelet. I want him to kiss me. I absolutely ache for him to kiss me.*'

Deep sigh.

'*He's dark and moody and gorgeous – just the kind of man I never, ever met in Kerry. His name is Alain. With an I. He's lived in Paris and everything.*' Oh, the innocent stupid girl!

'*Oh, no! It's 7.30pm and I haven't washed my hair! Toodle-pip!*' Caddy closed the diary firmly.

Ah, youth! What else was there to say?

She would not dwell on it. It was in the aquarium, but she didn't have to look at it. Instead she scurried around placing books on shelves and ornaments on the mantelpiece. She would throw that diary away one day soon, once she'd removed the nice sketches in the middle. It was so long since she'd painted anything apart from a wall.

Oh, good: there was Buddha. It was a nice version of him, too – plump and serene and smiling. She placed him on the floor beside a rampant cheese plant that might one day take over the neighbourhood. And there was her aromatherapy burner… Soon the room was smelling of lavender.

A tiny doubt about the letter entered her thoughts when she unpacked a multicoloured Indian cushion Jemma had given her. Jemma hated Dan. The very first time she met him, she had said he looked 'shifty'. She had been thrilled when they parted and had hugged her mother with relief. 'We're much better off without him,' she'd declared triumphantly. Jemma was often right about people, even ones she hardly knew.

Still, I've only invited Dan to lunch, Caddy thought. *And he*

17

probably won't come anyway, so I shouldn't worry.

Unpacking boxes had become almost unbearable. She wanted to fling them all out the window. Van Morrison was singing 'Someone Like You', so she turned off the stereo. It would be nice to lie down. How often she had thought this at college, or when talking to her mother, or when in the supermarket. And now she actually could. She could go upstairs and have a nice siesta.

She walked slowly and arduously upstairs and lay down on her futon. She shouldn't own a futon. She was not a futon kind of person. She needed something softer. Less hard and virtuous. Why on earth had she bought it?

And why on earth had she posted that letter?

She stared at the framed print on the bedroom wall. She and Dan had both been staring at that very painting when they had met in the National Gallery. Suddenly the memory of that long-ago Sunday afternoon flooded her with almost surreal clarity.

And, since she was clearly not about to break any old unhealthy emotional patterns, she decided to surrender to nostalgia.

She had remembered the ending, so why shouldn't she remember the beginning?

She closed her eyes and saw the gallery. It had not been crowded that day and, as usual, she had been drawn to her favourite painting. It was not the most beautiful painting on display. It was very old and had a biblical theme. Caddy was surprised that she liked it so much. Sometimes she wished she could step into it and feel the brushstrokes painting away her regrets. She had always wanted to find home – the place where she belonged.

She had stared at the painting for many minutes; she had only realised someone was standing beside her when he said, 'This is yours, I think.'

A stranger had picked up her cardigan. She had dropped it without realising. It was pink and soft and she would have been sad to lose it. 'Oh, thank you!' she'd said, grabbing it gratefully. Then she had looked up and found herself staring into the most beautiful dark-brown eyes she'd ever seen.

'Thank you,' she said again, blushing slightly. She felt shy and exposed just glancing at his face. Those eyes were darkening in invitation, but where would they take her? She felt a sudden need to sit down on a bench.

'Do you know anything about this painting? It's one of my favourites.'

'It's one of my favourites too.' Caddy smiled. Then, despite her shyness, she began to tell him its history in some detail.

'My name is Dan.' He held out a strong warm hand.

'And mine's Caddy.'

'Can I buy you a cup of coffee? To…to thank you for sharing your erudition.'

'Mmm…well, actually…' She had stared down very hard at her shoes. 'Actually, I…'

'They have some excellent cakes.' His smile was so broad and playful that she relented.

As they sat together, she waited for him to say that he was married. When you were forty you got used to that announcement. Nice man – married…the words themselves were almost wedded. She felt sorry for friends like Roz who kept hoping to 'meet someone' and ending up with eejits. It was far easier to just give up on men altogether, like Caddy had. But every so often you met an exception who reminded you of…oh, dear God…reminded you of all the needs and dreams and hopes you'd been pretending you didn't have.

She tried to give all her attention to her chocolate fudge cake but found herself staring at his hands. It was amazing how much affection you could feel for the hands of someone you'd just met. She hoped her own hand wouldn't tremble as she lifted her cup. It did, but somehow she didn't feel embarrassed. When two people are relieved to meet each other – yes, *relieved*, that was it – they cannot hide it. It is in every movement and every glance. A yearning surrounds them and they are as naked as the day they were born. This is what is so

19

terrible and so wonderful, what can break the heart or mend it. So much could be lost. Already she was scared witless. Why was it happening now, when she felt so unprepared and out of practice? And yet they were still two strangers.

This should be happening to Roz, Caddy kept thinking. *Roz is ready and I'm not.* But maybe it was all in her imagination anyway; maybe they would part any minute, drift away from each other like ships in the night.

She frowned, and he smiled. 'Do you like Chinese food?' He asked it suddenly, and she said, 'Yes.'

'Then why don't we go out for a Chinese meal sometime?' She'd fumbled with her napkin.

'I know a place you'd really like.'

'Okay.'

For the briefest of beautiful moments, it had seemed the only possible answer.

Chapter Three

TOM ARMSTRONG SAUNTERED HAPPILY towards a café. He was looking forward to a large mug of coffee, and he was pleased about a photograph he'd just taken. It was of a man cutting a garden hedge with a pet parrot perched contentedly on his shoulder. It was just the kind of unexpected suburban detail he liked to record, and he even wondered if the image might be included in his exhibition – if he ever had one. Tom hadn't spent much time on photography lately. He was very much caught up in the world of mobile phones, because he was going to marry a woman called Samantha.

How wonderful it was to feel this passion! And how sad it was that he'd postponed it for so long. If only they'd met earlier...but perhaps then he mightn't have recognised how wonderful she was. Because Tom was starting to see how callow and superficial he'd been in many ways, and how far he had wandered from the truth of his own heart.

Samantha had somehow handed him back to himself, and he had to marry her. She didn't know he felt this way, but he was wooing her assiduously. Eventually she would, of course, realise that they were meant for each other. In the meantime he would adore her and try to earn the kind of income she deserved. He wanted to provide her with a nice house and a big garden in a pleasant area, but he hadn't mentioned it. This was because Samantha was something of a feminist and already owned a flat, which had a considerable place in her affections.

Tom's intense, attractive face broke into a broad smile as he thought of his beloved. He was dressed in a very smart Italian suit, because selling mobile phones required him to look as plausible as possible. In fact, he cut quite a dashing figure as he walked, with long, lithe steps, towards his appointment with breakfast. When he caught his reflection in a shop window he couldn't quite believe he was seeing himself.

It was like a moment from a song by Talking Heads – he'd always been a fan of David Byrne.

For most of his adult life Tom had worn jeans and let his slightly curly brown hair follow its own bohemian inclinations. Sometimes he hadn't even shaved – freelance photographers were allowed as much designer stubble as they wanted – but now that he was a salesman he paid more attention to grooming.

And grooming took far more time than he'd realised. Regular and dutiful shaving was, in particular, a pain in the arse. So was hanging up his suit carefully, and delivering his crisp new shirts to the dry-cleaners. He'd even bought a special roller to remove lint. He'd never really noticed lint before, but it seemed to adore his suit; it clung to it with the kind of fervour that he himself reserved for Samantha.

Samantha… His step lightened just at the thought of her. The world seemed a different place now that he knew she inhabited it too. She made him feel like someone in an old Hollywood musical. If she had been a song, he could have listened to her for years and still wanted more.

He was the kind of man who bought CDs because of just one song, and then played that song many times over until it released its hold on him and left him free to appreciate the other tracks. He was glad when this happened, because music could stir passions in him and remind him of things he didn't even know he knew, or wanted. Now it seemed to him that all the songs he loved had been about Samantha.

She said they were 'just friends' at the moment, but that had happened before and had passed. She wanted him to take up full-time photography again, but mobile phones seemed to pay better. He'd never been very businesslike about photography. He was interested in faces, but not necessarily famous ones. You could tell so much from an expression, a gesture. Of course, you had to look to see these things – really look; it took patience, care and passion. That was his passion – looking at people. It was a kind of love, and for a long time it had been the only kind he'd felt comfortable with.

When he reached the café he ordered coffee and toast. Freshly ground coffee…what a wonderful thing it was! He drank deep and stared dreamily out the window.

'So have you asked her yet?'

His reveries were disturbed by a woman called Clodagh, who waved her wedding ring at him.

'No, I haven't asked her yet.' Clodagh was the café's proprietor and incredibly nosy. She was also very nice and was about to give him a free second cup of coffee.

'Oh, Tom, don't leave it too long, now.'

Tom removed a photograph he'd placed on the table. He didn't want Clodagh to spill coffee on it. She glanced at it eagerly. 'Is that Samantha?'

'No.'

Clodagh waited for him to explain himself. His top-up of coffee was obviously not going to be forthcoming until he did so.

'I don't actually know who the woman in the photo is. We went to the same college, but I never found out her name.'

'So it was taken a long time ago, then?'

'Yes.'

'It's lovely.' Clodagh sighed sentimentally. 'Pity it isn't in colour.'

Tom smiled and held out his mug.

Clodagh drifted off to another customer, and Tom's gaze settled on the young woman. She had found his lens twenty years ago, and she had seemed so beautiful and innocent. It was strange that you could feel such intimacy for a stranger, someone you'd never even spoken with. Just looking at her made him feel happy.

In Tom's photograph, which had been taken outside the National College of Art and Design, the woman was running, arms open, towards a tall, intense young man. Tom had been a photography student at the time and had always had his Leica camera handy – he still did. The black-and-white image was well composed. The buildings in the background, the evening sunshine, the metropolitan pigeons, all seemed just right; the

23

woman's cotton dress was billowing in the breeze, accentuating her slim figure. Her open, gentle face was radiant and her eyes were full of love.

He put down the photograph and once again read the utterly astonishing letter that accompanied it. Life indeed contained many surprises. And some of them were exceptionally nice.

Greatly cheered, he sauntered out the door of the café a few minutes later, waving goodbye to Clodagh. He was heading back to the mad, sad world of mobile phones. He hated the bloody things, though of course they had their uses. Despite this, he managed to sell three mobile phones in an hour and arrange a meeting with someone who might want the latest, hottest, coolest and most *impossibly fabulous* one on the market. After this he snuck into a bookstore and browsed through books about classic cars. One had to find ways to help one's mental health.

By 12.30 he was on his way to a pub called O'Byrne's, where he was meeting Samantha for lunch. He arrived twenty minutes early and sat at the bar. Samantha was always late; it still pissed him off, though of course he didn't show it. He ordered a Guinness and glanced at the man sitting next to him. He somehow looked familiar. Had Tom sold him a mobile phone?

The man looked up. 'Hello.' Tom smiled at him.

'Hello.' The man looked puzzled.

'We don't know each other, do we?' Tom suddenly felt embarrassed. 'Sorry…it's just…I sell mobile phones, and…'

'I don't own one.'

'Good for you. They're awful bloody things; I hate them.'

'Why do you sell them, then?'

'Because I am part of a global conspiracy to make people feel they have to be in constant communication with each other. What's the point of being on a train if you can't ring someone and say, "I'm on a train"?'

'Or in a pub,' the man suggested.

The conversation entered a long pause. The man returned

24

to his book, which was called *Cat Behaviour Explained*, and Tom wished he had a newspaper. He began to stare at a beer mat. Then he took out his BlackBerry and pretended to be interested in his afternoon appointments.

'So, Dan, are you in another play?' the barman asked. He was twisting a dishcloth inside a gleaming glass.

'No. I'm doing voiceovers in the studio next door.'

'Ah, yes.' The barman smiled at Tom. 'We get a lot of odd ones in here – actors and the like. This fellow's one of them. You probably saw him in that poncy costume drama – *Merrion Mansions*, wasn't it?'

'We'd never put up with Ted if he didn't pull such a good pint,' Dan whispered.

'Strutting around in those bloody breeches – you looked a terrible eejit.'

'Thanks, Ted. It's great to get the encouragement.'

'And where is our thespian Zia Andersson?'

'Is Zia Andersson a *lesbian*?' Tom couldn't hide his astonishment. She was one of Ireland's most beautiful and sultry young actresses.

'No, of course she isn't,' Ted laughed. 'Dan can vouch for that!'

Dan frowned and shifted in his seat. 'He said thespian.'

'Oh, right. Sorry. I misheard.' Not for the first time in his life, Tom felt very gauche and awkward. A 'cool' person would have shut up, but something impelled him to inquire about the book. 'Have…have you a cat yourself?'

Dan looked at Tom carefully, as though deciding whether he wanted to continue the conversation. He was obviously not a randomly sociable person, but he wasn't intimidating because his deep brown eyes were knowing and gentle. In fact, they began to twinkle with humour when he replied. 'Yes, I have a cat called Leonora. She's very bossy and beautiful.'

This led to a long discussion about why some people prefer cats to dogs. And about Samantha. Tom found it hard not to talk about Samantha. Some of his friends couldn't understand his need to mention her name at frequent intervals, but he sensed that Dan would be more tolerant. After all, he had spoken quite openly about his affection for his cat, and not every man would do that.

There was also something unusual about him – some quality that seemed both elusive and obvious, to Tom, anyway. Especially when he smiled. It was a great smile, the kind of smile you remembered. Tom would have loved to photograph it – and he *had* seen it before. On television. He leaned forwards eagerly. 'You were in that…that drama about pigeon-fanciers going to Germany or somewhere like that. You fell in love with the girl on the beach with the inflatable dolphin.'

'You've got a good memory. That was ages ago.'

'I thought it was great.'

'Thank you.'

'Dan MacIntyre,' Tom said. 'Now I remember. I almost photographed you once.'

'How do you almost photograph someone?'

'You were in a play and the PR woman wanted me to take the publicity photos, only then she found out someone else had been booked to do it already.'

'But fate has eventually brought us together.'

'Yes.' Tom grinned.

'So you're a photographer too?' Dan drained the last drops of his pint of Guinness.

Tom explained that he was indeed a photographer, but that, for the moment, he was a fake mobile-phone salesman because of his love of Samantha.

'Well, I hope she's worth it,' Dan remarked rather darkly, and it was then that Tom realised Dan was a bit sad. He had hidden it very well, but men could do that; Tom often had.

Dan left shortly after that, taking Tom's business card. 'My agent keeps telling me I must get a mobile phone,' he explained. 'I think I could only buy one from someone who dislikes them as much as I do.'

'Hope to hear from you, then,' Tom smiled. It was only after he said it that he realised it had come out as shiny salesman's patter. God, what was this job doing to him?

He tapped a beer mat against the table and looked at his watch. Samantha wasn't usually this late... and then he saw her, sashaying her way between the tables. She looked gorgeous. And guilty. This wasn't unusual.

'I'm so sorry, sweetie. Have you been waiting ages?'

'No.' He smiled at her with total forgiveness.

They wandered over to the buffet and Samantha took some time to decide on her lunch. As they found a free table and two firm velvet seats, some of the men at the bar glanced keenly at Samantha. Tom noticed this and felt indirectly flattered. What he didn't notice was that some women were glancing at him, too – casually but with a definite interest. Because, despite his smart Italian suit, there was something untamed about Tom Armstrong. His face had an openness that showed he had not spent his working life in an office, as did the athleticism of his movements and his slightly weathered skin. He was eager and curious and strangely determined. And there was a startling honesty in his clear blue eyes.

Tom would have been astonished to know he was being watched with such curiosity. He didn't have a very high opinion of himself. In fact, he often felt like a terrible fake. This was not, naturally, something he mentioned very often – especially when he was selling mobile phones. He knew that, deep down inside, there was a true Tom. And he felt far closer to him when he was with Samantha. Samantha knew the True Tom. With her he was more himself, somehow; more free; more everything. She was the first person he'd phoned to tell about the photograph. Now he was telling her about it again, and she didn't seem the least bit surprised.

'You're a very good photographer, Tom,' she said. 'It's a lovely picture. No wonder they want to use it.'

'Thank you,' he grinned, picking up his pint of Guinness and lowering his lips into the creamy froth. One of the nice things about Samantha was that she'd always believed in his photography. But he wished she'd stop claiming they now were just friends – 'it's a soul thing between us. We've

27

probably met many times before in previous lives and have done all the passionate stuff already,' she often said.

He tried not to look at her elbows. He loved kissing her elbows. He didn't want any part of her glorious terrain to feel forgotten.

'Are you listening to me, Tom?' she asked rather bossily.

'Yes,' Tom answered, thinking that Samantha was a bit bossy – and beautiful – just like Dan's cat. She was probably being elusive to make him more attentive. Some women did that; they didn't want to appear too available. But there was no need for Samantha to resort to such ruses. Surely she must know this by now.

'What are you going to do with the money from the photograph?' she asked.

Tom looked down at his slice of quiche. 'I'm not sure yet. I think I'll just enjoy that conundrum for a while.'

'You could go somewhere exciting!' Samantha had become quite animated. As she leaned forwards, her cheesecloth blouse loosened and he glimpsed the lush, fruitlike fold between her breasts. He was very fond of Samantha's breasts. How he'd love to hold them, cup them like ripe melons in his palms…

'Yes, I suppose I could,' he agreed. 'But where?'

'What about America? You've always said you wanted to go to California.'

'Would you like to go there with me?' The words left his mouth in a rush of eagerness, and he immediately wished he'd moderated them.

Samantha looked at him with great warmth. Then she began to laugh. This was not the reaction he had hoped for. 'Oh, Tom, you're so sweet!' she smiled. 'But you should go off and have your own adventures. Travelling alone would be exciting, and…' She paused. 'And you might meet someone.'

But I've met you! Tom wanted to shout. Of course he didn't. Samantha didn't like to feel pressurised. She also had her period. She'd informed him of this as soon as she'd arrived. It was very precious to Tom that he was privy to the mysteries of Samantha's monthly cycle. It was such a strange business, and he knew he must be tolerant of her moods and whims and, yes, even slight off-handedness.

Samantha was sipping her glass of Guinness, which had a dash of blackcurrant juice in it. He looked at the whirl of purple on its creamy head as she placed it back on the table. Then she looked up and seemed to study him intently. *What is she thinking?* he wondered. *Does she know how much I love her? Should I say it again? Now?*

There was no need for Tom to say these words, because Samantha already knew them. She was watching him as he drank his pint, registering his enjoyment. She knew that time felt different to him when he was drinking. He savoured it, just as much as the hops and barley in his glass; it was a way of slowing down, of letting things leave him. His face softened as he looked up at her.

And as she looked back she felt frightened for him.

Tom replaced his glass on the cardboard coaster with enjoyable precision. Then he looked out the window at the canal. It was great that Dublin had canals. On a sunny day it was lovely to sit on the grass beside the water and eat a sandwich and dream. During lunchtimes, the canal banks were strewn with carefree, happy escapees from various offices. The sun made such a difference.

When he had taken the photograph of that woman, it had been sunny too .. .

'I still don't know why they chose my photograph,' he said. 'They could easily have created the same effect with a couple of models in a studio.'

'But it wouldn't be *real* then,' Samantha corrected him firmly. 'The woman's expression is what makes your photo so special. She's obviously in love.'

As Tom looked at Samantha, he wondered if his own expression was as revealing. But she was looking into her bag – the big embroidered one she'd bought in a market in Tangiers. That bag was one of her many mysteries; unexpected things were always coming out of it. He watched,

29

fascinated, as she extracted a lemon scarf from its depths and slung it loosely round her shoulders. As she did so Tom thought, once again, how very desirable she was.

Hers wasn't a conventional prettiness. 'Gamine' didn't describe it either. Samantha had an unusual face, he decided. It was unguarded and yet not naïve. It changed, too: sometimes she was beautiful, and the next minute, in a different light, she could be quite ordinary. But those weren't the important things. What he really cherished about her couldn't be named – not adequately.

She looked younger than her twenty-eight years, almost girlish. She was dark enough to be Italian, and yet one would not have been surprised to hear her speak French. Her eyes were perhaps her most compelling feature. They were brown and looked right at you – into you, almost through you – and there was a little sadness in them that made her laughter special.

'You really must do more photography, Tom. This is a sign,' Samantha was informing him.

'What do you mean?' He frowned.

'It's an encouragement. You have poetry in your soul, sweetie. You're meant to share it.'

'I'm not sure.' Tom sighed. He wished he could be more open with her, match her gift for self-revelation. Sometimes he was quite distant, when he feared she was going to suck him into emotional territory he didn't know how to navigate. All his life, intimacy had been a bumpy business for him – it had never felt safe or comfortable, and yet it was something he craved. Sex seemed its simplest expression. It didn't require him to talk or explain himself or demonstrate deep personal insights. It was almost enough – and yet afterwards Samantha always asked him what he was thinking, and he could never come up with a satisfactory response. Because what Tom really liked was listening to Samantha – hearing her say all the things he didn't.

There were books about this kind of thing, he knew that. And Samantha seemed to have read most of them. 'You're in your cave again,' she'd say, and he hadn't known what the fuck she was talking about until she'd shoved *Men Are From Mars, Women Are From Venus* under his nose. 'Read that,' she'd said sternly, but he hadn't; he had flicked through it and had been put off by the fact that it was American. Though he was intrigued by the New World, Tom had come to believe that it had rather too many bossy opinions. In a strange way he felt that the book's stark yet cosy summations diminished a mystery that he cherished.

But perhaps the deeper reason, he saw now, was that he was scared. After Samantha had softened him up and made him blubber out his secrets, his needs, his terror, she might find out what a terrible fake he was and leave him. But this no longer seemed an adequate excuse. With Samantha, the True Tom would surely become more recognisable...

He moved a vase from the middle of the table so that he could see Samantha's face more clearly. He was just about to speak when a suave young man entered the pub and waved in their direction.

Samantha waved back, but she looked surprised to see him; she seemed uncomfortable, as if she wanted to be friendly but also wished he'd go away. But the man wasn't going away. He'd started to walk towards their table. His broad, handsome face broke into a boyish grin as he approached, and Tom watched him worriedly. He definitely had charisma.

The man paused by Samantha, looking down at her. He was at least six foot two. Samantha was shifting in her seat, but their eyes were meeting. As the man placed a proprietary hand on her shoulder, Tom began to tap a beer mat angrily against the table. The man seemed repugnant to him – an intruder; Tom was ready to fight him off if Samantha showed one tiny trace of distress. Only she didn't. Her whole body seemed to have eased at his touch. He was...he was leaning towards her face – he was kissing her gently on the lips... A sudden jolt of anguished realisation shot through Tom. *This man was Samantha's lover!*

'Tom, this is Brian,' Samantha said briskly. This was not

31

the way she had wanted him to find out about her new boyfriend, but he had to know sometime.

'Hi!' Brian smiled his huge, charismatic smile.

'Hello,' Tom said stiffly. He watched Samantha as she tucked a stray hair behind her ear. Her gentle face had grown solemn, implying an impassiveness she did not feel. Samantha could feel concern without necessarily making it obvious. Tom knew this, but it didn't comfort him.

'Tom's had some very exciting news about a photograph he took. Haven't you, Tom?' Samantha said.

'Oh, it was just a letter,' Tom replied dully. How could she have looked at Brian like that? He wasn't right for her. He was too… *too not me*, Tom decided. He would have liked to do something vicious to send this despicable creature on his way, but he knew he couldn't. He had to somehow remain calm while he watched his dreams of Samantha disappear.

And to think that, all this time, he'd thought she was simply waiting – waiting for him to improve so that they could love each other for ever.

As Brian's hand lingered lovingly on Samantha's shoulder, Tom suddenly feared he might cry. Why hadn't she told him? Why had she led him on and made him feel he was special? He blinked firmly, then looked across the table with a kind of hate. Samantha winced. She seemed unsure of herself now, miserable. *Good*, Tom thought as he grabbed his jacket and rose. In the second before he turned to leave, everything seemed surreal, magnified; strange details jumped out at him. He noticed that a woman at the bar was rolling a cigarette and that, as she licked the gum, some of her crimson lipstick smudged onto the white paper.

'You're not leaving, are you?' Samantha asked. She was looking up guiltily.

'Yes, I am.'

'Don't go on account of me. I just came in to use the phone.' Brian had removed his hand from Samantha's shoulder and was gesturing towards a corner of the pub.

'You should get a mobile,' Tom spat contemptuously.

'What?'

'Oh, nothing.' He looked away and clenched his jaw.

'But you haven't even finished your quiche,' Samantha remonstrated.

'I don't want it.'

As he turned on his heel, Samantha called out, 'I'll phone you.' Tom didn't look round. He pushed his way through the crowded pub and paused for a moment when he reached the sudden brightness of the pavement. In the newsagent's, Barry White was singing loudly about sexual ardour, which seemed very insensitive of him.

Tom felt like falling to his knees on the pavement and screeching out his wretchedness. But men in smart Italian suits weren't supposed to do that kind of thing. They were supposed to care about mobile phones and politics and sports and their new stereo systems. But he didn't care about anything, now that Samantha had gone. She had taken part of him with her. She'd softened him up, and now he would have to be all hard and fake again. Just like he had been before.

A sob rose in Tom's chest, but he managed to ride it out without changing his expression. As his feelings tightened he thought of his father, the silent figure in his childhood home. He walked aimlessly until he found himself in St Stephen's Green, where he slumped onto a bench beside the pond.

If this were an old black-and-white American movie, I'd be wearing a trench coat, he thought grimly. *And Samantha would be called a dame, and it would suit her*.

He sat staring at the ducks, wishing he could cry now that there was no one around to see him. But the tears he had felt earlier seemed to have hardened into a kind of blankness. It was as if they had joined some ancient grief inside him.

Love had proven so very hard to find. Maybe there was something so fake about him that everybody saw it. Maybe he should go to a pub and drink until it didn't matter. How could he ever love again, after this?

His mobile phone started to ring. He pulled it from his pocket and flung it into the water. It was probably Samantha.

He was about to rise and head for a nearby hostelry that had a quiet respect for misery when a small boy approached. He was carrying a boat, which he placed carefully on the water. As he tugged it along with a string, he looked at Tom and smiled. At first Tom flinched, but then he managed to ease his mouth into the semblance of a greeting.

The boy was about the same age as his own son. Eoin, the son he hardly ever saw. Eoin was the result of a casual coupling with a woman called Avril, who seemed to have almost forgotten that Tom's sperm had been involved. Recently he'd been wondering if he should re-establish contact with his son, but now, on this summer afternoon, it seemed unnecessary. What would he have to offer Eoin but his own confusion? It seemed such a clear-cut decision, and yet, strangely, Tom's eyes began to mist at the thought of it. Suddenly there was such a yearning in him that he had to force it away unnamed.

He stood up and headed purposefully towards his car. He was no longer in a daze, and the long walk back to the pub car park seemed annoying and stupid. Why had he walked so far? And what if he met Samantha and Brian outside the pub?

He reached his car, got in and turned on the ignition. 'Ticket to Ride' by The Beatles blasted out of the radio at full volume. Tom left it on and started up the engine. Then he pressed his foot down hard on the accelerator and drove towards an afternoon full of nothing at Techniware Mobiles Inc.

'It's pink,' Caddy was saying to her mother. They were talking on the phone because, thankfully, Ava Lavelle lived some distance away, in County Kerry.

'Oh, that sounds nice, dear,' Ava said. 'Though, if you change it, I'd recommend magnolia.'

'It's fine as it is,' Caddy replied firmly. 'And it has green wooden shutters.'

'Like in France?'

'Yes.'

34

There was a pause, and Caddy suspected that her mother would have liked to ask if the shutters were entirely necessary. But Ava managed not to point this out, which made Caddy realise that she was trying. Suddenly she began to feel rather contrite about the electric blanket. Her mother had felt she might need one. That was why she had phoned.

'I'm sorry I don't need the electric blanket,' she said. 'But I really do appreciate the offer.'

'It was your dad's idea, really.'

'How is Dad?'

'He's in the shed. He sends his love.'

Caddy frowned. Her father rarely spoke to her these days; he wasn't comfortable on the phone, and when he did use it he sounded extraordinarily formal. 'Dad spends a lot of time in his shed, doesn't he?' she ventured.

'Yes. It's good for a man to have outside interests.' Ava's tone had grown philosophical; it always did when she was generalising about men.

'What does he do in there?'

'Potters about, mainly, I think. I haven't asked him.'

'Aren't you *curious*?'

'No. A marriage needs its mysteries.'

Once again Caddy marvelled at her mother's phlegmatic attitude towards communication.

'I got a lovely letter from Jemma yesterday,' Ava continued. 'She seems to adore Arizona. And she has a new friend called Randy.'

Caddy stared at the rampant cheese plant, which needed watering. Her daughter hadn't mentioned this Randy person. Just the name made her shiver with fear.

'Caddy,' Ava said querulously. 'Caddy, are you still there?'

No, I'm on a hill-walking holiday in Tunisia, Caddy wanted to reply, but her mother wouldn't have found it funny.

'Sorry, I was just…'

'Just what?'

Caddy decided not to explain. 'Nothing.'

'It must be very lonely for you, dear. All alone in that lovely new house.'

'It must be very lonely for you, with Dad in the shed so much,' Caddy countered.

Ava decided not to comment. 'And it must have been so hard, moving all that furniture and all those boxes.'

'I hired removers.'

'Poor Matthew Connell's divorced. I met his mother yesterday. She was beside herself.'

'Oh, dear. I'm sorry to hear that.'

'He lives in Maynooth.' *Which is quite near Dublin.* Caddy could almost hear her mother thinking it. 'So I said that you might have him over to one of your dinner parties.'

'Mum, I don't have–'

'He'd like that. You used to be such good friends.'

'When I was fourteen.'

'And he's an accountant now.'

'Good for him.'

'Try to sound a bit more enthusiastic, darling!'

'Why should I be enthusiastic about Matthew Connell? I hardly remember what he looks like.'

'But he's available.'

'Well, that settles it, then.' Caddy sighed. 'Should I send out the wedding invitations now or wait until the menu is finalised?'

'Don't get sarcastic, dear. Now that Jemma's away, this is the ideal opportunity.'

'For what?'

'To go out more. She's very possessive of you. She wants you all to herself – which is only natural. But she won't feel like that for much longer.'

Caddy decided not to comment. The truth was, she hadn't really minded that Jemma misbehaved when she brought men home 'for coffee'. The dates had been few, and not one of those men had touched her heart or even known where to look for it; Jemma had almost done her a favour by frightening them off. The alliance had worked perfectly…until she had met Dan MacIntyre.

'Have you seen anything of Dan MacIntyre, dear?'

Caddy clenched the receiver. 'No, I haven't.' Was her mother telepathic?

'Oh, well, I suppose what will be, will be.' Ava sighed eloquently. 'I'll never forget that wonderful dinner he treated us to. He's *The One*, you know.' The phone was almost vibrating.

'What do you mean, *The One*?' Caddy demanded.

'The One you've been waiting for. And maybe the one you'll always miss. Anyway, I must go now, I have to make a raspberry soufflé. Byeee.' Emotional ambushes are swift and efficient, and Ava Lavelle was very good at them.

How does she know? Caddy grumbled to herself as she squeezed drops of Rescue Remedy onto her tongue. *And, anyway, it's not just about meeting the right person; it's about being the right person. You need to be ready.*

She stared at the phone. Would she ever be ready? It could get so lonely, waiting.

How strange it was, learning to be alone. It had taken her half a lifetime to make peace with it. And always – yes, of course, always – something was missing. Something beautiful – too beautiful, maybe. When it went, life was almost unbearable – for a while, anyway, until you partly forgot. That was the thing she couldn't bear: loving someone with all her heart again and then having it end.

But maybe it was just as sad to refuse even to let it begin.

Chapter Four

IT WAS ANOTHER NEW day, but this time Caddy did not wake up to a swirl of feathers. Instead she made herself a big mug of coffee and fed Chump. Then she settled back on her plump new pillows and started to read a book that explained absolutely everything about relationships.

She had already read it twice, and each time she had remembered what it said for twenty-four hours. During this time she had felt very wise and serene, but then she had forgotten it all – or nearly all; she had been left with just enough quotes to repeat to people until it annoyed them. She quoted things like, 'No one can make you happy unless you are already happy in yourself.' Roz said this was a load of rubbish, because she could think of a number of men (who were married, or Hollywood film stars, or very wise and attractive and for some reason totally unavailable) who could make her very happy indeed.

Come to think of it, chocolate biscuits could also make you very happy, if you learned to feel the guilt and eat them anyway. Caddy had an unopened packet of them in the kitchen, and, though they weren't the best kind of breakfast, she would make up for it by eating some of the fruit in the blue ceramic bowl. Lately she had started to tyrannise herself into eating more fruit by buying loads of it; it went off so quickly that she didn't have time to procrastinate.

She rose and padded downstairs. She had bought the biscuits because she'd forgotten Jemma was in Arizona. After they were eaten she would have absolutely nothing to do with biscuits or cakes for the rest of the summer – or with crisps, or popcorn. Jemma was really into popcorn and had converted Caddy to a version that tasted of cheese and some nameless delicious thing that was possibly addictive. Sometimes they sat watching telly with their cheeks so full of popcorn that they looked like hamsters.

The phone rang. Caddy rushed over to it with a half-eaten biscuit – it could be Jemma... Why was Jemma phoning? Were her cousins Brad and Cheryl looking after her properly? Was she ringing from a gas station in the middle of the desert? Caddy picked up the phone like a tigress ready to protect her cub.

'Isn't it a lovely morning!' Not Jemma. For a moment Caddy was almost astonished. It was Roz, and she was obviously in her aggressively happy mode. Aggressively happy was not the same as plain joyful: there was a tinge of desperation to it.

'D'you fancy going for a swim?'

'Mmm...' Caddy paused. Part of her wanted to swim and part of her didn't. She didn't like the bit in the changing rooms, where you had to stuff things into lockers and everything seemed damp and you kept bumping into people with newer bras.

'I've spent a fortune joining that leisure centre, Caddy. Not going there is making me miserable.'

'Can't you go on your own?'

'No. I need support.'

'For goodness' sake, Roz, all you're doing is getting into a swimming pool.'

'But there are so many stupid little fecky things you have to do beforehand.' Roz sighed. 'And then you get wet, and then you have to get dry again, and your hair goes funny.'

'Well, then, don't do it.'

'But I *like* swimming. It's one of the life-balancing things we said we'd do.' Roz and Caddy often talked about balancing work, rest and play. This was clearly essential for happiness.

'I don't know, Roz...I–'

'We'll talk about small, pleasurable things and try to float above our female sorrows,' Roz continued poetically. 'Please say yes, Caddy. If I don't get away from these loo rolls for a while I think I'll scream. It'll be my treat.' Roz was an advertising copywriter and sometimes felt the need to vacate her house immediately.

'Oh, there's no need for that,' Caddy protested. The leisure centre accepted paying guests and was fairly reasonable.

'So you're coming!'

'Oh, okay, then…'

The doorbell rang fifteen minutes later, just as Caddy realised she hadn't packed any hair conditioner. She planned to put it on in the steam room, because Roz claimed hair absorbed it better in damp heat.

'Coming!' she shouted, as she dashed into the bathroom. She could see the top of Roz's head through the stained-glass sunflower in the front door. Roz was astoundingly punctual and prone to impatience.

When Caddy yanked open the door, she was relieved to see that Roz was waiting calmly. 'Hello, dear.' Roz gave Caddy a light kiss on each cheek; she was French in her heart, though she had been born in Galway. She was looking formidably well groomed and attractive in a rather un-pretty way, as usual. She had big features and used very expensive make-up. Her hair was the colour of soot, her eyelashes were enormous and her big, friendly mouth was adorned with dark-purple lipstick. Caddy often wondered how Roz managed to appear so streamlined. None of her buttons ever seemed to be loose, her jumpers didn't bobble, and bits of her hair didn't suddenly decide to poke out in strange directions. What was more, her bottom was just the right size.

'I still haven't had a baby,' Roz revealed as they reached the pavement.

'Well, you weren't even pregnant last week.' Caddy smiled tolerantly. 'Have you found any suitable sperm yet?'

'Oh, I've had offers,' Roz declared mysteriously. 'I'll have to make a decision about them soon.'

'There's no need to rush it.'

'Of course there is. I'm thirty-eight.'

'It's a huge commitment.'

'Look, Caddy, everyone has a baby. Haven't you noticed? Absolutely everyone. They look so smug and nurturing. And they say things like, "I have so little time to myself."'

'That's true,' Caddy said. 'I don't know why you want one, quite frankly.'

'I want to be able to say, "I have so little time to myself!"' Roz declared. 'I want pity and admiration. Mothers get a lot of pity and admiration.'

'Not all of them,' Caddy said firmly. She was thinking of her own.

'I also want to be able to say, "My baby has changed how I look at my entire life…" They keep saying that in magazines. It always sounds very impressive.'

Caddy smiled and they fell into an easy step beside each other. They knew each other well enough not to feel they had to talk. As they walked past a newsagent's, Caddy noted that she had not entered it and bought a bar of chocolate. Instead she had proceeded with the calm resolve of a woman who would soon be taking virtuous exercise. She also began to wonder if she should ask Roz about Rufus, her ex-boyfriend. Rufus was very liberal with his sperm, but Roz rarely mentioned him these days.

When they reached the leisure centre, Caddy was relieved to see it wasn't too crowded. There were, of course, the inevitable small number of fanatics who were ploughing through the water like tanks, one length after another, but they could be dodged if she kept her wits about her.

Ten minutes later she was easing herself into the water, which wasn't quite as warm as she'd like but nice enough anyway. Swimming was good for sensitive people like herself; it gave them the sensation of being supported and comforted. Exercise in general was good for anxiety, and if you cried no one noticed because there was so much water. Roz was doing solo aqua-aerobics, but Caddy managed to ignore her. That was the nice thing about swimming: you were in a little world of your own, but you were all in the same water. She waved an arm through it and watched the gentle swirls.

Her serenity was interrupted by the appearance of a man standing beside the deep end. He was medium height, wearing small and suggestively bulging trunks, and his blond hair gave

41

off a Nordic sheen. Caddy recognised him immediately. He was Rufus, Roz's former boyfriend.

And Roz was glaring at him with considerable rancour.

Chapter Five

AH, THE STRANGENESS OF daughters!

Ava Lavelle sighed expansively and wished life were more like the short stories in her favourite women's weekly. The illustrations that accompanied them were also comforting: the young women wore lovely blouses or jumpers and tended to stand outside rose-covered cottages with dashing young men at their sides.

She wondered if she should make herself a cup of tea. No; it was not yet noon, and she had already had three cups. She'd be sloshing around the place like a hot-water bottle if she didn't monitor her intake. Jim, her husband, no longer shared her morning elevenses. He brewed up on his primus stove in the shed and used a mug – which he must have bought; Ava never kept mugs in the bungalow. Certain standards must be maintained. She always used elegant bone china, which she washed and dried immediately after use.

She stared at the pristine blue paper before her. She was about to write her daughter a letter – she had recently taken to sending Caddy occasional letters and carefully chosen presents. Because Ava was a person with regrets. She didn't let her regrets bother her too much, because she was also quite tough and knew that excessive rumination about things one couldn't change might affect one's domestic standards. Domestic standards were incredibly important. Somehow her daughter had never learned this, though she was a great one for lighting candles and burning incense and tossing swathes of white muslin over stacks of things that weren't in their proper place. One day Ava had even found an old bra wedged between the magazines on Caddy's coffee table. Pointing these things out to her made no difference: she thought they, like marriage, were unimportant.

The fact that her daughter remained unmarried was a great sadness to Ava. How she longed for a wedding! So many of her maternal capabilities would come to the fore. The hors d'oeuvres would be talked about for *months*. There was still an outside chance that Caddy might walk up the aisle, but she would probably have to be dragged. She had become the kind of woman who talked a lot about 'friendships' and the pleasures of slow, dreamy walks beside the sea. And she was besotted with that dog of hers. Which, at least, wasn't a cat. Cats were clearly one of the greatest threats to marriage in modern Ireland. Even the ads for cat food were like Mills & Boon novels. 'Darling, I'm home!' thousands of women now declared to tabbies and Burmeses. A man with a cat was entirely different. He regarded it as a pet, not a furry significant other.

Ava's bridge partner, Beth, had despaired when her daughter Ali got a Siamese. He had attacked any man who came into the house – but an engagement had still been achieved. Beth had located a suitable candidate called Stan, who fortuitously turned out to be a plumber, and the cunning plan had commenced. Beth and Ava had slipped into Ali's house while she was at work and loosened bits of various appliances so that they would act up but not flood the house. Stan had had to be called, and Ali had declared him to be 'expensive and bossy'. Then Beth had offered to buy Ali a new bath for her birthday (her old one was ancient and looked like a water trough), and Stan had installed it.

Gradually Stan's charms had become more apparent, especially when he had offered to put up shelves in Ali's bedroom in return for dinner. Ali was a very practical person, and the advantages of having a handsome resident handyman who brought her cat titbits and put up with the scratches were not lost on her. Ava and Beth had pretended to be surprised when the ring was bought, though they had broken open a bottle of champagne when they were back in Beth's sitting-room.

Yes, the ancient skill of matchmaking was as useful and important as ever – though some assignments were far more difficult than others. Ali was a straightforward girl who didn't read books about the unparalleled pleasures of being a spinster. She had just needed loosened washers and a little nudge. Caddy would require a heave. There was no doubt about it.

Those self-help books she kept reading didn't help, of course. Ava had taken a book called *While You're Waiting* to bed last time she had visited Caddy, thinking it was a romantic novel (it had a heart on the cover). It had turned out to be about how waiting for a relationship can be the perfect time to discover that *you don't need a relationship at all*. Ava had almost bounced off the mattress and hit the ceiling when she'd read the opening paragraph. No wonder so many women were single these days. Those books made 'having a relationship' sound like something you'd need a doctorate for, along with continuous therapy and army survival training.

She picked up her Parker pen and felt its firm, shiny expensiveness. Beth had given it to her some months before, for her seventieth birthday. 'I did my best, you know,' she wanted to write. Along with, 'I think you may now realise that some of my advice was well founded.' She also wanted to tell her daughter to contact Dan MacIntyre immediately and to marry him as soon as possible. The minute Ava had seen him, she had known he would be a more than adequate son-in-law, because of his eyes and the shape of his mouth.

Ava had firm opinions about mouths. She didn't like thin ones or ones that were too full. Dan's mouth was very nice and in the right proportions. It widened into a charming smile that could be both mischievous and kind. His eyes did not remain aloof from his expressions; they joined in, which showed he was sincere. His gaze was firm and steady and softened every time he looked at Caddy.

He was handsome, though not in a clothes-catalogue kind of way. He was not, for example, the chiselled, perfect type whose photograph sold Aran jumpers or up-market gumboots to the sitting-room shopper – his nose was slightly too long, his eyebrows could have been thinner, and one of his side teeth overlapped its neighbour; no, his type tended to appear in those odd ads for jeans and aftershave. But Ava could forgive him for this; after all, he was available – which, when a woman reached forty, was surely the most seductive word in the dictionary. His humour could, at times, be slightly sardonic, but this too was pardonable, especially since he had broad shoulders – Ava liked strong, broad shoulders in a man. Even though he was an actor (if only he had been an architect!) he owned his own house and made extra income from commercials. *He's The One*. She had known almost as soon as she met him.

When they had all had dinner together in that expensive restaurant, it had been clear that he was falling in love – but Caddy had kept commenting about the 'snootiness' of the waiters. It had been so rude of her. After all, Dan was treating them to this meal in honour of Ava's visit, and it had only happened because Dan had rung when Caddy was out shopping. Now that she thought about it, that had been the last time she had visited Caddy. These days Caddy always had some excuse or other to put her off.

Ava smiled as she recalled the phone conversation. 'Oh, Mrs Lavelle!' Dan had said in a welcoming way. 'I didn't know you were visiting.' The invitation to dinner had occurred completely spontaneously, though Caddy had tried to get out of it – luckily she had not come up with any plausible excuse. Ava had realised that Dan must be fairly serious about Caddy if he wanted to meet her relatives.

The restaurant he had chosen for them was exquisite, full of those unostentatious little touches that show one is dealing with serious luxury. Even the bathroom had freshly cut flowers and individually stacked pure white towels. They must have spent thousands on laundry alone.

Everything they had eaten was still imprinted clearly in Ava's mind. When she later told Jim about each course, he had become stupefied with boredom – his eyes had glinted with panic, like a trapped animal's – but Beth had been on the edge of her seat as Ava relived the entire evening. As she had sat down at the table, she had even begun to wonder if a wedding might be planned without her daughter realising it. Perhaps she and Dan could spring it on her, just like this dinner! From that moment she had regarded Dan as an ally in the difficult business of reaching her daughter's heart.

Dan had translated the French menu for her and laughed at some of its excesses. They had both swiftly decided on their first and second courses, but Caddy had taken ages. She said the only thing she was absolutely sure about was the pudding: she wanted chocolate mousse.

'Dan, you must both visit us in Kerry,' Ava had said while Caddy debated the merits of pâté, soup and something she'd never heard of that had prawns and fennel in it. 'Wouldn't that be lovely, Caddy?'

Caddy had stared up at her sulkily. She still didn't know if she wanted fish or chicken as a main course, or if she should just have two starters. She said she needed a menu coach and thought all expensive restaurants should provide one. She added that she felt bad about appearing ungrateful, but that this type of place specialised in intimidation.

Dan had quickly steered the conversation back onto the amazing things one could do with frozen raspberries. Ava had an enormous amount of frozen raspberries from the garden and their versatility never ceased to surprise her. But, in the middle of a description of meringues, Caddy had got up abruptly and headed for the ladies' room. When she returned, ten minutes later, her pâté had arrived and Ava told her how pretty she looked and said all sorts of nice things about her career as an art history teacher. Caddy had responded by drinking far too much wine and saying she was sure the waiters were just pretending to be French and were probably out-of-work actors. She had overheard two of them talking to each other and was prepared to swear that one of them had a Cork accent.

Ava had responded by saying that it was wonderful what one could do with linen napkins if one knew how to fold them. She added that she hoped Caddy was using the new set of napkins she had sent her for her birthday and had read the washing and ironing instructions carefully. Good linen napkins could last for years, with proper maintenance. Dan had held his own napkin to his mouth at that point and spluttered slightly – apparently he had been eating bread a bit too fast.

Caddy said she thought the fake French waiters had given them fresh rolls because they wanted to lure them into bread mania. She and Dan had laughed about this, and then Caddy had suddenly declared that it was a lovely restaurant and she was sorry for being such a pain in the arse about it (if only she could have used another expression!). She added that her 'monthlies' had made her a bit moody; Ava had looked down with embarrassment, but Dan had scarcely blinked.

Dear Dan – how polite and conscientious he had been during the entire meal... He was totally unlike that brute Alain, who had never invited any of them anywhere and had called Ava a silly old bag behind her back. She had actually heard Alain shout, 'It's that silly old bag for you,' to Caddy when she'd telephoned one evening. He'd been drinking; she could hear it in his voice. 'He's just come by for a meal,' Caddy had explained, but Ava knew they were probably living together. The shame of it! Her daughter was barely out of school. She'd always known it was a mistake to let her attend that art college.

After that Ava had made regular unannounced visits to Dublin, but Caddy never responded when she rang the doorbell. Then one evening she had stood very close to the door, so that no one could see her from the upstairs window, and managed to gain entry to the flat. Alain was in the sitting-room, angrily scraping paint onto a large canvas. The flat was shabby and student-like and full of cast-off furniture, but surprisingly tidy. It was Alain's painting that looked a complete mess; it vaguely resembled raw meat. But when Ava peered more closely, she realised he was painting a very large and abstract impression of a woman's bottom. Even thinking about it still made her blush.

'So, Mrs Lavelle, what do you think of this?' Alain had inquired nastily. The look in his narrow, suspicious eyes had made her shudder. Caddy had rushed forward and explained that he was there because his studio was being redecorated and that he was currently working on a very experimental painting of two melons. This announcement had caused Alain to fling his brush to the ground and leave the flat, slamming the front door loudly behind him. Then Ava had said that she and Jim were no longer prepared to fund Caddy's art studies, and that she must return to Kerry immediately. And Caddy had burst into tears and said that she'd almost finished her studies anyway and would never, ever return to Kerry because she belonged in Dublin, with Alain, who loved her.

'He doesn't love you. He doesn't even know what the word *means*,' Ava had declared.

'It's you who don't know that!' Caddy had shouted. 'Why did you come here if you just wanted to criticise me?'

Ava sighed at the memory. It wasn't easy being a mother and a born matchmaker. Many of her friends had children who had gone a bit off the rails; it was part of the way things were these days. But at least most of them had chosen 'partners' – oh, how inadequate that word was – who weren't thugs.

She gazed out the window at the patchwork fields and stone walls and fuchsia hedges. Alain had been attractive, in a dark, unpleasant, untidy way; even she could see that. He was tall and far too thin and hadn't shaved for days, and his long hair was tousled and careless. There was a mesmerising quality about him. You could easily lose yourself to someone like that, feel that your world turned on his smile, his approval. He knew it, too. The gleam in his hooded eyes was full of passion. With one glance Ava had known that he loved and hated without restraint and could do both at the same time.

Dear God, *he'll devour her*. That was what she had thought when Alain had returned from the pub and she had a chance to observe him more closely. And she had also known that he was wounded and frightened, underneath all the bravado. Her lovely lost girl loved the sad lost boy in him, and because of this it would sometimes be beautiful. When he let his guard down, Caddy would know he didn't do it for anyone else, and

49

it would feel heartbreakingly truthful and sweet. He would bind her to him with his shame and his secrets. And one day it would be over and almost impossible to forget.

Ava had not said any of this to Caddy, because she was not able to say these things to people – she was barely able to say them to herself. It was only the force of love that anchored these impressions in her. What she saw landed in her heart wordlessly, like music, and infuriated her because she was left with certainties she couldn't explain. She was a straightforward woman and couldn't understand how some part of her was in tune with all these mysteries. It only happened when her matchmaking skills were called upon; so, sadly, she did not have these almost miraculous perceptions about her husband, her daughter or other close relatives.

Ava sighed grandly. Yes, she had been born with the knack of recognising love, or the potential for love, when she saw it. Her skill was recognised locally and she had been involved in the formulation of at least ten weddings. Even the stout, bedraggled girl in the greengrocer's had benefited from her expertise and married a kindly farmer who was obsessed with growing prize-winning leeks. Caddy was aware of her reputation and distinctly unimpressed. She assumed that it was just a process of finding desperate people and shoving them together. Love, she was sure, played no part in it; Ava's insensitivity and bossiness must be the crucial factors.

Caddy... what a strange girl she was – in many ways a deep disappointment. She even refused to use her own name. She had been christened Catherine, which was a nice sensible name, but when she was little she hadn't been able to pronounce it. So Ava had shortened it to Cathy. Cathy was a nice name too – only her small daughter had refused to use it. 'My name is Caddy.' She kept saying it, and burst into tears any time Ava insisted that it wasn't: 'Caddy isn't even a real name, Cathy.' How many times Ava had almost cried herself with frustration! The odd new name had stuck when her daughter went to school. All her friends, and even her teachers, had used it. For years Ava had held out and referred to her daughter as 'Catherine'; but it had become too confusing, and eventually even she had relented. The battle about the name was when the tensions between them had started.

But this was not the time to dwell on past loss or victory. What Ava really wanted to say in her letter was that she didn't know what to say to her daughter any more. And that was a very odd letter for a woman of seventy to write. But if she could find the right words – how often they had eluded her! – then maybe Caddy would visit her, and they could find some way to negotiate all the awkwardnesses. It would mean so very much to Jim…

Jim and Caddy had always been close. There had been an ease between them from the very beginning, and Ava had often felt excluded from their laughter. They were so alike. Both of them bought huge Sunday papers they never got around to reading fully; they were prepared to watch films with subtitles, and purchased bottles of plain water when they could just turn on the tap; they liked things like olives and feta cheese and lasagne more than Irish stew, which was obviously far more nourishing. But at least they both adored Ava's home-baked chocolate cakes. There was never any dissent about their deliciousness.

A familiar growling noise broke the deep quiet. Oh, no: her neighbour Alfred was mowing the lawn again. It was nice having neighbours in the middle of the countryside, but this lawn-mowing was becoming excessive. Men became even odder as they got older, there was no doubt about it.

Why on earth is Jim spending so much time in the shed? she wondered. For it was clear to Ava that her husband had started to avoid her during daylight hours. When he disappeared into the toilet, he often brought the *Reader's Digest* with him and didn't emerge for ages. And then there were those 'errands' in Tralee that sent him scurrying off in his Volvo. Sometimes his face looked strangely furtive, as though he had a secret he was never going to share.

Ava sat reflecting about lawnmowers, sheds and marriages

for almost half an hour. She thought of poor, recently divorced Matthew Connell and how he might do, though her daughter would never love him. If Dan was a lost cause, then Matthew could at least be regarded as a backup. He knew nothing about art and he was obsessed with software, but he was available and fairly presentable, though balding, rather fat and prone to greasy skin. It was also very hard not to stare at the large pores on his nose.

One of the many clocks in the house started to chime, and Ava realised she would have to hurry to catch the afternoon post. She started to scribble quickly, though her handwriting remained tidy.

Dear Caddy,

It was nice speaking to you yesterday. We've had some drizzle here this morning. I went to Tralee yesterday. Your father was busy in his shed so I took the bus. I bought this linen tablecloth for you and I hope you like it.

Love, Mum

Ava didn't re-read the letter. Once it was dry and folded, she stuffed it in with the tablecloth and constructed a tidy package out of crisp brown paper. Soon she was walking quickly towards the village and hoping that Mrs Moore, the postmistress, would not inquire about her husband. The whole village seemed to have formed opinions about what he was doing in his shed and kept asking her for verification.

Sean, the postman, had spread the news about the shed to the village and was under the impression that Jim might be learning another language; after all, he had once ordered a set of Parliamo Italiano tapes. Mildred, who ran the grocery store, thought he might be reorganising his stamp collection because 'he used to be so keen on philately'. It was strange that they didn't just ask him themselves, but Jim could look rather aloof and forbidding when he wanted to. Anyway, people enjoyed the light-hearted conjecture and the mystery; it was almost like one of the TV soap operas they all followed keenly. Mrs Moore's guess was by far the most satisfactory. She thought that Jim was probably secretly involved in woodwork and making something 'very special' for his wife.

If only Caddy were here, Ava thought. *He'd tell her, I'm sure he would.* Then, as she bought the stamps and carefully placed them on the parcel, she hoped that her daughter would like the tablecloth; Dublin had made her complicated and fussy. Ava didn't say this to Mrs Moore, of course. Instead she regaled her with news of Caddy's new pink house and said she hoped to visit her there 'very soon'. She even found herself mentioning the green wooden shutters and going into some detail about the tablecloth. 'It may come in useful for her dinner parties,' she said, sounding as though she knew all about her daughter's social arrangements. Her life included many such small deceptions.

Another customer arrived, so Ava waved goodbye to Mrs Moore and headed across the street to Sally's Café. She chose a small table by the window. The tablecloth was plastic, faded red tartan. On the walls were dreadful amateur oil paintings, by local 'artists', of sea views and cottages and gardens; if anyone ever actually bought one, it would surely be out of pity. As her tea and iced bun arrived Ava said, 'Thank you,' and felt a familiar irritation towards the small stainless-steel teapot, which didn't pour properly. When she aimed it at her cup there was an excess that inevitably spilt. She dabbed it up with a paper napkin.

Then she picked up her bun and wondered if she should have married the beautiful black man who had sailed into Cork harbour, one very long-ago October day.

Caddy and Roz were also in a café. They were having cappuccinos, accompanied by carrot cake, because it was a well-known fact that people should eat more vegetables. They had heavy bags full of damp things beside them, and Caddy wasn't wearing a bra or knickers. This was because she had very cleverly changed into her pink swimming costume before she went to the pool, and very un-cleverly forgotten to take a bra and pants with her. At least she had been saved the usual humiliation of inadequate underwear standards, but now her

53

jeans were pinching her bottom, and when she and Roz were walking to the café some men had seen her bouncing breasts underneath her T-shirt and virtually salivated.

That was the thing about being blonde, even dark blonde. Men sometimes got completely the wrong impression. It reminded Caddy of that awful date, some years ago, with a man called Fergus, who had kept telling her about things that 'turned him on', including women not wearing knickers. Luckily, when he had virtually barged into the house for late-night coffee, Jemma had appeared and announced that Chump had fleas and they were all over the sofa. Single mother, inscrutable daughter, fleas… Fergus had leapt into his sports car like an Olympic athlete.

'Caddy, are you listening to me?' Roz was sounding very agitated.

Caddy banished the memory of frightful Fergus and smiled. 'Of course.'

'I'll never be able to go back there now. And I spent a small fortune joining.'

'Rufus probably won't be there that often.'

'But he might be.'

'Maybe he uses the gym more.'

'I didn't even know he was a member.' Roz reached into her bag for her lip salve.

'No, Roz. Don't start on the lip salve. Even though you're upset, you can do without it.'

'Just once,' Roz pleaded. She rolled some on her lips and put it back in her bag.

'So you still carry it, then?'

'Yes. But I've got it down to three times a day now.'

'Well done.' Caddy took a bite of carrot cake.

'I so much wanted to swim more this summer.'

Caddy decided not to mention that, only a couple of hours before, Roz had required support because swimming seemed so intimidating.

'Oh, *why* do I keep bumping into horrible past boyfriends!' Roz threw her hands in the air, sounding decidedly desperate.

'Well, at least he wasn't with his wife and two adorable children,' Caddy commented. Roz had told her many times that her awful ex-boyfriends always seemed completely different when she met them with someone else. It was as if they wanted to make it quite clear that 'I was only horrible when I was with you.'

'Rufus was even more horrible than the other horrible ones.'

'Oh.' This meant that he had been truly obnoxious, so Caddy listened respectfully as Roz elaborated.

Apparently Roz had often wondered why Rufus sometimes gripped her platinum necklace in his teeth during lovemaking. His insistence that they make love on radiators had also seemed a bit odd. But it was his suggestion that she should rub his genitals with a stainless-steel spoon that had robbed their relationship of all romance.

'He didn't love me at all!' Roz declared. 'He just wanted me to do these...these ridiculous things to him. He's got a fetish about metal. I think the only reason he asked me out was because of where we met.'

'Where was that?'

'In that very avant-garde furniture place near the quays. We were both admiring the aluminium tables.'

'Oh, dear.' Caddy groaned sympathetically. It was obviously time to trot out the line about Roz finding someone far nicer very soon.

However, Roz did not seem comforted. 'You keep telling me that,' she frowned, 'but it's just not true.'

'You'll have piles of boyfriends!' Caddy exclaimed. 'Look at you. You're an attractive young woman, and–'

'I'm thirty-eight, dearie.'

'Well, so what? You're still younger than some very glamorous Hollywood actresses.'

Roz picked up her spoon and started to make little ridges in the bowl of sugar.

'And you're very talented,' Caddy continued. 'That deodorant ad you wrote was wonderful. And...and everyone

55

loves the one about that car-spray stuff.'

'They've got me on toilet paper now.' Roz revealed this with such gloom that Caddy became quite worried. 'Look, it's kind of you to try to boost my morale,' she added, 'but we might as well just face it.'

'Face what?'

'That there's an extraordinary shortage of Quality Men and most of them have already been grabbed.'

Caddy found she couldn't contradict this, which was a great pity, because she would have liked to.

'We women have done so much more work on ourselves!' Roz continued feistily. 'Men have got away with being selfish bastards for far too long!' She thumped the table as she said this, and Caddy's spoon jumped into the air, swerved and landed under the chair of a young man sitting directly behind her. As she turned round to pick it up he smiled at her cautiously.

'See…see…he didn't even pick it up for you!' Roz hissed. 'Typical. No manners whatsoever.'

Roz got up and seemed about to thwack the poor bloke on the shoulder, so Caddy was very relieved when she said she was 'going for a pee'.

When they left the café, ten minutes later, Caddy summoned up the courage to ask The Question. 'Have you seen anything of Dan MacIntyre recently?' she said casually.

'Why do you want to know?'

'Oh…just curiosity.'

Roz glanced at her hopefully. She liked Dan, though she had stopped saying it. He seemed decent as well as attractive – though, of course, he could also turn out to be an absolute bollocks. What she knew about him didn't imply that he was a bollocks, but men were extraordinarily clever at hiding that sort of thing.

'Actually, I did see him quite recently.'

'Where?' The question flew from Caddy's lips, fast and frightened.

'In that new wine bar I keep telling you about. We should

56

go there sometime.'

'Was he with anyone?'

'Oh, just the usual crowd. They go around in a sort of pod, don't they?'

They walked on in silence. Roz remembered meeting Dan, ten years before, when she had been working in national broadcasting. She had been one of those heroic and not particularly well paid young women who play a key role in running the place but know it is unwise to point this out. What was nice about Dan was that he knew enough about the political manoeuvrings of television to realise that Roz was virtually producing the series of ten-minute documentaries he had been asked to present. The producer was away a lot, but it was an unwritten rule that this was not to be mentioned unless it was absolutely necessary.

The documentaries had been about the history of St Stephen's Green, and the ducks on the pond were to be prominently featured, only they kept flying off during filming. Roz was reduced to bribing them to return with cake and bread; she even tried soaking it with whiskey, to sedate them, only the ducks just didn't look right tottering around like late-night drunks. Dan offered to chase them gently from the trees and shrubberies where they were hiding. The documentary had contained many images of ducks flying and landing on the pond and then staring dubiously at bread.

The whole duck business had given Roz a warm, friendly feeling towards Dan, who had been a crucial ally. However, she didn't think about it too much, because she was crazily in love with the absent producer – who, it eventually turned out, was in love with someone else – and, anyway, Dan was involved with a camerawoman. Who knew what would have happened if they had met at a different time…but they would never have had the chemistry he and Caddy shared. Frankly, sometimes it was so embarrassingly strong you could almost see it. But, just like the errant producer's absence, this was absolutely not to be mentioned. This was now an unwritten rule of Roz and Caddy's friendship, along with not criticising each other's bottoms or saying things like 'But you *said* you were going to take up salsa.'

'Did you talk to him?' Caddy asked, after a full two minutes.

'No. We just waved at each other. He wasn't with anyone in particular. As far as I could tell.'

'Oh.' Caddy felt a rush of relief. Suddenly she didn't feel quite so awkward about sending that letter. But she wouldn't mention it to Roz. Not just yet.

'Mags O'Donnell was at his table,' Roz said. 'She was wearing the most extraordinary purple jumper. It almost covered her from head to toe. Her husband says she's never been the same since she was in *Hedda Gabler*.'

When they reached the supermarket, Roz said she had to do some shopping before sitting down at her desk and getting right into loo rolls. At least loo rolls were fairly straightforward, unlike sanitary towels, which were now deluged with flaps and general strangeness. 'By the way, I'm thinking of taking up Jamie's offer,' she added nonchalantly.

'Jamie's what?'

'Oh, you know. I told you all about it.' Roz leaned forward to kiss Caddy quickly, one cheek at a time.

Jamie's offer, Caddy thought as she strolled through the park. It must be something to do with sperm – but who was Jamie? Was he a suitable donor?

And then she remembered. Jamie was someone Roz had met through the deodorant ad. 'It would just be a purely practical arrangement,' she had explained enthusiastically to Caddy. 'His wife need never know. And he's *gorgeous*!'

Caddy suddenly felt like racing back to the supermarket. It would not be a 'purely practical' arrangement. Humans were not that simple, especially if they were married. But, after a bit of deliberation, she decided it would not be a good idea to confront Roz about sperm while she was shopping. People were bound to overhear, and perhaps they would conclude that Caddy was the one who was hunting for donors. Certainly her braless state might amplify this impression.

As soon as she got home she let Chump out into the garden, where he did his Happy Thing. This involved rolling over to have his tummy tickled, darting around and suddenly stopping, and jumping into the air after imaginary flies. He clearly enjoyed an audience. 'You are a very dear daft dog.' Caddy smiled as she caressed one of his long, silky ears.

She went into the kitchen and stared determinedly at the walls. She had partially covered them in bright yellow paint, which now seemed most impetuous. It also seemed a great deal more yellow than it had on the sample card. 'But I *like* this yellow.' Caddy said it aloud, surprising herself with her defiance. After all, Monet's house in Giverny had some rooms that were very yellow indeed. Jemma would like it too. She adored bright, daring colours, though Caddy wished she wouldn't use quite so many vegetable dyes on her hair.

'Do you like the yellow, Chump?' she asked.

Chump gazed up at her as if to say, *Of course I do, because I love you*. That was the wonderful thing about Chump: he loved people completely, without recriminations. He didn't mind that he had been left alone while Caddy was swimming; he forgot and forgave. He should clearly be giving intimacy workshops.

Caddy went upstairs to put on a bra and knickers and change into her house-painting T-shirt. It was so covered in squiggles of colour it could almost have been framed. Back in the sitting-room, she turned on the CD player, stood very still and listened as the soulful sounds of a saxophone filled the air. Roz had given her the album. It had been recorded in Los Angeles, and the musician was moody and marvellous and only twenty-one years old. There were no words in his music, no singing about being left or leaving or wondering if one should; most of all, there wasn't any singing about love and how wonderful it was and how it would last for ever. Many of Caddy's CDs expressed these hopeful sentiments, and they sometimes made her cry, in a nice way, with just a smidgen of despair.

This music was different. The notes dashed downwards and

soared upwards and glided across the room like skaters, with a comfortable, knowing wildness. As she listened, Caddy walked determinedly towards the kitchen and was soon zealously splashing yellow paint onto the walls.

They found Caddy sometimes, these golden moments that existed beyond doubt or delay. If she could have stayed in them longer, how different her life would have been... but just feeling them, however briefly, was changing her.

And one day they would present her to herself in a way that left no place to hide.

Chapter Six

WOMEN WERE A MYSTERY. A great big mystery that Tom Armstrong knew he would never understand. They were part of a cosmic riddle, and if he were more enlightened he would perhaps laugh about it. He tried, sometimes: he threw his head back and aimed for a gust of mirth, but it turned into the kind of defeated honk one might hear from a cornered wombat. He had never heard a wombat honking, but he thought it might sound like him.

Samantha was gone, and she would never come back. They didn't have A Groovy Kind Of Love any more. Only last week he'd sung that song to himself so happily. But now he was beyond lyrics.

Some of his friends had been sympathetic for a while, but they wouldn't put up with his whingeing for extended periods. Anyway, the only person he really wanted to talk to about Samantha was Samantha herself, which of course was out of the question. She had made him feel understood, and it was one of the things he now hated about her; because she must also understand how much she'd hurt him, and how rejected and lost he felt without her.

It was just as well that Tom's car was old and moody and required a considerable amount of besotted attention. She was a classic Citroën called Betsy, and only certain specialised garages understood her. She had an amazing, complicated hydraulics system that caused Tom endless fascination; her parts had to be imported, and he had long conversations with mechanics about her mysteries, which were not completely unfathomable. After enough experimentation, she eventually made her needs known. He liked her roomy, solid feel, and her trademark clamshell front.

After many hours spent pandering to Betsy's slightest whims, Tom realised that his longing for Samantha had somewhat receded. As he ate a Chinese takeaway they became even more distant. And, as he sat drinking wine with some mates, they seemed to have entirely gone.

Amazing: he was completely over her. In fact, he didn't even *like* her. He remembered the indescribable boredom of their visits to ethnic boutiques, and how she was always late for their dates. She had even been scathing about his mild interest in football. Brian could have her. There were plenty more fish in the sea.

In fact, one had almost dragged Tom home the other night. They'd met in a city centre pub and she had been voraciously eager for him to bed her. He hadn't taken up her offer, because he didn't feel quite ready; but it had reminded him that he was a supposedly attractive thirty-nine-year-old man who didn't need to spend his evenings pining for Samantha.

He hated that name now.

Last night his friend Joe had said, 'Us men are simple creatures, Tom. Point our penises in the right direction and we're content.' Tom's penis hadn't agreed with this, actually. It was sad and dejected and dozing lethargically in the folds of his boxer shorts.

His penis had been extremely fond of Samantha and had missed her dreadfully.

But that had been yesterday. Today was a brand new day. Something would have to be done about his life. And he was getting really tired of Chinese takeaways, too. There was something about seeing the leftover cartons the next morning that depressed him. Their smell seemed to intensify overnight, and bits of rice scattered onto the floor as he flung them out. He would have to learn more about cooking. This prospect did not displease him; if he was to be alone, he might as well do it with a certain panache. A wok was clearly required, as was a more rugged attitude towards sociability. He would have to get out and meet more people.

Which was one of the reasons why he was now in a nightclub called X, gingerly sipping a pint of Guinness.

He hadn't actually meant to wander into this strangely secretive-looking establishment, but the sounds of revelry had beckoned to him as he strolled home. He had spent most of the evening in José's Wine Bar with some colleagues. 'Now that you're free again, you should go to some nightclubs,' one of them had remarked. 'They're great places to meet women.'

'Especially if you're married,' a man called Nigel had interrupted, with unpleasant glee. 'I've got some great rides from nightclubs. There was a woman called Yolanda who…'

As Nigel proceeded to describe his extramarital gyrations, Tom felt an awful sense of gloom. Men were a mystery too. In fact, there were times when he felt considerable distaste for his entire gender. *But I don't have to share Nigel's attitude*, he'd thought as he left the wine bar. *I could just go into a club and have a few drinks and then leave.*

He'd decided to have a look around X out of curiosity. It had been years since he'd been to a club and he wondered what they were like these days. He suspected they might be full of 'cool' people, and if this turned out to be the case he would have to leave immediately. Once he was in X, however, he began to feel less detached. He even wondered if he might meet 'someone'. It was, after all, Friday night, so he didn't have to get up early the next day.

He looked around, fascinated by the shadows and shapes, the leers and glances. It was dark and noisy, and every so often bright lights flashed in his eyes. People were constantly pushing past him with glasses of wine and beer, and some of it was spilling. It was like being in an anthill. Suddenly the thought of being somewhere else became almost overwhelmingly appealing.

Tom was just about to leave when he saw someone he vaguely knew. She was a woman who regularly went to José's Wine Bar. They'd had a brief conversation about advertising and mobile phones, which they'd agreed were both 'rubbish'. Some weeks ago they had even shared a packet of peanuts and left the wine bar together, though a group of her equally inebriated friends had accompanied them; they had all headed into the Dublin night in search of chips, and then they had all gone home as strangers. He didn't even know her name.

'Oh, it's you again,' she said as he approached. She was wearing bright-purple lipstick and looked immaculately groomed and quite attractive – *though not pretty*, Tom thought. She appeared to be in her thirties and was alone and rather drunk. He smiled at her and she smiled at him, and he asked her if he could buy her a drink. She nodded. Her hair was the colour of soot and she had enormous eyelashes. She was totally unlike Samantha; this was her main attraction. She said she wanted a gin and tonic because the wine was crap.

When he returned with the drinks, they tried to talk, but the music was too loud and extraordinarily repetitive. It was jerky and jumpy, with no attempt at melody, and the drumbeats sounded like a herd of wildebeest stampeding over vast tracts of corrugated iron. It was yet another reminder to Tom that he couldn't do coolness. The woman's name was Roz; she was there with some people from her agency, and she said they were all as pissed as newts. She laughed uproariously at this comment, though not in an entirely natural way – Tom could discern a veneer of learned gruffness. Tom wondered why newts had come to be associated with alcohol. He shouted, 'Know the feeling!' and laughed too.

'What?' she shouted back, giggling.

He didn't reply. She wouldn't hear him. This place was so loud and agitated; no one was listening to anyone, not really. For a moment he experienced a distant sense of irritation. And then it was gone.

They started to dance. Tom had never been a confident dancer – while others moved their entire bodies, he concentrated on his arms and legs and occasionally moved his head – but the astonishingly expensive alcohol had loosened him up considerably. The main thing about this kind of dancing was not to care if you looked foolish. He followed Roz's cue and started to sway dreamily. Looking around, he saw that people were thrusting their pelvises at each other, so he did it too. The hypnotic noise seemed to demand it.

Their movements became more languorous, and when the music softened he moved towards her. She slung her arms absentmindedly around his shoulders – mainly for support, it seemed. The music was becoming very sensual. It was about people wanting 'love' – oh, how casually people used that word! And they wanted love now. Immediately. Great big fireworks to send into the night with no heed for their cascade and ebb, the small heap of spent longing they might leave in the morning. Part of him was aware of the night's manipulations, the strange strings of desire that were being played without harmony or care. An animal thrill ran through him, a sense of pure appetite with no guilt or reproach.

Yesss – this is what I want! he thought as Roz's hands started to roam towards his buttocks. She pressed herself hard against his groin, nibbling his ear. Her body felt so slight and warm. So soft. She said something; at first he thought it was an endearment, but when it registered he realised she had said, 'I hate your aftershave.' He laughed uncomfortably. They both laughed. It was not the kind of laughter he was used to.

'Share a taxi home?' He pressed the words urgently into her ear. The music was outrageously loud.

Roz hesitated for a moment. 'Okay,' she said slowly. 'Let's go now.' She untangled herself from him and headed towards the cloakroom. Her movements contained the eerie poise of the considerably inebriated. She chatted earnestly for some seconds with a woman, obviously a friend, who was standing near the bar. They stared at Tom as though he were a creature in a zoo.

As he waited, he decided that he would have to learn more about aftershave. Maybe it was the aftershave that was causing this discussion. It certainly seemed the most comforting explanation, and he settled into it with a strange detachment. It really wouldn't have bothered him that much if Roz had disappeared into the night, like she had when they'd eaten chips together. It would have been frustrating, but there were other ways of dealing with that which didn't require company. The thing was, when he resorted to them, he always thought of Samantha – even though he was completely over her, of course. The memories of breathing in the smell of her hair and tenderly touching the small mole near her belly button were just lingering nostalgia.

When Roz returned, he gave her a welcoming smile. They went outside. More waiting, this time for a taxi; Roz gestured dramatically and drunkenly to the ones that were full. By now, though, Tom felt reasonably sober – sober enough to worry that he mightn't perform adequately, or that he might shout out Samantha's name at a crucial moment, or find that his lust had suddenly deserted him. Women never seemed to fully realise the responsibilities of erection.

'Let's go to your place,' Roz said as they got into the taxi. She certainly seemed far more practised than he was at this kind of thing. Tom blurted the address quickly to the driver; then he kissed her as they sat, entwined, in the back seat. It was a deep, hungry kiss that surprised him. As he looked up from it, he sensed that the driver, who was probably in his sixties, was disgusted with this kind of carry-on. It was obvious from the solemn set of his back and his tank-like concentration on the road.

After they arrived at Tom's apartment, the night dissolved into a haze of alcohol and sensations. They drank more, and Roz insisted on trying odd concoctions Tom had bought on holiday – they tended to have small twigs in them. Then she looked carefully at some of his framed photographs before they descended, with a deep inevitability, into his double bed. He hadn't changed the sheets before he went out because he'd expected to return alone. Why on earth was he doing this?

The next morning the sheets were almost unrecognisable. They were in a state of considerable disarray, in fact. Tom decided he had obviously not tucked them in with sufficient firmness. It had been a very strange night, and now he was greeting the new day with a stranger. He looked at Roz's sleeping form and wondered who Rufus was. For that was the name she had whispered in the middle of some dream.

'We're having carrot-cake salad,' Caddy was saying to Dan. He had arrived for lunch and was swimming round her sitting-room. She was admiring his manly thighs and broad shoulders while she stood on the tiled section near the kitchen. It was the only part of the room that was not full of water. She herself was wearing a bra and knickers because she had forgotten where she'd put her swim suit. It all seemed absolutely normal.

'When did you get this put in?' Dan asked.

'It's Roz's really, but she hardly ever uses it,' Caddy replied.

'Come and join me.'

'No. I'm frightened.'

'Why are you frightened?'

'Because I don't know how to swim.'

Dan laughed. 'Of course you do! You learned when you were five. You were with your father in the sea and a wave knocked you over. You floated like a dolphin.'

'I never told you that.'

He didn't reply. He was swimming like a dolphin himself, splashing playfully, diving, grinning with a beautiful, absurd happiness. She wanted – needed – to join him. The yellow walls of her kitchen grew brighter and virtually pushed her into the water.

Splash! She landed right beside him and he took her in his arms. 'We're supposed to be swimming.' She looked at him bossily.

'This is swimming.'

'No, it isn't. It's…it's…wanting to kiss someone.'

'Do you want me to kiss you?'

'No.'

He kissed her. What would happen if she melted into the water? It felt so deep and tender and right. She could feel the hairs of his chest on her breasts – he must have taken off her bra without her noticing. How lovely it was to feel them pressed against him. He bent down tenderly and began to kiss her nipples. It was like getting little jolts of delicious electricity.

'Oh, Dan,' Caddy moaned. She looked up into his eyes.

Only they weren't Dan's eyes. They were hooded and dark and blazing with fury.

'Alain!'

She tried to pull away, but he wouldn't let her.

'Who's Dan?' He was holding her arm so tightly that a searing pain made her wince.

'Who is he?' She felt the first blow, and then another, and another. She was reeling in pain and shock. He grabbed her hair so tightly that she cried out, 'Stop! Oh, please stop!' She tried to kick him through the water. It was barely a nudge. She had to escape. Oh dear God, where was Jemma? She had to save Jemma!

She scratched his face and bit his arm. Then she lifted her knee between his legs. He let go of her for an instant, and in that moment she swam desperately away from him.

'You'll never love again, Caddy Lavelle,' he shouted after her. 'Not after you've loved me. *You still love me!*'

And then she woke up.

Chapter Seven

TOM WISHED HE COULD remember the name of the woman who hated his aftershave. Their meeting in X seemed like centuries ago. It was Fake Tom who had brought her home – and now she was sitting up in bed and drinking coffee very sleepily.

It wasn't me who had casual sex with you, he wanted to say. *It was Fake Tom. I don't do that kind of thing – in fact, I find this situation highly offensive, so I'd like you to leave my house as soon as possible. I'm sorry that you've been misled. Fake Tom can be a right bastard sometimes*. Instead he sipped his coffee and wondered how long she would stay. The memory of their coupling was still surprisingly clear to him. As the woman closed her eyes and leaned her head against the pillow, he reviewed the night's events.

Their 'lovemaking' – if only it had been! – had been quite noisy. He had been delighted at the new smell of her, the sense of exploration. Her breasts were quite small – it had been strange to feel them, after Samantha's – and her pubic hair was scant and brown, a different colour from her dramatically dark hair. Looking at her lying there naked, he had felt a moment of fierce protectiveness. It seemed to him that men and women, and perhaps even dogs and cats and parakeets, were more emotionally vulnerable than he'd realised. He had met the wrong person in the wrong place, and it had been wrong to sleep with her. But so many other things felt wrong too that he'd let the urgent sensations in his groin quell his conscience.

And how good those sensations had felt! For a while they'd obliterated all his doubts. He'd floated into their surge and felt their waves tug him from the shore into a vast sea of forgetfulness. Out there, nothing mattered but this moment… But then it was over, and becoming a very distant thing itself.

And it was then that he had felt a brief sense of hatred towards the woman. Because she wasn't Samantha.

This reaction appalled him. The casual way she had offered herself to him seemed a type of refuge. She probably didn't even realise how lost she was, but he felt sure that some deep part of her must be offended.

He didn't even know the exact colour of her eyes. He hadn't watched or wanted her enough. They were strangers – and yet, that was part of their reckless pleasure: the fact that it was random, that she could just as easily have been someone else. Even so, he'd decided to count her toes tenderly, one by one, stating each number carefully. Though they'd giggled, in the silences she had watched solemnly, as if grateful.

He watched her curled up in his bed and felt an awful blankness, an awful lack that had to be filled and smoothed over. He wanted her to leave. But of course he could not say this.

He had already made her coffee. What other offering would lend some meagre dignity to the night before? Toast? No, that wasn't enough. A baguette? *Croissants*! That was it. The bakery was just down the road. Tom tiptoed towards his jeans and T-shirt. Then he spent some time unlacing the trainers he had kicked off so heedlessly only hours before.

The fresh morning air came in a rush of newness. It was the kind of bright morning in which one could forget things – leave someone alone with a large mug of coffee and not return. He could go into town and have a large fried breakfast in Bewley's... But, being the person he was, he walked into Milly's Bakery and claimed five croissants instead.

As he walked homewards, the pavements suddenly seemed full of smiling couples with small children. *I should be one of those men*, Tom thought. *I shouldn't be thirty-nine and all alone*.

He thought briefly of his son, Eoin. Did he like the toy train Tom had sent him for his birthday? What did he look like now? Tom quickened his steps. He would deliver the croissants to the stranger on a heaped breakfast tray and chat breezily. Then, after an appropriate interval, he would announce that he was going to play some rigorous form of sport. Women respected that kind of thing – and it needn't be a lie: his friend Joe had suggested that they play racquetball.

He might also mention that he had recently parted from his girlfriend and drop large hints that he wasn't ready for a relationship. There was no way he wanted to give this woman the wrong impression. He didn't want to mislead her or say that he would phone. In the past, saying he would phone had seemed like a very inconsequential thing, but now he knew what it was like to wait for a call, to long for it, to pick up the receiver to check the dialling tone – Samantha often said she would call and then didn't. Yes, it was clear that Samantha had never fully returned his affections; but somehow Tom's disappointment did not make him feel vengeful.

'*Oh, feck!*' He actually said it out loud. He had suddenly realised that he had become a more caring and compassionate person. He was now lumbered with a conscience and a sense of empathy towards anyone who was seeking love and acceptance – which covered most people. He'd have to be careful or he might marry someone out of pure pity. Betsy the car would have to be his significant other until these inconvenient feelings subsided.

'Oh, I thought you'd gone for the day,' the woman greeted him when he returned to the house. She was still in bed and, though she was smiling, she looked tired and hung over, like himself.

'Of course I hadn't gone,' Tom replied jovially. 'I was getting us some breakfast.'

'Don't pretend you weren't tempted.' She laughed gruffly.

'What do you mean?'

'Tempted to sod off, sweetie. I've been around.'

Tom was unprepared for this veiled aggression. 'I've bought us some croissants,' he replied defensively. 'Here, look at them. They're still in the bag.'

The woman's face softened.

'Would you like some marmalade on them?'

She looked as pleased as a little girl. 'Yes, please.'

'I'm going to bring you breakfast in bed, so just stay there

71

for a while. Okay?' he said firmly.

'Oh, someone has trained you well!' the woman commented.

Yes, someone has! Tom yearned to shout. *Her name is Samantha – and I don't even know yours.*

As he disappeared into the kitchen, he wondered whether his gallantry was misplaced. He wasn't going to put up with crap this morning. It was Saturday and he was a free man. He decided not to put the milk in a jug; the carton would do just fine. In a way, this was easier than having breakfast at a table. Anyway, he didn't want her snooping around his kitchen. She would almost certainly chide him about the state of his sideboards.

As he re-entered the bedroom the woman sat up eagerly. She did not cover her breasts with the sheet, and her nakedness disarmed him. *But she probably knew it would*, he thought as he placed the tray carefully on the bedside table.

'My name's Roz, just in case you've forgotten,' the woman smiled. 'And you're? – you're...' She blushed.

'Tom.'

As she ate her breakfast, Roz could feel Tom watching her with a kind of wonderment. It was nice to be watched with wonderment. Maybe he was experiencing a profound sense of recognition because they'd met in a previous incarnation.

Suddenly she longed to run her fingers through his brown hair and touch his hand. It was amazing, the affection you could feel for a hand you hardly knew. It was a lovely tanned hand, firm and manly, with long sensitive fingers. She wanted to say that he was sweet and kind, and that the croissants were delicious...but then she remembered all the gratitude she had lavished on men, and what brutes they could be. So she took the fifth croissant without even asking if he wanted it.

'Mind if I use the shower?'

'Go ahead.'

As Roz walked determinedly towards the bathroom, Tom knew he wouldn't have to mention racquetball. She wasn't the kind of woman who was going to stare at him, doe-eyed and lost, and start talking about films and restaurants. She was obviously going to make a swift exit from his house, and he was immensely relieved. Five minutes later she was dressing quickly, though she did linger over her nylon stockings. She was wearing suspenders and, as Tom glimpsed them, he felt a brief return of lust. She really did have wonderful legs.

He picked up his laundry – he had been gathering dirty clothes for the washing machine – and left the room. She joined him downstairs soon afterwards. 'That was nice, Tom. Thank you,' she said in a businesslike way. 'I did enjoy it.'

Despite himself, he gave her a naughty smile. 'So did I. It was fun.' A slight shiver filled the air between them.

'Here's my card, to remind you what my name is!' She laughed as she thrust it into his hand, but her eyes were solemn.

'Do you need a lift anywhere?'

'No. I live nearby.'

'At least it's nice weather.' Tom wasn't sure why he'd said this. 'Nice weather for a walk,' he added.

'Yes,' Roz agreed, as they hugged quickly. Then she kissed him on the cheek and headed for the front door.

'*Au revoir*, Tom,' she called out. 'Might see you in José's again one of these nights.'

'Yes – yes, indeed!' he agreed, trying to smile broadly. Now that he was sober he found her rather intimidating, but he was also saddened that they were parting with so little longing or care. He almost said he'd phone her, out of habit, but stopped himself in time. 'I hope you have a great weekend,' he found himself adding. 'And I'll try to improve my aftershave!' This made them both chuckle and removed some of the awkwardness.

Roz fled out the door. Tom watched her leaving. He was about to turn away and get on with his laundry, but something told him she might turn around and wave. Thank goodness she wasn't driving. Watching people drive away was always awkward. They got flustered and self-conscious and the whole thing seemed to take ages.

She did wave, and he was glad that he was there to wave back. Such small civilities meant a lot to people.

Especially when so many other things hadn't.

Chapter Eight

DAN IS COMING TO lunch. The thought whooshed through Caddy's mind as soon as she woke up.

He had phoned the day before. This had been an enormous surprise, because she had just got used to the idea that he had completely gone off her and they would never meet again. For days she had jumped every time the phone rang; and, frankly, when she had given up on him it had been a relief. She didn't want an adventurous summer at all. This realisation had hit her with an enormous and sleepy comfort. She wanted to potter around and look after her geraniums and watch television. She wanted to embrace middle age like a lover and spend ages looking at catalogues full of things that made storage easier.

This was her peace and this was her contentment. The aquarium in her brain had become blue and serene. If she ever did find herself getting into another relationship, it would be with a man who had given up on all the same things and simply wanted a quiet life. She would say things like, 'Do you want toast?' and he would reply, 'Yes, please, and just a scrape of that new organic strawberry jam.' Rented DVDs and Chinese takeaways…their pleasures would be simple. They would doze quietly through life together. If she didn't meet him, she could quite happily do the same thing on her own.

She had even begun to wonder if she should invite newly divorced Matthew Connell over for lunch. She had bumped into him in town the other day and he had appeared cosily defeated, though still cheery and plump. He had talked about his new central-heating boiler and his new software, and she had talked about an art exhibition in London she would like to see but wasn't going to go to. Dan would have said she should book the airline ticket immediately, but Matthew had simply smiled and understood that she wasn't that kind of person.

Yes, Matthew clearly wanted an easy life; and so did Caddy. Sadly, this wasn't a priority for Dan. He thought life was like a big airy house; he said it was terribly important to get to know all the rooms, not just get stuck in one of them and think that was all there was. But Matthew seemed the kind of person who would *like* to be stuck in a nice room with her. He had hardly any hair left, but that was a minor technicality. His greasy skin and the large pores on his nose were a bit off-putting, but in a way that might even be an advantage: if one wanted a comfortable, easy life, passion and romantic yearnings were highly inconvenient. When Jemma fled the nest, as she inevitably would one day soon, Caddy and Matthew could attend the occasional film together, and he might be able to explain the mysteries of Microsoft Word over coffee afterwards. The fact was, most women spent part of their life desperately wanting to fall madly in love and the rest of it rather hoping that they wouldn't.

Oh, feck it, anyway, why hadn't she just invited Dan over for coffee? Caddy jumped out of bed and raced into the shower. Then she sprayed deodorant under her arms while holding her breath. Yuck. She should have bought a roll-on. Inhaling deodorant was horrible.

'I am old and calm,' she said to herself as she put on some expensive moisturiser. It had been a present from Roz, who thought skin maintenance was frightfully important. Roz wanted to stay young for as long as possible, whereas Caddy was becoming increasingly aware of the joys of carpet slippers and sherry and Saga holidays. She must start listening to more classical music on the radio, and think of more things she would like to do, and then not do them. There was tremendous comfort to be found in simply not bothering.

'I am unattractive and fat.' This non-uplifting affirmation also calmed her, though it was untrue. 'I do not make elaborate lunches because I am too slow and sleepy.' By this stage she was beginning to feel like a dormouse. When Dan arrived, it might be quite a struggle for her to stay awake. Then she looked at her watch and exclaimed, '*Oh my God, he'll be here in two hours!*' and started to rush around the place like a blue-arsed fly.

'Blue-arsed fly' was a strange expression, really. She had never seen a blue-arsed fly. Did they actually exist? And was Dan really dating a very beautiful young actress called Zia Andersson? *I won't mention her to him*, Caddy thought. *He can mention her himself, and I'll make it obvious that I don't care. He wants this to be a lunch of regrets, but it won't be. I'll laugh and chat gaily, and say that I'm thrilled he's found such a desirable and appropriate partner...*

'*Zia Andersson has at long last found true love.*' That was what the newspaper caption had said. It was a stupid photograph, anyway; they were both laughing and looked like halfwits. How very unoriginal of them to fall in love after they'd already done it on television. Zia had been Dan's love interest in *Merrion Mansions*. That passion had been completely unconsummated and mostly conducted over privet hedges, but they were clearly making up for it now.

'Feck it!' Caddy shouted at her alarm clock. 'The house is a tip and I lack the mental health to cook pasta. It's a cruel hard world and I don't even own a comfortable bed.'

Ten minutes later she was racing round the house in her 'Underachievers Unite' T-shirt. She was a slut, a complete slut, and she desperately wanted a cigarette. She had given them up five years ago, but now she'd mug for a Gauloise. The sofa was covered in dog hair. She frantically attacked it with a strip of Sellotape. It made absolutely no difference.

Minutes before Dan was due to arrive, Caddy decided she would not put on any make-up. She did change, but only into Jemma's 'Surfers Against Sewerage' T-shirt. Dusting was not even considered: women spent far too much time trying to impress the opposite gender. She sang 'One Day at a Time, Sweet Jesus' – it had become the theme tune of her summer – as she searched for the least fashionable CD she owned. It was country music and had been bought in a car boot sale.

The print of the painting she and Dan had admired in the National Gallery caught her attention. It had been up in her bedroom, but she'd wrenched it from view. Since she'd heard about Zia, it no longer evoked happy memories. Now it was propped against a wall and seemed to be taunting her. Caddy could hardly bear to look at it. It was grossly over-sentimental. She managed to shove it under the sofa before it offended her beyond toleration.

If Dan was rude and reminded her of how much she had disappointed him, she would say wonderful things about his acting. Actors could never get enough of that kind of thing. It was just a lunch, and soon it would be over and she could turn on the television. There was quite a good western on at 3.30, and before it started she must buy some cheese-flavoured popcorn.

Dan wondered if he had found the right villa. Country music was blaring through an open window, sounds of gunfire – he hoped it was on the television – emerged from next door, a dog was barking and it all combined to make the most frightful din. But it was number 3 Bluebell Villas, so he tried to open the ramshackle wooden gate. After a few moments' experimentation he realised you had to lift it up to open the catch and again to close it.

The house certainly was very pink. He liked the green shutters, though: they seemed a bit eccentric, like their owner. The front lawn could do with mowing and was festooned with weeds that bore small yellow flowers. When Dan glanced at the big bay window he saw Caddy had collected some of these weeds and placed them in a vase. It was a typical touch, and he was sure that he'd find stones and shells and bits of driftwood on the mantelpiece. When they'd gone for walks by the sea, she'd spent most of her time looking at the stones and extolling their shapes and their beauty.

The front door was painted dark blue and decorated with a stained-glass sunflower. Near the doorbell there was a sign that said 'Beware of the dog'; someone, probably Jemma, had scrawled 'Ha Ha Ha' beneath it in blue Biro. There was a statue of a naked man – he had an inscrutable smile and the first traces of moss were gathering round his genitals – near a large lavender bush. Dan started to hum to himself. He hoped

Caddy would like the roses he'd brought. They were expensive ones from a floristry shop, pink and tight and just about to open.

He rang the bell and waited. It was an old-fashioned bell, not one of those electronic ones that always sounded like ice-cream vans. Half a minute passed. Where was she? He heard sounds of scuffling and peered through the bay window, which gave a clear view of the sitting-room and the kitchen. Caddy was trying to hide a pile of magazines in the washing machine. She clearly hadn't changed all that much.

Dan waited tactfully for a minute and then rang the bell again. After some seconds the door was opened with a flourish.

'Hi, Dan!' Caddy had a large strip of Sellotape on her hair. She seemed rather anxious. Chump was panting excitedly beside her.

'Hello, Caddy.' Dan looked into her eyes, but she appeared to be staring into the distance over his right shoulder. 'These are for you.'

'Oh!' She was clearly taken aback. 'Roses! How lovely!' She took them from him. 'Roses,' she repeated. 'How *kind* of you.'

Dan waited. 'Shall…shall I come in?'

'Oh, yes, *of course*! Come in. Isn't the weather wonderful? Sit anywhere you want.'

'Here's some wine, too.'

'Oh, how nice of you! You shouldn't have.' Thank God he had, because she'd forgotten to buy some herself.

'*You'll never know how much I missed you when you left me in Ohio. I put a dollar in the jukebox for all the things I didn't say…*' The lyrics to the country song were becoming a bit too accurate. Caddy switched off the stereo firmly and fled to the kitchen.

Dan followed. She jumped when she found him standing behind her.

'Sorry. I didn't mean to surprise you.'

'You didn't surprise me. I mean, you…' What on earth was

she trying to say? She reached for some plates. 'I painted this room recently.'

'It's a lovely colour.'

'Is it?' She looked at him dubiously.

'Yes. Are you having doubts?' He was standing far too close.

'No, not at all. I…I *love* it.' Why had she used that word?

'Good. I'm glad to hear it.' Dan bent over and patted Chump, who had been looking up at him expectantly.

'Look, why don't you go into the sitting-room and relax?' Caddy looked up at him. He seemed taller than she'd remembered.

'Only if you will.'

'But I have to stay here and cook the pasta.'

'I mean relax. You seem a little uptight.'

'No, I'm not.'

'Yes, you are.'

There was an awkward silence, and Caddy wondered if she should refute this observation again. She decided to go for a complete change of subject. 'I've been doing a lot of swimming lately.'

'That's nice.'

'No, it isn't, really. It's all rather complicated.'

'Why?' He seemed solemn, but she could see his eyes were twinkling.

'Because, well, Roz's sex…' She gulped. 'I mean, Roz's ex-boyfriend is a member.'

'A member of what?'

'Of the same leisure centre. They argue every time they set eyes on each other.'

'Oh, dear.'

'It's very hot, isn't it?' Caddy opened a packet of spaghetti.

'Yes, it is pretty warm.' Dan was looking at a large bottle of extra-virgin olive oil.

'I'm sorry that I'm…' She hesitated. 'That I'm not more ready.'

He looked at her.

'For lush...I mean lunch.' What was happening to her tongue?

Surely he would mention Zia Andersson soon. But he didn't. Instead he said, 'I haven't quite mastered wrenching wine-bottles open with my teeth yet. Do you have a corkscrew?'

'Oh, yes. Somewhere.' She rummaged in a drawer. Sometimes it took her ages to find the corkscrew... 'Here it is!'

'Thanks.' Their eyes met for a moment, and Caddy got that same old quivery feeling in her stomach. He was being so pleasant. Last time they'd met... no, she mustn't think of it. She mustn't think of him grabbing his coat and leaving the café. The hurt and anger in his eyes.

'I didn't cook the pasta before you arrived because...'

'Stop worrying.' He said it firmly.

'I got the sauce from the supermarket. Oh, dear – I shouldn't have told you that. I should have pretended.'

'Look, Caddy, I'm not expecting anything fancy. Relax.'

'Yes. Sorry.' She stared into the pan of boiling water and then shoved the spaghetti into it. As usual, it just sat there and she had to shove it down as it softened. If she wasn't careful it would start to stick together, too. Why wasn't Dan in the sitting-room? It wasn't fair of him to watch her. But at least he was being friendly and civil. Not all exes were as unpleasant as Rufus.

'I think your new house is lovely.'

'Really?' She frowned uncertainly.

'Yes. I wouldn't say it if I didn't mean it.'

'Thank you.' She'd forgotten how kind he could be, and how the smell of him wafted from beneath his cotton shirt. It was a lovely smell, barely discernible; it was nature's lust cocktail, and she had to ignore it. Maybe the heat was him, not the weather. A trickle of perspiration was running down Caddy's forehead. Those spiritual books were right: all sorts of things that were hardly ever mentioned happened between people – vibrations and tingles and glows that you simply

81

couldn't stop.

'It's very hot, isn't it?'

'Yes. You said that already.'

And I'll say it again if I want to, Caddy thought. *Oh, why can't you be more like Matthew Connell? He wouldn't tell me if I repeated myself. He'd know it was only because I have a slow brain with odd things floating around in it.*

'That's a nice washing machine. Is it new?' As Dan stooped to examine it, Caddy shoved a glass into his hand.

'Have some wine.'

'Is that an order?'

'Yes. And I'll have some too.'

'I didn't expect this,' he said as the rich red wine glugged into the glasses.

She almost said, 'Neither did I,' but she stopped herself just in time. *And I didn't expect you to be so nice and forgiving*, she wanted to add. *It's almost as though we're friends, like I wanted us to be. You must have forgotten, or forgiven, my sad closed heart.*

'How's Jemma?'

'She's in Arizona for the summer. Staying with cousins.'

'Good for her. It's a great place.'

'You've been there?'

'Yes. When I was a student. I love that red rock. It's amazing.'

'She's working in a restaurant and saving up money for college. She has to recite the whole menu off by heart. She says she wants an Oscar at the end of it for Best Newcomer Specialising in Obesity.'

Dan laughed. She'd forgotten how his laugh burst on to his face with such warmth and wildness. He was the kind of person people told too much to. You could be sitting with him, talking about cream buns, and suddenly blurt out that men kidnapped you and dragged you off to salsa in your sleep. It was his eyes that did it. They were steady and unshockable and rarely entirely serious. Roz said they were the eyes of an 'old soul' who knew that very few things were really important.

'Oh, no!'

'What is it now?'

'I forgot to get garlic bread.'

'Well, then, I'll have to leave.'

She stared at him in consternation.

'Do you want me to lay the table?'

'Yes. Thank you.' Caddy smiled.

They discussed where things might be found, and why there was a hot-water bottle amongst the plates. Some of Jemma's incense sticks had got in with the cutlery and there was a badge that proclaimed 'I believe in unicorns' in the bowl Caddy planned to use for the Parmesan. She told Dan that everything would have been in its proper place if she hadn't moved recently, and he nodded as though he believed her. It was extraordinary: all the old awkwardness between them had vanished. It was obviously because of Zia Andersson. Now that he had a proper girlfriend, they could at last be friends.

When the table was laid, Caddy suggested that Dan should play with Chump in the garden. He loved people throwing squeaky toys for him. Squeaks, woofs, yelps, laughter… they were obviously enjoying themselves. As she poured the sauce onto the pasta, she reflected that it was very peevish and unpleasant of her to have resented Dan's new liaison. So many of her own liaisons had been dangereuses – but Dan and Zia's partnership would be different.

What was more, Dan was quite right to want someone younger. Zia could give Dan children, and Caddy didn't want to have another baby. He and Zia would have bonny, beaming sons and daughters. And subtle bathrooms with stacks of fresh towels. Their paint would be weathered Mediterranean, and their sitting-room would not be littered with unread Sunday supplements. Their animals would be large and boisterous and affectionate. When they eventually moved to a beautiful house in the country, a river would flow nearby; on sleepy Sunday afternoons, they'd have picnics beside it and paddle lazily in their rowing-boat. Photographs of them would appear in the features pages of up-market newspapers. And they would probably be asked to describe their day.

Any time Caddy read a 'describe your day' article she felt woefully inadequate. The people in them always got up extraordinarily early and did yoga, before having a carefully prepared breakfast of exotic fruit, oatmeal, fresh orange juice and a glass of algae. At about 7 a.m. they got down to their correspondence and made international calls, then crammed in some quality time with their adorable offspring before showering and changing into beautiful clothes in soft, expensive fabrics. The rest of the day was usually spent doing important things in interesting places with fascinating people. During lunch they nurtured deep and enduring friendships. And in the evening they returned to their besotted families to share sushi and watch *Coronation Street*, or went to dinner parties and concerts and other cultural activities. 'I'm actually a very lazy person,' they often claimed, with astonishing implausibility. 'There's nothing I like more than lounging around and eating chocolates. And I can't bear to miss the omnibus edition of *The Archers*.'

Soon Dan and Zia would be saying these kinds of things. And Caddy could point to the articles and say casually, 'I knew him once.' It would certainly impress her colleagues. They would crowd round her and ask questions, and she would say that Dan MacIntyre was 'a really nice person' and that they had met in the National Gallery 'when he picked up my cardigan. I didn't even know I'd dropped it.' And they would laugh and find this snippet fascinating and unexpected. Some women in the staff room might wish they had dropped their cardigans in the National Gallery that day, because then Dan MacIntyre would have become their friend and they could say he was 'a really nice person'. And Caddy would never correct this impression, though it was so far from the truth it was almost offensive.

Things being over was never easy, even when you *wanted* them to be over. The truth was, every person was at least twenty different people. Perverse parts of you could suddenly lunge forwards and want to kiss someone and bury your head in his strong, broad chest...

Caddy took a very deep breath. Being a parallel woman meant she could feel all these things and still remember that she had forgotten to buy olives.

Despite feeling as though she had drunk five glasses of Chardonnay, Caddy managed to put together some edible substances and find the orange paper napkins. She couldn't get the smell of smoked salmon off her fingers, but since she also reeked of garlic and lavender aromatherapy oil – lavender was supposed to be very calming – it probably didn't matter.

As Dan returned, she realised the roses were still lying on the sideboard. It was terribly rude not to put flowers in a vase as soon as you got them. She started to hunt for a vase but couldn't find one; this provoked a mild panic, until Dan pointed out that the glass jar that had contained the sauce would probably do.

They sat down to lunch. It was tasty and pleasant and the pasta wasn't overdone. Caddy even remembered to comment on the wine and the fact that it came from Australia. She also contrived to ask Dan about acting and his life in general without mentioning Zia Andersson. She had forgotten he could be such easy, undemanding company when he wasn't trying to storm his way into her heart.

'I almost decided not to come here, you know,' Dan said as she handed him his coffee. It was freshly ground, not instant.

'Oh. Really?' Caddy was resting languidly on her tropical-lagoon sofa. 'What made you change your mind?'

'The note from your mother.'

'*What?*' She almost catapulted towards the ceiling. 'What note from my mother?'

Dan shifted in his seat. 'The one that...you know...explained why you'd invited me to lunch.'

'But I never *told* her I'd invited you!'

Dan was beginning to look irritated. 'Well, she must have found out somehow.'

'What did she say?'

'She said she knew you hoped I would call around to see your house, especially given the date.'

'The date.' Caddy was on her feet. 'What the fuck does she mean by *the date*?'

Dan's face had grown still and his eyes were icy. 'The date of our first meeting, of course. Tomorrow's the anniversary.'

'The woman's mad! How dare she!'

Dan stood up.

'She doesn't even know the date we met!'

'Yes, she does. That evening we had dinner, she asked me and I told her. You're the one who's forgotten it.' All expression had left his face.

'It's so bloody typical of her! She's always interfering!'

'Are you listening to a word I say?'

'I can't even have a…a friend over for lunch without her pushing her nose in.'

Dan glanced ostentatiously at his watch.

'She didn't know about my letter, so…' Caddy was pacing the room like a detective. 'So she must have just wanted you to turn up and catch me unguarded.'

'Yes. Unguarded. You would have hated that, wouldn't you?' He glared at her. 'It means nothing to you, does it?'

'What?' She was suddenly aware that his eyes were glinting with anger.

'The day we met. What it was like.'

'Oh.' She looked down at the floor. 'Of course it does.'

'Thanks for lunch, but I think it's best if we don't meet again.'

'Fine. I didn't expect to meet you again anyway.' Caddy tried to look defiant, but her hands were trembling. 'Oh, Dan…why aren't you angry with her instead of me? She's the one who's…who's a silly old bag. Alain was right about that.'

'Who's Alain?'

Caddy flinched.

'Fine. Don't tell me. I don't want to know. This was a mistake. I'm sorry that I've embarrassed us both by thinking…'

'Thinking what?' Caddy's chest felt so tight she could hardly breathe.

'Oh, nothing that you'd want to know about.' Dan reached into a pocket for his car keys and bent to pat Chump, who solemnly offered a paw.

'So you're…going.' She could hardly believe it.

'Yes.' He turned away from her and went to the front door.

'Dan! Dan!' Caddy called after him as he walked down the pathway. She didn't know what she wanted to say, but it didn't matter, because he didn't even look around.

He got into his car and turned the key. In a moment he was gone.

Chapter Nine

'YOUR FATHER HAS MOVED into the shed.' The message greeted Caddy when she returned from swimming. Her mother's voice on the answering machine sounded very clipped and resigned, and not particularly surprised.

Caddy knew that she herself should feel surprised. She knew that this was a very strange occurrence and that the small solidities of her parents' marriage were, perhaps, melting. She should be feeling sticky and swampish, but she wasn't.

The first thought that flashed through her mind was that her father had escaped. He had escaped from his wife, who had never understood him. Perhaps now he would play the harmonica with greater eloquence. His endearing honkings on that instrument had always seemed an attempt at inner harmony. *Poor Dad*, she thought as she recalled his dear balding head. She liked to run her hand over it and feel its smoothness. How often she had done this in wordless comfort – for he had comforted her so many times himself...

He hadn't regarded Caddy as a 'fallen woman' when she had become pregnant. He had said that her mother 'didn't really mean' her waspish comments about single mothers and the necessity of adoption. 'She still loves you,' he had declared, but Caddy had seen very little evidence of it. If her mother had truly loved her, surely she would have shown more compassion?

'You can't stay here,' Ava had announced on that miserable weekend when Caddy revealed her secret.

'I don't need to stay with you. I have a home. With Alain.'

'No, you don't. He'll go.'

'He loves me.' Caddy's eyes had glowed with indignation.

'People use that word too easily. If he loved you, he wouldn't have put you in this situation.'

'We used a condom, but–'

'I don't need to hear this.'

'Darling, let the girl speak,' Jim had interrupted. It had been one of his very few moments of rebellion.

Ava had then pronounced that it was out of the question that Caddy should marry Alain, because he was feckless and couldn't be relied upon. 'You must go to a home and have the baby and give it up.'

'I don't want to.'

'You must. And no one must know – no one.'

After this conversation, Caddy had gone to the lake. It had been the favourite place of her childhood. The water was smooth and forgiving, framed by hills and rippled in the sunlight. Local folklore said that many mysteries lay in its depths. *The lake knows*, she had thought. *The lake knows my secret and is still calm.*

She had taken off her shoes and socks and paddled in its brackish water. Small fish had nudged her toes and the rocks beneath her had been cold and round. She had picked up a pebble and put it in her pocket. And, as her fingers closed over it, she had known what she had to do.

On the train back to Dublin she had not cried. She had known that Alain would be waiting for her at the station, and that he would pronounce her mother 'a silly old bag' and firmly take her suitcase. He was her family now – he and their unborn child. There was so much in her past that called this shameful, but she mustn't listen to those voices. Why was there all this talk of virgins and whores? Surely there must be someplace in between.

Caddy had not returned to the village until Jemma was ten years old. Her father had collected her at Tralee station. He had visited Dublin four times in ten years to see his daughter and her child. He had told his wife that he was travelling on business, and she hadn't challenged him. It was unusual for him to strike out on his own, but very occasionally he did so.

It was during that homecoming that Ava fell in love with Jemma, the child she had tried to banish. Some of this love spilled onto Caddy, who realised her mother was forgetting all the terrible things she had once said. She proclaimed that she hoped Caddy would marry because 'Jemma would love to have a proper father'. She took her granddaughter into the village, and Mrs Moore the postmistress extolled her beauty and gave her a Snickers bar. Everyone seemed to warm to this lovely child, but Caddy knew she herself was not completely forgiven. There were sometimes gaps between recognition and greeting. She was a person with a past. But surely everyone had that.

These days she thought of her mother as someone who was divorced from her; but, as ex-partners often do, she tried to be civil to her because of other family members. They had parted because of irreconcilable differences, though sadly her mother did not realise this. It was only Caddy who knew that all significant communication between them was over. To her, Ava Lavelle had always been a problematic figure. When Caddy was small, Ava had not been a symbol of security and constancy. Her moods varied dramatically, though this never affected her talent for criticism. Caddy had never had the sense of someone safe and sure whom she could run to. Often she had found Ava staring mournfully out the window, too lost in some dream to notice a small girl who needed comfort.

'Why do black babies need milk-bottle tops?' When she was small it had seemed an urgent question. Her mother saved milk-bottle tops very carefully. They were washed and placed in a big plastic bag, where they didn't smell very nice. Caddy felt very sad for the black babies who would eventually receive them. They would tear open the wrapping and find these smelly cast-offs.

'Why don't we send them toys?' She hoped her father might be more forthcoming.

'Don't worry, Caddy,' he explained gently. 'We're not sending them the tops. They're going to be sold for money, which will buy what the babies need.'

She developed a considerable respect for the silver tops after that. When she squished them down and took them off, she raced to wash them. And Ava smiled. Yes, in those early years her mother had sometimes shown her tenderness and affection – though she had also spent a great deal of time gazing sadly out of the kitchen window as if she longed, ferociously, to be someplace else.

She was missing something. Even as a toddler, Caddy sensed it. Ava's life had not turned out as she had hoped, and the people around her couldn't make up for it. Maybe she even blamed them for keeping her somewhere she didn't want to be.

I've made her cry. Caddy had thought it so many times as she saw her mother's eyes well up with tears.

'Why are you crying?'

'I'm not crying.'

'You are.'

'Go outside and play.'

Being indoors had become even more problematic as Caddy grew older. She had breasts and pubic hair, and parts of her were curving. The free and freckled country girl that her mother had tolerated suddenly became subject to a host of containments.

'That dress is too short.'

'What have you done to your hair?'

'Take off that lipstick at once.'

'I will not tolerate this wildness.'

Yes, it was the wildness in her that her mother feared.

'Men don't respect women they sleep with – unless they're married to them.' The stodgy nutrition of Sunday lunch was made even heavier by such comments.

'I don't know if I want to get married.'

'Of course you want to get married! Every woman wants to get married.'

'That's not true. I have friends who–'

'I told you we shouldn't have allowed her to go to that college in Dublin.'

'Let the girl speak, Ava.'

'If only she'd enrolled in that secretarial course in Tralee. Then she could be at home. With us.'

Caddy had often heard herself discussed in the third person. In a way, her eventual banishment from the village had been simply a confirmation that her mother was deficient in imagination and compassion and that this could make her heartless. She thought of the world solely in her terms and was rarely aware of how much her words could wound. She seemed incapable of understanding that other people might feel things just as deeply as she did; she was sensitive when she was hurt, but rarely displayed the same interest when someone else was in the same situation. Caddy suspected that she remained happily unaware of the anguish her lack of support had caused her daughter. There were certain standards when it came to pregnancy. Ava had adhered to them so that an untidy situation might seem more orderly.

I must write to Dad and say he can stay here if he wants, Caddy decided. *That shed can't be very comfortable.* She scribbled a hasty note. How nice it would be to have his company again! And her mother would hardly miss him anyway.

As Caddy posted her letter, Ava was deciding that she would never allow her husband back into the house. This was because he was having numerous affairs with foreign women. She had the evidence. It was a terrible thing, and she couldn't tell anyone, not even Caddy. Not yet, anyway.

She had walked into the village that morning intending to tell Beth, her bridge partner, but had ended up discussing Scandinavia. 'Seamus and I are going to Finland for a couple of weeks,' Beth had announced. 'We got cut-price tickets with those supermarket coupons. You should get some yourself. I'm sure Jim would like the fjords.'

'Yes, he probably would,' Ava had said brightly, though she was feeling distinctly fjordish herself. Life held many cavernous crevices, she realised. And you could be right in the middle of their lonely depths without anyone noticing.

'You could come with us. We could make a foursome. And it might make him – you know…' The shed was rarely referred to directly in Ava's conversations with friends.

'Mmm.' Ava's gaze had settled on the bright-orange

curtains in Beth's otherwise sedate sitting-room. 'Actually, we may be going to Dublin to visit Caddy. She's a bit lonely at the moment, with Jemma away.'

'Yes. Yes, of course.' Beth had smiled. 'Have you ever been to Finland?'

'No, but I think it's very nice,' Ava had answered vaguely. She had not taken up Beth's offer of a cup of tea.

Later, in Sally's Café, she had had a scone with a skim of butter and some gooseberry jam. The teapot was, as usual, rather leaky, and she decided to finally comment upon this to Sally herself. With some vigour. People had to mention such things. One couldn't ignore them indefinitely.

Sally had not seemed offended, and had offered her a handful of napkins to mop up the spillage on the table. 'Let me make you some fresh Darjeeling,' she'd said, but Ava had replied that she had an adequate quantity of it already. Not too much had spilt, really.

'And how's your husband?' Sally had inquired – rather keenly, Ava had thought. A slight hush had fallen over the café at these words, and Ava had realised her reply was eagerly awaited.

'He's…he's doing some work in the garden at the moment,' she'd announced. This was, in fact, the truth. The shed was in the garden, and Jim had been washing up after breakfast when she'd left. Sally had smiled and said something about geraniums before drifting off towards a cluster of tourists.

Ava was normally friendly to tourists. Irish people were friendly; it said so in the brochures, and it was largely true, though not as true as it had been. Sometimes she had to work a bit at friendliness with foreigners – but then, all national traits required a certain degree of dedication. For example, when she sat beside, say, an American on a bus, she exhibited a great deal more bonhomie than she would have with a local. It was quite cheering, in a way, seeing how it pleased them. But today Ava felt a great disapproval towards foreigners. Especially if they were female, like the olive-skinned beauties sitting near her.

They were Italian, and they were talking volubly and fidgeting with their long black hair. As Ava ate her scone, she glowered at them occasionally and wondered if any of her husband's paramours shared their features.

How innocent she'd been about his escapades! When he had joined the Mountain Minstrels, she had truly believed it was entirely above board. Every so often the all-male group had gone abroad to give concerts, and Jim had sent her effusive postcards. *Those poor people, listening to him playing the harmonica*, she thought now. *Maybe he didn't even do that. Maybe it was just a cunning ruse to meet foreign women.* One of the great mysteries of Ava's life had been her husband's inclusion in a group that purported to produce soothing melodies. He probably went off on his own as soon as he arrived at the airport, she decided. Yes, it was on those trips that he must have met Conchita and Paloma and Drusilla, and the other names she'd glimpsed.

And all the village probably knew about his infidelities.

Ava had only found out about them the day before. She hadn't really meant to sneak into the shed, but Jim had left the door unlocked and her curiosity had overwhelmed her. She had darted inside, hoping to find a large cupboard under construction, or at least his Parliamo Italiano tapes or his stamp books. Instead she had been confronted by a sheaf of letters on a desk with numerous ring marks – he was obviously completely ignoring her advice about using mats for all beverages.

She had moved cautiously towards the correspondence. She didn't like reading other people's private papers, but they probably were about trifling matters anyway. Since he'd retired, Jim had seemed to have a great capacity for inane enthusiasms.

'Dear Conchita,' she'd read quickly, aware that her husband might return at any moment, 'I think about you every single day. You are not alone. I will never forget about you. You are a very special person, and when I look at your photograph I so wish that you were sitting here with me now in my shed…'

Ava had blinked with disbelief and then flicked to the next letter in the pile. It said almost the same thing, only it was to a woman called Paloma. The letter beneath was to Drusilla and was nearly identical. Her husband wasn't just cheating on her – he was cheating on his foreign women!

She had been about to slump onto a decidedly scruffy chair when she had heard the sound of his car. With frantic movements, she'd managed to re-stack the letters so that they looked undisturbed. Then she had fled the shed, just before her husband's Volvo crunched onto the pebbles in the driveway.

Now, as she sat in Sally's Café, Ava felt her whole marriage was a farce. People laughed at farces. They threw their heads back and great gusts of mirth burst into the air. All her devotion, all her tender domesticity and selfless patience, seemed derisory in the face of Jim's disloyalty. If she didn't know him, how could she know anyone? She should have left him years ago. She had often wanted to.

I must get away, she thought. *Far, far away… but where to?* That was the awful thing about being seventy and a loyal, diligent wife and mother: 'away' was taken from you. You didn't know where to go, apart from the well-trodden paths.

Ava left the café and plodded sadly homewards. The landscape and the familiar houses annoyed her. She had seen them too often. *I thought that being a wife and mother would bring me love*, she thought. *But it hasn't. Being a wife and mother is terribly difficult, and it means you get blamed for things. Someone will probably march up to me someday soon and say I caused Third World debt.*

I must distract myself, she decided as she arrived at her pristine bungalow. *I'll send Caddy that tea cosy I bought for her last week.*

She went to a cupboard and extracted her present, which was multicoloured and hand-knitted and had a large pom-pom on the top. It was a very nice tea cosy, and just the sort of thing a metropolitan young woman mightn't have. Tea did cool quite quickly, and if you had friends over it was important to keep it warm. Even the look of the tea cosy was friendly. There was nothing sharp or critical about it... Ava gazed out the kitchen window with a sigh of deep regret.

She had been sharp and unforgiving once. That time when Caddy had said she was pregnant. Ava had been angry – and not just for herself: for her daughter, who hadn't found true love. Why, oh, why hadn't Caddy heeded her warnings? She couldn't bear to witness Caddy's unhappiness, so she had found other ways to love her.

She should have told her – she should have told her years ago. But now it was too late.

Chapter Ten

DAN AND CADDY WERE reading the same holiday brochure, though not in the same place. They had both contacted a man called Malcolm who was a travel agent. Dan knew Malcolm from university, and Caddy knew him because he was a former neighbour. He was married to Harriet, who was constantly trying to clear clutter – only the week before, Caddy had almost ended up with a framed print of a huge tomato.

'I need to travel as quickly as possible,' Caddy said. 'It's been a very odd summer and it's still only July. I need to get away.'

'Where?'

'Anywhere, as long as it isn't too expensive... anywhere apart from Belgium.'

'Belgium can be very nice. Bruges is a beautiful city.'

'Warm,' Caddy said. 'I'd like it to be warm, too, and by the sea. And restful.'

Dan said much the same thing when he phoned, but he talked to Harriet, who sometimes manned the office switchboard. 'I'll get Malcolm to call you,' she said briskly. As soon as she put down the phone, she consulted Caddy's travel details. Caddy's holiday had already been booked and it seemed supremely sensible to send Dan to Rhodes too. All of Caddy's former neighbours felt it was a terrible pity that Caddy and Dan had parted for no good reason. Harriet was particularly vexed about it because she'd had a long chat with Ava about Caddy's loveless state, during one of Ava's infrequent visits.

'We need to mount a campaign,' Ava had declared. 'I have allies in County Kerry, but I hardly know anyone in Dublin.'

'Allies?' Harriet had been fascinated.

'Yes. I'm a matchmaker, but I can't do it on my own. A friend called Beth usually helps me, and Sally from the café.

The women in my knitting circle are also very helpful.'

Harriet hadn't said anything, but from that moment she had decided to use her own matchmaking skills as soon as a suitable opportunity arose. If Dan and Caddy stayed in nearby and relatively small hotels they were very likely to bump into each other. Their holidays would overlap by a week, and romance might blossom with the aid of retsina, scant clothing and the absence of Zia Andersson. Zia was far too young for Dan, anyway. They didn't look right together.

It was just the sort of project that gave Harriet immense pleasure – though some of her introductions had proved less than satisfactory. She had, for example, introduced Caddy to a man who seemed ideal until he announced that he hated dogs and could only be phoned on Wednesdays between three and four-thirty. He also wore a hairpiece, which had somehow fallen off while Caddy and he were watching *Some Like It Hot*.

Harriet sighed. She feared that this and other sobering blind dates – at least she'd *tried* – had contributed to Caddy's great romantic apathy. Decisive action was clearly called for. Harriet had already surreptitiously placed a photo of a couple embracing in Caddy's feng shui relationship corner, when she'd visited the new house. It was hidden behind a peace lily she had also brought with her.

Fortunately, Caddy was completely unaware of the campaign that was being waged on her behalf. If she had known about it, she would have been tempted to flee to Outer Mongolia.

Instead, she was dashing desperately towards Samantha's bright, minimalistic apartment. This was the ridiculous thing about having massages. The whole thing was supposed to relax her, but she always left the house far too late and ended up stressed out and exhausted as she virtually ran down the road. Her T-shirt was wet from perspiration and her heart was pounding. Oh, the pressures of self-improvement!

But the minute she stepped into Samantha's serene massage room, all these pressures evaporated and she was left with only her usual guilt about not having better underwear.

Caddy had started visiting Samantha for occasional massages during the Easter holidays, and it no longer seemed a luxury. Harriet had made the introduction. Harriet seemed to know everyone. She was a great believer in 'networking' and often attended high-powered breakfasts and lunches for 'professional women' – Harriet regarded herself as a professional woman, while Caddy said that she herself was still an amateur. It was at one of these breakfasts (she never had more than one croissant and a cup of very strong black coffee) that Harriet had learned about Samantha. Apparently she was great at 'getting you back into your body' and 'reminding you of your feet', which was essential for 'grounding'. She was also very spiritual and didn't mind if you burst into tears – Harriet sometimes felt the need to burst into tears, though she didn't quite know why.

At the start of the massage Caddy always gave Samantha a description of her current angsts so that she could select the appropriate aromatherapy oils. 'I want something for indecision and dread and impatience,' she said this time. 'And I'd like more clarity about things in general.'

Samantha accepted these statements with complete sang-froid. She was a very calm person.

She had said something rather odd when Caddy had first met her. 'Have we met before?' She'd surveyed her new client curiously. 'You seem very familiar.'

Caddy had said she was sure they hadn't met before. Samantha's was the kind of face she would have remembered. 'But I have seen you somewhere,' Samantha had persisted; and then she'd stood very still, as though suddenly recalling where.

She hadn't spoken about it. In fact, the subject had never been mentioned again. It was Caddy who talked most during their appointments. This time, as Samantha kneaded her flesh, she found herself saying that she kept changing her mind about things. Did she want adventures or a quiet life? Should she give up on relationships completely or partially? Was the paint in her kitchen too yellow? What would she do if Jemma got pregnant in Arizona? Why did everyone keep going on about how great love was, when it was clearly so bloody difficult? Samantha massaged her back wordlessly, and gradually the sound of whale song made her drift towards the deep.

Caddy preferred Samantha's whale-song tape to the panpipes one, which could sound slightly agitated. Listening to huge mysterious creatures calling to one another was very liberating. Sometimes Caddy imagined that she was a whale too and had forgotten everything she didn't really need to know. Out there in the blue vastness there was no call for urgent improvement. She couldn't speculate on the whale that she once had been or might become. The journey itself was the becoming, and it was sufficient. Out... how far away she was drifting – drifting to a place of dreams and sleep and another kind of waking.

She was swimming in Moon River. That was her parents' special song. They had heard it at a restaurant on their first wedding anniversary. Jim often tried to play it on his harmonica, and Ava said, 'How can he stand to play that thing so badly? Doesn't he hear himself?' But in Caddy's dream her dad's blue river sounded bruised and beautiful. She hadn't known you could swim in a song, lie back and let it lift you. That was the thing: just to let it. Not to struggle, but to trust.

Oh, Dad, I love you! she cried out inside. *I love everybody, really, deep down in this place I've forgotten. It's another kind of love. A bigger kind.*

'Love...' She was saying it out loud when Samantha trailed long, sensitive fingers through her hair. This was the signal that the massage was ending and she must return to life's surface.

That place where Dan was gone. And she had to keep flossing her teeth and shaving her legs and pretend she didn't care.

Chapter Eleven

'SOMETHING'S HAPPENED TO THE sperm.'

From the outset Caddy knew this was not going to be a normal conversation.

'The sperm. Something's happened to it,' Roz repeated.

'I didn't know you had any.'

'Can I come round?'

'Yes, of course.' Caddy hung up the phone and stared at her partially packed suitcase. She was going to Greece tomorrow and she didn't feel like discussing sperm. It wasn't the kind of thing people talked about much. In fact, in some circles it was almost never mentioned.

A few minutes later, Roz was sitting at the distressed-pine kitchen table. 'Bernice put it in her coffee.'

'What?'

'Jamie's sperm. Bernice put it in her coffee.'

Caddy sat very still. This was a most extraordinary development and she was trying very hard not to laugh. 'She – she works with you, doesn't she?'

'Yes. And she's extremely short-sighted. I really shouldn't have put it in the milk compartment of the fridge.'

There was a long pause.

'The phone rang, you see, and when I went to answer it she decided to make some coffee. Why on earth didn't she keep her glasses on?'

'When did you get the…sperm?'

'Jamie dropped it round this morning. He's going away for a while and he thought I might want it.'

'He's very keen about it, isn't he?'

'Yes, well, he likes me. And he probably wants to spread his genes.'

'I think it's more than that.' Caddy frowned. 'I bet he wants another woman in his life. Men don't go around offering sperm quite so casually.'

'He did suggest we have an affair once.'

'You must have absolutely nothing to do with him,' Caddy declared. 'No man can be trusted. Especially one who's already married.'

'What do you mean, "no man can be trusted"? That's a terrible thing to say.'

Caddy looked at a carton of margarine guiltily. She normally tried to keep this belief, that men were simply not worth the bother, to herself. It was not a belief that suited all women, and it didn't suit Roz, even if her romantic experiences completely confirmed it. All rules have their exceptions, and Caddy wanted Roz to find the exception to this one.

She turned back to more practical matters. 'Was it in a bottle?'

'Yes. Bernice thought it was soya milk. She's trying to avoid dairy products at the moment.'

'Did she drink the coffee?'

'I grabbed it from her just in time.'

'What did you say?'

'I just shrieked.'

'Did you tell her what it was?'

'No, of course I didn't. I just mumbled something, and she got the impression it was a buttermilk culture. "If you get more of it, will you give me some?" she kept saying. "I really want to start making my own organic wholemeal bread."' Roz laughed in a hollow way.

'Well, at least you can see the humour in it,' Caddy said gently.

'It was funny peculiar, not funny ha ha,' Roz sighed. 'The ridiculous thing was that we were discussing an ad for baby powder.'

'It's nice that they let you work from home sometimes,' Caddy commented. Roz looked as though she could do with some distraction. 'Have you thought any more about writing a film script?'

Roz was not about to be deflected. 'Bernice said, "Oh, this

seems a bit gooey." That's what alerted me.'

'I see.'

'What's happened to my life, Caddy? Last night I realised I'd watched the same episode of *Friends* four times.'

'Well, they do keep repeating them.'

'Do you have any wine?'

'Yes. I'll get some.' Caddy went over to a cupboard and extracted a Cabernet Sauvignon from Chile. 'I tried some of this in the supermarket the other day,' she said chattily. 'It's surprisingly fruity.'

'I don't care if it smells of stale socks,' Roz said listlessly. 'Are we women just plain stupid?'

'What do you mean?'

'We want things that are so very hard to find.'

Caddy struggled with the bottle opener. Between yanks she said, 'Maybe happiness is learning not to want them so much. That's what I believe, anyway.'

'You're so disciplined.'

'No, I'm not, but I've found I don't need someone else to feel contented. Sometimes I get weird longings, but they come and go. You can watch them like clouds floating across the sky.'

'But you get lonely. I know you do.'

'Yes.' The cork popped gently. 'I often feel very lonely. That's the hard part – being on your own when it was the last thing you expected.'

'So many women never find anyone.' Roz held out her glass. 'Films and books are full of people finding someone. It's not fair. They should tell the truth.'

'It's true for some people and not for others.' Caddy sighed. 'I think true love may exist, but it's a fairly rare flower. Look at Harriet and Malcolm – they probably only stay together out of habit and a shared fondness for Mozart and roast chicken.'

'And yacht clubs and champagne and gossip,' Roz said. 'It suits them.'

'Yes, maybe it does.' Caddy sighed again. 'It seems sort of

103

sad, but they're the ones who feel sorry for us.'

'That's another thing that keeps them together. Feeling sorry for us,' Roz commented grimly. She took a gulp from her glass. 'Tom never even thanked me for the aftershave. I shoved it through his letterbox personally, and he didn't even phone me.'

'Men have a very strange relationship with telephones,' Caddy said. 'It's all part of that horrible game that one gets so weary of eventually.'

'He counted my toes, and now he's probably forgotten my name.'

'Well, it was a rather slender link, Roz. Men in nightclubs aren't often looking for long-term relationships.'

'I knew that at the time, but then I somehow forgot it. Desperate women do that.' Roz tore open a crisp packet with great ferocity. 'He seemed decent and ordinary. I thought it was very mature of me to find him so attractive.'

'So he's ugly?'

'Oh, no!' Roz exclaimed. 'He's quite handsome, but he isn't dark and brooding. And he doesn't think most people are beneath him. That sort of elitist nonsense doesn't attract me any more.'

Caddy remembered all the snooty and high-handed men who had cavorted carelessly through her friend's hopes.

'His photographs are beautiful,' Roz continued dreamily. 'You can tell a lot about a man from his photographs.'

'Forget him,' Caddy said decisively. 'It's far easier than it seems.'

They sat pensively for some moments. Roz traced a finger round the edge of her glass. 'I've decided I don't want to rear a child on my own, Caddy. I know you did, but you're much more patient than I am.'

'I didn't think I'd be doing it on my own.'

'I know.' Roz reached out and patted Caddy's shoulder. 'We've had to do without the E for a very long time, haven't we?'

'What?'

'We've had love, now and then, but it hasn't been the full-on thing. Men have said, "I love you," but it's always been as if they didn't want to finish the word. It's been lov without the E.'

'There have been plenty of times when I've put up with just the L.' Caddy laughed grimly. 'I think we should get a really good DVD. Love is much safer when it's rented.'

'Oh, don't make jokes about it.' Roz sniffed. 'It's too sad to make jokes about.'

'It's too sad not to make jokes about,' Caddy said briskly. 'Sometimes I sit here and just laugh and laugh.'

'Do you really?'

'No.'

As Caddy rose from the table to get some more snacks, she became aware that she was slightly drunk. The bottle of wine was a large one and they had already drunk most of it. 'I hope this doesn't make me sound like a very superficial person' – she tilted forwards conspiratorially – 'but I'm beginning to find a lot of things rather ridiculous.'

'Join the club, dearie,' Roz snorted. 'I studied farce at the Sorbonne, but I never thought I'd get this close to it.'

'I dance alone sometimes.'

'Do you?'

'Yes, I pull the curtains and turn up the stereo.'

'Why don't you put something on now? It might help me forget about the sperm thing.'

'Okay.' Caddy started to rummage through her CDs. 'What about some reggae?'

'Sounds good.'

When Caddy returned to the sofa, her hips were sashaying gently to the music. As she and Roz reached for more crisps, their shoulders began to undulate and their feet started to tap against the wooden floor.

'My legs feel funky,' Roz said.

'So do mine. I think we need to move around a bit.'

They shoved the coffee table against the wall, and moments later they found themselves dancing, wildly and unselfconsciously, with the curtains open and no shoes on their feet. Chump sat on a chair and watched.

Tom saw them through the window as he passed the house on his way to O'Donnell's pub. He recognised the dark-haired dancer as Roz. Very briefly, he glimpsed a woman with long blonde hair who looked startlingly familiar, though he didn't know where he had seen her before.

Chapter Twelve

AVA HAD DECIDED TO do something about her hair. A woman whose husband was having numerous affairs with foreign girls needed to boost her morale. This was why she was entering an up-market salon in a relatively large town in Kerry. She had one hundred and twenty euro in her purse, and she was going to get her hair completely restyled.

One hundred and twenty euro seemed an incredible amount to spend on a hairdo; but then, a lot of things seemed incredible these days, even euro themselves. You would have thought people would have had enough of fiddling around with money after decimalisation. Anyway, Roderick was supposed to be excellent. Beth had gone to him before she left for Finland and he had made her look at least ten years younger.

As she took her seat on a fake-leather sofa, Ava began to feel slightly alarmed. The salon was full of young, very confident-looking women. And the magazines on the table beside her were extraordinarily brazen. She almost blushed as she read the headlines. 'Extend Your Orgasm'... 'Sizzling Sex'... 'His Favourite Positions'... It was just as well she'd bought a copy of her favourite magazine en route.

As she extricated the magazine carefully from her handbag, she looked round and wondered what Roderick looked like. She was a bit anxious about him because Beth said he was 'rather odd but very talented'. 'He's a bit like one of those modern chefs,' she'd added by way of explanation, but this didn't explain anything to Ava, who had never heard of Marco Pierre White. Maybe I should have gone to Alexandra's, Ava thought. Alexandra's was the sedate salon she usually frequented. It was small and cosy, and Alex herself did a good perm and made an excellent cup of tea; the music was soothing, unlike the clashing harmonies in this establishment. What was more, Alexandra's magazines were full of knitting patterns and recipes for chocolate cake and stories about beautiful babies that had been adopted from far-flung lands. And they gave you a cup of tea as soon as you arrived. Ava was beginning to long for a cup of tea.

Beth is probably visiting a fjord at this very moment, she thought as young women with angular hairdos darted around her. *Perhaps I should buy one of those cheap air tickets and go away somewhere too...*

She opened her magazine and noticed that there was an interview with Dan MacIntyre. She stared longingly at his handsome, calm face and dearly wished he were her son-in-law. Since no one had rushed over to attend to her hair – in Alexandra's they rarely kept her waiting – she decided to inspect the interview. She hoped Dan would talk about *Merrion Mansions*. Those tight breeches had looked very good on him. And he had longed for the affections of that young actress with the unusual name in a way that was deeply satisfying. It was sad that they hadn't married or even kissed. But it was the love-filled glances that had really united them.

She sprinted through the opening paragraphs – Dan was being rather too philosophical for a person who was waiting to have her hair completely restyled. 'I have a cat,' she read. 'I'm very fond of her, but I wish she wasn't so fussy about her food.' It was good that Dan had a cat, and that she was fussy. A man who kept a cat would inevitably learn something about respect: cats demanded it.

A teenager with an earring through her right nostril said,
'Are you Mrs Lavelle?'
'Yes.'
'Roderick's doing you, isn't he?'
'I – I think so. I haven't actually seen him yet.'
The teenager smiled and asked her to move to a seat near the window. As Ava was being swathed in a bright-blue protective smock, a man with a long black ponytail darted forwards and started to yank her hair.
'Are...are you Roderick?' she inquired cautiously.
'Mmm,' he muttered. 'Who did this last time?'

108

'Alex.'

'The perm will have to go.'

'Why?'

'It doesn't suit you.'

'Oh.' Ava was unused to being stared at with quite such intensity.

'Shorter, okay?'

'What?'

'I think it would look good shorter.' Roderick dug his fingers towards her scalp. The effect was not displeasing.

'My friend Beth says–'

'And some easi-meche tints.'

'What?'

'Colour, to bring it up a bit. It'll look very natural.'

'Will it?' Ava peered up at him fearfully.

'You won't know yourself, Mrs Lavelle.' Roderick smiled with sudden softness.

'Oh…' Ava was about to question him further, but he darted off towards another customer.

She became determined to interrogate him further about his plans for her hair. One had to stand up to hairdressers sometimes. They could be very bossy. Her resolve deepened when her tea arrived; it was in an oddly shaped cup, with a solid handle that had no space in the centre for one's fingers. *I'll say I just want a tidy-up*, she decided. *And if he gets angry about it, I'll leave. It's quite warm out today; my hair would dry on its own. Or I could use one of those drier things they have in ladies' rooms.*

The longer Ava sat waiting for Roderick, the more she felt like she was preparing for a getaway. In the many mirrors she watched him moving, swivel-hipped, amongst his clientèle, grabbing at the scissors in his back pocket like someone in a western. He made odd, jerky movements while cutting, stood back to gain perspective, lifted a handful of hair and seemed about to cut it, but instead let it drop, as though following some inner motivation. Despite herself, Ava became fascinated. He was an ordinary-looking fellow, apart from the ponytail. Though he seemed to be in his twenties, his face was broad and boyish; he was wearing a loose cotton shirt that was not tucked in, and everything about his clothing seemed casual. But he wasn't a casual person; that was obvious. He was a man with a mission, and it was hair – her hair; for he was at last coming over to her.

'Roderick, I've been wondering if...' she began determinedly, but then she stopped. Roderick had plunged his long, olive-skinned hands into her perm and the pleasure of it startled her. There was a delicacy to his movements, and her hair sensed his confidence. It became sinewy and sensuous in his hands, and when he gathered it together it felt like golden wheat.

'What were you about to say, Mrs Lavelle?' Roderick inquired, as he began to brush her hair very carefully. His eyes followed the movement of the brush right down to the split ends, and Ava was strangely moved, though still quite fearful. It was such a long time since anyone had displayed this level of interest in her hair. And her hair wanted it. It yearned for it, and she could not ignore its pleadings.

'I – I was wondering if I could have a biscuit,' she said softly.

'Oh,' Roderick said. 'I'll ask.'

After a brief conversation with a girl with pink streaks, Roderick decided upon the colouring mixture that Ava's hair required. 'Cindi will look after you,' he said as a young woman approached with a trolley and several bowls of thick liquid.

As Cindi began to paint segments of her hair with this concoction and then cover them in squares of see-through plastic, Ava realised she would have to stay. She couldn't go out on the street looking like a recipe. And they had brought her a chocolate-covered digestive biscuit.

Once her hair was covered, she had to sit under some heated lamps, which were uncomfortably hot. At last her hair was ready; but having it washed was, as usual, rather uncomfortable. 'Someone should come up with pads for these basins,' she told the young girl, who didn't ask her if she'd like another cup of tea. At Alexandra's they gave you as many cups of tea as you wanted, and biscuits. And everyone said her perm was very nice.

Once she returned to her seat near the front of the salon, Roderick appeared and reached swiftly for a comb. He swept it agilely through Ava's tresses while she squinted at the mirror and tried to discern what her highlights looked like. She couldn't really tell, because her hair was so wet, but at least they weren't magenta. Jemma had turned her hair magenta once. She had a passion for dramatic vegetable dyes.

Roderick whipped out his scissors from his back pocket and stared at them for a moment, as though drawing inspiration from them; then, with quick, deft movements, he began to snip, moving Ava's hair this way and that at unexpected angles. Every so often he dug his fingers through his work in progress.

Ava's toes were beginning to curl, even though, outwardly, she was a matronly woman reading about imaginative uses for old wine bottles. Jim had loved her hair once. He had fondled and flicked it, and sometimes kissed it when he thought she was asleep.

Roderick was obviously not going to indulge in chit-chat about holidays and family and the weather – which was, in fact, quite a relief. It meant Ava could luxuriate in curiosity and wonder what she would look like when he had finished. She knew she would be greatly altered.

Might she even look a little beautiful? It would be so wonderful to feel attractive again. Then Jim might look at her and realise what he was missing. And when she spurned his amorous advances, he wouldn't understand, and she wouldn't tell him why. Then he would know what it was like to be rejected, apparently without cause.

Tears briefly misted Ava's eyes, and Roderick glanced at her as though sensing her sadness. He was a sensitive young man, she realised, although he was also capable of considerable rudeness. She had made some comments about

111

getting pads for the basins and he had completely ignored them.

'Okay,' he said at last, taking some final snips and standing back. 'It's done.'

'Thank you.' Ava beamed. 'You've worked really hard.'

He didn't reply, just reached for a large hair-drier. After some moments he put it down and got some mousse, which he squirted on his hands and rubbed onto her hair. It was creamy and thick and smelt of something very nice. It was not the smell of a perm. It was not the smell of containment and tidiness. It was foreign and unexpected and somehow right.

A few minutes later, Roderick was holding a mirror up to show Ava the back of her new hairdo. 'It's lovely,' she told him. 'It really is very nice.'

She went to the girl at reception and paid her, leaving a large tip for Roderick, and said again how nice her new hairdo was. She put on her coat and gathered her bag and remembered to fetch her magazine from her seat.

'Thanks again,' she called out, as she opened the door and reached the muted sunlight of the pavement. Her smile was broad and beaming, but as soon as she was a few doors away it disappeared. What she needed now was a very large headscarf. And it might be many weeks before she could remove it.

Chapter Thirteen

THE GREEK CAT WAS an amazing concoction of colours. Some parts of it were brown, some cream, some orange, and there even seemed to be a dab of yellow by its left ear. It had a dear pink nose and big blue eyes, and it wasn't scrawny and frightened like the other cats Caddy had seen. She glanced around to see if anyone was looking, and then quickly gave the creature a small piece of chicken from her plate.

It guzzled it gratefully and peered up at her with intensified interest, which deepened into wide-eyed pleading. More morsels of chicken were furtively offered, until the owner of the taverna looked over and smiled with only the slightest hint of irritation. She was a pleasant woman, and her daughter played the violin with great proficiency. The colour photographs on display above the salad ingredients testified to this fact: they frequently included large silver cups and beaming faces.

This was the fifth time Caddy had sat under the taverna's jasmine-covered canopy and ordered a meal. She usually pointed to the photographs on the menu. When the meals arrived, they were accompanied by bread and salad and the inevitable small plastic bottle of water. She ate slowly: the heat made her feel languorous, and she liked to pause every so often and stare out at the sea, which was turquoise near the shore and a calm deep blue in the distance. She had been in Greece for a whole week, and the backs of her legs were still not brown.

She had visited Greece before, but this town was not like the small villages she had explored when she was younger. Instead of old men herding goats, there were scores of tourists intent on purchases, tans and sightseeing. Many of them spent part of the day on the crowded beaches, and this afternoon Caddy planned to join them. As she looked at her honey-coloured arms, she felt a glow of contentment. She hadn't been this shade for many years.

The hotel where she was staying was quite small, tucked away from the melée of the main tourist quarter. It had a pleasant, palm-rimmed courtyard, which was regularly doused with water by its owner, Sofia, who was spectacularly conscientious about cleaning. She scrubbed, swept and polished, and she wiped the breakfast tables seconds after they were vacated. Every so often she and Caddy exchanged philosophical looks. Sofia seemed to appreciate it when Caddy clucked sympathetically or made vague consoling gestures in the international language of put-upon women. Sofia's English was adequate enough for Caddy to know that her husband had left her and her five children and that he was a 'no-good man – better gone'.

'You have man, yes?' Sofia sometimes inquired hopefully. Her marital disappointment didn't seem to have diminished her romantic ambitions for her guests. 'You pretty lady. He hold you like so.' She embraced herself eloquently.

'No, I don't have a man at the moment,' Caddy explained cheerfully. 'But I have a lovely dog.'

'Pretty dress. Very nice,' Sofia replied tactfully. Foreigners were an odd bunch, but she had been strangely moved by the small teddy bear propped up on Caddy's pillow. Some big strong man should come and give this particular guest a huge hug and many kisses. The timing was right, for Kaadi – that was how Sofia pronounced the name – had learned the considerable comforts of solitude. Romantic love was always far nicer when it wasn't essential. Then you could suck on it like a fat luscious olive, and know when to spit out the pit.

Caddy had been eating lots of olives and cherries in tavernas. Occasionally she even bought them in one of the small supermarkets. She walked up and down, staring at the shelves in a pleasant daze, before deciding on her purchases. It was extremely hot, and she was grateful for the cooling breezes that often swept across the sea.

Her fellow guests in the hotel welcomed the breezes too. Some of them were visiting the town for a cultural conference.

114

She tended to meet them in the hotel's dining-room, where strange things happened to their words. Babs, an elderly English lady, believed this was because of the room's unusual acoustics. Caddy began to suspect that she was right; conversations did sometimes seem to float upwards to the extraordinarily high stone ceilings, or ricochet off the stone walls, or curl out the door. The fact that most of the participants came from different countries was a complicating factor that, added to Babs's almost silent speech, united them in a host of routine misunderstandings. After some days, Caddy had realised it reminded her of talking to her mother.

One morning, for example, she had announced that she needed to buy some bread for a picnic, but Babs had heard her saying that she was going to the beach. 'Which beach?' Babs had asked. As Caddy was explaining that she wasn't going to the beach just then, Josef, a Slav whose English was sparse, had thought they were talking about the local buses and proceeded to ask the way to a square Caddy had never heard of. Just then Sven, a Swede, had arrived in the room and joined in with some comment about Hellenic architecture. 'Could you say that again?' Caddy had asked; but by then Josef was pressing for further information about local transportation, and Babs was saying she might go to the beach too. At this point Caddy had begun to giggle. Their breakfasts were becoming ludicrous. Sven clearly agreed with her; she often saw his eyes sparkling with amusement.

Josef's English was not good enough to allow him to get the joke, however. He seemed to have taken an interest in Caddy and often waited for her to sit so that he could choose a seat beside her. His inquiries were so halting and obscure that it often took many minutes to decipher them. After a while Caddy had ceased to ask him for clarification; she just smiled and nodded in reply. 'We... much... many waters... swim,' had apparently been an invitation to go swimming, but she had greeted it with an expansive smile and a gesture towards the bougainvilleas. 'Many flowers – beautiful,' she'd remarked, and Josef had said, 'Yes. Many,' and looked down

115

disappointedly. In this way a certain harmony was preserved by a liberal scattering of incomprehension, for Caddy had no wish to be accompanied by this intense and decidedly intellectual gentleman who seldom smiled and had a great fondness for boiled eggs.

She had thought that travelling alone might be lonely, but she was finding it surprisingly liberating. In an odd way it made her feel closer to Jemma, who was also exploring foreignness and gorging on unfamiliarity. Perhaps when they returned, with this strangeness within themselves, they would have more in common. They'd had so much in common once. Their love had felt like swimming in a large warm pool and feeling the depths beneath them grow.

It hadn't been like that at first. In the raw days after Jemma's birth, Caddy had felt her daughter had arrived far too soon. She had stared at the demanding little face and realised how much of her freedom this child had taken. In moments of deep fatigue, she had almost believed another mother would arrive and claim the baby.

And then, one day, Caddy had found herself surrendering to the fierce love she sensed had always been there. Having done so, she realised that her resistance to it had been far harder. But she had also needed those weeks of adjustment and reluctance and tired small-hours tears while Alain slumbered. He had never seemed to hear Jemma's bawlings. Or Caddy's own, which were more silent.

'Alain.' Caddy tested the name on her tongue very cautiously. Perhaps she really was over him now. The bruises and welts, the puffed skin around her lower lip had, after all, long healed.

She felt so calm, sitting here contentedly. The island's exuberant colours delighted her. She loved gazing at the abandoned villas, with their soft, sunbleached layers of pastel paint. Just beneath her hotel window was a jacaranda tree cascading with purple flowers; Caddy stared at it every morning before she showered and made her bed. The rooms were designed to offer coolness in the searing heat, and the

116

shutters outside her window were not unlike the ones in her Dublin home. Sven said the hotel's blankets looked like they were made from teddy bears. Caddy had frowned before laughing at that: she had brought one of Jemma's smallest teddies with her, and the idea of him being hunted for his eminently huggable fur was extremely distasteful.

Caddy walked slowly homewards, buying ingredients for a Greek salad on the way – there was a fridge in her room, and a table by the window, for such simple repasts. She also bought a bottle of wine and some honey and yoghurt. The bulging bags added a comforting prosaic feeling to the warm late afternoon.

When she reached the hotel, she washed some clothes and hung them on the line at the back of the building. As she went indoors she was greeted by Sofia, who was taking a break from her cleaning and smoking listlessly while listening to Greek music. Its ebullient melodies regularly cavorted down the corridors.

'Come in,' Sofia gestured, so Caddy did. She drank a small cup of tremendously strong coffee and listened while Sofia spoke of the deviousness of men and the irritating qualities of daughters – at least, that seemed to be the general gist. Caddy tried to nod sagely and with sufficient sympathy, until the aggressive whirrings of a Vespa motorcycle vibrated from the courtyard. This announced the arrival of Spyros, Sofia's oldest and much-adored son. He regularly arrived for food and general cosseting.

As Sofia commenced her maternal cluckings, Caddy thanked her for the coffee and headed for her room. She decided to sit on her balcony and sip a glass of wine very slowly. She would also eat some olives and read the letter from her mother. It had arrived on the morning of her departure and she had barely glanced at it, which now provoked a slight sense of guilt. *But I did phone her to tell her I was going away*, she thought. *And I dealt with those inquiries about the tea cosy very tactfully.*

She delved into her canvas bag and cautiously extracted the

envelope.

Dear Caddy,

*I was very pleased to hear that you have booked a holiday.
I may go away myself for a short break. Beth seems to be
enjoying Finland. She sent me a postcard and says she's been
eating a lot of pickled herring.*

*The weather has been very mixed here lately. I don't see
much of your father these days, but, in the circumstances,
that's quite a relief. He's a very different person from the man
I married. I'll tell you more about this when you visit. You
must visit soon, dear. I'm not getting any younger, and it
would be so nice to see you. Have you done up the spare
bedroom yet?*

*I've finally finished embroidering that cushion you kindly
ordered for me from Country Living. It looks lovely, though
Gertrude has left cat hairs all over it. I let her into the house
more often these days because she's getting old and needs her
comforts. I think she was lonely sleeping in the utilities room.
Cats get lonely, just like people, I now realise.*

*Jemma's postcards seem to be getting shorter, which
probably means she's busy enjoying herself. I read an article
about your friend Dan MacIntyre when I was in the
hairdresser's the other day. He looked very nice in the
photograph. Why don't you invite him round to dinner and use
that nice linen tablecloth I sent you? It would, of course, need
to be ironed.*

Love, Mum

Caddy frowned and stuffed the letter back into her bag.
Why did people say they weren't 'getting any younger'? Did
they expect time to suddenly start running backwards? Those
references to her father were meant to provoke her curiosity –
and that inquiry about the spare bedroom was a clear signal
that Ava intended to visit. She would probably bludgeon down
the front door if her stay was deferred for much longer.

How on earth did I end up with such a mother? Caddy
thought, although not with the usual irritation. Ava hadn't
even apologised for sending Dan MacIntyre that note – though

118

Caddy had firmly told her that she must never contact Dan again – and she never would apologise. It was easier just to accept this.

Caddy reached lazily for an olive, poured herself a glass of wine and surveyed the garden of the neighbouring hotel. It had a swimming pool and sun-loungers. She enjoyed watching intriguing developments amongst her fellow tourists; she had already witnessed the tentative beginnings of various holiday romances.

The wine was making her feel pleasantly sleepy. She was about to go indoors for a nap when she spied a man who looked extraordinarily familiar. He was sitting by the pool and dangling his long, attractive legs in the water. He was probably a new arrival; he wasn't tanned yet.

Caddy rubbed her eyes. She had obviously drunk too much wine. *I should have had some bread with the olives*, she thought. Then she rose and leaned over the wrought-iron railing. The resemblance was quite amazing…

It *was* Dan.

And he was talking to a beautiful, red-headed young woman who looked remarkably like Zia Andersson.

Chapter Fourteen

AVA WAS LOOKING AT her husband through the sitting-room window. He was mowing the lawn, even though she hadn't asked him to, and was wearing a blue shirt with rolled-up sleeves. His arms were tanned and his grey hair was tousled. Every so often he stopped and peered at the underside of the machine to check some mechanical detail.

Jim liked machines. He liked taking them apart and oiling them and putting them together again. Ava had bought him a special soap to remove the grease. He wouldn't be using it today, because it was stored in a kitchen cabinet. He was doing without all sorts of things she believed he needed, including herself. It was turning him into a stranger; but perhaps he always had been one.

She wondered if he would be leaving soon to visit one of his foreign women. Perhaps he might do a tour of them and never return. He was certainly very far away now, even though he was in the back garden. As she studied him Ava saw that he was still quite handsome. He had never put on weight, like she had; he was quite fit and lithe, and his broad, muscular shoulders might be appealing to some. The moustache, a recent development, made him look almost distinguished. *How can a man live with so many secrets?* she thought. Then she restrained the urge to go out and give him a hefty kick on the shin.

Jim became aware that he was being watched. He looked up, and Ava looked down at a begonia on the window-ledge; when he recommenced his mowing, she looked up at him again. If they'd had a son, would he have shared Jim's features?

A son... Ava experienced a moment of almost unbearable sorrow. Jim had never really understood her grief about the miscarriages. Some of her friends did, because they had felt the same grief. Perhaps that was the unspoken bond behind their talk of recipes and new sitting-room suites.

There were so many things she couldn't say. Mentioning love, for example, had always been a problem for her. Her own parents had rarely alluded to it, though her father had bought her those delicious penny sweets in the village shop and her mother had been most diligent about lengthening her summer dresses. This was the language of affection Ava understood. But it obviously hadn't reached Caddy or Jim. All these years, she had been reaching out to them in ways they didn't recognise, ways that often only caused them annoyance.

She felt a sudden fatigue and went to make herself a large cup of plain tea. Caddy had many kinds of tea; on her very occasional visits, Ava was given a bewildering choice of beverages. But then, her daughter's whole life contained more freedom than her own. She had been brought up to believe that selflessness was the core of female virtue, but women today demanded something for themselves. Perhaps her criticisms of Caddy often contained a certain envy. And perhaps her daughter sensed it...

As Ava drank her tea, she knew she had to get out of the house. She would buy a romantic novel in the newsagent's and hear a bit more about Finland from Beth, who had only been back for a few days and still had plenty of holiday stories to tell. She might also go into Sally's Café.

As she walked down the fuchsia-lined lane, she glanced out at the sea and wished she were on it. She'd always wanted to go on a cruise, but it hadn't appealed to Jim. It was just another example of his selfishness. At the crossroads she met Beth, who was wearing a blue tracksuit and walking quickly. Since she returned from Finland Beth had been taking more exercise and tying her hair back in a chignon. Also, her earrings had got larger.

'Ava – your hair!' Beth exclaimed.

Ava cringed. She had forgotten to put on her headscarf! 'I – I got it done at that new place you told me about,' she said, as though explaining a misdemeanour. 'I wanted to have a perm, but Roderick wouldn't let me.'

'But it's beautiful.' Beth touched Ava's short, stylish tresses. The headscarf had flattened the layers somewhat, but Roderick's expertise was still very much in evidence. It was neat and modern and took years off Ava's face. 'And the colour!' Beth enthused. 'So natural… is this what you've been hiding under that headscarf?'

'I…I wasn't sure it suited me.'

'It does, darling. You look very attractive.'

Beth had planned a two-mile walk and obviously wanted to finish it, so Ava continued her journey, taking her attractiveness with her. It was a pleasant cargo and made her walk with a lighter step. She glanced at her watch. She had time to catch the afternoon bus to Tralee if she hurried. It would be nice to go to town, and she did need some new teacloths. She thought of Caddy sunning herself in Greece and decided that she might even go into a travel agency herself, for an exploratory chat.

There were foreign women on the bus, but Ava paid them scant attention. She was thinking of where she wanted to go and for how long. It should be somewhere foreign, but not too far away, and the journey had to include a sea voyage. She would not tell Jim she was going. That was the most thrilling part of the whole escapade.

When she reached Tralee, she went to the travel agent immediately. She had decided where she wanted to go with astonishing rapidity, and all she had to do was purchase her ticket.

She spent half an hour discussing her voyage with the young woman behind the desk. She wanted to be clear about every detail. Then she headed for a café that played soft, soothing Irish ballads. En route she glimpsed her husband scurrying towards the post office with a bundle of letters. Normally this sight would have dismayed her, but the ticket in her handbag shielded her from his infidelity.

So many husbands were unfaithful. Ava had read about their disloyalty in magazines and heard women weeping on the radio. On those American television shows, some men even talked about sleeping with their sisters-in-law, and people booed and hissed and clapped. What had happened to common decencies?

The music in the cafe was, as usual, pleasantly soulful. Ava's face relaxed as she listened to the uileann pipes. They seemed to go to the very heart of things in a way that was both plaintive and uplifting. Sometimes the tunes became more cheerful, and the pipes could express that too. Music was indeed a great solace – though her husband's tuneless honkings on the harmonica were excruciating.

The bun she had ordered was soft and delicious, and the sweet cream oozed out at the first bite and had to be wiped from her chin with a paper napkin. She stared idly out the window at the words on a large poster. 'Affinitie Perfume,' she read. 'Because True Love is Forever.'

Suddenly the image of a huge ship loomed into her mind. The huge ship that had brought Him, her sailor, into Cork harbour. And taken him away…

'You went to a dance together!' That was what her mother had shrieked. 'You stupid, stubborn girl! Have you listened to anything I've said?'

'I'm not stupid.'

'Don't you dare talk back to me.'

'I love him!'

'Of course you don't! You're young and ignorant. You don't know the ways of the world.'

'I know my ways.'

'I will not put up with this wildness!'

'Is…is it because he's black?'

'He's not one of us.'

'But–'

That 'but' had sent Ava's mother into a fury. She was a frightening woman when she was displeased. There was much talk of what had happened to Fidelma Moran, who had got drunk and 'dropped her knickers' for a sailor. The baby had been adopted, and Fidelma had gone to Birmingham, where she had become a waitress. No man would ever want her – not

123

the kind of man you married, anyway. Because there were women men married and women men just wanted for sex. Eventually, just hearing Fidelma's name made Ava shudder.

Fidelma had often sat with her at the village dances and told her that her dress looked nice. Fidelma wouldn't have cared that Luigi was the wrong skin colour – he wasn't that dark, anyway, because his grandfather was Italian. Even before she had got pregnant, Fidelma had said she would leave the village as soon as possible and go to a place where Father Z. Flannary didn't roar at you from the pulpit. Father Flannary's voice became very agitated when he spoke about fornication, though it softened when he spoke of Jesus.

'Jesus...' Ava said the name to herself as she stirred her tea. There had been a time when she had thought that even he was angry with Fidelma Moran, but now she suspected that he wasn't. Jesus knew about love and innocence. He knew what it was like to be human and make mistakes. His skin would have been quite brown, too, because he was, after all, a foreigner. What would her mother have made of him? It was most unlikely that she would have invited him in for soda bread and her famous gooseberry jam.

'I'm sure he must be nice if you liked him.' That was what Ava's grandmother had said when they were alone one Sunday afternoon. 'The world is a strange place, Ava – stranger, perhaps, than your mother realises. You should finish that shorthand typing course and go to Dublin. Every woman needs a taste of freedom.'

But Ava hadn't gone to Dublin. Her mother had forbidden it, so she hadn't gone.

'You should write to Fidelma.' Her grandmother had said it so many times. 'She'll be feeling very alone; she must be missing her friends.'

Ava hadn't written to Fidelma. She had decided to completely forget about her and the waywardness she represented. Sometimes Fidelma still sent her a card on her birthday – it was amazing that she remembered the date – but Ava never replied. The last one had contained Fidelma's new address in London. 'Chiswick,' Ava said softly, wondering if she was pronouncing it correctly. For years she had left in the H when she said 'Thames'.

Dymphna, an acquaintance, passed her table.

'Ava, what have you been doing to yourself!' Ava peered up at the beaming, gossipy face. 'You look different.'

'It's my hair.'

'Of course. It's lovely.' There was an awkward pause. 'So what are you up to these days?'

Ava brushed some crumbs from her skirt. 'Actually, I'm planning a trip to England.'

'Really! Are you visiting relatives?'

'No.' What a nosy woman Dymphna was. She asked questions and then she told other people, anyone who would listen, all your answers. You had to be careful what you said to her if you cared what other people thought of you.

But perhaps I've cared too much about what other people think of me, Ava thought. She took a deep breath and added, 'Actually, I'm travelling on my own.'

'On your own? Ava!'

'Yes. They have some great bargains on the ferry.'

'But on your *own*!'

'I may drop in on a friend in London.'

'Is it someone I know?'

Ava decided to change the topic of conversation. 'I'd better get on with my shopping. I've been wondering if I should buy a wok.'

'A wok? Goodness, you are getting cosmopolitan!'

Ava did not deny this.

When Dymphna left, Ava wondered why she'd mentioned London. Her ticket was to Holyhead. But London now seemed to be her true destination – even though she knew nobody in that city.

And then she remembered that she did. She knew Fidelma Moran.

Chapter Fifteen

CADDY SPENT A FULL hour wondering if she should spend the rest of her holiday in her bedroom. The thought of bumping into Dan and Zia Andersson was truly appalling. Had they somehow followed her here just to annoy her? It seemed highly unlikely. Maybe it was just an extraordinary coincidence – a horrible coincidence. Of all the countries in all the world, they would choose this one. And the next hotel, too!

Oh, God, fate had brought them all together. Was it something to do with karma and past lives? Perhaps they'd had a ménage à trois in a previous incarnation. Roz believed in reincarnation. She was sure she and Rufus had had a very complicated affair in the Court of Versailles.

Since Caddy was hot and sweaty, she decided to wash, and had a noisy argument with the shower arrangements in the bathroom. There was no curtain; the water sprayed over everything in the room before disappearing down a drain in the middle of the ceramic floor. After venting her anger on numerous inanimate objects, Caddy felt surprisingly calmer. Buddha was completely right: life contained much suffering. It could even contain suffering on holiday, when you expected it to be easy. Buddha said there were ways to transcend the suffering, but it was hard to remember them because it was so hot. When it was terribly hot, you kept telling yourself it was terribly hot, and that took up a lot of thinking time. Even her bedroom, with its thick stone walls, was hot now.

And would she ever find the vanilla tea?

She had drunk it in a Danish restaurant some days ago. She had never tasted vanilla tea before, and afterwards she had decided that she needed more of it. But it had been the very last tea bag in the box, and there didn't seem to be any on the local shelves. She had searched and searched but hadn't found it. Now, in this heat haze, it had joined her more urgent priorities. These included finding a really wonderful present for Jemma and getting an early flight home.

She clearly couldn't stay here. Perhaps she should just go to a neighbouring island... Either way, she would leave tomorrow at dawn. Surely Dan and Zia wouldn't be up by then – unless they'd decided to watch the sunrise. They were just the type that would. She'd have to sneak out the door in dark glasses and a headscarf.

As she began to pack, Caddy suddenly felt frightfully indignant. It was just like Roz and Rufus and that leisure centre. Roz had stoically continued to swim despite the arguments, and it was Caddy who kept telling her she must 'feel the fear and do it anyway' – the only thing she remembered about that book was the title. Yes, since life was often difficult, one simply had to get used to feeling uncomfortable sometimes. This was *her* holiday too. And it was a perfect opportunity to prove that the whole daft thing with Dan MacIntyre was absolutely over.

After ten minutes of prevarication, she decided she would and could leave the hotel building. She wandered out into the hotel's garden and sat on a faded wooden bench beneath an orange tree. Almost immediately, Josef, the solemn Slav, attempted to join her.

'I feel like being alone right now, Josef.'

'No, Caddy. We must have talks.'

She spent some minutes trying to persuade him that his presence wasn't required. Then, when his hand seemed about to linger on her right knee, she told him very firmly to fuck off.

Josef's jaw dropped in astonishment – he was acquainted with this crude and emphatic expletive. 'You...you are not so nice, maybe, I think,' he commented.

'Yes, perhaps I am not so nice, maybe, Josef,' Caddy agreed.

A few minutes after he left, Sofia appeared. 'Oh, Kaadi! My poor lady! What is wrong?'

'Hello, Sofia. Isn't it a wonderful evening?' Caddy replied. 'I'm having a wonderful holiday. Everybody has been so kind.'

'But…but you look sad. It is some man, yes?'

'No.'

'It is terrible when a man, he is no good. But you are pretty. You find another.' Sofia stroked Caddy's back protectively.

'I don't want another, Sofia. But I do wish I could find that tea.'

The word 'tea' did not register in Sofia's mind. She adored talking about romance's awfulness and beauty. 'Love – yes, she is sometimes shy.' She smiled sagely.

'I found all the other kinds.'

'Yes; love, she has many kinds,' Sofia said dreamily.

'The supermarket said they'll have some next week, but I'll have gone home by then.'

At the mention of the supermarket, Sofia reluctantly realised they were having parallel conversations. 'What are you looking for, Kaadi?'

'Vanilla tea,' Caddy answered. 'I love vanilla, Sofia.' As she said 'love', she blinked slowly and sighed.

'What is his name?'

'Dan.' The name leaped from Caddy's lips before she could censor it.

'He is here?'

Caddy stared down at the big turquoise ring on her right index finger. 'Yes. It's the most extraordinary coincidence.'

'And now he is with someone else?'

'Yes.' Caddy gave a steely smile.

Sofia clucked disapprovingly. 'He shows his happiness with this woman and makes you need vanilla.'

'No. I would have needed vanilla tea anyway. It's all over between us, Sofia. I knew that before I came here. I wanted it to be over.'

'I get retsina,' Sofia said briskly. She realised that comforting words would not adequately penetrate her guest's confusion and unhappiness. As she clattered indoors in her slip-on sandals, she felt a deep distaste for men in general, though her son Spyros was not included in this condemnation.

As Sofia poured the retsina into two large glasses, she wondered if Caddy should be introduced to Dimitri from the garage. 'Do you eat at hotel tonight?'

'Well, maybe I should, in the circumstances.' Caddy looked at her anxiously.

'You must go out,' Sofia declared. 'Show him you will not hide.'

'I...I suppose I could go to that taverna.'

'Which one?'

'The one with the friendly cat.'

'There are many cats.'

'The one near the supermarket, with the jasmine. The owner's daughter plays the violin.'

'Ah, yes.' Sofia smiled. 'You go there. Promise me.'

Caddy had never seen Sofia look quite so adamant. 'Oh, all right then.'

'Good.' Sofia beamed at her. 'I go now and make moussaka.' She scurried indoors to the phone. And Caddy climbed arduously upstairs to change into her pink cheesecloth dress.

At first she wondered if she even wanted to eat anything, but the process of reaching into her wardrobe and putting on clean knickers emboldened her. She felt like an actress as she prepared for her foray. After all, she now looked like a woman who was on holiday and enjoying herself. As she pressed some lipstick onto her lips, she suddenly realised what a vast relief it was that Dan could now be completely forgotten. A stubborn part of her had always longed for him, but it wouldn't any more.

Despite her determination to be brave and rugged, she decided to get a taxi to the taverna. She chose a table next to a large potted palm: if Dan and Zia appeared, she could duck behind it and make a quick getaway. She had brought a headscarf and dark glasses with her, just in case. It was nice to eat out of doors. The smell of jasmine was so sweet and soothing. Being abroad made you different, it really did.

As she waited for her salad, Caddy began to wonder

whether Dan's arrival at a neighbouring hotel could have had something to do with Harriet. 'You might meet someone special on your holiday,' Harriet had winked conspiratorially. 'It's amazing, the people you bump into when you're away.'

Seeing Zia had distracted Caddy from the enormity of the coincidence, but now she was fairly sure that Harriet had played a part in it. After all, Harriet's husband was also Dan's travel agent, and Harriet loved matchmaking. How appalled she'd be to learn that Dan had brought his lover with him! Malcolm must have booked her in without Harriet knowing about it. Oh, when would people learn to leave well alone?

Caddy looked up and discovered that a swarthy man was staring at her.

'Hello.'

'Hello.'

'My name is Dimitri. I am friend with Sofia.'

'Oh.'

'I see you in hotel garden yesterday. Sofia, she tells me you are very nice pleasant lady.' Dimitri paused significantly.

Oh, Sofia, you naughty sweet woman, Caddy thought. *Why will people never believe that I'm perfectly happy on my own?* She picked up the menu and pretended to scrutinise it thoughtfully.

'You are eating alone?'

'Yes.'

'I also am eating alone.' Dimitri made 'alone' sound very sad.

Caddy wondered if she could tolerate having dinner with Dimitri, or with any man, ever again. But he did have a kind face. And if Dan and Zia appeared it would be rather humiliating to be seen dining solo. She took a deep breath. 'You can join me at my table… if you like.'

'You are sure?' Dimitri feigned considerable surprise.

'Any friend of Sofia's is a friend of mine.'

He pulled out a chair.

Dimitri was, in fact, quite good company. Caddy laughed and laughed, because women who were abroad were supposed

130

to do that kind of thing. There was a certain hollowness to her mirth, but that would pass and she would begin to find the whole thing tremendously funny. Dimitri had a nice smile. And he had very broad, manly shoulders. Perhaps she should sleep with him and become his wife. She could open a little tourist boutique and spend a lot of time doing things with aubergines.

No. His eyebrows were too large.

They had eaten their main meal, and Dimitri was steadily plying Caddy with ouzo. 'Maybe you come with me for coffee?' he whispered over the plastic tablecloth.

'We can have coffee here.'

'My house. It has view of sea, and stars. Very pretty.'

Caddy did not feel like having coffee in Dimitri's house. She felt very opinionated about it, suddenly. 'I think we should have coffee here, Dimitri,' she said, peering under the table.

'What are you looking for?'

'The cat.'

'There are many cats near my house.'

'But I've made friends with this one. Someone else must be feeding her this evening.'

'It is that man over there. He is looking at us.'

Caddy turned around unsteadily. 'Who's feeding her?' she demanded. 'I want to feed her. I even kept some chicken especially.'

She found herself staring into a pair of very familiar and very astonished deep brown eyes.

Chapter Sixteen

CADDY WONDERED IF SHE should throw the bottle of retsina at the vile, deceitful and most un-nice person who had been feeding the cat morsels of grilled beef. The bottle was almost empty and she'd drunk most of it. She looked at the carafe of water, but she simply wasn't sober enough to get involved in armed combat.

'Hi, Dan.'

'Hello, Caddy.' His face was rigid with astonishment.

'It's a very nice taverna, isn't it?'

'What are you doing here?'

'I'm having dinner with my friend Dimitri. Have you met him?'

Dan didn't reply.

'Dimitri, this is Dan.'

'Hello, Dan.'

'Hello, Dimitri.'

'It's very hot, isn't it?' Caddy took another sip of ouzo. She'd moved on to ouzo after the retsina, but she absolutely must not drink any more. She had to be on her guard.

'When...when did you arrive here?'

'About... What day is it today?' Caddy began to count on her fingers. The ouzo seemed to have suddenly gone straight to her head. 'Lots of days ago. I'm almost a native!' This was good. She was sounding light-hearted and jocular.

'What a coincidence!'

'Yes, it's absolutely extraordinary; but then, a lot of things are, when you think about it.' Ten out of ten: philosophical resignation was always a sign of considerable maturity. If she'd allowed herself to love him, he would have left her for Zia anyway. Dan was amazed that Caddy seemed so unsurprised.

'I suppose you booked the ticket through Malcolm.'

'I did, actually.'

'So did I.' Caddy paused. 'Did you talk to Harriet when you were deciding where to stay?'

'She answered the phone, and I–'

'Thought so.'

'Sorry?'

'I'm surprised Zia isn't dining with you.' Caddy paused significantly. 'Did she decide to have an early night?'

'What does Zia have to do with this?'

'Well, she's on holiday with you, isn't she?' Caddy looked straight into his eyes without blinking. 'I saw you together at the hotel pool.'

'Zia isn't here.'

'Of course she is. I saw her.'

Dan frowned and threw a piece of meat to the cat.

'Why are you lying to me?' She said it calmly. Excellent: she was simply stating the truth, without becoming angry. Jealousy was terribly undignified.

'I'm not.'

Caddy looked at him with tranquil mistrust. 'That woman did – hic – look very like her.' Oh, dear, her fake sobriety was slipping. Deep breath.

Dan tore a bread roll in two and began to eat it. He clearly wasn't going to comment further on the subject, and Caddy decided not to pester him. He had 'gone into his cave', or whatever that expression was. Men were always in caves or sheds or something. She stared fondly at the cat. American surveys said that loads of women felt closer to their pets than to people.

'Are you all right?' Dan suddenly inquired.

Now that Caddy noticed it, she was swaying slightly. 'Of course.' Her stomach felt like it was doing the samba. That was what could happen with emotional earthquakes: when you decided not to register the fact that the earth was heaving, the aftershocks jittered through you and made you feel all strange and jumpy.

Dan looked down at his plate and wondered if he was dreaming. Sometimes his dreams were very real. Perhaps he should just get up and go, dreaming or not.

Caddy also wondered if she should flee, but she decided she didn't feel up to a swift departure. If she tried to grab her cardigan and leave haughtily, she was almost sure to knock over someone's beer and have to spend ages mopping it up with napkins. Maybe she was just the kind of person who always bumped into people she knew on holiday. It had happened before. When she and Jemma had had that big treat vacation in Italy, they had met that woman from the library who kept going on about the inadequate filing system in the biography section and how various colleagues were bullying her. Even in the Sistine Chapel, she'd wailed about how she always had to make the tea and was the only one who bought biscuits.

But Caddy knew that, now she had met Dan, she should at least try to converse with him. Why on earth was he being so secretive about his new romance? If she was polite to him, he might eventually tell her the torrid details. It was always better to face the truth.

'I'm…I'm sorry that lunch was such a mess.'

Dan looked out to sea.

'I always go apeshit when my mother interferes. I'm sorry. I mush – I must have seemed very…' What was the word? Dan looked at her.

'I must have seemed very…' Caddy looked down at her plate. 'Oh, dear, I've forgotten what the word is.'

'Insensitive?'

'Oh, yes! Well done.' She felt as if she were doing a crossword. 'I thought it began with an S.'

Dan resumed his meal.

'I think you're being rather insensitive too, actually,' Caddy said.

Dan threw some meat to the cat, who gobbled it in one gulp.

Feck you, anyway, Dan MacIntyre, she thought. *You've been canoodling with a beautiful young actress and you're still being haughty and unforgiving.*

'You could at least try to be polite to me, since it's all over between us,' she continued.

Dan ran a hand through his hair and sighed. 'Look, you don't understand, okay? Things aren't quite what they seem.'

'I take you to old part of city tomorrow,' Dimitri interrupted. He was tapping his fingers on the table.

'Oh, thank you, Dimitri, but I've been there. It is very old and very beautiful, but it's also very crowded.'

Silence.

The memory of beautiful Zia sitting by the pool in a tiny bikini lunged into Caddy's brain. Zia was probably staying in tonight because she was exhausted after hours of torrid sex. For a moment Caddy felt she might explode with... with what? What on earth was she feeling, anyway? Surely it should be relief.

I am a parallel woman, she thought. *And that means I can chat and be civil even if I feel like hitting someone over the head with a loofah.*

'My father's moved into the garden shed. Did I tell you that?' She leaned towards Dan and almost fell into the potted palm. 'Oops!'

Dan steadied her just in time. 'No, you didn't.'

'I think he may stay there for ever and ever. It's a very nice shed, you see, and he likes it.' She took another large gulp from her glass. Perhaps she should order a bottle of water.

'I think we maybe go for coffee?' Dimitri suggested hopefully. There was a distinct frisson between Caddy and this stranger. He thought of his large double bed with Caddy curled inside it. The straps of her pink cheesecloth dress were straying from her shoulders and she was looking very pretty. Sofia had said her guest needed cuddles and kisses and... Dimitri's eyes darkened with erotic thoughts. He was a very good lover. All his women said it, even Sofia.

'But I want to have coffee here, Dimitri,' Caddy announced. 'I like it here. It's very nice.'

'My house, it is very nice,' Dimitri said softly.

'I'm sure your house is lovely, Dimitri. But I like this one.

And it has a cat.'

'I think the lady is trying to tell you she wants to have her coffee here,' Dan interrupted. He'd wake up soon, but he might as well play along with the dream while it lasted.

'I think maybe I go. Three is a cloud.'

'You mean *crowd*, Dimitri,' Caddy corrected. 'But it isn't. Three is very nice.'

'I think you and this man… you have many feelings for each other.'

'Oh, no, you've got completely the wrong end of the branch.'

'The stick,' Dan corrected.

'Yes, the stick,' Caddy agreed. 'You've got the wrong end of it.'

'What is this stick?' Dimitri inquired.

'It's a piece of wood,' Caddy explained. 'Oh, dear, I should have brought my dictionary with me.'

'I do not understand. I go.'

'Oh, Dimitri, don't go!' Caddy implored dramatically. 'Tell me more about your nephew and the squid. I'm tremendously fond of squid… and plankton,' she added, remembering her whale world.

'I have told you about the squid,' Dimitri answered. 'But I can show you my boat. It is near my house.'

'Oh, why do you have to keep mentioning your house, Dimitri?' Caddy asked sadly. 'Is it because you want to rip off my dress and ravish me?'

Dimitri was not acquainted with the word 'ravish', but he did understand the part about the dress. He leaned across the table. 'Is it so bad that I want to hold you?' he said gently. His experiences with foreign women had taught him about persistence.

'I have been held by many men, Dimitri,' Caddy replied. 'And none of them – hic – have been very nice in the long run.'

Dan, who was feigning deep interest in the menu, glared at her.

136

'Many men have deceived me, Dimitri,' she continued. 'Do they have cake here?'

'What?'

'I'd like some cake. And coffee. You're a very strong, special man, Dimitri. I'm sure you can find me cake. That one with the honey in it. I'd adore the one with the honey in it.'

Dimitri rose dubiously from the table.

'Have you known him long?' Dan inquired, as Dimitri sloped obediently indoors.

'No. We just met this evening. But we've become tremendously close and intimate.' Caddy refilled her glass. Just one more teensy-weensy drink and that would be it. She was, after all, on holiday. She stared closely at her paper napkin. It was amazing, the patterns one could get from dried food. One of them looked remarkably like a butterfly.

'Flutterby,' she muttered wistfully to herself.

'You're drunk,' Dan commented.

'No, I'm not. I was thinking about how… you know…'

'What?'

'How caterpillars become butterflies. It must be a great surprise to them. Maybe it can happen to people, too. One day they're pulling themselves along like a great big… sack of radishes or something. And then suddenly… you know… they turn into a proper person.' Caddy sighed expansively and scratched her arm. 'I've always wanted to be a proper person.'

'You don't feel you're a proper person already?'

'Well, of course I am, in a way,' she said. 'I'm not a sack of radishes, but I'm definitely an amateur woman. I should have a big L-plate on my back.'

'You think about things a lot, don't you?' His tone was more tender.

'Yes. Too much.'

'Sounds like you could do with some drama therapy.'

'Oh, no, I don't want drama,' she replied firmly. 'Now that I'm middle-aged and wrinkled and resigned, I want to do more gardening.' She reached down to pat the cat, but stopped when she noticed some fleas hopping around on its back. She pulled

137

her hand away quickly.

Dan didn't appear to notice. 'Sometimes, when you pretend to be something, it helps you to become it.' He sucked pensively on an olive. 'If you act as if you're feeling brave, it can actually help you to feel more courageous.'

'How do you know?' Caddy skewered a slice of tomato with her fork. The tomatoes in Greece were so much sweeter and riper.

'I used to do some drama therapy with people.'

'What…what kind of purple?' The minute she said it, she knew it didn't sound quite right.

'Purple who were suffering from depression and anxiety and low self-esteem.'

'You said–'

'So did you.'

'Oh, dear. Sorry. I'm beginning to sound like the spelling checker on my computer. It turned "erratic" into "erotic" the other day.'

'Erotic,' Dan repeated. He was staring at her.

Caddy shifted in her seat. God, she was blushing, and she was also covered in fleas. She had to be. She could feel the little varmints hopping all over her. She squirmed in disgust. 'What's wrong with you?'

'The cat has fleas. They're jumping around on its back like Michael Flatley.'

'Oh, well. I suppose we'll just have to be covered in them for the rest of the holiday.'

'Oh, no!' Caddy wailed. 'Sofia will make me sleep in the garden. I'm infested. Can you see them? I think they're in my hair too!'

'I can't see any fleas.'

'But they're all over me!'

'No, they're not. Stop worrying,' Dan said firmly. 'Do some drama therapy. Imagine that you are an entirely flealess woman.'

Caddy took a deep breath and imagined she was Samantha. Amazingly, it did help a bit. The entire cast of Riverdance was no longer jumping around on her thighs.

Dan's brown eyes started to twinkle mischievously. 'Cat fleas don't like humans all that much. They'll hop off somewhere else in a year or two.'

'A year!'

'I'm joking.'

Caddy sat very still for a moment. Now that she considered it, she hadn't even patted the cat. She had just thought about it.

It was horrible being drunk when you wanted and needed to be sober. Every so often a big jolt ran through you, saying, 'I'm drunk! Help!' and you couldn't even get your elbow to rest on the edge of the table without slipping. Still, she was giving a fairly good impression of someone who wasn't pissed but merely tipsy. She stuffed another wad of bread into her mouth. Normal service must be resumed as soon as possible.

What had they been talking about before the fleas? The word 'erotic' immediately floated into her brain. Erratically erotic. That pretty much summed up the situation. The space between them was full of some sweet wild thing she would never be able to name.

She remembered the drama therapy. 'Wow... drama therapy,' she gushed. 'That sounds *great*!' Oh, dear, she was doing it again. She always said people's careers or hobbies sounded great. Even if someone said he was a specialist in corrugated metal, she fell over herself trying to sound impressed.

'Thank you.' Dan gave the flea-ridden cat another piece of meat.

Caddy scratched her left armpit. 'Somehow I didn't think you'd be into that kind of thing.'

'Why?'

'Because... life isn't a rehearsal.'

'What has that got to do with it?'

'I don't know, really. I suppose I thought you'd feel that people should try to be more rugged.'

'We all need help sometimes.'

Caddy gazed into his eyes. 'Yes.' Her voice had lowered to

139

a whisper.

'Here is your cake and coffee.' Dimitri reappeared just in time. When Caddy had turned round, a minute before, she had seen him talking to a very nubile and scantily clad young woman by the cash register.

'Hello, Dimitri,' she beamed. 'Did you meet someone you know?'

Dimitri appeared not to hear her.

'Because if you want to take her back to your house, I don't mind at all. You could show her your boat.'

'This cake, it is local speciality.'

'I think you want to show someone your boat this evening, Dimitri. And I wouldn't want to prevent you from doing so.'

'But I am with you.'

'Yes, and it's been very pleasant. But I'm going back to the hotel soon.'

'With him?' Dimitri glanced at Dan sullenly.

'There's no call to be jealous. Dan finds me far too complicated.' Caddy smiled sweetly at Dan. 'We're only being nice to each other because we're on holiday. It's a new EU directive: "Thou shalt be nice to compatriots in a foreign country." Ireland is a small place.'

'But you are now in Rhodes,' Dimitri replied.

'Yes, but Irish people can never get away from each other. Even if I went to the Sahara, I'd probably meet the woman from the corner shop. She threw her knickers at Tom Jones once.'

Dimitri frowned. 'So – so you leave soon?'

'Yes. Any moment.'

'And really you do not mind? Because Sofia, she–'

'I'll tell Sofia you've been a wonderful companion. She'll be very pleased.'

'I walk with you to–'

'No, go and join your friend, Dimitri.'

'But–'

'Go, Dimitri. Go and enjoy yourself. Maybe I'll see your boat another time.' She stood up and shook his hand firmly.

140

Dimitri departed, and they heard tinkling laughter coming from the taverna's interior. Caddy drank her coffee; when she turned round, she saw that Dimitri and the woman were dancing. It was clearly time to leave. Alone.

She rose carefully and reached for her handbag. Then she leaned over to say goodbye to the cat and almost fell into a bush. Dan reached out to steady her, and she let his hand linger on her naked skin. It felt so warm and reassuring. Zia was right to choose him. He was a good man.

Dan studied her. 'Are you cold?'

'No. Of course I'm not.'

'But you're…you're trembling.'

Caddy took a deep breath. 'I'm going now, Dan. Thank you for being such – hic – such pleasant company.'

'I've upset you.'

Oh, no, there were tears in her eyes. 'Well…well, maybe you have, just a little.' She blinked firmly.

'Why?'

She didn't answer.

'I think I should walk you back to the hotel.'

'No!' Caddy protested. 'You said you didn't think we should meet again, and now you're on holiday.'

'What's that got to do with it?'

'When people are on holiday, they should only do what they really want to do.' She looked at him closely. Dear God, his eyes seemed so sad…

Dan took her arm and steered her to the road.

'I said I didn't want you to walk me to the hotel.'

'I know you did. Where is it, anyway?'

Caddy gestured vaguely in the direction of the hillside. 'It's near yours.'

He stared at her for a moment and then resumed walking.

'Zia was here, wasn't she? That's why you're sad. She's left.' Dan sighed but didn't comment.

'Oh, Dan, you say I don't open up to you, but now you're the one who's being all closed and defensive.'

Dan scratched his elbow.

141

'Now you've started me off again.' Caddy bent down and scratched her knee.

'Oh, okay. I might as well tell you.' Dan took her arm. She had almost collided with a German man who was studying postcards of big-breasted women. 'Zia was here today. She flew out this evening because she's making a film near Athens. When you saw us by the pool, we were having an argument.'

'Oh.'

'We're very close, but not in the way you think.' He stared hard into her eyes. 'You must believe that. We truly are—'

'Just close friends.' Caddy completed the sentence for him. That was what people said when they were almost married, wasn't it?

'Yes.'

She blinked and watched a discarded ice-cream wrapper fluttering in the breeze.

They reached a complicated bit of pavement, with tables and chairs and inflatable dolphins. 'Zia has some problems at the moment, and she's confided in me. I can't tell you more than that, I'm afraid,' Dan continued. 'She's sworn me to secrecy.'

'She must really trust you.'

'Yes, she does,' Dan agreed solemnly.

Oh, the poor man. What had he and Zia argued about? He looked so bereft – but it mustn't stop him enjoying his holiday.

Caddy stared at her feet. Samantha had told her that remembering her feet was terribly important for grounding. What she was about to say would require enormous maturity and self-discipline.

'Look, Dan,' she began carefully, 'if you feel you'd like a bit of company while you're here, just…just leave a message at the hotel reception desk. I won't contact you because I don't want to impose. You're on holiday, and when they're on holiday people should only do what they really want to do.'

'Yes. You've said that already.' They had reached a yellow villa with a large sculpture of a yellow horse. Caddy stared at

142

it with great affection.

'Dan...' She patted the horse's muzzle and ran her fingers round the contours of its nostrils. 'I think I should point out that it's a teensy bit rude to point out to people what they've already said, especially if they're a bit pissed.'

'So you admit it, then,' he smiled. 'You've spent the whole night claiming to be sober.'

She could feel the heat of his skin beneath his T-shirt. How nice he smelt, musky and clean... She leaned forwards and took a deep sniff.

He laughed. 'What did you do that for?'

'I was just checking to see if you smelt of vanilla.'

'You're a very odd person.'

'Oh, Dan.' She looked up at him fondly. 'This is my chance, and I'm going to grab it... but only if you want me to.'

'What do you mean?' His eyes glowed darkly.

'To show you that I'm not a bad person. That I can be your friend. Friendship is so much more enduring.'

Dan straightened and took a deep breath. 'Is your hotel far away?'

'No, it's quite near here. Listen to the cicadas. Aren't they – hic – wonderful?'

'Indeed.'

They were walking up the hillside again, and Dan was watching Caddy carefully. Sometimes she lurched and he had to grab her.

'You know something?' Caddy turned to Dan solemnly. 'I think Harriet probably booked us into hotels near each other because – well, you know what she's like.'

'I don't, actually. I've rarely met her.'

'She's a bit of a matchmaker. She wasn't to know that...'

'What?' Dan asked quickly.

'Oh, nothing. I wanted to be alone, but now that I've met you I'm really glad. It's almost as though I'm meant to be here, to comfort you.'

Dan did not reply.

'I don't mind if you go into your cave. Men do that, don't

143

they? They go into their caves when they're upset.' Caddy stopped to gaze at a cascade of bougainvillea. 'But women go into caves too. I've been in one for years, sort of.'

'Why?'

'Because of things that happened. Things I thought would be... you know... otherwise.' She reached up and touched the flowers. 'That colour is gorgeous, isn't it?'

'Yes.' She could feel his breath on her cheek.

They resumed their journey up the hillside. The air was full of the scents of dry earth and blossoms and sea. The path was dusty now, and narrower. Stars twinkled brightly in the sky. It was amazing to think that light came from so far away that it took years to be visible here, on this funny old planet.

'This is my hotel,' Caddy said. They had reached an immaculately clean courtyard.

'Really? Mine is just across the road.'

'Isn't it a beautiful evening? It's warm, but not too warm. And there are so many lovely smells, especially the jasmine blossom. I adore jasmine blossom.'

Dan gently removed a stray hair from her cheek

She leaned against his shoulder. 'If we do meet up again, we'll keep it simple. We won't talk about love or relationships or anything tiring like that.'

'What will we talk about?'

Caddy hesitated. 'I don't know, really.' She looked up at him. 'And maybe it's all right that I don't know. That's a kind of knowing in itself – knowing that you don't know.'

'Yes, it is.' He squeezed her left elbow gently. 'Good night, Caddy Lavelle.'

'Good night, Dan MacIntyre,' she called after him. 'Sweet dreams, and sleep tight, and don't let the bedbugs bite... or the fleas or the mosquitoes.'

And then she scratched her nose.

Chapter Seventeen

TOM HAD BEEN SENT three free bottles of Affinitie perfume, and he was wondering what he should do with them. Perhaps he should give one to Roz. After all, she had given him some aftershave. He had come down one morning to find a neatly wrapped parcel waiting for him. It had been an unexpected gift, but not unwelcome. He had her address somewhere… yes, here it was, amongst a pile of business cards on the mantelpiece. Wow – she lived just down the road! He'd pop the present through her letterbox. It would be a nice gesture, and people needed nice gestures.

Samantha hadn't made nice gestures because she was a horrible person. It was sad, but he had come to realise this lately.

As Tom started to clean some camera lenses, Roz was reaching for one of her large cream French cups. She would make herself a cup of coffee and then sit down and write the film script that would free her from advertising. She had to get away from advertising because she had been propelled into yet another fecking life reappraisal. How many more of the bloody things would there be?

It was Saturday. She had already done her shopping and spent at least ten minutes squinting at a cash-dispensing machine outside the supermarket. It was almost impossible to see the computerised figures in strong sunlight. She'd virtually had to press herself into the wall to get a proper look at them.

Chump was looking at her expectantly. Dogs did a lot of that. They were so randomly optimistic. Should she take him for another walk? No; she would do that after she'd written something absolutely brilliant.

'Darling, I do love you, but I can't pander to your every whim,' she said. 'Why don't you go out and play in the garden?' She opened the back door, but he didn't move.

'Do you need a hug?'

Chump placed a paw on her knee, and she bent down and scooped him into her arms. He was quite heavy. She began a slow waltz, humming 'Some Enchanted Evening'. Chump started to wriggle, so she deposited him on a very expensive sofa, which was covered with a protective blue rug.

She picked up one of his toys and pressed it. It made a squeak, but he was not amused.

'Oh, poor dear, you're missing Caddy – but she's coming back very soon.'

Chump yawned dolefully.

'Perhaps there's something interesting on the National Geographic channel.' Chump seemed to enjoy the occasional wildlife documentary. Roz plugged in the television and reached for the remote control. Soon they were both watching whales calling to each other in the Pacific. It was very restful and pleasant. And there was that Australian soap on later... Roz decided she could sit here quite happily and watch television for the rest of her life.

No. Perhaps that was a slight exaggeration. She rose determinedly from the sofa and wondered if she wanted a beach house in Malibu. If her script was accepted by a major studio, these were precisely the points she needed to be clear about. Perhaps she was more a canyon kind of person. Up in the Hollywood Hills, you could really get away from it all – though she hoped there wouldn't be too many earthquakes. Maybe she would be bi-coastal and spend part of the year in Connecticut. Provence was also a possibility; after all, she really should have been French. It would, of course, be absolutely essential to have a jacuzzi.

This is ridiculous; I haven't even written the thing yet, she thought as she sat down at her word processor. *If I spent a little less time worrying about what to wear to the première, I might have done a first draft by now. Maybe I should set it on a submarine. Though there should be some car chases. Or the heroine could live on a cattle farm in Arizona and...*

She sighed deeply. *Come on, Roz, you don't know anything about that stuff. If only you'd led a more interesting life!* She

146

started to type, but the words were 'Blah blah blah blah blah.'
Tears began to mist her eyes.

Face it, Roz, she thought sternly. *You're just going to have to stay in advertising, which is becoming more tough and cynical by the day. Soon men will be abandoning their wives and children in the desert because they're frightened of getting chocolate on the seats of their new cars.*

When the doorbell rang, she ran ecstatically towards the hallway. Maybe it was someone very chatty and demanding who had no respect for people's schedules. She yanked the door open with a flourish of relief.

Standing before her was Tom.

'I…I have a present for you.'

As Roz gawped at him, she realised she should be looking far less surprised and not too drastically pleased.

'I was going to pop it through the letterbox, and then I thought I'd say hello.'

Roz tried to assume the demeanour of a woman who has not been phoned. If only she'd put on some mascara! 'What is it?'

'It's perfume. They sent me some samples.'

'Who?'

'The people who're using my photograph in an advertisement.' He handed the package to her. It was nicely wrapped. When a man wrapped something nicely, it meant something, surely.

'Thank you.' She managed a muted smile. 'Would you like to come in?'

'Oh, no, I don't want to impose. I should have phoned.'

'I've just made some coffee.'

'Are you sure?'

'Yes.'

Tom stepped carefully into the tasteful hallway.

'Make yourself comfortable and I'll bring you a mug.' Roz gestured airily towards the sofa.

Tom sat down on it and found that he was being regarded curiously by a cocker spaniel. Chump barked, and then did it again for good measure.

'He only does that to pretend he's a guard dog,' Roz called out from the kitchen. 'Rub behind his ears and he's anybody's.' Oh, why had she said that! Anybody's... Tom probably thought she was just like that, too!

When Roz returned with the coffee, she sat on her best chair and folded her legs elegantly beneath her. She wanted to appear very self-contained, so that Tom would know she was an extremely contented woman who led a balanced and fabulously fulfilled life. *She was that woman*. Why didn't she remember this more often? Only last week she'd been asked to describe her day for a marketing magazine. She'd made up the bit about adding papaya to her porridge.

Oh, feck, what on earth was she going to say to him? She remembered the photograph. 'It's wonderful that they're using your photograph, Tom. But in many ways I'm not surprised.'

'Really?'

'You have poetry in your soul. You're meant to share it.'

God, Tom thought, *Samantha said exactly the same thing!*

'The ones I saw that... evening were special. You're very talented.' Roz smiled, but the word 'Bastard!' lunged into her thoughts. He had used her and forgotten her. Now he probably wanted to sleep with her again. He was just a horny little creep.

She pulled her brown leather skirt primly over her knees. She seriously considered handing the package back to him, but she found herself opening it instead. 'It's lovely,' she said, as she sprayed some perfume on her wrist.

'Oh, I'm so glad. I wasn't sure if it was your kind of thing.'

'It is my kind of thing. I like it very much.'

There was an awkward silence.

'So...so how's advertising?'

'Awful. I'm trying to get out of it. I want to write a film script.'

'Really?'

'Actually, I was trying to work on it today, but I didn't get much done.'

'Oh, dear, I've interrupted you.'

'Don't worry about that. It's good to see you.' Roz immediately regretted sounding so pleased. If only the phone would ring so that he would see how tremendously in demand she was.

And then Tom smiled. It was a very nice smile. It didn't seem full of guile and low cunning. It was not the smile of a man who had called by for a quick shag and brought some perfume along in payment. Maybe he was just very good at faking sincerity; but Roz found herself thinking he was, perhaps, fairly tolerable.

Then, amazingly, they began to talk with each other quite easily. It was as if they were re-starting an ancient conversation.

Tom revealed that he was so bored with mobile phones that he sometimes shouted the lyrics of 'YMCA' when he was driving. And Roz said that she could, perhaps, introduce him to some people at the agency. He would, of course, need to bring along his portfolio. Tom said he knew an actor who might give Roz some advice about her script.

'What's his name?'

'Dan MacIntyre.'

'I know him too!'

'What a small world it is.'

'Would you like another cup of coffee?'

'Are you sure?'

'Yes.'

As Roz padded elegantly and non-promiscuously towards the kitchen, she felt pleased that she was being so friendly and serene. She was giving every appearance of being a contented single woman. And there was so much to be said for being a contented single woman. They were the Western world's most significant and fastest-growing consumer group. No wonder the matchmakers of this world were getting frantic. One of the pleasures of marriage had always been pitying those who were unattached, and now the unattached were cool and savvy and enjoying themselves. If men weren't careful, they'd soon be replaced by cats and aromatherapy massages and Italian Stallion cocktails… she handed Tom his mug with deepening, but very mature and calm, affection.

The doorbell rang. 'Maybe I should go.' Tom seemed about to rise.

'Stay there and look after Chump.' Roz smiled. 'And have some more biscotti.'

Tom reached eagerly towards the tangerine-coloured ceramic plate. 'They are very nice and crunchy.'

Roz sashayed towards the hallway. Sashay was a nice word; she should do more of it. She opened the door. It was probably one of her small neighbours wanting to retrieve a ball from the back garden.

Only it wasn't. It was a very stylish woman, as slim as a whippet and wearing a trouser suit. What on earth did she want?

'I want the sperm,' the woman said loudly.

Roz almost fell over. 'Who are you?'

The woman's eyes were flashing dangerously. 'I'm Helen. Jamie's wife.'

Chapter Eighteen

AT FIRST ROZ DIDN'T believe this was happening. When she realised it was, she tried to close the door, but Helen gave it a vigorous push and propelled herself into the hallway. 'You whore!' she shouted. 'You predatory little slut!'

Roz froze in horror. It was like something from a French film, but not the bits she dreamed of. '*Je ne parle pas l'anglais*,' she declared.

Helen wasn't fooled. 'Liar!' she screamed, and lunged at Roz's hair.

'Ouch!' Roz aimed a kick at Helen's shin. 'Get off me!' Helen's jaws loomed towards Roz's cheek. 'Don't you dare bite me, you crazy person!' She scratched Helen's arms.

'Aargh!' Helen leaned forward and bit Roz's elbow.

'Stop it!' Roz felt a thud on her cheek as she was pushed against a wall. The shock made her forget for a moment that she was a dynamic and forceful person, but then some of her robustness returned, and she gave Helen a clout on the shoulder and pushed her towards a corner of the hallway. Helen was almost snarling, so Roz grabbed her arms and held them very firmly.

Roz was absolutely determined that this woman should not gain access to the sitting-room and Tom. Despite not phoning, he did vaguely resemble a Quality Man; and if he found out about the sperm, he'd be out of there like an Olympic athlete.

She stared determinedly at Helen's wide, glinting eyes. '*Look*,' she said with extraordinary composure, 'I'm sorry that you're upset. Can we discuss this later?'

'No.'

Roz wondered what *The Little Book of Calm* would have to say about this situation. Then she attempted to forcibly remove Helen from her house.

Tom was returning to the sitting-room. The dog had become very agitated, and Tom had decided to let him out into the back garden. It was quite a nice garden, and he had thrown a few sticks, though the dog hadn't bothered to retrieve them. He'd just barked. Perhaps he was trying to tactfully advise Tom that it was time to leave. Roz had another visitor, and he didn't want to overstay his welcome. Still, he'd enjoyed their conversation. Roz seemed much softer and considerably less aggressive than she had before.

'Get out of here, you bitch!'

That was her voice!

'I don't have the sperm. I threw it away.'

'I don't believe you.'

Tom edged nervously towards the hallway.

'It would have gone off by now anyway, even if I had it.'

'Sperm thief!'

'I didn't take anything. Jamie offered it to me.'

'You are not having my husband's baby!'

'No, I'm not. I'm really not.'

'Bitch!'

These words immobilised Tom for a minute. It was the strangest conversation he had ever overheard, and he wondered if he should flee unobtrusively, but the walls of the back garden were very high and he wasn't sure if he could scale them. Perhaps he should just remain in the sitting-room until the argument subsided. Suddenly he dearly wished he had shoved the perfume through the letterbox.

As he returned to the sofa, he felt a rising sense of panic. He was stuck in a house with two wild and angry women, and that was not a situation any man would choose to be in. He tried not to listen to the raised voices and wondered why an attractive and relatively young woman should collect sperm in the first place. Surely there were more pleasurable and traditional ways of obtaining it. He felt a flash of intense anger as he began to wonder if sexual intercourse would one day be completely passé. Perhaps the closest the sexes would come to intimacy was in the handing over of small phials of viscous liquid. He sighed deeply and thought how very strange modern life could be.

It was no good; he couldn't distract himself from the warfare in the hallway. He began to wonder if he should intervene in the altercation. Some sort of physical combat seemed to be taking place, and it was surely unchivalrous of him to remain this detached. He had photographed many weddings and was therefore not unused to open hostility. One ploy was to appear almost inhumanly unaware of what was going on. Men had mastered the art of selective idiocy far more than women realised.

Tom prepared his lines as he walked with considerable trepidation towards the hallway. Once there, however, he allowed his expression to flatten into a sort of bovine insouciance, and pretended not to notice that Roz was trying to look as though she knew something about karate.

'Roz,' he said, with as much dimwittedness as he could muster, 'I've let the dog into the back garden.'

Both women stared at him.

'I think he wants to go for a walk.'

Their eyes widened and then narrowed in a desperate attempt to gain perspective.

'It's quite a nice day for a walk, actually. Though they said there might be showers later.'

Their eyes blinked slowly, like camera shutters at twilight. Then Helen released her grip on Roz's hair.

'I like to try and get a bit of exercise at the weekends,' Tom continued airily. His palms were sweating.

'Who are you?' Helen demanded.

'My name is Tom.' He held out his hand, but Helen did not shake it. Instead she glared at him in amazement at men's obtuseness. Some of this irritation settled on her husband and slightly softened her fury towards Roz. Especially since Roz had burst into tears.

'I am not here to discuss dogs and exercise,' Helen said with steely impatience. 'I am here to discuss the return of my husband's sperm.'

Roz visibly drooped. The humiliation of it! She would never, ever find a Quality Man now.

'I believe my friend says she's thrown it out,' Tom said calmly. Roz blushed. He had heard the whole thing!

'And if my friend says she's thrown it out, I'd believe her,' Tom continued. 'She's an honest kind of person.'

'She's a brazen hussy!' Helen shouted. 'And now she wants to take my husband!'

Roz was appalled to find herself sobbing copiously. Men didn't like women who sobbed copiously – especially if they were desperate and pathetic and kept sperm in the fridge. Tom would go right off her now. Her shoulders sagged and her hair suddenly felt greasy. She'd probably developed about twenty wrinkles in the last ten minutes. There was no point in pretending any more. She began to shudder inconsolably.

'What is it, Roz?' Tom asked gently.

'I'm upset.'

'I know.'

'Then why did you ask me?'

'I didn't know what else to say. I'm sorry. I–'

'It's me who should be sorry!' Roz wailed wretchedly. 'Can't you see, Tom… can't you see what this whole situation says about my life!'

Helen smiled with satisfaction. Roz noticed, but she didn't care; what was there to hide now? Her toughness had deserted her and she plunged into the mire of her own humiliation. Her romantic experiences had so often contained humiliations. She'd reacted to them with anger and denied herself the consolation of tears, but now she was hurt, and offended because her predicament was not even aesthetic or poignant.

'I didn't want to be this kind of person.' She made a dramatic gesture. 'I just thought… you know… I'd find the things I needed. And that…and that there might even be some moments of…' The sobbing increased. 'Moments of beauty. Sunsets and kisses and… snuggles.'

'Snuggles,' Tom repeated.

'Yes, and…and I wouldn't be all alone, and I'd belong. And…and I wouldn't have to be so tough.'

Helen was looking slightly less vindictive.

154

'I don't want to hurt anyone. I really don't.' Roz's face was blotched and swollen with tears, and there was a red patch beneath her left eyebrow. 'I wouldn't have taken the…the sperm if he had not just arrived with it. I did wonder if I should use it. Then I decided not to, and…'

Tom and Helen waited.

'And then Bernice put it in her coffee.'

'*What*?' Helen leaned forwards.

'She's a colleague of mine. She thought it was soya milk. She'd taken off her glasses.'

'And…and she just poured it in, did she?' Helen was smiling ever so slightly.

'Yes. Go on. Laugh. I know you want to.' Roz's tears grew fatter and warmer and some trickled into her ears.

This revelation seemed to convince Helen. It was not the kind of thing one would make up.

'How did you find out about it, anyway?' Roz sniffed.

'Jamie told me.'

'*He told you!*'

'Yes, just before he left on a business trip. He said he'd met this poor sad single woman called Roz who needed his help. He didn't seem to think I'd mind.'

'The little fecker.'

'He's not a little fecker. He's a generous and compassionate man.'

Tom listened in awe. Helen was obviously an expert at compartmentalisation.

'How did you find out where I live?'

'There was only one Roz in his address book. I thought he'd taken it with him, but I found it this morning. It was under the sofa.'

Helen was studying Tom closely. He was quite a handsome man, and he seemed to care for this despicable woman – who was actually quite attractive and surely could find plenty of sperm in a more conventional way if she chose to. A terrible feeling of discomfort assailed her as she realised that her anger should also be directed at her husband. Jamie could be very difficult and impetuous and was capable of considerable manipulation.

'He wants me to have another baby,' she mumbled miserably.

'Your husband?' Tom inquired.

'Yes, of course. Who else would I be talking about? I...I think that's why he did this. He wanted me to know he was going to have another baby one way or another. He wants a son, you see. We already have four daughters.' Helen burst into tears and seemed about to sag onto the hall mat. Tom dragged her into the sitting-room and propped her up on the sofa.

And Roz made tea and tried not to howl with disappointment and humiliation.

Chapter Nineteen

'Y – M – C – A!' Caddy was roaring into a microphone. She'd already done 'Dancing Queen' and 'Blue Suede Shoes'. That was the great thing about being abroad: it didn't matter if you made a total arse of yourself.

Going to a karaoke bar had been Dan's idea. He'd said that, if they weren't going to talk about anything complicated, they might as well sing or dance, though Caddy had pointed out that they could also watch cable television. She hadn't wanted to sing at all. It seemed terribly intimidating. Dan had said that doing intimidating things was sometimes good for you. He said that before he went on stage he always felt like throwing up, but once he was out there it seemed absolutely right and natural.

Amazingly, Caddy's singing was going down really well. Perhaps it was because she'd borrowed a feather boa and sometimes wriggled her bottom. She was sweaty and scared and her hands were trembling, but she had a good voice. Somehow she'd forgotten that.

'Well done!' Dan congratulated her as she stepped off the stage. A Japanese man grabbed the microphone and started attempting 'Sergeant Pepper's Lonely Hearts Club Band'. Where were earplugs when you needed them?

'Was I okay? Was I all right?' Caddy asked breathlessly.

'Yes. You came completely up to scratch,' he grinned mischievously.

'Oh, no, don't use that word!' She scratched her elbow. 'I still have them, you know.'

'No, you don't. It's just your imagination.' He handed her a glass of wine.

Was it her imagination again, or were she and Dan really enjoying each other's company? The strain of that meal in the taverna seemed to have disappeared entirely. Deciding not to talk about anything really significant had helped enormously.

It was almost impossible to be friends with someone if you kept analysing whether you were friends with them or whether you should perhaps be something else. Your brain got so busy that you forgot the rest of you, which was supposed to be on holiday. And your brain was supposed to be on holiday too, wasn't it? It didn't want to go down the same sad old roads; it wanted to find new things to look at.

'Oh, Dan, it's nice here, isn't it?'

'Yes.'

'I didn't think I'd like karaoke, but…but it was fun to make a fool of myself.'

'You didn't. You were very good.'

'Was I?'

'Yes. I told you so.'

'And I'm brown, too, aren't I?'

'Very.'

'I should have sung something by Joni Mitchell. I love her.' Caddy's eyes were shining. 'Or Carly Simon… or Cat Stevens. There are so many songs I love, and now they hardly ever play them on the radio.' She trailed a finger round the rim of her glass. 'You were brilliant doing The Eagles.'

'Thank you.'

'Are you feeling a little better about… you know…' She couldn't bring herself to mention Zia's name.

'Yeah.'

She smiled at him. 'Jemma would like it here.'

'You worry about her, don't you?'

'Of course. I dream about her almost every night.'

'Who's she staying with?'

'Cousins called Brad and Cheryl. I'm glad she's with them. They'll keep telling her that she's wonderful and talented and as pretty as a little peach – or possibly a pumpkin – and she'll squirm and feel horrified, but the words will stay locked in her heart.'

Dan smiled. 'How do you know?'

'Because they're locked in mine somewhere. Brad and Cheryl said them to me when they visited Dublin about ten years ago. The thing about people like that is that they drive you a bit mad, but…but they also make you feel you're just fine as you are.'

'And you don't know that already?'

'No. I come from the kind of family where everyone isn't quite what other people wanted.'

'Been there, done that–'

'Oh, please don't say "bought the T-shirt",' Caddy pleaded.

'I wasn't going to.' Dan pretended to be offended. 'I was going to say "bought the armadillo".'

'Much more imaginative.' Caddy nodded approvingly.

'We're both a bit crazy, you know.'

'Yes, and we've also sold out. Remember all those times we've gone into swanky cafés in Dublin? What happened to the stewed tea and leaking teapots that we used to say we loved so much?'

'We still love them,' Dan said authoritatively.

'Do we?'

'Of course we do. Next time we'll meet at that place where even the white bread is stale, and the tomato sauce explodes onto your lap after you've thumped it twenty times, and they'd think you were swearing if you said "foccacia".'

Caddy giggled. 'Remember how the waitress almost fell over when you asked her for Earl Grey tea?'

They sat in silence, smiling at the memory.

'It wasn't all bad, was it? We had plenty of good times…' She searched his eyes. 'I felt so guilty about not being ready. I wanted to be ready, but I wasn't.'

Oh, dear, I shouldn't have said that. She knew it the minute the words were out. He'd be on to her like a Rottweiler.

'So, anyway…' Dan stared closely at a black dot on the tablecloth. Fleas were never far from their minds these days. 'So did you take the magazines out of the washing machine?'

'Oh, God, you saw me!'

'Yes. Through the window. I was wondering if you were going to put them on the non-fast-coloureds cycle.'

Caddy kicked him under the table.

159

He left for the loo and was back within a minute. 'How on earth do you do that?' she inquired.

'What?'

'Go to the loo in fifty seconds.'

'I dunno.' Dan leaned back in his chair and surveyed her solemnly. 'Maybe I just wanted to get back to you as fast as possible because I thought you might run off with the armadillo.'

The laughter made her splutter, and big droplets of wine landed all over his denim shirt. She reached forwards to brush them off, and he caught her hand and held it to his chest. She could feel his heart beating. She could feel his heat and warmth and strength.

'I'm sorry.' She withdrew her hand gently.

'I'm not.' He leaned across the table until their foreheads almost touched. 'I've been wanting to do that since you said you had fleas. I want them too.'

'Oh.' Caddy felt her cheeks grow pink. 'But what about your shirt?'

'I don't care about my shirt.'

'But you should. It's very nice.'

'And so are you.'

'I'll get you another one.'

He frowned. 'What are you talking about?'

'Another shirt like that. I think I've seen them in Marks and Spencer's.'

'Look, it will come out in the wash. I'm not going to discuss it any more.' He closed his eyes and started to tap a spoon on the table.

'What are you doing?'

'I'm playing you the opening bars of one of Bach's Brandenburg Concertos.'

'It doesn't sound like it. It sounds like someone tapping a spoon on a table.'

'You're not listening properly.'

She grabbed the spoon from him. 'Stop it, it's very annoying.'

He held her wrist. 'And so are you, but I still think you're… fairly nice.'

'Only fairly?'

'Yes. I'm afraid I've deducted a few marks for the wine.'

'Oh, no! That Swedish man's got up again – the one who sounds like a coffee-grinder.'

They both burst out laughing at the same time. The Swedish man was trying to be Barbra Streisand.

'Let's go.' Dan grabbed Caddy's hand.

When they reached Caddy's hotel, she asked him if he'd like some vanilla tea. She had found some just that morning.

'Yes, that would be nice.' He followed her up the stone steps. Caddy saw Sofia peeping out at her from behind a curtain. She had a broad smile on her face.

'It's very hot, isn't it?' Caddy said as she plugged in the kettle. 'Too hot, really. They should have air conditioning.'

'Yes, it is terribly hot.' Dan sat on the edge of the bed.

'There should be two chairs in here, too. That wooden one is very stern and doesn't even have a cushion.'

'The bed's fine.'

Caddy sat beside him. 'Don't look at the kettle or it will never boil.'

'Okay. I'll stare at the teddy bear.'

'He's got a lovely expression, hasn't he? I put him on the windowsill every morning when I go out. I feel he should at least have a sea view.'

'I'm sure he appreciates it… God, I'm knackered.' Dan lay back and rested his head on the pillow.

'Are…are you going to drink your tea there?'

'I thought I might. If that's all right with you.'

Caddy got up and looked for some milk in the fridge. 'Here you are.' She handed him the mug.

He sniffed it. 'Mmm… lovely. It smells like cake.'

She watched as he took his first sip.

'Excellent,' he declared. 'The nicest tea I've ever tasted.'

Caddy sat down on the bed beside him and cradled her mug in her hands.

'Do you know what would make it even nicer?'

'What?'

'A hug.'

'I don't know, Dan. I–'

'Pretend I'm a teddy bear. I won't jump on you, I promise.'

'But what…what about Zia?'

'I've told you, she's just a *friend*.'

'Oh, dear…' Caddy let out a long sigh.

'We need this, Caddy.' Dan rubbed her back gently. 'Everyone needs a bit of human warmth and comfort.'

'Yes, I suppose everyone does.' She gazed pensively at her turquoise ring. 'And… after all, we are on holiday.'

'Do you want to lie down?'

'No,' she answered quickly. 'I want to drink my tea first.'

'*Okay.*' He gazed out the window.

Dan was being so much more understanding, Caddy could hardly believe it. Maybe she had changed a bit, but he had too. 'Thank you.' She drained the last drops from her mug.

'For what?'

'For making it so easy to be with you.'

'Ditto.'

She lay down beside him, and they both stared at the ceiling. Dan sighed and nestled his head deeper into the pillow.

'It's very hot, isn't it?'

'Yes. We've said that already.' Caddy sat up suddenly.

'Was that a mosquito?'

'No. I don't think so.'

She lay down again. 'I suppose that's why we come here, really.'

'To be chased by mosquitoes?'

'No, of course not!' She punched his arm playfully. 'To be hot, and brown. The backs of my legs aren't, though.'

'Aren't what?'

'Brown.' She rolled over to demonstrate their lack of brownness, and felt Dan's hand caressing the inside of her left ankle with exquisite care.

162

'That feels nice.'

'Does it?'

'Yes, very nice. Have you studied massage?'

'Ages ago.'

'I must have been more tense than I realised.' Caddy tried not to let out a moan of pleasure as his hand made sweeping motions up her calf. 'I get massages in Dublin sometimes.'

'Really?'

'Yes. Samantha's very good at it.'

'The backs of your legs are a bit brown, actually.'

'Oh, I hope so!'

'I wonder if they're brown all the way up.' Dan began to extend his caresses.

Caddy squirmed with pleasure. 'Oh, Dan, that's…that's enough.' He didn't seem to hear her.

'Dan, I'd like you to stop that now, please.'

'Why?'

She rolled over and looked at him sternly. 'Because I'm tired and it's very hot.'

'You'd be less hot if you took off your dress.'

'But I'm not going to.'

'Fine. Keep it on, then. You're certainly not going to get me out of this T-shirt.'

'Good.' Caddy smiled. 'That seems very sensible.'

Dan reached out to touch the tip of her nose. 'It's funny, isn't it?'

'What?'

'Being this comfortable with someone.'

Caddy rested her cheek on his shoulder. It felt warm and firm and slightly damp from the heat. 'Yes. It's very… nice.'

'You've been very hurt, haven't you?'

'Would you like an olive?'

'Not just at the moment.'

'They're very nice olives.'

'I'm sure they are. Who's Alain?'

Caddy stiffened. Surely it was time to tell him. She clenched her hands over her stomach. 'Someone I loved far too much. For a while he was everything. I let him be everything.'

'Why?' Dan whispered.

'Because…' Her lower lip was trembling. 'Maybe I felt I wasn't enough in myself. That I didn't matter… compared to him.'

'Oh, Caddy, how did you come to feel like that?'

'I don't know. I wish I did. It's still there, somewhere inside me – that feeling that…that I lose myself in someone's expectations and demands. Their anger. That…that I don't have a strong enough sense of myself to say, "No, this isn't fair."'

'But you left him, didn't you?'

'Yes. I did it for Jemma.'

'And for yourself, too. I'm sure of it. You've been stronger than you realise.'

'Oh, I don't know.' Caddy sighed.

'It's true. Why don't you remember all the good things about yourself? You should. You need to.'

'I know. I've been trying to. I've been… I've been reading books about it.'

'You won't get it from books. You'll get it when you know it – and you know it already, somewhere deep down inside you.'

He brushed some hair from her eyes and noticed the small scars on her forehead. He had seen them before but hadn't dared mention them.

She saw him looking at them, and lay very still. 'Now you know why I have a fringe.'

'Where did you get them?'

'From him.'

'Alain?'

'Yes.'

Dan's jaw clenched. 'What can I do? What can I do to make it better?'

'Nothing,' Caddy said blankly. 'Let's just not talk about it any more, okay? I feel so tired even thinking about it.'

They turned to look at each other at the same time, and their noses almost collided. Dan smiled; then he said, 'Yours makes that noise too.'

'My what?'

'Your cistern. It gurgles just like mine.'

'It's a comfortable bed, isn't it?'

'Yes. Very soft,' Dan agreed.

'I own a futon. It isn't soft. I wish it were.'

'Why did you buy it?'

'I don't know, really. I suppose I liked the look of it. I wanted to be someone who had a futon. Freud called that kind of thing "the narcissism of small differences".'

'There's a lot of that about these days,' Dan said.

'Maybe that's why people are so lonely,' Caddy whispered. 'I see it in my students. They're searching so hard for something… you know… something that endures and matters. And people keep trying to sell them cars.'

Dan ran a finger lightly along her arm. 'Why did your father move into the garden shed?'

'How do you know that?' She was genuinely amazed.

'You told me the other evening.'

'Did I?'

'Yes, you said he might be in there for ever and ever.'

'Oh, I suppose he may move back into the house eventually. He just needed to escape for a while.'

'From what?'

'From my mother.'

'I thought they were fairly happy.'

'They seem to be, Dan, but that's only because she subjugates him.'

Dan did not reply. He was thinking of the day he had met Ava Lavelle in that Dublin restaurant. She had been very friendly. She had talked about what a wonderful granddaughter Jemma was and how good Caddy was at teaching. But after the meal Caddy had only seemed to remember her mother's 'insults'. 'She only went on and on about how well that tablecloth was ironed because she knows I rarely iron things myself... I know she thinks I'm too lenient with Jemma. She made that very obvious, didn't she?... She has this need to control people. I just can't stand it.'

Dan looked out the open window at the stars and marvelled at how two people could have such dissimilar recollections. What he had seen was an elderly woman trying very hard to say the right things and demonstrate her approval. It had been done clumsily, because tact was obviously not her forte.

'What is it between you and your mother, Caddy?'

'That would take at least a year to explain.'

'Try to.'

'She's never really tried to understand me.'

'Have you tried to understand her?'

Caddy glared at him. 'So you're taking her side now, are you?'

'No... I just feel she may care for you more than you realise.'

'She hasn't shown it.'

'Maybe she finds it hard to show it.'

'She should learn.' Caddy was sitting up in bed now, sucking furiously on an olive.

'What happened between you?'

'Lots of things.'

'Such as?'

'I came to Greece to forget all that stuff, Dan.'

'But you haven't, have you?'

Caddy stuffed another olive into her mouth. 'I...I suppose I can't forgive her for not forgiving me.'

'For what?'

'For having Jemma. She banished me, Dan. I didn't go back home for ten years.'

'I see.' Dan reached for an olive. 'That must have been very hard.'

'It was. She didn't even contact me. She sends me these stupid presents now, but she should have sent them then. Even a card would have been something. She knits wonderful jumpers for other people's children, but she didn't knit one

166

thing for Jemma. Not even a pair of socks.'

'Don't feel embarrassed about crying if you need to.'

'I don't need to. I've cried too much.'

'I don't think I've cried enough.'

'About what?'

'Oh, I don't know. Just things.'

They both lay back and stared at the darkness. The cistern was gurgling again; it seemed like the sound of loneliness.

Dan yawned. 'I'm tired.'

'So am I.' Caddy snuggled against his shoulder.

'It's lovely being here with you.'

'Ditto.'

'I can see why you like vanilla tea. It has a very… vanilla flavour.'

'Yes. It's special. Like you.'

Dan rolled over and looked at her solemnly. He would have to say it sometime.

'I'm not in love with Zia Andersson.'

'Of course you are. You must be. She's *gorgeous*.'

'No, I'm in love with you.'

'What?'

'You heard me. And you love me too. There's nowhere to hide any more, Caddy, because we both know it's true.'

Chapter Twenty

Ava was on a large ship and drenched in Julio Iglesias. That wasn't actually the name of the perfume – it was called 'Only' – but she preferred using the name of the singer, which was also on the bottle. 'I'm just going to put on some Julio.' It always made her friends laugh. Even Jim laughed at her jokes sometimes.

Ava gazed at her fellow passengers and felt a terrible heave in her stomach, so she recommenced her knitting. A woman who was embarking on a journey to God-knows-where needed to keep her hands busy. Knitting, like tea, was one of Ava's crucial allies. It helped take her mind off her worries and gave her a sense of pattern and purpose. She could certainly do with a pattern now, because she had embarked on the construction of a jumper. She had visited a knitwear shop the day before, as soon as the bus from the train station had deposited her in central Dublin – she had decided not to make the journey from Kerry to London all in one go, and had stayed the night in a B&B. She had purchased a startling variety of wools in vibrant colours. She had also purchased an assortment of knitting needles, but not a pattern. 'I'm an experienced knitter,' she'd told the assistant. 'I often knit without a pattern.' This was, in fact, true, but now Ava wished she had one. Though the jumper was growing, she didn't know what shape it would take. She wove in the colours and the decorative motifs in a kind of daze.

Her note to Jim had been gloriously understated. '*I have gone to a foreign country.*' How he would frown as he read it! Thinking of this made Ava glow with satisfaction. She was an enigmatic woman, and her husband might regret having taken her for granted. He would know that she was foreign, too – foreign in ways he would never understand.

As the newfangled ferry zoomed between Dublin and Wales, Ava's knitting needles clicked determinedly. She felt as though she were gliding along in a huge modern building, and, frankly, she found it rather intimidating. Of course, it was also very comfortable and speedy… but it wasn't like the ship that had carried Luigi into Cork harbour that misty October day.

What on earth am I doing here? Ava thought. *I am completely alone and abandoned.*

All through her life, she had dreaded abandonment. In truth, she didn't really know what made others leave or stay. She tried hard to make people need her because she knew they would never love her for herself. Earning love involved a complicated series of offerings and demands.

How guilty they would all feel if she never returned!

She decided to purchase a cup of tea. The restaurant was extremely large, and when Ava had made her purchase she scanned the restaurant, hoping to see a familiar face. At home she sometimes felt oppressed by the smallness of the village, but now that seemed a comforting haven from the world's large and anonymous spaces. People knew her there – sometimes they knew too much about her, and what they didn't know they guessed.

That had often annoyed her, but if this was the alternative, then she would gladly choose the village and the voluminous gossip that came with it.

As the ship glided towards a foreign land, a dreadful sense of insignificance assailed Ava. Maybe she wouldn't get off in Holyhead at all, just take the ferry straight back to Ireland. She gripped her handbag and stared bleakly at a child who was scattering sweets across a colouring book, chocolate-mouthed and innocent. Then she set out in search of a table that was clean and unoccupied and not scattered with used plastic cutlery.

Eventually she found a pleasant refuge by one of the large windows. As she meekly sipped her tea, she studied the faces around her. You could tell so much from a face if you really looked. No one would look at her like that again. She was old and therefore partly invisible. Other people saw you were old before you knew it yourself – and then they reminded you of it, over and over again.

Many of her fellow passengers seemed bored by their peregrinations. They had probably done this kind of thing quite often, but Ava hadn't; and now she was too timid to enjoy it. *Why on earth did I tell Fidelma Moran I'd visit her in London?* she wondered. *I hardly recognised her voice on the phone. She's virtually a stranger.* Suddenly she wished she had flown straight to London. When the ship arrived in Holyhead she'd have to get on a train, and she was already tired.

She stared gloomily out the window. Tears began to mist her eyes and she blinked them firmly away. It was silly, crying about things one couldn't change. But perhaps that was precisely why one needed to cry. She folded a paper napkin carefully and decided that she needed a chocolate muffin.

There wasn't much of a queue at the counter. She purchased the muffin and another cup of tea, but when she headed back to her table she found it was occupied by a group of teenagers. They were laughing and one of them had a plastic cup between her teeth. Where was she going to sit now?

She looked around and saw an empty seat, but she would have to share the table with a stranger. He was elderly and looked quite civilised.

'Is this seat taken?'

'No, it isn't, dear. Do sit down.'

Dear. He had called her '*dear*', and in an English accent. This probably meant that he wouldn't talk much. English people didn't tend to talk as much to strangers, though they were incredibly polite if you asked them about directions and buses.

She probably wouldn't be talking much to anyone, apart from Fidelma Moran, while she was away. If she got desperate she could, of course, remark on the weather to people who worked in transportation.

'My name is Henry.'

Goodness, the man was talking again!

'Mine is Ava.'

'Pleased to meet you, Ava.' The man extended his hand and she shook it politely.

'Have…have you been visiting Dublin?' As soon as she'd said it, she realised how stupid it sounded. He had hardly been on a trip to Copenhagen.

'Yes, I have been. I had a very pleasant little holiday.'

'Oh, I'm glad to hear that,' Ava said. 'It's a very big ship, isn't it?'

'And fast.'

'Indeed.'

Henry gazed out the window, and Ava wondered if he had run out of small talk. She reached into her handbag and extracted her knitting.

'So you knit?' Henry said.

'Yes.'

'My wife used to knit.'

'Oh, I'm sorry – is she…?'

'Ran off with an Italian waiter twenty years ago.'

Ava stared at him.

'They're in Sorrento now.'

'I…I believe it's a beautiful city.'

'Never been there.'

'Neither have I.'

'What are you knitting?'

'I don't know.' Ava cringed as soon as she'd said it. 'I…I think it's a jumper.'

'Are you travelling on to London?'

'Yes.' She took a careful sip from her cup of tea.

'I live in London.'

Ava didn't answer.

'Where are you staying?'

'South Kensington.'

Henry proceeded to tell her about a Viennese café that she should visit. He wasn't a particularly handsome man, but he still had his hair, though probably not all his teeth. His eyes

171

were brown and his skin was very wrinkled and quite tanned. What was more, he was wearing a perfectly ironed cream linen jacket, and his mouth was almost in the right proportions. He offered to queue for Ava when she said she might try the shepherd's pie. They had both suddenly realised that they were hungry.

'Thank you, Henry,' she said. 'I'll stay here and keep our seats.'

She tried to stuff some coins into his hand, but he said she could pay him later when they knew the exact amount.

When Henry returned with the heavily laden tray, Ava saw he had bought two small bottles of wine. He refused to let her pay for them. 'They're my treat,' he said jovially. 'I like a bit of wine with a meal.'

As they ate, he told her he liked travelling and hoped to visit France sometime soon. 'I tend to go by boat,' he added. 'I like to feel the miles.'

Ava nodded.

'I often wish I had a companion to come with me. It can get a little lonely, though I sometimes meet lovely people.'

'Do you live alone?'

'Yes.'

'Oh.' Ava took a gulp from her glass.

'And what about yourself, Ava?' His smile was very pleasant and cultured.

So she found herself telling him how she was married to a black man who had sailed into Cork harbour when she was very young, and how, after all these years, they were still tremendously close and happy.

'I notice you aren't wearing a wedding ring.'

Oh, bugger, Ava thought. She had removed her ring when she had boarded the ship, because Jim probably didn't wear his when he was with his foreign women. She reached into her handbag and extracted the ring. 'I took it off when I was in the ladies',' she said with a bright smile. 'Thank you for reminding me.'

'Where is your husband now?'

'He's visiting his relatives. In the Caribbean.'

'Have you been there yourself?'

'Oh, yes. Many times.'

By the time they disembarked, Ava and Henry were quite pally. Ava was not attracted to him, but he was an entertaining and sympathetic companion. He was also something of a man of the world. Before his retirement he'd been a Customs officer.

'This is my daughter, Oregano.' He carried pictures of his grown-up children in a special plastic wallet. 'It's an unusual name. My ex-wife was very fond of herbs.'

On the train Henry told Ava that he and Oregano were 'very, very close'. He went on about it a little too much, actually, and she found herself feeling slightly irritated.

'I'm not very close to my daughter,' she admitted. It was one of the very few times she had said this.

She looked out the window at the countryside. The train was going very fast – unnecessarily fast, she thought. It snaked through town and country, under bridges and beneath mountains. If only there were more time to look at it all properly.

'Does your husband mind you travelling alone?'

'No. Not at all. We lead very independent lives.'

Ava stared across the aisle at a young woman with a portable computer. She was typing things into it in a very businesslike fashion, consulting a notebook every so often. Beside her was a contraption, which Ava knew was called a BlackBerry. Beth had one, even though she didn't really need it.

The young woman was quite pretty, but her face looked tired and tense, and her skin implied that she didn't spend enough time out of doors. She looked fiercely efficient. Ava decided that she was probably quite important and about to attend some high-powered meeting. She yearned to understand the mysteries of these modern young women with their BlackBerrys and their mobile phones. Did they tell their male colleagues when they had their periods? Were they lonely?

Did they ever feel like getting on a boat and running away? Did they know how much they didn't know? Perhaps not; Ava was only just beginning to realise it herself.

The young woman realised she was being watched and glanced quickly at Ava. She didn't smile, she just looked, and Ava felt shocked by her impassiveness. She flinched slightly as Henry leaned forward and tapped her arm. 'Would you like a cup of tea? I think I'll toddle down to the buffet.'

'No, it's my turn to queue. You got the lunch.' She rose from her seat.

'Are you sure?'

'Yes.'

'Because I'd happily go if–'

'Oh, Henry, let me. Would you like a biscuit with it?'

'Yes,' he beamed. 'One of those shortbread snacks would be nice.'

Ava bustled off down the carriage, holding on to the edges of the headrests. Minutes later she returned. 'I'm so impressed with the little straps they've put on these cups,' she exclaimed. 'It makes the tea so much easier to carry.' She handed Henry his cup and watched to see how much milk and sugar he used.

'Thank you, Ava.' Henry started to fastidiously clean the small table with a napkin. 'And you even got the shortbread biscuits! What a very pleasant travelling companion you are.'

Ava almost blushed with pleasure. She was in a foreign country and had a new friend. The busy young woman had smiled at her when she returned. Even the train's speed was beginning to feel quite exhilarating. She opened her slice of cherry cake and savoured it carefully, while Henry watched her.

'Isn't this nice?'

'Yes, it is,' she agreed.

'Ava…'

She looked at him. 'What is it?'

'Ava…' He leaned forwards. 'Ava, I have a small proposition to make.'

Chapter Twenty-One

'ROZ HEADON.' IT WASN'T aesthetically pleasing. Roz had said it a number of times, for experimental purposes, but its attraction had not increased. When she and Rufus married – which they probably would – she would keep her own name. She was stuck with a man of such Non-Quality that he was glad to get anyone at all!

She hadn't meant to get back with Rufus, but it had happened in a resigned and inevitable kind of way, as unsurprising as losing one's socks in a launderette. They'd bumped into each other in José's Wine Bar, and after a bottle of Chardonnay Roz had decided he wasn't all that grotesque. He said he still cared for her; and she needed someone to care for her, though she often wished she didn't. Being a contented single woman seemed more and more appealing. If only she had the temperament for it!

The best thing about Rufus was that he spoke fluent French because his mother came from Poitiers. He specialised in fitted kitchens and had a particular penchant for chrome. He was slightly plump and balding and always tanned, and he wore very colourful ties in an attempt to have a colourful personality. The ties, if anything, made him less interesting: you saw the tie and then you saw the face, and, frankly, the tie won out. The second nice thing about him was that he was rich, and the third was that he wasn't already married. If he had been nicer, of course, he probably would have been married, so this third merit was somewhat questionable.

Being back with him was a terrible disappointment, but at least Roz had been trained to deal with this dejection by her mother, Fern. Fern McCarthy had always known that men would prove to be a terrible disappointment. 'They do their best, dear,' she had told Roz on numerous occasions. 'But, frankly, they're rather dimwitted about the things we women cherish. They don't notice, you see. We baffle them, and then they get frightened. You have to talk to them softly but with a certain firmness. And never, ever make them feel rejected in bed, because that's where the poor little things feel most vulnerable.'

'They don't behave as if they're feeling vulnerable.'

'Don't be fooled by the bravado. And never let them see that you're desperate or lonely, or need them too much.'

'Why?'

'Because they completely lose respect for you, dear. That's just the way they are.'

Roz had spent a good deal of her life waiting for men to disprove her mother's notions, but they hadn't. Her own father had left only months after her brother Sig was born. And now Tom Armstrong had completely lost respect for her because of the sperm incident. He hadn't made this obvious; but then, men never made things obvious. He had even phoned to ask how she was, but that had been purely out of pity. And Roz couldn't bear to be pitied by a man.

'You seemed very upset,' he had said.

'Oh, I just did that to get rid of that stupid woman,' she'd replied airily. 'I don't get upset by that kind of thing. I'm a very tough person.'

'You don't seem like that to me.'

'Look, Tom, it's sweet of you to be concerned but there's no need for it. I'm sure you must be very busy.'

She'd thanked him again for the perfume and wished him well with his photography. 'Goodbye, Tom,' she had added, in a very final, unsentimental way.

'Bye, then.' He had sounded rather bewildered, but, on reflection, Roz realised that he had also been enormously relieved.

She was relieved too. She would try to avoid him and get on with her relationship with Rufus. She knew how to have a relationship with Rufus. She would do things for him, and he would do things for her. The transaction would be clear-cut, mercenary and tremendously superficial. Marriage would be mentioned quite soon. They would have two children,

176

preferably a boy and a girl.

She'd give him ten years and then go.

At least I'll have a really nice kitchen, she thought. *I must start looking at catalogues.*

A strange thrill ran through her. What a relief it was to roam towards the vast and uncomplicated tundra of superficiality! Roz's mother went from lover to lover with an exemplary lack of longing or regret; at fifty-nine she was still in demand, and she was currently staying in a French villa with a man who specialised in plastic CD racks. He would never be allowed to see Fern without her make-up. Her face was a canvas, and every day it underwent an amazing transformation. Sig said he hated her, but that was only because he was getting in touch with his inner child in Manhattan. Therapists had a lot to answer for. You could be quite contented until they persuaded you that your mother was narcissistic and that your father was an alcoholic whom everybody had enabled. Poor Sig; he was probably paying two hundred bucks an hour just to be made more miserable.

Roz squared her shoulders and decided she would spend the afternoon in the office. The agency was very understanding about her need to work away from interruptions, but they did expect her to return to her desk at regular intervals, and attend meetings, and go for those long silly lunches with clients – her John Rocha skirt with the seductive slit had, she suspected, clinched a number of accounts.

'Chump, I hope you don't mind, but I'm going out for a while.'

Chump looked up at her dolefully.

'I'll put on the Brandenburg Concertos if you want. You seemed to like them yesterday.'

Chump rested his head on his paws. He clearly didn't care.

'Would you like some gourmet dog food? They have some in the delicatessen.'

Chump blinked in a melancholy way.

'Oh, Chump, darling…' Roz was appalled to find that her

177

eyes were brimming with tears. 'Caddy hasn't forgotten you. She's flying home tomorrow.'

Half an hour later she was sitting at her desk. It was a very nice desk made out of cherry wood; she had chosen it herself. Her best advertisements were framed and hanging on the walls, and some awards were tastefully displayed on a side shelf, next to a small lemon tree that needed watering. She reached for the large bottle of spring water that she kept for this purpose and poured it onto the dry earth.

'Poor little thing, no one even noticed you were thirsty,' she said. Somehow this made her feel terribly gloomy.

'Hello, Roz!'

'Hello!'

She beamed cheerful greetings to the strange stream of humanity that passed her open door. It was important that people should see her at her desk, and speak with her, and learn that she had been 'very busy' and was therefore tremendously dedicated to the sale of corn cream, which was her current assignment. Some of her colleagues were rather jealous of the flexible working arrangements Roz had negotiated. There had been some snide comments and bitchiness, and no one ever watered her lemon tree.

There had been a time when this would have made her miserable, but the years spent working in television had taught her it was impossible to please people all of the time. You could make yourself utterly dejected thinking about colleagues who didn't like you for their own peculiar reasons. Being liked by everyone on the planet was no longer Roz's priority, though it was a great relief that Bernice was loyal and non-judgmental.

After Roz had paraded her presence by ostentatiously fetching a cup of coffee from the communal cafetière, she walked briskly and enthusiastically back to her office. Once she had closed the door, however, she slumped into a kind of torpor and thought about how wonderful Tom had been with Jamie's wife. He had calmed her down amazingly; he had even persuaded her that she didn't need to have another baby.

The wretched creature had scoffed nearly all Roz's biscotti and left looking immensely cheered up and almost happy.

But these ruminations would not lead to the increased sale of corn cream. And the sale of corn cream was, of course, extraordinarily important.

By the time Bernice tapped gently on her door, Roz was almost crawling on the carpet with frustration.

'What is it? You look a bit glum.'

'Oh, it's nothing.' Roz beamed manically.

'Have you time to talk about the concept for the corn-cream ad?'

'Of course!'

'I'd like to get the storyboard done soon, but the brief from the client was pretty vague.' Bernice was the art director on the project.

'Has Clint said any more about it?' Clint was the creative director. He wore suede shoes and turquoise braces and had recently taken to making origami at meetings.

'No. He just muttered something about synergy. He's using that word a lot lately.' Clint went through favourite-word phases.

'I don't know how we can make the bloody stuff sound sexy.' Roz was no longer looking quite so enthusiastic. 'The client says they want it to be sexy, but there is simply nothing seductive about corns.'

'You made blackheads seem sexy.'

'I made the absence of them seem desirable,' Roz corrected. 'That was relatively easy.'

'And what about those products for whiteheads and pimples? You put them right up there with coffee, in the romantic sense.'

'Oh, please stop it, Bernice. You're making me feel nauseated.'

The cream softened corns, apparently, and made them easier to bear while you waited for an appointment with the chiropodist. 'I think the person with corns needs to be extremely attractive.'

179

'Yes, I'd already figured that out,' Roz replied irritably.

'She needs to have corns and a really hot date.'

A slight glimmer shone in Roz's eyes. 'Yes. You're right! She's getting home from work, tired, and her corns are driving her crazy. We can use that "eek eek eek" kind of music to symbolise her immense discomfort.'

'She slumps into a chair in her apartment.'

'It's a very beautiful apartment.'

'Of course,' Bernice said. 'Only she can't appreciate it, because of her corns.'

'She looks at her diary, which is open on a table, and sees, "Brad, 7.30". But her corns have made her lose all interest in romance.'

'And then she remembers the cream in her handbag. She takes it out and we get the product shot.'

Roz was frantically scribbling notes on a pad. 'Of course. Then she rubs the sperm on her corns and–'

'What are you talking about?'

'The cream. She rubs the cream on her feet.'

'You didn't say cream. You said sperm.'

'I didn't!' Roz was blushing furiously. 'Why on earth would I say that?'

Bernice decided not to debate the point.

'Anyway, she rubs the cream on her corns and this blissful smile appears on her face as she leans back in the chair. The music is soft and sensuous and her apartment immediately seems brighter.' Roz shifted in her chair. The S word had made her want to lie under her desk and stay there until the cleaners arrived, although she knew she would feel rather guilty as they vacuumed round her. 'And the next time we see her she's running to answer the door in a short slinky dress. Brad is, of course, absolutely gorgeous.'

'They kiss very passionately,' Bernice added dreamily. 'Then she grabs her handbag in the manner of a woman who's just found the right sanitary towel.'

'Or a detergent that removes intransigent odours.'

'She and Brad leave for a wonderful evening unaffected by

the discomfort of corns – and probably fall in love and marry and have beautiful children.'

'And all because of a cream!' Roz declared happily. Then she burst into tears.

'Oh, poor Roz – what is it?'

'I don't want to do this any more,' Roz wailed. 'It's…it's just too silly.'

'But people *need* corn cream, Roz. I'm sure it's a very helpful product.'

'Yes. Yes, I'm sure it is.' Roz sniffed. She should have known that Bernice wouldn't fully sympathise with her dilemma. Bernice liked advertising. Lots of people did; it was, in fact, quite an interesting and varied profession – if you wanted to do it. Which Roz didn't.

'Are you really going to leave advertising?' Bernice inquired gently.

'I'm…I'm not sure. Please don't tell anyone what I said.'

There was a lengthy silence.

'Hmm.'

'Hmm what, Bernice?'

'I was just thinking – we've used that hot-date formula so many times. Do you think the corn-cream people will want something more original?'

Roz thought of chiffon scarves floating over purple oil-rigs and frowned. 'We both know you have to train clients into originality,' she declared. 'I think the corn-cream bunch would be terrified if we came up with anything too creative.'

At five-thirty, Roz almost ran down the road to her appointment with Samantha. Caddy had given her the name and number of her masseuse, but it wasn't until the sperm incident that Roz had felt the need of her services. Though she was a very tough, steely person, she knew that her superficiality could only be maintained by occasional spurts of honesty. Caddy had said that Samantha was very discreet and patient, and Roz desperately needed someone with those qualities.

By seven o'clock, Samantha knew all about Tom

Armstrong and how he would never want Roz now. She also knew that Roz's father had abandoned the family and that her mother hardly ever phoned. She even knew about Rufus and the awful things Roz had to do to please him.

'What I really want is someone to love, someone who'll love me back,' Roz blubbered into a soft white towel. 'I want a man who sees things – you know, the little things that other people might not notice. And...and I want to help him, and make him less afraid and more open. But only if he wants. And I want us to be honest and kind and forgiving. And...and I want us to count each other's toes.'

'You're in love with Tom Armstrong, aren't you?' Samantha smiled.

'Yes,' Roz agreed miserably. 'But I don't know why I'm telling you all this. It's probably the geranium oil.'

Chapter Twenty-Two

ROZ HADN'T PLANNED TO share her double bed with Rufus. They'd seen a bit too much of each other recently, and she wanted a bit of peace. He had just turned up with a bottle of wine. Now it was early morning and he was tugging her elbow.

'Open your mouth.'

'What?' She peered at him blearily.

'Open your mouth, I want to look at your fillings.'

Roz squinted at the clock. It was 5 a.m. 'Feck off.'

'Oh, darling, you know how it excites me.'

'I'm knackered.'

'I'm not.' He pressed against her.

'This is getting ridiculous.'

'I love you. *Je t'aime,* Roz. *Je t'aime beaucoup…*'

She flexed her jaw reluctantly, but as Rufus lowered his lips towards her mouth she pulled away. 'You haven't washed your teeth.'

'I'll do it now.'

'No. It's too early. I want to go back to sleep.'

He stared at her mutinously.

'If you're feeling frustrated, deal with it on your own. I would have thought that you'd be tired after last night.' She rolled so far away from him that she was at the edge of the bed. It was obviously high time she made some demands of her own.

'Rufus, I want you to send some flowers to my office,' she announced. 'A really big bunch. And a note saying, "With adoration from You Know Who."'

'Of course.' Rufus's hand was moving towards her left buttock.

'Stop that.'

'But it's nice.' He tugged playfully at her pubic hair.

Roz sat up furiously and glared at him. 'Look, Rufus, if

you don't behave yourself, our arrangement about radiators, teaspoons, steel-rimmed sunglasses and fillings will have to be completely revised.'

Rufus looked suitably alarmed. 'I'm sorry. I've been very selfish.'

'Yes, you have been,' she agreed. 'Now leave me alone. I want to get some rest.'

She put her head back on the pillow and started to doze. Last night's massage had been so nice. Samantha had been so very kind and caring. Tears formed in the corners of Roz's eyes.

Lots of people probably knew about the sperm incident by now. It was the kind of thing that tended to leak out. Jamie's wife would probably confide in someone, who'd confide in someone else. People found it very hard to keep juicy gossip to themselves. It would be mentioned as something 'just between ourselves' and eventually become a spectacular indiscretion. Eventually the secret would reach someone in the agency; after all, Jamie was one of their key clients. Tom might talk about it too, but not with the same degree of pleasure.

Tom... His name seemed like another country. A beautiful big land where you might watch someone sleeping and feel glad to be beside them.

Rufus was quietly masturbating. He was trying to do it without ostentation, but the mattress still bounced a bit in a determined, lonely kind of way. Little hisses were escaping from his mouth and the rhythm of his solo stimulation was intensifying.

I've been driven to this, Roz thought. *I've been driven into this small, sad corner of desire. And it isn't even my own.*

When she heard a muted 'Ahhh,' she sat bolt upright in bed. Rufus was fumbling for Kleenex as she ran towards the bathroom; she locked the door and sank to the floor like a crumpled feather. Huge sobs heaved right through her. How could she have become this kind of person? It wasn't as if she was ugly. As far as she knew she didn't have halitosis, and her clothes didn't reek of objectionable odours. She even used the right brand of coffee and had a university degree. There were people she could talk with – people who understood and liked her. But the right man had always eluded her, fled from her, to the point of farce.

And now everybody in the agency would know she was reduced to hunting for sperm – oh, how weary she was of that word! – and she would have to try to reclaim some status via the regular delivery of flowers. Rufus would have to be mentioned, frequently and with a feline purr of contentment. And she would have to stay in advertising, because getting into films required great determination and patience, and lots of other things that no one would ever fully understand.

'Roz? Roz, what is it?' Rufus was tapping at the door.

'Go away.'

'Please let me in.'

'No. I'm…I'm meditating.'

This silenced Rufus for a moment. Then he said, 'I don't believe you.'

'I'm tired.'

'I know. I'm sorry. I shouldn't have woken you up.'

'I have a very complicated life, Rufus. I don't think you realise that.'

Rufus tried to switch to listening mode. Sometimes women just wanted to be listened to, apparently. He'd read about it in a newspaper article. 'Come back to bed and talk to me about it,' he said gently.

'No,' Roz mumbled. 'You wouldn't understand.'

'I could try to.'

Roz's sobbing recommenced.

'I won't ask to look at your fillings ever again.'

'Oh, Rufus,' Roz sighed. Then she reluctantly rose and opened the door.

Back in bed, Rufus stared at her solemnly. 'This isn't going to be enough for you, is it?'

'Why do you say that?'

'This – us… it's not what you want.'

185

Roz yearned to agree with him, but then she would have no one. This was her very last chance. The facts were depressingly clear. She had squandered her youth on unsuitable men, and now the quality ones were beyond her reach.

'Say "*je t'aime*" again, Rufus,' she whispered. 'I like hearing you say it.'

'*Je t'aime.*'

Yes; now that she listened closely, she could tell the E was missing. And the M was too.

Chapter Twenty-Three

TOM HAD DECIDED TO cook something tasty in his new wok. It was evening and he was hungry. He had become the sort of man who regularly went to the supermarket and remembered to buy things like sesame oil. Sometimes he even gave small dinner parties.

He placed a jazz record on the stereo and moved to the music as he sliced the vegetables. At least that whole business with Samantha was over. And he was taking photographs again, though not full-time.

He'd been taking photographs anyway, in his head. It was instinctive. Even as he sold mobile phones, he often found himself thinking: *that* would make a good photograph. But what did make a good photograph? The human lens saw the image first, selected it and gave it value. Lately Tom had been wondering if he had valued certain people enough.

Once again he remembered the silent, withdrawn figure in his childhood home. His father wasn't a man of eloquence. He couldn't say beautiful things or make people sit in awe. He was easily overlooked, and maybe that was why Tom had looked so hard at him: because he loved him, and he wanted to know why.

I must go home, he thought. *I must go home and photograph my father*. It was a familiar resolution and easily forgotten, but now he had an extra motivation: a gallery owner he knew was planning a photographic exhibition entitled *Fathers*, and he seemed very keen for Tom to send him some prints.

The photograph in the Affinitie advertisement had really impressed people. It was up all over the place – the first time Tom had seen it on a bus shelter, he had been quite startled – and it no longer felt like the image he had taken. To celebrate its launch, he'd gone to O'Donnell's pub and bought several bottles of champagne for his friends. He'd also paid off part of his mortgage. He still couldn't get over how much they'd paid him.

'I wonder who the woman is,' someone had said. 'She'll certainly get a surprise when she sees herself.'

Tom frowned. He was realising that his photograph was, in a way, a considerable intrusion. He had never wanted his photographs to interfere too callously with their subjects. He had never chased celebrities unless they were at a public function and, in a sense, fair game; he had tried not to exploit very private moments or feed on others' emotional hunger. He could have made a lot more money if he had. That was one of the reasons he had turned to mobile phones.

He tried to outpace these thoughts by turning up the music. He was listening to the Boogie-Woogie Trio and there were no lyrics about love. He still didn't like listening to songs with lyrics about love in them. Bryan Adams, in particular, had to be turned off any time he came on the radio, though Tom could still tolerate Aretha Franklin. He'd always be able to tolerate Aretha; she was so gutsy and great.

He was preparing the mangetouts when the doorbell rang.

'Coming,' he shouted, as he removed the wok from the heat. It might be a Mormon. A number of people of various religious persuasions seemed to be calling at his house recently. Sometimes he felt like shouting at them, but he didn't. They looked so polite and enthusiastic. He just said, 'Thank you, but I can't talk to you now. I'm in the middle of something.' Come to think of it, he was always in the middle of something… but what?

He squared his shoulders as he opened the front door.

And found himself facing Her.

'Hello, Tom.'

Tom tried not to look at her beautiful smile. 'Hello, Samantha.' His voice was hard and unfriendly.

'Can I come in?'

'Actually, I'm in the middle of something at the moment.'

'I – I thought I should let you know…'

'What?'

'I'm going to Nepal.'

'Oh. I hope you have a nice holiday.' He said it with complete lack of emotion. 'Is Brian' – the name came out in a kind of hiss – 'going with you?'

'Oh, he's…' Samantha looked down at the pavement. 'He's in Australia.'

Tom tried not to whoop with delight. 'When did he go?'

'Last week. We…we kind of drifted apart.'

Tom decided not to offer Samantha any comfort about Brian's departure. She was a cruel, callous and unpleasant person, and he wanted to get back to his wok. He should do this immediately, because Samantha was looking sad, and he didn't like to see her looking sad…

So Brian was gone. Perhaps he should let her into the house after all. But he would not share his dinner with her.

Half an hour later, Samantha had eaten much of Tom's stir-fry. She said it was very good, and he was absurdly pleased by her pleasure. He didn't say this, of course. He tried to look distant and moody. The thing was, he couldn't keep up the pretence for very long, because Samantha saw right through him. And Tom wanted someone to see through him. He wanted it very much.

He didn't open a bottle of wine. Wine might make him drop his guard, and he needed to be very guarded with Samantha – especially now that he'd learned she wasn't going to Nepal for a holiday. She was going there for a whole year. Twelve months. Three hundred and sixty-five days. *Come back!* He was almost shouting it already.

He looked at her as she spoke and thought, *I don't want to love you, Samantha. My love for you is a great burden and it gives me very little pleasure. Why can't I forget you? What have you done to me? Did you know you were doing it? I'm tired of wanting you. I want someone who wants me. Why did you have to come here and tell me this? I wanted to watch that documentary about classic cars on Channel 4.*

Samantha sensed his distraction. 'What is it, Tom?'

'Nothing.'

189

'Oh, that again.'

'Yes.'

'You're angry with me, aren't you?'

Tom mumbled something incomprehensible.

'Yes, you are.'

'Maybe a little.'

'More than a little.'

Tom was aware that he could easily become furious. 'Look, I don't want to talk about this,' he said. 'There's no point. And don't tell me I'm going into my cave. I don't need one of your lectures.'

'I'm sorry.' Samantha's voice sounded very small. 'I'm sorry I disappointed you, Tom. You're such a lovely person. I wish I could love you. I mean, I do love you – but not in the way you want.'

Tom was moved by her contriteness. 'Thank you for being sorry. I've been waiting for you to say that. I wanted to believe you cared.'

'I do care, Tom.' Samantha's eyes were shining with emotion. 'That's why I called you. I called you so many times.'

'I know you did.' Tom sighed. 'But it wasn't to say you loved me. That's what I wanted to hear, Samantha. That was the only thing I wanted you to say.'

Samantha reached out and took his hand very tenderly. 'They say one of the important things about getting older is integrity.'

'What do you mean?' Tom eyed her warily. He hoped she wasn't going to start spouting popular psychology.

'Coming to terms with your losses and recognising your gains. Seeing how the pieces fit together. Or something like that,' she added lamely. 'I keep reading these books, and then I feel I should quote them. I get a bit tired of it, actually. And it sometimes pisses people off.'

Tom decided not to mention that it had often pissed him off. And, anyway, the quote about integrity sounded quite wise. Perhaps he would open a bottle of wine after all.

Samantha seemed so soft now – soft and sweet and womanly. If only she'd agree to go to bed with him. She didn't have to love him for that. His eyes lingered on her breasts.

'I'll probably be alone for a very long time,' she said as he filled her glass.

'Why?'

'I don't know. I just feel like I need to be alone for a while. I don't have this longing to find Mr Right – not yet, anyway.'

They both stared at one of Tom's framed photos. It was of a man with a parrot on his right shoulder.

'I often wonder what it's like,' Tom said softly.

Samantha peered at him. 'What are you talking about?'

'What it's like to be you. I don't know what it's like to be you, Samantha. Maybe I'm only beginning to see what it's like to be me.' He sighed expansively. 'There are so many things that I don't know.'

He looked into his glass. He'd bought a new set of glasses the other day. He had all the accessories of a plausible life, as long as you didn't look too closely. He began to wish that he hadn't been so open; how could a woman respect a man who didn't know so many things and admitted it? This was what was left when you stopped pretending. It was very stark and scary.

'Oh, Tom, that's a wonderful thing to say.'

He looked at Samantha cautiously. 'Is it?'

'Yes. It's very sweet and moving.'

'I thought it sounded rather pathetic.'

'No, it didn't.'

'So – so you like it when I admit to being emotionally inadequate?'

'That's not what I heard.'

'What did you hear?'

'I heard someone letting me share his loneliness.'

Samantha leaned over and brushed her lips against Tom's cheek. Oh, how he'd missed the scent of her, the softness and the comfort! A low cunning suddenly made him wonder if he should exploit this moment of intimacy. It wasn't a particularly noble response, but desire did not encourage scruples.

'I think my loneliness would be eased even more if–'

'I'm not going to bed with you.'

Tom looked at Samantha and realised she meant it. 'If you'd have a cup of coffee,' he said sharply, feigning slight offence.

'Oh, you rogue, Tom Armstrong!' Samantha pushed him playfully. 'Okay, I'll have some coffee. But I want to hear about your love life first.'

'It's a vast and arid desert with occasional mirages.'

'Surely you must have met someone?'

'Not really.'

'Come on, Tom. I don't believe you.'

'Well…' Tom hesitated. 'There was a woman I met in a nightclub. But she's a bit complicated.'

'In what way?' Samantha leaned forwards eagerly.

So Tom began to tell her about Roz, and how cool she had been on the phone – and how surprised he had been by his disappointment.

Chapter Twenty-Four

CADDY DIDN'T WANT TO know her exact altitude, but the pilot had just announced it. He had also told the passengers that they were somewhere over Italy and that he hoped they were enjoying their flight, although this last sentence had been so perfunctory that it had sounded like a technical detail. He had obviously said it innumerable times before.

Caddy thought that people who flew for a living were incredibly brave. The air hostesses didn't seem to know they were being brave as they handed out lunch; for them it was just another afternoon spent hurtling through the atmosphere in a large piece of machinery. The bit where they explained about the lifejackets and things was always horrible. How on earth would you remember how to find and inflate them if you needed to? And then there were the oxygen masks and the lights and... oh, dear.

It was best not to think about it.

Caddy had loved flying when she was younger. It had all seemed terribly glamorous and cosmopolitan and part of a world that was wonderfully distant from her parents. Maybe Jemma had felt like that too, as she'd soared into the sky towards Arizona. Caddy had watched that plane until she couldn't see it any more. Then she'd gone to the bar and had a large whiskey.

Oh my God, I'm on an airplane! The realisation lunged at her as the hostess was pouring her some coffee. *I'm on a plane and I want to get off it. Now.* She took a deep breath. *Surrender*, she thought.

Just let yourself be on an airplane – because that's where you are, and, though you'd like to get off it, this is not currently feasible.

She leaned back and remembered Dan's tenderness. It absolutely should not be analysed or dissected, or it would immediately turn into something strange and odd. She'd disappear up her own bum if she continued this constant rumination. Things happened, and then you didn't have to think about them. That was what this holiday had taught her.

She was sitting on an airplane, and she didn't even know how it stayed up in the air. Love was the same way: you didn't have to understand the entire business to know it was nice and necessary. Love was all about faith and trust. How could she have lived so long without them? But once they returned, they made you feel so different. You were back on your journey, not stuck watching life go by you any more; going somewhere, opening up to possibilities.

Caddy closed her eyes, and as she began to doze she felt herself floating towards a brightness that felt very comforting. Something was pulling her away from the past, away from everything that was over and empty and misleading. In this new space, she could begin again.

The plane jerked in the sky and Caddy awoke with a bump. Turbulence usually terrified her, but, amazingly, she felt quite calm. She knew what she had to do. She would meet Dan for that dinner. He'd said it would be his treat, but she would insist on paying her share. They would sit and talk and not rush or try too hard. The main thing was to make a space where their feelings for each other could live and grow, if they wanted to.

If only I could get a sign, she thought; *a sign that shows me I'm not being foolish.* But she had the sign already, surely: the kisses and the cuddles, the fleas and the laughter. He was telling her the truth about Zia – of course he was; she would have known if he was lying. How wonderful it was to feel that she knew things again – that she could trust her instincts!

Caddy's luggage took a while to emerge on the conveyor. She'd tied a small yellow scarf around the handle of her suitcase; so many suitcases looked the same these days. It would be awful to lose it, especially the lovely silk blouse, hand-painted with shells and starfish and tropical fish, she'd got for Jemma... Thank God – there it was, trundling towards her. Next she had to go through Customs without looking guilty. She had nothing to declare, but it was so easy to look as if one did.

But no one even looked at her. It was time to head home – and it was wonderful that it wasn't raining. Rain was awful when you came back from somewhere warm. It reminded you that you should really be sitting under an olive tree eating figs.

As she left the airport building, Caddy found herself staring at the words of an advertisement on a bus shelter: '*Affinitie Perfume. Because True Love is Forever.*' That was nice. So many ads these days were cynical about relationships. There wasn't a large queue for the taxis. She decided to sit down on her suitcase. Oh, how good it would be to see Chump and her friends… She gazed dreamily into the distance; the advertisement caught her eye again, but this time she looked at the large black-and-white photograph above the words. Her heart leapt with joy. *This was the sign!*

The photograph was wonderfully romantic. A woman was running, open-armed, towards a man. Caddy couldn't make out the details, but distance could not obscure the passion and conviction. That was the thing about love: when it was there, it was so obvious. Even when you wanted to hide it, you couldn't. She thought of Dan and smiled.

Caddy got into her taxi, almost giddy with excitement. Maybe one day she would be like the woman in that photograph, running towards Dan with no doubts or fears. She could still feel his kisses on her lips and his breath in her hair. They hadn't made love, but they had done just about everything else. Just thinking about it made her feel all warm and melting and moist. Who would have thought that someone nuzzling your bare shoulder could be so delicious?

When the taxi stopped at traffic lights, she saw the advertisement again, this time on the side of a building. *Goodness, the model looks quite like me!* she thought. *That's rather flattering. It must be a sign, if we look so similar. How wonderful! I wonder who she is.*

She closed her eyes and was glad that the taxi driver was listening to the radio. During one of their longer halts, she opened her eyes and looked dreamily out the window. There was the photograph again, on a wall, beside an ad for Danish lager. Caddy studied it more carefully and felt a dreadful heave of recognition.

It's me, she thought. That's me in the photograph. It can't be, but it is.

It was like being hit. She felt the thud and the incomprehension. Then she tried to numb out the pain. She looked determinedly at a lamppost and hoped that she was dreaming.

The taxi moved on. Caddy jumped when the driver spoke to her.

'I stayed in a hotel, but I ate out a lot…'

'Yes, the cheese does come from goat's milk…'

It seemed extraordinary that she was saying these things. She shouldn't have been able to say them when her heart was breaking. Someone should notice. Someone should know and hold her and comfort her and make that photo go away.

How on earth had it got there? Who had taken it, and why? And why was it being used now, after all these years? Surely someone should have asked her for permission to display it… but of course they wouldn't know where to find her. It was just a moment someone had noticed and captured. And now she was trapped in it. She had always been trapped in it. That was what the sign was. That was what it was trying to tell her.

She got out of the taxi and paid the driver. He carried her suitcase to the door. 'Thank you,' Caddy said as she reached for her key. Inside, she looked at the heap of letters on the hall mat.

She stiffened as she saw the small, slanting writing. It was Alain's handwriting. She would have recognised it anywhere.

This was just the chance he'd been waiting for. He'd written three years before and pleaded to see her; Caddy hadn't replied, and he hadn't pursued it. But now, with this bloody photograph everywhere, he'd probably think it was worth trying again.

'*I've changed and I still love you*,' he had written last time.

'Don't you remember how beautiful it was sometimes? How we said we'd always be together?'

Caddy fled upstairs, leaving the letter lying unopened in the heap of bills and bank statements. She was too shocked to know what she was feeling. She didn't want to feel anything. She just wanted to burrow under the duvet and wait until it didn't matter.

She had learned how to make things not matter, to ignore them, to distract herself. If you felt it all at once, it wasn't bearable.

She would think about it tomorrow. Now she would just watch the bright sky darken as warm, fat tears ran down her cheeks.

Chapter Twenty-Five

'TO ROZ, WITH BEST wishes,' was on the card that came with the flowers. Roz wanted the entire office to know about the flowers.

She wanted people to admire them, and smell them, and listen while she said they came from her boyfriend, who was a dear man and so sensitive. This might dilute rumours of 'the incident' – the abbreviation was necessary because Roz couldn't bear to use the word 'sperm' any more.

Though the flowers were lovely, Roz felt disappointed that Rufus hadn't complied completely with her instructions. His card should have read, 'To Roz, with adoration, from You Know Who.' She would have to train him further, and be far less available. Harriet was adamant that rationing was required.

'There must be some sort of carrot,' she'd declared firmly.

'Oh, I hope he doesn't start getting into vegetables!' Roz had replied in alarm.

'I mean some incentive,' Harriet had said. 'Why should he marry you if you're already doing everything he wants?'

Harriet is absolutely right, Roz thought. But at least Rufus had remembered the flowers. Bernice was the first to sniff them – they were freesias and beautifully fragrant. But it was a busy day, and the freesias did not attract as much attention as Roz had hoped.

Finally she shoved them into a vase and sighed. Then she rang Rufus's mobile, which for once was not switched off or out of range.

'Thanks for the flowers, Rufus. They're lovely.'

'What?'

'The freesias. They're beautiful.'

'Could you speak up a bit?'

'*Les fleurs*,' she hollered, '*sont très jolies.*'

Rufus pondered for a moment, then decided Roz was being

198

sarcastic. 'Oh, I'm…I'm sorry, darling. I meant to send them, but–'

'But you did!'

Rufus was tempted to agree with her, but his lies to women were usually discovered. 'No, I didn't send them. Someone else must have.'

'Are you sure you didn't?'

'Yes. Yes, I think I am.'

Roz frowned, and Rufus heard it. 'Shall I call around this evening? I could bring you flowers then.'

'No,' Roz said firmly.

'When can I see you?'

'I don't know. I'm rather busy at the moment.'

Their conversation ended in a disjointed and rather unfriendly way, and Roz wondered if she had been *too* unavailable. Getting the balance right was such a delicate art. The flowers must be from a grateful client. They might even be from the corn-cream people. If they turned out to be from Jamie, she'd fling them in the bin.

It was almost time to go home, but Roz didn't reach for her bag. She watered her lemon tree, because no one else would, then turned to her laptop computer in a kind of daze.

A jolly cleaning lady called Stella turned up just at that moment. Roz made a point of chatting to her, because people like Stella were a reminder of the world's terrible inequalities. Roz asked Stella about her family, and Stella asked Roz what she planned to do this weekend. 'Oh, I…I plan to meet up with some friends and…' Roz muttered vaguely. Why did people have this obsession with what one was doing during the weekend? It was the most frequently asked question in the office.

After Stella left, Roz realised her computer had turned itself off. It was one of its many 'helpful' little quirks that someone, somewhere, presumably understood. She turned it on again, and an hour later she had partially written the outline for a film script.

It was about a woman called Chloë who worked in

marketing and had a horrible boyfriend. He was repulsive, actually. His obsession with vegetables was, perhaps, the most trying aspect of his personality. *I am worth more than this*, Chloë often thought, but in truth she didn't really believe it. She would never be wanted purely for herself – that fact was quite plain to her; she had dreadful flaws secreted deep in her personality, which was why she dressed so well and knew so much about Scandinavian furniture.

When she got to the Scandinavian furniture, Roz burst into tears. The script was pointless. It was clearly about herself, and nobody else was as foolish as she was. Other people knew who they were and what they wanted. They sat on commuter trains with their wedding rings and their shopping. They were going home – but she wasn't. She had never found home. It had always eluded her.

Maybe I'm affected by previous incarnations, she thought. *Something happened to me in ancient Rome and it's left me deeply fucked up*.

She tried ringing Caddy's number again, but the answering machine was still on. Perhaps the flight had been altered, or Caddy had run off with a Greek waiter. *I must have got the date wrong*, Roz thought. *She would have phoned by now if she were back*.

She decided to face the stresses of the train trip home. She carried the flowers dutifully. They weren't love-flowers. Love-flowers made people look at you and smile. The platform was crowded; Roz studied the faces and noted that many of them looked tired and harassed and even a little lost – though she envied the woman with the boy who was talking about flying saucers.

If she married Rufus, there would be flying saucers, and many other types of speeding crockery. She would eventually detest him. This fact was suddenly quite clear to her. She was, in many ways, an ordinary woman, with ordinary hopes and dreams. She cared about love – real love – and if she couldn't find it, she would much prefer to be alone.

Roz felt lighter as she stepped off the train. It was a lovely evening, just right for a walk by the sea. The sea was wonderful company when you were in the right mood. She might even swim in it. She knew women who went swimming every morning in the sea, whatever the weather.

Of course – that was the answer! She didn't need the leisure centre at all! Every time she went there she would meet Rufus, and it would just be too bloody stressful. She would get up early every morning and go to the nearest beach; it was only a fifteen-minute walk if she was brisk about it. How invigorating it would be! Her skin would glow for hours afterwards.

A big smile settled on her lips as she looked at her flowers. How wonderful it was that they hadn't come from Rufus! Perhaps she didn't need to walk by the sea tonight, since she would be in it first thing tomorrow morning. She'd have a night in, watching television, with a Chinese takeaway as her Significant Other. Now that she was taking regular exercise, or was about to, it was really important to get the right nutrition.

Roz fantasised about spring rolls and beef with black-bean sauce as she strolled homewards. She passed a newsagent's and decided to get a paper. It was awful devoting an evening to television when you didn't know what was on.

As usual, she completely avoided the tabloids – they were full of rubbish; she only read the front pages, though she did sometimes have to flick through them a bit to find out why certain people were behaving quite so oddly. One couldn't help being a tiny bit curious. Tonight, for example, a country-music 'artiste' had decided to have wild sex in a stalled lift with a man dressed as a gorilla. A well-known model had enlarged her breasts. (What was this thing about breasts, anyway? The way the papers went on, you'd think they'd just been invented.) And there was another glamorous actress kissing someone goodbye at an airport – actresses were always getting photographed at airports. Roz leaned forwards to study the image more closely. Goodness, it was Zia Andersson, and the man was Dan!

'*Zia Andersson was in tears as her "close friend" Dan*

MacIntyre left Athens for Dublin yesterday,' she read. '*She is currently making a film in Greece with co-star Mel Nichols.*'

So things were really heating up between Dan and Zia – and in Greece, too! Oh, dear… still, perhaps Caddy hadn't heard about it. She never read the tabloids either. Roz grabbed a copy of *The Irish Times*. Maybe she should pop into Caddy's house on the way home and check that everything was ready for her return. She'd buy a bottle of milk and put it in the fridge for her. Returning from somewhere warm and wonderful was always awful – but at least Caddy had *been* somewhere warm and wonderful.

Roz frowned. People in the office kept asking her where she was going for her holidays, and she kept muttering about doing yoga in Tunisia. She'd seen the poster in the leisure centre: '*Yoga in Tunisia! The perfect holistic holiday, with renowned American teacher Doug Mansur.*' There was even a picture of Doug doing extraordinary things with his legs on a beach at sunset. If Roz said it any more she would be forced into actually doing it. Perhaps she should just buy some fake tan and hide in her house for a week…

She headed briskly towards Bluebell Villas. Goodness, the light in the sitting-room was on; Caddy must be back! Roz walked eagerly up the path and pushed the bell. She wanted all the juicy details, fast!

She could hear the sound of the television, but Caddy didn't come to the door. Perhaps she was in the bathroom. Roz pushed the bell again. Eventually she heard slow footsteps heading towards the hallway.

'Who's there?' Caddy's voice sounded dubious.

'Roz.'

The door opened. Caddy looked very brown and very bedraggled, and there were huge dark circles under her eyes.

'Hi, Roz.'

Roz was appalled but decided not to mention this; if someone said you looked dreadful, it never made you feel better. She searched her brain for something positive to say. 'Wow, look at how *brown* you are!'

'I'm sorry.'

'Why would you be sorry for being brown?' Roz laughed uneasily.

'I'm sorry for not answering your calls.'

'So…so you didn't just get back?'

'No, I've been here since… I think it was the day before yesterday.'

Roz listened to the American voices coming from the sitting-room. She recognised the dialogue.

'And you're watching *How to Make an American Quilt*, aren't you?' she said solemnly.

'Yes.' Caddy lowered her head.

Roz sighed. She and Caddy had both seen that film at least twenty times. They only watched it when something really disturbing had happened.

'Can I come in?'

'Of course.'

'What bit are they at?'

'She thinks he's sleeping with someone else. Now they're making the quilt again.'

They sat on the sofa and watched the women talking and sewing. It was very much a women's film, about things that really mattered and would therefore bore men witless. There were no car-chases or gun-fights or wars or explosions. It was just a bunch of women trying to understand things and making a quilt. And the love part made you cry.

'It's nice when they help her get all the bits of paper that float out the window, isn't it?' Caddy muttered. 'And when she puts the quilt round her. We haven't got to that bit yet.'

'That's at the end.'

'Yes. I wish I had a quilt like that.'

'Maybe we could make one.'

'Yes. We'd have to buy some rocking chairs, though. It wouldn't be the same without them.' Caddy stuffed half a Snickers bar into her mouth. 'Do you have any cigarettes?'

'No.' Roz frowned.

'I suppose I'll just have to break into Dad's present, then.'

Caddy rose lugubriously from the sofa and dug out a cigar that was the size of a fairly large sausage.

'I thought you'd given up smoking.'

'I dunno. Maybe I have.' Caddy inhaled ardently and blew a cloud of smoke into the air. 'I wonder if I can make rings. I used to be able to.'

'Caddy.' Roz patted her arm firmly. 'What is it?'

'I'm a sack of radishes.'

'Of course you're not! Tell me what's bothering you.'

'Oh… a few things, really.' Caddy reached for a small bottle of Rescue Remedy and drank it all in one gulp. 'I'm probably over-reacting. Do you have any popcorn?'

'No. *Details*, Caddy,' Roz said grimly.

'Okay…' Caddy sighed and looked down at Jemma's rabbit slippers. They were a bit too small for her, but very cosy, though the ears flopped a bit too much when you walked. 'Well, first of all I sort of got involved with Dan in Greece. He was there too and he told me he loved me. And I'd found the vanilla tea. I thought I wouldn't, but it was in the little shop with all the postcards of nude women.'

Roz gawped at her.

'And then I flew back here and found…' Caddy delved into the pocket of her jogging pants and took out another Snickers bar. 'And found I'm in a big advertisement for some kind of perfume. The posters are up all over the place. It must have been taken years ago.' She stuffed half the bar into her mouth and scratched her leg.

'And I think I still have fleas. Dan said they'd go, but I don't think they have.'

Roz's eyes were as large as saucers.

'Oh, yes, and there was a letter from Alain waiting for me. I haven't opened it, but it'll be about him wanting to get back with me again. I don't know how he got my new address. He may turn up at any moment.' She leaned forwards. 'Oh, look, the quilt's finished! I love this bit.'

Roz stared in a daze at the television.

'And then…' Caddy took off one of her slippers and started

to play with the ears. 'What part have I got to? Oh, yes. I went to the shop today and saw that photo of Dan with Zia. It's quite a nice one, really, but I think it makes Dan's nose seem a little longer than it is.'

She sat back and took a deep breath. 'So that's my little tale. What have you been up to?'

Roz looked as though she was about to fall off the sofa.

'Oh, dear, Roz, what is it?' Caddy exclaimed. 'Have there been more problems with sperm?'

'No. No, there haven't been,' Roz said carefully.

'How's dear Chump? I feel so guilty about not telling you I was back, but I just felt very tired, for some reason. Travelling can be very tiring, can't it?'

'Yes.'

'It was a nice holiday, but the backs of my legs still aren't really brown. Maybe I'll just have to get some fake tan.'

'Yes. I think I might get some too.' Roz reached into her bag for some lip salve.

'Oh, no, Roz, you're not back on–'

'No, just a few times a day,' Roz said as she rubbed it carefully onto her lips.

'Oh, look! This is the bit where she finds him. I *love* this bit!'

They watched in silence.

'Gosh, I'm not crying!' Caddy exclaimed. 'I *always* cry at that part. That's very strange, isn't it?'

'No, it isn't,' Roz said. 'You're in shock.'

'No, I'm not!'

'Of course you are. With everything that's happened, you must be. Just listening to you makes me feel I need counselling.'

'Is Chump on his own now?'

'Yes.'

'Oh, we must get him. Poor little thing!'

'You stay here. I'll fetch him, and I'll get a Chinese takeaway while I'm at it. What would you like?'

Caddy scratched her head. 'Oh… mmm… you choose. My

brain's a bit fuzzy.'

'It's all that popcorn.' Roz smiled, then grew serious. 'Do you really have fleas?'

'Oh, probably not. It just feels like I have.'

'And…and are you really in an advertisement? Are you sure it isn't someone else?'

'No. I'm sure it's me.'

'Why?'

'Because…' Caddy's lower lip trembled. 'Because Alain's in the photo, too. I even know the day it was taken.' She gazed distantly out the window. 'It was my birthday, and that evening we went out to dinner. That night he hit me for the first time.'

Chapter Twenty-Six

AVA'S VISIT TO FIDELMA Moran was very odd. Fidelma was *happy* – far happier than Ava. She was not terribly miserable and isolated, or a waitress in a seedy café where men pinched her bottom. Decent men didn't shun her because she'd dropped her knickers for a sailor and had a son to prove it. Her son had not been adopted, though that was what the gossips in the village had told everyone who would listen. He was now something important in new technology and visited most weekends.

Fidelma had married a very nice man who didn't have affairs with foreign women. His name was Craig. Ava had known this from Fidelma's occasional cards, but she had never suspected that he was so nice; she had thought he would probably be a drunk who returned home late and made Fidelma wish she'd never met him. But he wasn't like that at all. He even cooked them lunch while she and Fidelma chatted in a very tasteful if somewhat untidy sitting-room.

Ava knew Fidelma and Craig had a daughter who was in her thirties and unmarried. She assumed that at least they could talk about what a disappointment daughters could be, but it turned out that Fidelma just wanted Jocasta to be happy. 'I don't really care what she does,' she said, 'as long as it makes her contented.'

'Yes, of course,' Ava agreed. 'But…but I'm sure you'd like to see her settled.'

'Oh, she's getting married next month – didn't I tell you?'

Ava felt a surge of misery. Of course it was wonderful that Fidelma was so contented, but a little bit of misery would have made her a more suitable confidante. Ava dearly wanted to confide in someone. She wanted to tell someone about the shed and the foreign women, and the enormous silences.

'Oh, that's great. I'm sure you're very relieved.'

But Fidelma said she hadn't been worried about Jocasta's

single status. A lot of young women remained single these days; it wasn't that unusual. Ava pursed her lips and felt resentful of Fidelma's tolerance. It was unnatural for someone to have so few opinions about other people's behaviour. If she told Fidelma about Jim's disloyalty, Fidelma would probably say that foreign affairs could broaden the mind.

Inquiries about Caddy followed, and Ava said she was an art history teacher and had a lovely house in a very desirable part of Dublin. 'She likes giving dinner parties,' she added. 'I sent her a lovely linen tablecloth some time ago.'

When Fidelma asked if Caddy was married, Ava decided not to answer the question directly. Instead she said that Caddy had a daughter. 'She and the…the father parted some years ago,' she added. 'But she's become very friendly with a well-known actor. You probably saw him in *Merrion Mansions*.'

'Which one was he?'

Ava explained, and Fidelma became very excited. 'But he's *gorgeous*!' she exclaimed. 'I'd grab him myself if I were thirty years younger!'

Ava laughed, because she didn't want to seem like an uptight person, even though she was. This was becoming quite clear to her: she was uptight and difficult and intolerant and did not know enough about love. Fidelma Moran knew about love. She knew about wanting for others what they wanted for themselves. She knew what she wanted, too. Where had she learned all these things?

When it seemed that she and Fidelma had nothing more to talk about, Ava removed a photograph album from her bag. She'd grabbed it on impulse just before she'd left her home. 'This is Jim,' she said. 'And this is Caddy. And…and this is a photograph of our wedding.'

She frowned at the image and was about to put the album away, but Fidelma took it from her and stared at the smiling, apparently happy faces. 'Oh, they're lovely, Ava,' she beamed. 'I'm so glad you came to visit. Would you like to stay for a while? It would be great to have you here.'

'Ah, no, Fidelma. Thank you, but… actually, I'm going to

France, with a friend.' This was in fact true, only Ava hadn't known it until that moment. Henry had asked her to go to Le Havre with him. She had said she would phone him about his 'proposition' after her visit to Fidelma Moran.

Now she wished she hadn't paid the visit at all. Fidelma didn't need her solace. Ava was the one who needed understanding. As she started to gather up her belongings, she felt Fidelma studying her. What was she seeing? Was it the creases on Ava's dress? She really should have brought a portable iron, or at least packed clothes made from synthetic fabrics that didn't wrinkle.

But Fidelma didn't comment on the state of Ava's clothing. Instead she leaned forwards and said, 'Ava, are you happy?'

'Of *course* I am, Fidelma!' Ava exclaimed. 'Of course! Why would you ask that?'

Fidelma took a swig of sherry. She had often been sad herself, and admitting it had helped her. There was a lot of kindness in the world, if you learned to recognise it. A long time ago she'd decided that love – the kind of love that lasted – involved a decision to reach beyond yourself into another person's truth. Ava seemed disinclined to share her truth just now; but her silences spoke for her, and contained their own mysterious honesty.

Ava rose from her chair. 'It's been so nice seeing you again, Fidelma. The lunch was delicious. I must get you a present.'

'Your company was the present,' Fidelma smiled, and Ava feared she might sob in gratitude. Oh, to be enough – enough in yourself! That would be so wonderful…

She was about to shake Fidelma's hand when her friend moved forwards and hugged her very tightly. Ava was embarrassed, but she didn't say it. And Fidelma didn't say that news of the shed had filtered through to her from the village, where people wondered whether Ava and Jim were about to part. The village was also deeply curious about Ava's sudden disappearance. But why shouldn't she be a woman of mystery if she wanted?

Ava had so much more love inside her than she showed. Fidelma knew it was there; she had seen it for herself. Just before she had made that lonely trip to Birmingham, all those years ago, Ava had shoved a package into her hands. She had been furtive about it, shy and embarrassed. The package had contained a box of chocolates, a necklace, a bottle of perfume and a small teddy bear.

'It's only little things,' Ava had blushed.

But they hadn't been little things. They had been very big to someone who felt lonely, abandoned and lost. Fidelma had eaten the chocolates on the ferry. One by one, they had helped her to travel those miles, and when she got to the strawberry fondant she had arrived in Liverpool. We all have to find our sweetness somewhere, and on that day Ava had provided it.

But as Ava left Fidelma Moran's house she didn't remember the package. What she remembered were her mother's words, and how she hadn't contacted Fidelma, though she had wanted to. Just like she'd wanted to contact Luigi, and that college in Dublin that taught Italian. Italian was a nice language. The words were like airplanes; they took you far away.

She was far away now – far away from the people whom she loved and who didn't love her. Ava wondered whether she would ever be able to tell Caddy the truth – tell her that she hadn't been forgotten during Jemma's first years; that Ava had 'interfered', the very thing her daughter disliked most.

Ava quickened her step. She must try not to get too depressed.

She must also try to forgive Fidelma for being so disinclined to complain about anything. Some people were like that; and, deep in her heart, Ava realised Fidelma's tolerance had embraced her too.

Maybe I'm changing, she thought, and the idea did not alarm her. It seemed to her that a woman whose husband was having numerous affairs with foreign women should undergo some sort of transformation. And she wanted it. She embraced it. It seemed long overdue. She had always been different; she must have been, to fall in love with Luigi so suddenly and to know that, despite their differences, they were similar – similar in ways her mother would never understand.

Yes, she, Ava Lavelle, had great passion stored inside her, and a capacity for rebellion that had never been fully expressed. She had seen these very same qualities in her daughter and they had terrified her. She had been sure the world would not understand them, so she had tried to stamp them out.

It had been terrible watching Caddy become the sort of person Ava herself had abandoned. It had been wretched to watch her be hurt and disappointed, dreadful to see her passion pummelled until her dreams were so frayed they almost ceased to exist. Ava had turned away eventually, unable to witness these barbarities.

If only she had listened to me, she kept thinking. For Alain had done things to her daughter – and Ava wasn't just thinking of how he had got her pregnant and left her. There was something else; something Caddy wouldn't speak of. It had turned her into a cautious, hesitant person, a woman with a great fear of needing anyone.

She's become just like me! Ava thought suddenly. The idea was so startling that she almost sat down on the pavement.

She tried to distract herself by thinking of travel irons and creases, but smoothness no longer tantalised her. Life could be creased and wrinkled and bumpy; to pretend that it was always smooth was to be less than fully alive. Caddy had been right to take risks – to sometimes succeed and sometimes fail. She must not be allowed to retreat into her own seasonless world where safety was more important than love.

It was strange that Ava should begin to hear the whisperings of her soul amidst the roars of a London street, but that was where it happened. *I've rejected Caddy for what I've rejected in myself*, she thought. *And it must stop, because I'm too alone and too tired of feeling shortchanged.*

Then she returned to her more usual contemplations. The whole afternoon had put a great strain on her niceness, and she

211

was beginning to deeply dislike mobile phones. People had the most casual conversations as they walked along the streets. As she hunted for a phone box, Ava overheard strange snippets: 'But what about the tassels…?' 'Ten o'clock. In the foyer. But don't say I told you…' 'I'm just outside the tube…' 'Of course not! No, really, I wouldn't – not with a man who owns an Alsatian…'

Ava spotted a phone box and walked determinedly towards it. She would ring Henry and tell him she wanted to join him.

When she had completed this task she went into a café, which obviously regarded itself as more than a purveyor of refreshments. It was very smart and Spartan and made sure that its close connections with Italy did not go unnoticed. Ava had thought she wanted a large cup of tea, but she found herself ordering a cappuccino.

As she sipped this exotic beverage, she took a postcard from her bag and began to write, in small, tidy letters.

Dear Jim,

I have just visited a friend in Chiswick and plan to go to France tomorrow. This card comes to you from an Italian café where I am having a cappuccino.

I know about your foreign women. I saw your letters to them in the shed. The weather has been quite nice, though rather windy. If you've gone before I get home, could you please leave a forwarding address?

Your wife, Ava Lavelle

She took a stamp from her purse and licked it. It was strange, putting an air-mail sticker on a card to Kerry. She wondered if she should put 'Ireland' or 'Republic of Ireland'. She added 'Republic of' just in case. *I'll just shove it in the post-box and forget about it*, she thought. *I'm going to France. I, Ava Lavelle, am going to France with a man I hardly know.*

Her hand was trembling as she wiped some froth from her mouth, but a small smile settled on her lips.

Ava's eyes were bright with tears because of the harsh wind and flecks of sea water.

212

'Smile, Ava!'

He was at it again.

'Lean over the railings and look out at the sea. Then turn round and wave. Yes, that's right… brush the hair out of your eyes.'

Ava found herself smiling idiotically and for no good reason. Henry cared far too much about video photography for her liking. The visit to France had been nice, but it had been too intensely documented. In recent days she'd gained some insight into what it might be like to be a celebrity. He had even filmed her eating snails. She hadn't wanted to eat them, but the camera had demanded it.

Henry said that no trip to France was complete until you'd eaten snails, and that the event should, naturally, be recorded. Videoing something made it more real to him. It was as though he needed proof that it had happened. His visit to France would, in a way, be retrospective. He'd watch it on his TV screen with his daughter and a cup of tea.

As Ava smiled at the sea, she felt a strange longing for Jim, who would never ask her to behave like this. Jim was a pleasant travelling companion. He knew her ways and she knew his – or, at least, she had thought she did.

But at least now she could return home with a small infidelity stored amongst her other mementoes. For Henry had kissed her last night. It had happened when they were walking back to the hotel – Ava had, of course, insisted on separate bedrooms.

The kiss had occurred in a park and had not been entirely satisfactory. Henry had popped a peppermint into his mouth just before it, so it had lacked spontaneity. In the slim, bright romantic novels Ava sometimes read, men pushed women against walls and kissed them until they begged for mercy. Kissing Luigi had been beautiful. There had been a feeling of melting and sweetness, and wonderment that it was happening at all. His lips had been very full and extraordinarily soft.

Henry's mouth felt hungry – hungry and somewhat embarrassed; anxious, too. His arms had felt stiff as he clasped

213

her. Then he had suddenly remembered he had to take off his spectacles – he had put them on to read the menu. He was a practised kisser, though. Ava had known that as soon as she felt his tongue negotiate the various barriers she placed before it. As it slid over her teeth, she wondered if she still tasted of garlic; and she tried to pretend he was Luigi.

Luigi, who was married to a nice woman and living in California. He had sent her a letter, many years ago. It had arrived at the village post office, and it had been full of chat and resignation and news about his recent marriage.

'*If only it could have been you,*' he'd written just before the 'Best wishes'. '*I'll always love you. At night, Ava, when you look up at the moon, please think of me.*'

The moon was shining while Henry kissed her. Ava looked up at it and allowed herself to feel some pleasure. Someone wanted her. His arms were around her. She wasn't alone – not at that moment.

I wonder if you're still alive, Luigi, she thought as she stared at the moon. *I wonder if we'll meet again, somewhere far from here.*

The cuddle that followed the kiss was the part she had liked most. It had been warm and affectionate, and later Henry had placed his cheek against hers very tenderly.

'I'm sorry, Ava,' he had said. 'I shouldn't have kissed you. You're a married woman.'

'I know I am, Henry,' Ava had replied. 'But we did drink quite a lot of wine at dinner.' She'd said this in a very pragmatic tone, and it had almost seemed a sufficient explanation.

Now Henry wanted her to throw some bread for the seagulls. So that was why he'd been collecting rolls from various restaurants. 'Smile, Ava!' He had a big thing about smiling. The photo album in her bag was full of her and Jim smiling. Sometimes she felt like throwing it into the sea.

After the seagulls dispersed, Ava said, 'Excuse me, Henry, I need to freshen up a bit.' As she walked towards the ladies', she noticed some French people staring at her stridently patterned floral dress. French people had a lot of opinions about style, and they made sure you knew it.

I don't care what they think, she decided. *I like this dress. And that's enough for me.*

In the ladies' she sprayed on some perfume. She hadn't been away from home for long, but it seemed like months. So much had happened – and some of it had been very nice. She would miss Henry, in a small way. He had been kind.

Ava had a deeper respect for kindness now. It didn't blare its presence; but it made all the difference when you found it.

Chapter Twenty-Seven

RARELY HAD A ROMANCE ended so euphorically. Parting from Rufus had been pure joy, and afterwards Roz had bought herself a huge bouquet of pink roses. She'd completely gone off the whole marriage thing. Perhaps she'd been married many times and had loads of children in previous incarnations. She needed a rest from all that stuff.

In order to celebrate her new contentment, she decided to have lunch at José's Wine Bar. She would sit voluptuously in a corner with her notebook and get on with her brand-new script.

The pasta was exquisite, and the glass of Beaujolais was fruity and unassuming. Roz's serenity would have been complete if Caddy had been sitting with her. Poor Caddy – that bloody photograph had stirred up so many painful memories. Roz's own memories of romantic disappointment seemed so soft and insubstantial now.

Then Tom Armstrong walked into the room.

At first Roz was tempted to duck under the table and prepare a suitably fascinating expression, but then she remembered that he had completely lost respect for her and that she didn't care. She continued to scribble in her notepad, and when he said, 'Hello, Roz,' she said, 'Hello, Tom,' and smiled broadly.

'Are you mitching from advertising?'

'Yes.'

'I'm mitching from mobile phones.'

There was a pause; then he said, 'Do you mind if I join you?'

'Fine. Go ahead.' She moved her bag off a chair. Feck it, anyway. Couldn't he see she was luxuriating in her solitude?

Tom bought a bottle of wine and invited Roz to share it. It was red and full-bodied and made her feel a little less resentful. She decided she wanted dessert, and Tom was very keen to try the pasta she had recommended. As they tucked in, they admitted that they were not, in fact, mitching, though it sounded more fun. They had both done a great deal of overtime on their more zealous days, which meant they could take the occasional day off in lieu.

'You have to grab the time off, because no one's going to remind you about it.' Roz frowned. 'They take it for granted you'll stay late. It only makes sense if you're really ambitious.'

'I'm not ambitious,' Tom declared. 'Not about mobile phones, anyway.'

'And I don't give a piss about corn cream,' Roz said. 'The profiteroles are delicious.'

As Tom ate his tagliatelle, he was relieved that Roz had overcome her coolness towards him. He didn't know what had caused it, but she was certainly friendlier this afternoon. When she was relaxed she was very good company.

'Have you ever been to Nepal?' he asked as he refilled her glass.

'No. Why do you ask?'

'A friend of mine is going there for a year.'

Roz only knew one person who was going to Nepal for a year. 'Is her name Samantha?'

'Yes.'

'I know her too.'

'I know you do. She told me.'

This made Roz feel considerably less serene. '*What* did she tell you?'

'Just that you're a nice person. She's very discreet. She didn't tell me any of your secrets.'

'How do you know I told her my secrets?'

'Because people tell Samantha their secrets.' Tom sighed. 'I certainly did.'

'Do you love her?' The minute she said it, Roz realised the question was far too direct.

'I'll always love Samantha in a way,' he replied dreamily. 'She knows who I am, better than I do. It's hard to forget that

217

kind of thing.'

'Poor Tom.' Roz felt quite misty-eyed. Now that she'd completely given up on men, she could feel sincere sympathy for his situation. 'Do you want to talk about it?'

'No.'

The subject was obviously painful for Tom, so Roz decided to change it. She leaned forwards to sniff the yellow freesias that were in a blue vase on the table. 'They have a lovely smell, don't they?'

'Yes, I thought you'd like freesias,' Tom replied. Then he suddenly looked extremely bashful.

'Why did you say that?'

'What?' He was rummaging in his briefcase.

'Why did you say you thought I'd like freesias?'

'Did I say that?'

'Yes. You know you did.'

Tom began to fiddle with a complimentary box of matches.

'Someone sent me a bouquet of freesias the other day.'

'Oh, how nice.' He was gesturing towards the waiter.

'The note just said, "To Roz, with best wishes".'

'Do you want some coffee?'

'Why are you looking so embarrassed?'

Tom stared at a sauce stain on his suit. 'Actually, those flowers were from me.'

'What!'

'I sent them.'

Roz gawped in astonishment. 'Why?'

'Because Samantha told me to. I tend to take her advice about that kind of thing.'

'Why on earth did Samantha tell you to send me flowers?'

'Because I told her that the last time we met you were upset. I didn't say why,' he added quickly.

'You've been talking about me!' Roz's lower lip was trembling.

'We hardly said anything. Really. She just said you were a sensitive, sweet person – deep down.' He paused meaningfully.

'I told you I wasn't upset about the…the incident! I told you I didn't need your pity.'

'You were upset about it,' Tom said firmly. 'And I didn't send the flowers out of pity.'

'Why did you do it, then?' Roz braced herself for the humiliating explanation.

'Because I like you.'

'Oh.' She gazed down at the tablecloth.

'I'm sorry if that's inconvenient.'

'No, no – not at all.' Oh, God, she was blushing!

'I suppose I should have put my name on the note, but you were so offhand when I phoned…'

Roz's toes had started to tingle with disbelief and pleasure. She felt disarmed and shy and very embarrassed. 'I'm sorry for being so offhand. It's just that I thought you'd…'

'What?'

'Oh, nothing. It's women's stuff. You don't want to hear about it.'

'I don't think women's stuff is that different from men's stuff.'

Oh, what a sweet – if stupid – thing to say! Roz felt like flinging herself at him in gratitude. But she couldn't fling herself at Tom Armstrong. Some self-composure was definitely called for.

She rose and reached for her handbag. 'Could you excuse me for a moment? I need to pop into the ladies' room.'

Once she reached the ladies', she sank onto a chair.

So Tom Armstrong liked her. And she liked him. Ardently. Passionately. She had never liked any man quite so much. Like wasn't love, of course; but the E was rarely missing.

Yes, it was very nice to have a kind, sensitive friend like Tom Armstrong.

Who, inevitably, loved someone else.

Chapter Twenty-Eight

AVA LURCHED TOWARDS THE ship's railings. It was very windy, and the sea was swelling; it lashed against the old ferry with great thumps, and its spray cascaded over the deck. She almost fell a number of times and had to steady herself against various benches. She wanted to find a quiet corner where no one would see her. Most of the passengers were in the lounge. It wasn't a day for gazing at the waves too closely.

She reached into her bag and extracted the large plastic book. She had taken out the photos of Caddy; they were safely stored in her suitcase. She stood on tiptoe as she lowered the album towards the water. It seemed to cling to her fingers. She must open her hands and watch it drift towards the deep and her own forgetting.

She leaned right over the railings, her feet no longer on the deck. She must let the thing go, and with it so much else... She edged closer to the water and felt it mix with her own salty tears. She was so lost in remembering that she didn't even notice the huge waves forming in the distance.

It was only when they were upon her that she felt their thunderous embrace.

'Caddy, could you stop rocking quite so fast?' Roz pleaded. 'It's making me feel giddy.'

'Oh, sorry.' Caddy slowed down. 'It's got a lovely bouncy feeling when you speed up a bit.'

'I thought rocking chairs were supposed to be calming.'

Caddy smiled and patted the chair's embroidered armrests. 'It's lovely, isn't it? And it was twenty per cent off.'

'Did you open Alain's letter?'

'Yes. I did what you do when you get bank statements: poured myself a neat gin.'

'Oh, I don't do that any more,' Roz said virtuously. 'I chant in Sanskrit. What did Alain say?'

'Oh, it was okay, really. He just said he wanted to see more of Jemma. He said that last time he wrote, too. I don't know where he got my new address.'

'Well, I'm glad to hear he's not about to storm the building.' Roz smiled. 'I must say I was a bit worried.' She paused and sniffed her mug. 'What is this?'

'Blackcurrant and ginseng. I asked you if you wanted it.'

'Did you? Oh. I must have been distracted by the rocking.'

'I'm completely off caffeine at the moment. Do you want a coffee?'

'Mmm… no. I plan to completely cut back on caffeine as well,' Roz said. 'I've taken up yoga again, did I tell you? That's where I learned the chanting. It's very calming. I don't know what I'm saying, but I'm sure it's enormously uplifting.'

'Yes, it's so important to build these things into one's life, isn't it?' Caddy commented. 'I've been doing much more gardening.'

'But I didn't swim in the sea again today.' Roz frowned. 'I almost did, but then there was something good on the radio.'

Caddy gazed at the photograph of Jemma on the mantelpiece. She was beaming delightedly as she removed a supermarket trolley from a river. She spent a lot of time saving rivers.

'I'll come with you if you want,' she said, somewhat reluctantly.

'Oh, would you?'

'Yes. Just to help you get into the habit of it. I don't want to swim in the sea every day myself.'

'It's been a very challenging summer, hasn't it, Caddy?' Roz commented. 'But I think we're learning to…to balance our lives a bit more. We're no longer so caught up in silly dramas that don't matter.'

'Yes. I'm tired of the hurly-burly too,' Caddy said. 'In fact, I've been thinking a lot about early retirement and organic gardening somewhere nice and rustic.'

'Really?' Roz said excitedly. 'Oh, I've always dreamed of moving to the country too!'

'I didn't know that.'

'Oh, yes! Remember that passionate phase I went through with the Laura Ashley wallpaper?'

This led to a discussion about how they both wanted to move to the country immediately, if not sooner. How could they have failed to notice how restless they were feeling? They decided that they were tired of city life and rampant materialism; and, since they had both gone right off men in the romantic sense, the prospect of meeting far fewer of them was enormously enticing.

'We should buy a cottage in the wilds,' Roz announced grandly. 'I'd write film scripts and you'd grow enormous parsnips. We could rent out our houses here for big bucks and Totally Transform Our Lives.' She slapped her knee in delight.

Caddy nodded eagerly. After such a summer, who wouldn't want to Totally Transform her life as soon as possible? 'Would you like some more blackcurrant and ginseng tea?' she asked.

'Well... it was lovely, but... do you have any white wine?' Roz asked, a bit shamefacedly. 'I'm almost completely off alcohol, too, but I sometimes have a little sip in the evening.'

'Of course.' Caddy rose and padded barefooted into the kitchen. How well she had adjusted to all the recent startling events! One couldn't be a teacher without learning something about stress management. She had stepped onto a roller-coaster for a while and had simply let it plunge and soar and hurtle; now she was back on land again, though there were still occasional lurches.

It had been a vast relief to discover that almost nobody recognised her as the woman in the poster. This might be because she had immediately taken to tying her hair back and wearing dark glasses, but it was also because of her fringe, which considerably changed the proportions of her face. Sometimes strangers did stare at her for slightly longer than was polite, but when this happened Caddy hardened her expression and looked so unlike the young woman in the photo that they knew they must be wrong.

She reached for the bottle of wine and hunted for the corkscrew. It was still hard to find things in this house... There it was. How on earth had it got into the bread bin?

Thank God Roz was such a good confidante. Caddy had told very few friends about her secret fame, but a number of them had formed the opinion that she looked very like the successful young Affinitie model. 'Maybe now you'll realise how pretty you are!' Harriet had commented. It hadn't even occurred to her that the woman might be Caddy, for ordinary people rarely found themselves plastered on advertising billboards all over Europe. And, anyway, the girl was so much younger and more trusting; her expression was completely different from Caddy's.

'Do you want me to go out and get some crisps?' Roz shouted from the sitting-room.

'Yes. But get the low-fat kind. I've started a diet.'

'Cheese and onion?'

'Fine.'

Caddy heard the front door close. Things almost seemed normal now, though only a week ago she had been in the middle of another earthquake. The cork sprang from the bottle. Good; getting corks out of wine bottles wasn't always that easy. Dan was much better at that kind of thing than she was...

She felt a familiar heave in her stomach. Every time she thought of that name, it fizzed in her brain like the leftovers from a firework. The part where it had burst and blazed was gone; it had joined all the other things that were over. Caddy had a whole zoo of these melancholic and bewildered creatures – but the wonderful thing was that she needn't think about them. This very strange summer had taught her that life was enormously odd, and that it was amazing what one could get used to. She had asked for some sort of sign, and she had got it; and it had told her she wasn't ready. She was still too like the young girl who believed everybody's lies. And they were such beautiful lies, too; sometimes they were the sweetest things you might ever hear. But they didn't break her heart this time. They just seemed familiar and sad.

She hadn't said this to Dan, of course. When he had phoned, she'd said that he had been a wonderful holiday companion but that, considering the circumstances, it might be best not to socialise together in Dublin.

'What circumstances?' he had demanded.

'Look, Dan,' she'd replied calmly, 'I'm sure you had your reasons for lying to me about Zia, but I'd prefer not to continue this charade any longer.'

'It isn't a charade. Why don't you believe me?'

'Have it your way,' she'd sighed. 'But it all seems very complicated, and I don't need that at the moment.'

'It's that bloody photograph, isn't it? It's shoved you back into your cave again.'

'Oh. You've seen it.'

'Of course I've seen it. It's plastered all over Dublin. I assume the man is Alain.'

Caddy hadn't answered.

'Oh, God, I wish I could tell you the truth!' Dan had sounded genuinely distressed.

'So do I.' At least he'd sort of admitted he'd been lying.

'Let's have that dinner and talk. We need to talk.'

'No. Sorry, Dan. I just don't want to.'

The phone call hadn't upset her. It was amazing how many things you didn't need to feel, if you really put your mind to it.

Their time together in Greece had been so like a Mills & Boon novel that Caddy had forgotten about the giant worms. But watching *How to Make an American Quilt* had helped. There was an awful lot to be said for just sitting around and sewing. And, of course, deep down it was about how life was like a quilt and how you had to put all the different pieces together. It was the differences that made the quilt beautiful.

She would never think that photograph was beautiful. The girl in the perfume company had said it had been found in a photo agency in London. Photographers were continually taking pictures of strangers, of course; as you admired their work in exhibitions and magazines, you never thought it might one day be you. Caddy had rung all sorts of people, but no one would take the photograph down. When she realised she was stuck with it, she'd spent a whole day sobbing. It was good to get the grief over with quickly and dramatically. She'd walked around in a kind of stupor and had bought nearly a whole shelf of natural remedies in the health-food shop. What a summer it had been – and it wasn't even over yet! Why, oh, why had she said she wanted adventures?

Now she just wanted everything to be very calm and ordinary. That was why she had bought the rocking chair: it seemed a symbol of cosiness and comfort. Thank goodness she'd made a profit on the sale of her old home. For the first time in years, she had some cash to spare – though it was far too easy to spend it. Yesterday she'd gone into town and spent seventy euro, but all she seemed to have returned with was a new pair of knickers.

The phone started to ring, and Caddy decided to ignore it. The phone could be a terrible tyrant. There had been a time when it had almost completely dominated her evenings. But the fact was that you didn't have to answer it every single time. Caddy had come late to this revelation. What was the point of having an answering machine if you didn't use it?

She was serenely pouring the wine into the glasses when the thought lunged at her: God, *it could be Jemma!* She tore into the sitting-room.

'Hello.'

'Hello! Hello!' a male voice boomed uncertainly.

'Hello, Dad!' It was good to hear his voice again.

'Is that you, Caddy?'

'Yes.'

'I need to come and stay with you, dear.' Jim tried to say it calmly.

'Oh, great! I was hoping you would. My holidays are almost over, and–'

'The circumstances aren't entirely social.'

'Why?'

'Because...' He hesitated, sounding agonised. 'Because your mother's handbag has been washed up on a beach in

225

County Dublin. There were some clothes and…' His voice broke with emotion. 'And some wedding photos, too.'

'*Oh, dear God.*' Caddy leaned against the sofa.

'She's behaving very oddly.'

'So she's *alive*?' Caddy almost sobbed with relief.

'Yes. She's been to Wales, England and France, and now she's in Dublin.'

'*She's here?*'

'Yes. I told the police she was missing, and then she was spotted in a bank. They showed me the security video.'

'Hasn't she contacted you?'

'No. She says our marriage is over. I got another postcard yesterday.'

'Are you *certain* it was her in the video?'

'Yes. She used our joint account.'

'What on earth is she doing?'

Jim sighed dramatically. 'Oh, Caddy, I'm not sure even she knows that.'

Chapter Twenty-Nine

WHY DON'T I HAVE a photograph of Eoin? Tom thought. *I have one of him as a baby, but he's seven now. My own flesh and blood, and he's almost a stranger. Samantha's right. I should visit him.*

Samantha... If she got married at all, it would probably be to some wise, hairy person with large hiking boots and a highly developed soul. Tom might even be best man at their wedding, because Samantha said he was her 'best and beloved friend'. How awful those words sounded – how final and dismissive! But he clung to them for comfort. And they helped him get into his car.

It wasn't Betsy; she was at the garage, having all sorts of nice things done to her. A classic car of her quality deserved a bit of pampering. Tom turned on the engine of his borrowed Ford Fiesta and started to sing 'Five Guys Named Moe'. He was driving to some stupid meeting. Mobile phones... would he ever be free of them?

He and Roz were alike, really: they both needed to be free of something and to find something else. *I must show her the perfume photograph,* he thought. *I think she'd like it.*

He tapped his fingers on the steering-wheel. The great thing about singing in a car was that it didn't matter if you sounded shite.

Tom drove onwards into town, but then he found himself turning left down a side road. At first he was deeply bewildered. The road didn't even look familiar. What on earth was he doing there?

Suddenly he knew.

He had been down this road before, but he should have travelled it more often. It led to a huge suburban sprawl with small gardens and net curtains. It led to a small boy called Eoin, who wouldn't even know who Tom was.

I should turn around, Tom thought. *I really should.* But he didn't.

The garden was slightly overgrown and there were toys on the pathway. Tom parked behind a truck, some distance from the house; he didn't want Avril or Eoin to see him. His son might scamper on to the lawn at any moment. What would he look like? It was five years since their last meeting.

Tom reached for his Leica camera, which was on the seat beside him. Perhaps he would take the photograph today. He was glad he'd brought a telephoto lens: it meant he didn't have to get too close. He checked the light meter, placed the camera on the dashboard and picked up his newspaper. If Eoin appeared he would have to act quickly. He would develop the prints that evening in his darkroom. One day he might even show them to Eoin, as evidence that he had been watched, and wanted, though his father hadn't been able to say it at the time.

Tom thought of his own father. It was only when he had listened to opera on the radio that his face had softened. *Maybe that was how I grew to love faces*, Tom thought. *My father studied faces, too. He studied mine. That was how I knew he loved me.*

He could never say it, but somehow I knew.

But why didn't he say it to Eoin? What prevented him from walking towards that house and declaring it? It was mainly embarrassment and fear, Tom realised – and a dread of being a disappointment, which he clearly was already. It would be something too long postponed, too perplexing. Maybe he would do it someday soon… but he had been saying that for months.

Avril had a boyfriend called Sean, who lived with her. Acquaintances told Tom that Eoin was happy and that Sean treated him like his own son. It would be terribly confusing for him to have some stranger visiting his home and claiming his affections.

Tom sat in his car and waited. Every so often he looked anxiously at his watch.

Suddenly an image returned to him: himself, walking along the beach with his father, when he had been a tiny boy. His

228

father's footprints had seemed enormous in the sand, and he had placed his own small feet into them so carefully. He wanted to feel the space they made, the little ridges from Dad's shoes. They seemed the shape of something he couldn't name; maybe, if he followed carefully, he would know what it was. He would be closer to this big man who rarely spoke, but who watched, who saw things.

Sometimes, when Tom had thought he was forgotten, his dad had said something that pulled him back into the love that was their secret. 'You like that stone, don't you, Tom? You've looked at it for a long time. Are you going to take it home?... Don't be worried about that dog. It's only playing... Your mother didn't mean it when she said she was leaving... If you're tired, Tom, you can take my hand...'

There had been a time when Tom had thought his father would always, in a way, be close beside him. And then he had learned that following those footprints was not going to be enough – that he had to make his own. His father could not answer many of his questions, so many that he became a question in himself. *Am I going to be like him?* Tom thought. *An apologetic figure in the corner with my pipe, drumming my fingers to a song that only I can hear?*

He was so lost in his memories that he was startled when he heard a tapping at his side window. A small boy with large brown eyes was studying him. The face looked familiar, and Tom realised he recognised it from photos of himself at the same age.

The boy had to be Eoin. He and his son were staring at each other.

Tom stiffened with panic. What on earth should he say? He had a sudden desire to flee.

'Hello.' The boy looked so trusting.

'Hello.' Tom smiled cautiously. Then he saw the bicycle. It was the bicycle he had sent some weeks ago. Though it lay discarded on the pavement, it seemed to form a slender bridge between their hugely separate worlds.

'Is that yours?'

'Yes.'

'Do you cycle a lot?'

'Sometimes.' The boy looked into the car and saw the camera.

'It looks like a good bike.'

'My father sent it to me. He lives abroad.'

'Oh.'

'He's a photographer. I want to be one too.'

Tom was unprepared for the wave of tenderness he felt towards this small stranger. He wanted to sweep him into his arms and cuddle him, to smell his hair and pat his pudgy knees.

'Is that your camera?' Eoin was pointing to the Leica on the dashboard.

'Yes. Would you like to see it, Eoin?'

The boy's face brightened in surprise. 'You know my name!'

Oh, God, why did I say that? Tom groaned inwardly. *How can I explain my way out of this? Will I tell him the truth?*

'Eoin!' The moment was snatched away by the sound of a woman's voice. She sounded frightened, imperious. 'Eoin!' she screeched. 'Come here this minute! I've told you not to talk to strangers.' She was standing at her front door and seemed about to run towards them.

'But it's Daddy!' the boy screamed.

'Stop saying that!' Avril shouted. 'I've told you not to say that.'

'But–'

Avril started towards the car. 'Come here!' she repeated.

Eoin obeyed, though his eyes were brimming with tears. He picked up his bicycle and looked wistfully back at Tom for a moment. His little shoulders seemed to sag and his face was downcast. Avril was squinting her eyes in the sunlight, trying to peer past the truck.

She'll come over if I don't leave, Tom thought. *She'll march up and recognise me, and demand an explanation.* For a second he thought he might stay and face her; but then he

230

switched on the ignition and swerved out on to the street.

He pressed his foot down hard on the accelerator and drove away as fast as he could.

Chapter Thirty

WHILE JIM AND CADDY were adjusting to the enormity of Ava's transformation, Ava herself was feeling enormously grateful that she was a fast knitter. She was still reeling with relief. Her new jumper had saved her: part of it had attached itself firmly to a spike on the ship's railings when she was leaning towards the deep.

It had anchored her as the huge waves grasped her bag and her hat and the album. Her wedding pictures were just flotsam and jetsam now. Like her marriage.

The many shocks of the past weeks could have made Ava more timid, but they didn't. Instead, she found herself thinking that everybody dies eventually and that mere existence wasn't enough.

She was free – she'd been free all the time, but she hadn't known it. She had cared too much about what other people thought. But now the wildness her mother had tried to eradicate was back. She was a feisty old lady and she didn't care who knew it.

And this afternoon she was going to suck Milky Mints in a cinema and watch the soppiest film she could find.

'You go in first.'

'No, *you* go in first.'

'You're the one who said you wanted to swim in the sea.'

Roz jogged on the spot to keep warm. 'But it looks so cold.'

'It won't be cold when you get into it.'

'It'll be bloody freezing.'

'No, after a while you'll feel warm.'

'Why do you keep saying "you", Caddy? You're going to go in too, aren't you?'

'Yes.'

'Oh, no! Now it's raining.'

'Look, we're going to get wet anyway.'

'That man with the greyhound is staring at us.' Roz pulled her towel round her.

Caddy took a deep breath. They'd be here all night at this rate, and she wanted to get back in time for *Coronation Street*. She threw her towel off and started to run towards the water.

It felt like ice, and it was getting deeper. She gasped. How could water be this cold? She could barely move her limbs!

'Oh, well done, Caddy!' Roz shouted.

'It's… lovely and warm,' Caddy shouted back. Her teeth were chattering. She'd turn blue if she didn't get out fast.

'Is it really?' Roz was edging gingerly towards the waves. She dipped a toe in the water. 'Liar!'

'Just do it!' Caddy yelled.

'Oooh… no, I can't.'

'Come on!'

Roz threw her towel onto the beach and held her nose.

'Why are you holding your nose?'

'I don't know. Aaah… yikes!' A large wave drenched her. She shook her fist at it.

'Just plunge in. Get it over with.'

'Oh no, oh no, oh no,' Roz gibbered. Caddy splashed her.

'Eeeeek!' Roz plunged forwards and almost immediately stood up again. 'That's it. I've done it.' She was running towards the shore.

Caddy followed her. 'It got warmer after a while,' she said, as she scrubbed herself down with a towel.

'Don't sound so bloody virtuous,' Roz frowned. 'You were only in there for a minute.'

'Which is fifty seconds longer than you were.' Caddy laughed. Her skin was glowing and the air felt warm. 'It's all about how you feel afterwards.'

'Oh, dear…' Roz sighed. The rain had stopped, but the wind was very chilly. 'I don't think I can do this every day. But at least I've taken up yoga again.'

'Now we've got to have a mug of tea and a big slice of chocolate cake,' Caddy declared. 'There's a really nice café just down the road.'

'I thought you'd given up caffeine.'

'Well, I did, for three whole days,' Caddy replied.

'Remember that time we tried to detoxify ourselves and almost ended up starving?' Roz giggled.

'Oh, yeah – and that time we were virtually living on rice and carrots and avoiding anything that had the slightest connection with yeast.'

'Or anything that yeast grew on, especially sugar,' Roz said. 'I was working in television, and the canteen was full of cakes. They had a kind of revolving display. I'd stare at it going round and almost cry with longing.'

Caddy bent over and tried to get sand out of her socks. It was pointless, of course. When she got home, she'd be leaving bits of sand on the floor for weeks. The sand was also in her ears and threatening to take over her handbag. And her mobile was ringing, and it could be Jemma... she pulled everything out of her bag again. Her mobile was locked in a fierce embrace with a scarf.

'Hello.'

'Hello, Caddy.'

It was Dan.

'Sorry to bother you, but I wondered if you wanted your Van Morrison CDs back.'

'Oh... okay.' She dug her toes deep into the sand and wiggled them around a bit.

'I'm leaving for America soon, and a friend is moving into the house for a while. That's why I've been... you know... sorting through stuff.'

America. Caddy gulped and took a deep breath.

'I could leave them somewhere for you.'

'What part of America are you going to?'

'California.'

'Where in California?' Somehow she felt impelled to know the details.

'Hollywood. We'll be staying in Beverly Hills. It all sounds terribly glamorous, but I bet it won't be.'

234

We. He'd said 'we'.

'Are…are you making a film?'

'No, but my agent has set up some meetings.'

'Oh, that's great. *Great.*'

'I could leave them at the college for you.'

'Fine.' She was sounding very bright and cheerful.

'Okay. Bye, then, Caddy.'

'Bye. Dan…' She couldn't let him go without asking. 'Are you going with Zia?'

'Yes, I am. Where should I leave the CDs? Do you have a pigeonhole?'

The brazenness of him! He didn't even sound bashful about it.

'With the caretaker,' she mumbled. 'His name is Albert.'

The phone went dead. So that was the last thing she would say to him. '*His name is Albert.*' And it was raining again.

'I've put all your stuff back in the bag.' Roz was studying her anxiously. 'That was Dan, wasn't it?'

'Yes. He's going to Hollywood with Zia.'

'Oh, poor Caddy!' Roz rubbed her back. 'He's turned out to be a right bastard, hasn't he?'

'Yes, he has.' Caddy sighed as she started to put on her socks. 'But at least I've discovered something comforting.'

'What?' Roz asked, as they walked towards the café.

Caddy turned to her and smiled wanly. 'Sometimes there's an awful lot to be said for not being ready.'

Chapter Thirty-One

THE FEATHER LANDED SOFTLY on Caddy's pillow, but she didn't notice because she was asleep. 'Stop it!' she was screaming silently. 'Just stop it.'

Alain stared at her, his hand still raised.

'If you don't stop it I'll call the police.'

'You always say that.'

'This time I mean it.'

His eyes glowed darkly. They bored through her, into her very soul. When he looked at her like that, all thoughts of herself evaporated. He stole the light and condensed her into nothing. The world was his and she inhabited it on sufferance. At any moment she might make a mistake. She *was* a mistake. But this morning, in this dream, she was something else too.

She could feel her feet on the ground beneath her. She was standing in her own space and her own life – *her* life, not his; not the place where only his pain mattered. A howl escaped her lips. She was more than this. She must believe it before she had the evidence. It was only by believing it that she would know it. No one could save her except herself.

'Those aren't real tears.' That was what he sometimes said when she cried. She wasn't real to him. She was a blank space. He threw his hopes and fears and furies upon her absence. He made her feel the pain he could not feel or heal himself.

'I've leaving.'

'No, you're not.'

'Yes, I am. And you can't stop me.'

He grabbed her arm and flung her against a sideboard. She shuddered at the impact, but as he lunged forwards she sprang away from him. She raced into the bedroom and snatched Jemma, crying, from her cot.

He was waiting for her at the front door.

'Get out of my way.' Everything in her said it. She had never spoken to him like that before, with the same cold fury as his own.

She could see people walking in the street. She would call to them for help if she needed it. She held Jemma tightly. She would do anything to protect her.

'This is no longer our secret.' She said the words very slowly and firmly as she stared past him. He stiffened with disbelief. She could sense him, coiled and ready. She looked at him with such conviction that he stood back from her and leaned against the wall. And he began to cry.

She didn't say his tears weren't real. She didn't say anything; she just walked away. She was in her slippers and she didn't know where she was going. She blinked in the sudden sunlight, and a neighbour asked her if she needed help.

'Yes, I do.' How hard it was to say it!

She could hear Alain pleading with her from the driveway. How many times she had stayed because of his words, his promises. What was she without him? Nothing. That was what he had tried to teach her. 'We can heal each other.' That had been her hope. For weren't they both, in a way, lost children? She loved that he saw the lostness in her; but, despite her scars, it was he who was most wounded. 'I need help.' One day he would have to say it too.

Chump jumped onto Caddy's bed, but he didn't waken her. She saw that the neighbour who had offered help wasn't a stranger. It was herself as she was now. She was comforting the young woman and her baby. She was offering them refuge and protection. She was saying that she understood, that there was nothing to be ashamed of. And then her voice gradually became more distant, until the sound of the ocean replaced it.

She had drifted out to sea, but she wasn't frightened. The water lifted her when she lay back and let it. That was what the huge creatures were telling her: let it. You don't have to understand anything; it just happens. They were singing to her, a sweet bruised melody that lifted and fell like the waves, loving and scarred, disappointed and hopeful, ruthless and merciful, lost and yet somehow home…

It was Jim's harmonica playing that finally woke Caddy.

237

She rubbed her eyes and glanced at the clock, and felt as though she had travelled back in time. Her dream about leaving Alain had been uncannily accurate, and its wretchedness made her hug the pillow; but, somehow, it hadn't been as desolate as it could have been. The part about the neighbour had seemed different, but Caddy couldn't recall why. The dream was fading as she tried to remember it, but her heart still held the traces of a distant melody.

Goodness, that must have been her father practising the harmonica! It was amazing how sleep could dull one's critical faculties. Now the sound was just a desperate warbling that pushed its way determinedly through the maple floorboards.

Rarely had any melody been more brutalised. Poor man – he was obviously using the harmonica as an outlet for his considerable frustrations. Caddy hadn't joined him on his long searches through the streets of Dublin. If her mother decided to go AWOL, that was her own business.

She got up and padded gingerly into the bathroom, where she studied her face in the mirror. She touched her forehead cautiously. The jagged white scars were still slightly raised. The woman at the shelter had been surprised to see that Alain had marked her. 'They usually hit where people won't notice,' she'd explained.

Still, the special make-up hid them quite well. And with the fringe they were hardly visible. It was all so long ago that maybe it hadn't even happened.

Caddy began to hum a song she didn't know she'd heard.

Ava couldn't believe how glad she was to leave the National Gallery. A sense of oppression had descended on her as soon as she'd walked into the place. There were so many paintings, and she had put on the wrong shoes for culture. *I'll look at five paintings properly*, she thought. *There should be a room with five paintings for women like me.*

Her visit to the gallery had been vastly enhanced by her decision to sit on a bench and look at the paintings nearest her.

'Hello, Ava! On a visit to Dublin?' An acquaintance from

Tralee, Liam, had suddenly appeared.

'Yes.' She could hardly say she was in Stockholm.

'That photo of Caddy is lovely.'

'Thank you.' What on earth was he talking about?

'Are you enjoying the paintings?'

'Oh, yes, they're… delightful.'

Liam's eyes had glinted with a not entirely pleasant curiosity. 'So when are you coming home to us?'

'I don't know.'

'Oh.' He had gawped at her, obviously stupefied by her candour. 'Oh – well… the wife's waiting, so I'd better go.'

Now, as she sat in a café, Ava wished she had asked Liam about the photo. It was probably in a newspaper. Caddy did sometimes go to openings of art exhibitions. At least in an art exhibition there weren't so many paintings. It was a dubious merit, but it seemed a substantial one after her visit to the National Gallery.

When the waitress arrived with her cream bun, Ava managed not to mention the inadequacy of the stainless-steel teapot. It probably *wanted* to pour properly; it probably wanted a big gush of tea to emerge, unencumbered, from its spout. It was doing its best under the circumstances. *I'm like that teapot.* The ridiculous words flew into Ava's brain, and suddenly they seemed terribly true. Her love leaked and often didn't reach its target. It had spilt all over Caddy's childhood and her marriage. And her misery at the mess had made it worse.

'Sometimes I sit at the kitchen table and feel I can't go on.' That was what she had confided to various doctors. 'I have a daughter, and I often shout at her when she hasn't done anything. It's not like that all the time; there are whole months when I'm quite contented. It's like a big cloud that lands on me… But I shouldn't waste your time with this silliness. You must be very busy.'

They had wanted to give her antidepressants, but she wouldn't take them. Antidepressants meant you had something wrong with your head, and that was a terrible thing. It was

239

better to be sad than to admit to such weakness. But the tears had still come at the oddest moments, and she hadn't been able to stop them.

She hadn't wanted Caddy to see her snuffling at the kitchen table, but it had happened many times.

'Why are you crying? Is it because I didn't eat all the sandwiches in my lunch-box?'

'Go outside and play.'

'I want to stay here.'

'Stop being difficult, Caddy! Life's hard enough without that.'

These memories were so painful that Ava ate her cream bun in three bites. She didn't feel guilty about the extra calories. Dr Armitage had said that we all need our treats and that cream buns could be very medicinal in certain circumstances.

Dear man – he had come to live in the village at just the right moment. He had been young when they first met, but wise beyond his years. She had scurried to him with swellings and inflammations and stiffnesses. Sometimes she had been so worried about all her crucial organs that he had set aside a whole half-hour to listen to her plight. She had found herself telling him about Luigi, and about the miscarriages. She had found herself telling him that she had wanted to live a completely different kind of life.

'What kind of life?'

'I don't know, but it wouldn't be like this one. I serve everyone else, but I don't have any pleasures of my own.'

'You must have some pleasures of your own.' Dr Armitage had said it so firmly it had been virtually a prescription. 'Have you thought about golf?'

'Certainly not.'

'Playing a musical instrument?'

'Never.'

'Set dancing?'

'Only if you paid me.'

Eventually Ava had agreed to take up bridge and pay

monthly visits to the hairdresser. Dr Armitage had also recommended regular exercise and good nutrition. She had promised to tell him if she felt utterly miserable, so that he could give her a mild 'tonic'.

But it wasn't just a tonic; they both knew that. She had the small bottle of pills with her now. Just knowing that it was there and that someone understood was sometimes enough.

Why is it that I can say these things to a doctor, but I can't say them to other people? she wondered. *Everything would be so different if I could. I've led a life of secrets, and now I don't know how to tell them.* Tears filled her eyes but she blinked them away firmly. Happiness had eluded her, but perhaps her daughter might find some contentment.

She opened her newspaper and scanned the entertainment pages. Première – the word jumped out at her as she read the theatre listings. It was attached to a play called *Turf and Roses*, which was, apparently, a 'compelling new drama' by a playwright Ava had never heard of. If she went to it tonight, she could discuss it with Dan MacIntyre when she visited him tomorrow. And she was going to visit him tomorrow. She knew where he lived; even though there were numerous D. MacIntyres in the phone book, she had been able to identify the right address because she already knew his phone number. She had noted it down that time he had rung and invited her and Caddy to dinner, and she had kept the piece of paper. Matchmakers needed all the information they could acquire.

Ava gulped down her tea. This was perfect. She couldn't spend all her visit talking to him about the desirability of her daughter; she would have to sidle up to the subject stealthily, and talking about the play would allow her to do that. She would have to book the ticket immediately. Oh, dear, maybe there wouldn't be any seats left... She grabbed her coat and bag and almost ran out of the café.

Ava now knew she could not be like Fidelma Moran. Her own type of motherhood, when unleashed, was ardent, bossy and tender. She had stood back from her daughter's life for too long, and now she wanted to plunge through the hesitations and interfere in a magnificent manner.

Life didn't last for ever. If you froze in fear, you missed so much.

People might never know who you truly were because you'd never shown them. That was the greatest loneliness: locking all those things away.

Chapter Thirty-Two

TOM HAD COME TO share Ava's belief about loneliness. He had been heartbroken as he drove away from Eoin. Looking back, he could hardly believe what he had done.

That evening he rang Avril and told her that Eoin had been right: he had been talking to his father.

'I didn't recognise the car.'

'I wasn't driving Betsy.'

As they spoke, in short, perfunctory sentences, Tom realised that Avril didn't despise him. She had very few expectations of him, which was a sobering judgment in itself. He knew that to her he must seem feckless, casual and flimsy in his affections. She made it clear she didn't particularly like him; but then, perhaps she never had. They had been brought together by mild desire, boredom and many pints of lager. Now they had this beautiful boy who needed their love. And offering it to him wasn't always going to be comfortable.

But comfort wasn't Tom's priority any more. He felt older and less shielded. Though he didn't know how to be a father, he would try to learn. He would run towards this love instead of away from it. He would be more like the woman in his photograph. For months, she had been a silent presence reminding him of the man he could become.

'I want to have Eoin to stay some weekends.'

'He'll have to get used to you first.' Avril sounded very cautious.

'Of course. When can I visit?'

They made an appointment, and Tom kept it. He sat in the toy-strewn sitting-room and watched his son, who watched him back and made things out of Lego. It wasn't a sentimental reunion; Eoin didn't run towards him crying, 'Oh, Daddy!' or anything like that. There was a mercenary flavour to it, actually: when Tom handed Eoin gifts, Eoin told him about other ones he wanted. Many toys seemed to be part of a set these days, and children told you about the various members of these collections with astounding precision.

When Eoin went out to play with his friends, Avril asked Tom some questions, but she didn't batter him with accusations. Life seemed to have taught her that people's feelings couldn't always be judged by their behaviour – though it was surely the most revealing gauge. She acknowledged that she hadn't done much to encourage Tom's paternal participation. Her boyfriend, Sean, treated Eoin like his own son. She had wanted this child anyway, so she didn't resent his presence.

'Did you… plan to have him?' Tom asked.

'No. But I wasn't using the most reliable method of contraception.'

'We were both drunk.'

'Yes.' Avril sighed. Then she went to fetch some Earl Grey tea and ginger biscuits.

It was only when Tom was about to leave that Eoin shyly came up to him. 'Daddy.'

'Yes, Eoin?'

'Can I take some photographs with you?'

'Yes. We must do that soon.'

'When?' Eoin's eyes had narrowed with suspicion.

'Maybe…' Tom looked up at Avril, who nodded. 'Maybe next weekend.'

'Okay,' Eoin said solemnly. He was clearly not going to get too excited about it just yet.

'He likes the bicycle,' Avril said as they moved towards the hallway. 'And all the other presents. You were good about the presents.'

Eoin watched from a window as they walked towards Tom's car. Then he suddenly raced out of the house and ran desperately across the lawn. 'Daddy!'

'Yes, Eoin?'

'I like calling you Daddy.'

'I like calling you Eoin.'

'That's my name.'

'I know it is.'

'Are you going for ever now?'

'I hope not.' Tom blinked hard and hoisted his son tenderly into his arms. He hugged him very tightly, and Eoin didn't protest.

'We're supposed to take photographs together at the weekend. Don't you remember?'

'Yes, I know, but…'

'But what?'

'But… I thought you mightn't know it any more.'

Chapter Thirty-Three

JIM'S NEWS WAS WONDERFUL and awful. Caddy lurched when she heard it. It was as though the very foundations of her life were shifting.

Her mother had helped her after Jemma was born. She had sent Caddy money, via a priest, and never told a soul. The revelation provoked a sweet relief, and then a hope that frightened Caddy. What was she to make of this astonishing discovery?

Suddenly anger seemed the most familiar and safe response. 'It's ridiculous!' she exploded. 'I can't believe she didn't tell me.'

'Maybe she thought you'd be angry.'

'Oh, come off it! Why would I be angry?'

'You're angry now.'

Caddy gulped. This was true.

'You've always hated it when we interfere in your life.'

Caddy blinked slowly. This, too, was entirely accurate.

'Your mother does many tender things, Caddy, but I think she's lost any hope that they'll be understood or even noticed.'

'I don't understand.' Caddy picked at a bit of loose fingernail.

'Maybe we never will.' Jim thought of the polishing and the sponge cakes and the insistence that he bring a jacket with him on the sunniest of afternoons. 'And maybe we don't need to.'

'You're just making excuses for her.'

'No, I'm not,' Jim said firmly. The insight about his wife had dawned on him just yesterday morning, as he was playing the harmonica. It was frustrating to feel such beauty, and to hear the notes leave him in such discord. The attempt was not unlike Ava's tenderness: amateurish and incomplete, but entirely sincere.

'Ava's not a great one for words, dear,' he continued. 'She

hides away from her true feelings, like you do.'

'I don't hide away!' Caddy thumped the table and pouted miserably. She suddenly felt five years old.

'You and your mother have a great fear of needing anyone,' Jim persisted bravely. 'That's why love has become a terrible dilemma for you both.'

'Love is not a terrible dilemma for me!' Caddy shouted desperately. 'If I could find the right type, I'd grab it, and nothing in the world would make me let it go.'

'What's the right type?'

'The one that lasts. The one that doesn't almost… kill you.'

Jim regarded his daughter tenderly. Life could be so brutal. There were so many scars, so many barbarities that he couldn't even bear to think of. The tears of the world sometimes grew so heavy that he lost the heart to continue. But, each time he lost faith in love, he found the best solution was to give it – just give it away, without asking the reason or counting the cost.

'Offer what you seek, dear,' he said softly. 'Open your heart.'

'That's what *she* did,' Caddy replied stonily. 'And look where it got her.'

'Who's she?'

'The girl in the photo.'

Jim sighed. His daughter had shown him the offending image, and he had found it very sad and very beautiful, both a warning and a comfort. If Caddy could understand the impulse that had made her run into those cruel arms, she would face her own despair and hope; and one day they would guide her to her reason and her song.

'Love her.' The words hung perilously in the air.

'Who?' Caddy stiffened. She assumed he was referring to Ava.

'Love the girl in the photo,' Jim said. 'Even though she was wrong. She needs it far more than if she had been right.'

Tears clouded his eyes. He had rarely spoken to his daughter with such passion. He fumbled in a pocket for a handkerchief, and when he looked up he saw that Caddy had left the table. Her face looked blank and her eyes held the same dullness. She hadn't heard him. She would never hear him. She was as stuck in the past as the girl she could not forgive.

'Where are you going?' He tried to hide his disappointment.

'Upstairs.' Caddy chose not to explain why. She was going to the window on the landing. Every day she cleaned it, and every day it briefly shone. It felt like the one part of her life she had some control over. If the neurosis spread to ironing, she would definitely seek medication.

As Caddy carefully wiped and polished, she thought of the manila folder on the kitchen table. Her father had found a small key under a geranium pot and had somehow instantly known it would open the locked drawer in the walnut cabinet. Ava had been so careful to conceal those letters.

They explained why Father Ignatius had so often arrived on Caddy's doorstep. His explanation had been that he liked to keep in touch with single mums in the diocese. He had said it in his chummy, modern way, and she hadn't asked him how he knew where she was living. She hadn't asked him about the cheques, either. He had said they came from a philanthropist who preferred to remain anonymous. 'If I hear of a nicer place, I'll contact you,' he'd added. 'This bed-sit isn't really suitable.'

Sure enough, Father Ignatius had located a pleasant, though very small, flat. The rent was reasonable because it was subsidised – he had never explained why. He had also arrived with large soft toys – toys that were clearly expensive – on Jemma's birthdays.

'Have you contacted your family?' Now that she thought about it, he had said it quite often.

His visits had become less frequent when Caddy got a full-time job as a teacher. When he was about to move to another parish, he had decided to deliver a little homily at her kitchen table. 'The people we should know best are often the hardest ones to understand,' he'd announced. 'Silence doesn't always mean indifference. You haven't been forgotten.'

Caddy had assumed he was referring to God's infinite love. But now she realised that her mother was included in the statement, and that Ava had worked in Sally's Café to fund her largesse. The cheque stubs and carbon copies of Ava's letters were in the folder. Father Ignatius's replies were in there too.

'*I think I should tell your daughter that you are in contact with me,*' he had written.

'*I don't want her to know,*' Ava had replied. '*It's simpler to leave it as it is.*'

'*Simpler.*' How typical of her to use that word. Tidier and neater and so much less demanding than the truth.

Caddy gave the window a final wipe and went slowly downstairs. She was about to make lunch when she noticed the painting. It was no longer underneath the sofa but propped up beside the washing machine, awaiting delivery to Oxfam. Yesterday she had realised she couldn't keep it – not after reading the ebullient report in a tabloid newspaper about Dan and Zia moving to Hollywood. She'd been waiting to buy milk when the headline had lunged at her. There was a photo on page eight of them sitting, hunched and intimate, in a restaurant.

She was about to store the painting in a black plastic rubbish bag when a sense of indignation overcame her. It was hers; she had chosen it. And she had loved it long before she had met him.

I'm not giving it away. I've let go of so many things I love, but I'm not letting go of this. The decision came with a fiery surge of battle. Caddy lifted the painting tenderly and carried it into the sitting-room. Five minutes later, her father found her banging a hook into the wall above the mantelpiece.

'What are you doing?'

'I'm reclaiming a painting. Could you hand it up to me?'

Over lunch, Jim told Caddy that someone called Melanie Swan had phoned earlier, when she was at the corner shop.

'She mentioned something about an appointment... Is she

your hairdresser?'

'No.' Caddy shifted uncomfortably in her chair. 'She's a therapist I see occasionally. I haven't been to her since the start of the holidays.'

Her father remained silent, surprised, so she added, 'I need to see her before I go back to work. It's always a terrible wrench.'

'So she advises you on your career?'

'And other things. She helps me to advise myself.'

Caddy seemed unwilling to talk more about her therapist, so Jim decided to plunge into another controversial topic. 'Have you seen anything of Dan MacIntyre recently?' The words were mumbled through a sticky mouthful of Wensleydale cheese.

'Why do you want to know?' Caddy bristled.

'You're in love with him, aren't you? Ava keeps saying it.'

'Well, if she says it, then it must be true, mustn't it?' Caddy gave a brittle laugh. 'There is, however, one minor consideration.'

'What is it?' Jim leaned forwards anxiously.

'He's a liar and a cheat and he's in love with someone else.'

Chapter Thirty-Four

AVA WAS IN A compact artisan dwelling, being stared at by a cat. The cat did not approve of her presence; she stalked around the table and arched her back suspiciously. She was big and fluffy and very dignified. Her name was Leonora.

Ava hadn't planned to spend the night at Dan MacIntyre's house. It was something that had just happened. A lot of things had 'just happened' in this manner recently. Sometimes she felt as though there was a current beneath her, and every so often it reached up and dragged her in a direction she had not anticipated. Her magnificent interference had been a terrible mistake – another mistake in a life that already contained so many errors and omissions.

'Ava, would you like some marmalade?'

'Thank you.'

'Did you sleep well?'

'Yes.' It would have been rude to mention that she had tossed and turned and cried at her own stupidity.

When she had seen Dan in the theatre foyer, the night before, she had been sure it was a sign. She was obviously meant to make this magnificent interference – he had gone to the première of *Turf and Roses* too! It had seemed extraordinary; but, now that Ava thought about it in the clear light of day, she should have known he might be there – he probably knew some of the actors in the play and was there to support them. But at the time it had seemed obvious he was only there because he was meant to marry her daughter.

She had taken a deep breath and marched up to him. Then she had announced that she urgently needed to speak to him. Since the play was over and they had both been about to leave the theatre anyway, he had suggested that they speak in a nearby pub.

Once they were installed on the firm velvet seats, she had given him a little homily about the importance of perseverance and love, and how some people were meant to be together. Somehow she had felt her words would influence him. She had remained silent about so many things that she had, perhaps, overestimated the power of speech.

'It's pointless talking to me about Caddy,' Dan had replied. 'It's over between us.'

It was then that Ava had realised that this openness was too late. It should have occurred with Caddy, and Jim, and her own mother. She almost wished her jumper hadn't caught on that railing. She was at sea, completely at sea. Perhaps she had been all her life.

Ava was not used to copious amounts of alcohol. When she realised that Dan didn't want to discuss Caddy, there had seemed no further point in speaking. The Bordeaux, however, had had other notions. She had muttered something about numerous affairs with foreign women, and Dan had insisted that she should explain herself, and then the story had tumbled out. 'I wouldn't be telling you this, only I haven't had a proper supper,' she had explained. 'I should go. I've delayed you far too long already.'

'Nonsense,' Dan had declared grandly. 'I'll get you some sandwiches.'

Sandwiches weren't usually available at that hour, but Dan was friendly with the barman, who had concocted something out of coleslaw, cheese and chicken. Kindness, when one has ceased to expect it, is one of life's most disarming potions, which was why Ava had not even noticed the drop of mayonnaise that landed stealthily on her cotton skirt. Suddenly it had become a night of revelations. She had told Dan about Jim's affairs, and then wept about eating snails with a man called Henry and losing her handbag. A handbag was such a *personal* thing.

'How did you lose it?' Dan had inquired gently.

'I almost fell into the sea.'

Ava had buried her face in her hands, aghast at how inconsolable she was. Dan had put his arm around her as she spoke of the vast waves and the rusty railing and the bloody photo album that had defiantly floated. She had needed a confessor, and in the absence of Dr Armitage or a priest she had chosen Dan.

Women had confided in him in *Merrion Mansions*. He had been so kind and understanding, though a bit moody at times... There was nothing moody about Dan this morning, though, as they sat together at his kitchen table. It was his cat who was moody. She obviously wanted him all to herself.

Ava's sobbing had led to the invitation to stay. 'You can't go back to the guesthouse like this,' Dan had said. The news of the foreign women had particularly touched him. 'My own father was unfaithful.' He had flung the words at the pavement as they got into the taxi.

Now Ava wanted to hear more about Dan's unfaithful father and his dear departed mother. It was a wonderful thing when a child loved a mother – and a terrible one when a father was feckless.

'Do tell me about your father, dear.' She had taken to calling him 'dear' last night. She leaned towards him sympathetically, the way Fidelma Moran might have.

Dan leaned defiantly back in his chair. 'I don't want to talk about it.'

His words didn't carry the sting of rejection. From someone closer they would have, but Ava's dance with him was new. She didn't have to follow the old steps. She could take risks and not feel like a failure. There was no past to divide them, no expectation or reproach.

'You've been terribly sad, dear boy.' Dan looked embarrassed, but Ava persisted. 'You've been very sad, and you've been grieving. It's all been locked up inside you.'

'I said I don't want to talk about it.'

'But you're crying.'

'No, I'm not.'

A tear plopped onto his hand and he stared at it. The deepest tears were the ones you scarcely noticed. They were warm and fat as they flowed without remorse. He let them flow, because he had to; they had waited so long for this moment. And Ava watched with golden attention. It was a very special gift, this silent witnessing, and not everyone could do it. Silence, the right kind of silence, was such a solace. It took away the need to explain and made explaining so much easier.

'I wasn't...' Dan had to heave the words into existence. 'I wasn't with her when she died.'

'Were you away?'

'No. I'd left the room to get a sandwich and a coffee. They said I needed to get out and eat something. I was exhausted.'

'Of course you were.'

'I said goodbye to Gran and Grandad – even to my great-aunt, who was a right old battleaxe. But I wasn't with her.'

'Where was your father?'

'Abroad, on business. He was travelling back but he didn't make it in time. Pretty typical.'

Ava took a deep breath and fingered the beads on her cultured-pearl necklace. Oh, to be missed like that – to be loved and regretted that much! For a moment she almost resented Dan's mother for the devotion she had inspired, but she dived past the feeling into someplace more forgiving. She reached out and patted Dan's hand very tenderly. 'Oh, dear boy, how pleased she must have been to have you as a son.'

'But I wasn't there!'

'You'd only gone for a snack.'

'I could have waited.'

'Oh, Dan... we could all have done so many things.'

'What are we here for, if we're just going to leave eventually and cause other people so much sorrow?'

'I don't know.'

'I was visiting that place for weeks. I saw the people in the ward of that hospital, suffering and waiting for God knows what.'

'But some of them got better.'

'Yes, but some of them didn't. It disgusted me that I couldn't do anything to help. We come into this world alone, and we leave it the same way, and in the meantime we try to

254

make some sense of things. But sometimes there is no sense to things, is there?'

'No, there doesn't seem to be,' Ava agreed. 'We just have to learn to live with the mystery while we're here.'

'Do you believe there's more than this?'

'I try to.' She smiled at him. They sat together sharing solidarity, toast and silence for a full five minutes. It was a satisfied silence, Ava thought; one that was far more eloquent than anything that might fill it. She had so rarely sat in that kind of silence.

She might never sit in it again. She could not risk being this open with Caddy or Jim. They might use it against her, misread her intentions; their memories of her would not allow for this newness. So it would have to be another secret. She was so tired of secrets!

Leonora began to scratch moodily at the door; she wanted to go out. It reminded Ava that she, too, should be leaving. Dan might have his own plans for this Sunday morning. He had been extraordinarily kind. In some ways it would have been far easier if he'd been less pleasant. Now she knew what a wonderful son-in-law he would have been.

Whenever he mentioned her daughter, there was a strange hardness in his eyes. There were lots of half-packed boxes in his sitting-room because he was going to live in America. Her dream was over. And that was all it had been: her dream – not Caddy's.

Maybe Caddy was meant to be alone. What was the point of all this matchmaking, Ava wondered, when love so often went astray? From now on she would have to let Caddy live her own life, and stop wanting things for her that she didn't want for herself. That was the kind of love that sustained people.

'Thank you, Dan.' She smiled at him warmly. 'This has meant a great deal to me.'

'I've enjoyed it too.'

'Let me do the washing-up.'

'No, please don't. I'll do it later. I let it pile up a bit first.'

It was only supreme self-discipline that prevented Ava from scurrying to the kitchen sink. Unwashed plates never stayed long in her presence. For a moment it felt like the world was ending: there were plates that needed washing, and she was not to attend to them. She stared longingly at the washing-up liquid.

But change involved discomfort. She would have to sit here and feel it. The tablecloth was un-ironed, and Leonora had left hairs all over the rug beside the open fireplace. Ava could stare at these things until she exploded, or she could watch herself and all the strange emotions that flew in and out of her heart.

When you watched them like that, somehow they didn't seem quite so important. Every person was so many things at once; no particular thought or feeling could ever define you. Ava would never have guessed that she herself contained quite so many ingredients. No wonder so many young women chose to travel and stay independent and have adventures. Now that she'd had a little taste of their freedom, she could see how much it taught you.

She stealthily took a cotton handkerchief from her pocket and attempted to rub a bit of dried egg out of the tablecloth. There – it was almost gone; and Dan was looking at her and smiling. His eyes were twinkling in a way that made everything seem less serious. Ava loved that steady, playful gaze of his. It reassured you, somehow, and made you feel that you were enough.

She began to explain that she needed to collect her belongings from the guesthouse and deliver some presents to Caddy. 'I want to catch the late-afternoon train to Tralee, so I'd better get a move on. Could I call that nice taxi-driver we had last night? I liked him.'

Dan said that there was no guarantee she would get the same driver; it was a big taxi company with many cars. 'I'll drive you to Bluebell Villas,' he said. 'Caddy can order you a taxi to the station. Do you want to phone her to say you're coming?'

Ava nervously fingered a coat button. This was clearly a situation that involved another plunge. 'No. I think I'll just turn up at her front door and see what happens.' She smiled unsteadily. 'Oh, I do hope she likes the linen napkins I got for her in Dieppe!'

Chapter Thirty-Five

AVA HAD NOT EXPECTED her husband to open Caddy's front door. She took one look at him and bolted down the path, pulling her luggage trolley after her. 'Oh, bugger!' she mumbled at frequent intervals, for her trolley did not seem in full agreement with her desertion; it lumbered arduously over the paving slabs and caught on tufts of shrubbery. Just as it seemed about to topple over, she heard her errant spouse calling, 'Ava! Ava, come back.'

'Feck off!' she shouted. 'Feck off to your foreign women.'

Jim joined her on the pathway and she took a swing at him with her new handbag. It was as though a volcano had erupted, and its molten lava, fumes and sparks were engulfing her as she tried to get away. She had to get away, though she didn't know where she would go. She was just a piece of flotsam in the life they had built together. For weeks she had been drifting without rhyme or reason. And it was all his fault.

'Ava!' he implored. 'Ava, please let me explain.'

'You're a big phoney!'

'No, I'm not.'

She pummelled his shoulders. They were big and strong and made her feel exhausted.

'Ouch!'

She aimed a kick at his shin, but he dodged.

'Ava, those letters–' She tried to open the gate, but he sped in front of her and barred her exit.

Then Dan appeared. He had waited in his car to make sure someone answered the door.

'Calm down, Ava.'

'Why should I? I didn't know *he'd* be here.'

'Maybe it's good that he is.'

'Horseshit!' Ava screamed. At least her trolley had disengaged itself from the lavender bush. 'None of this should be happening. This is not the life I planned to lead.'

This was not the life Jim had planned to lead, either. He fumbled desperately for the right words and found himself mentioning tea. Tea had always been a word of peace in their household. They suggested it, made it and then drank it. It gave them something to do when nothing else made sense.

Ava glanced at him contemptuously. 'What are you doing here, anyway?'

'I came to look for you.'

'Oh, cut the crap – I've had enough of that.'

Jim's eyebrows launched a vertical take-off. Ava had never spoken like this before.

'Where's Caddy?' Ava demanded. 'I came to see Caddy.'

'She went to see a friend. She'll be back any minute.'

'I'll wait here and give her the presents,' Ava said firmly. 'And then I'll go.'

'There's been a terrible misunderstanding.'

'And you're it,' Ava glowered. 'You've been misunderstanding me ever since we met.'

'I haven't been having affairs.'

'They all say that, even American presidents.'

'Especially American presidents,' Dan interjected.

'Keep out of this,' Jim snarled. 'Just because you're in love with our daughter, it doesn't give you the right to interfere.'

'Who says I'm in love with your daughter?'

'Ava does, and she knows these things,' Jim replied with great authority. 'So why are you going to America with another woman? Explain yourself.'

'Oh, shut up, Jim!' Ava snapped. 'He doesn't have to explain himself to us. I was wrong. I don't know these things. I don't know anything.'

'Of course you do, dear. You know a great deal more than I do.'

These words slightly mollified Ava, because she felt they were entirely true.

'Come inside for a while.'

'I don't want to. I should have married someone else.'

'Don't say that,' Jim implored. 'That's an awful thing to

259

say.'

'I kissed a man in France,' she said defiantly. 'The moon was shining and I thought of Luigi.'

'Who's Luigi?'

'The man I should have married.'

Jim looked as though he was about to slide into the herbaceous border.

'Perhaps we should go inside for a while,' Dan sighed. He had obviously been assigned the role of peacekeeper. It was a role he was, sadly, far too used to.

Ava didn't respond to the suggestion. She was staring at a statue. It appeared to be smiling at her, as if to say that none of this was all that important in the grand scheme of the universe... A certain detachment was probably necessary if you had to stand stark naked in a front garden.

'We're all little grains of sand,' she muttered dismally. She felt terribly tired and small and far too old to be so indignant, and her corns were hurting her. 'And we try so hard to think we're important.'

'We are important,' Jim said firmly. It was something he had decided in the shed.

'You don't treat me as if I'm important!' Ava screeched. 'You're a big phoney.'

'You said that already.'

'And I'll say it again if I want to.' She glared at him and realised she was running out of insults. If she sat down, she might remember more phrases used on those American TV arguments – they weren't really programmes. She relented. 'Okay. I'll go inside for a while.'

Dan took charge of the luggage trolley, and the trio sloped indoors. Chump was gambolling around excitedly and Dan let him out into the back garden. He stared at the painting for some moments. It was hanging over the mantelpiece, but he decided not to lend this fact any great significance.

'Do you want me to go, Ava?' he asked hopefully. 'You and your husband would probably like to discuss these... things in private.'

'Oh, please stay!' Ava begged abjectly. 'I don't want to be left alone with *him*.'

Jim winced at being tossed into the third person.

As Ava sank onto the sofa, she realised her husband was genuinely distressed. He kept repeating that the letters were 'of a supportive nature' and that many of the recipients were 'complete strangers'.

'Oh, cut the bullshit!' she hollered. 'I don't want to listen to your ramblings.'

'They are not ramblings,' Jim said fiercely. 'And I have no intention of shutting up. I need to say these things.'

The tone of his voice silenced her. He sounded like the old Jim, the man she had met and married – a man who knew what he wanted and didn't wander into rooms searching for things he couldn't even name. They had shared some years of conviction. It was easy to forget that, amidst this anger.

'Spit it out, then, Jim,' she said wearily.

Jim said that he regularly sent letters to prisoners of conscience – he got their addresses from Amnesty International. This had sparked his new vocation as a compassionate correspondent. During his travels with the Mountain Minstrels he had met some nuns who were finding their vocations rather lonely, so he wrote to them too. There were even some Italian music students who welcomed his encouragement and understanding; Jim, of all people, knew that even the harmonica was a deceptively demanding instrument. And there was a woman in Barcelona who liked postcards featuring the Irish landscape. She was trying to finish her Ph.D. thesis on post-feminism and had recently fallen in love with a hill farmer who wouldn't change his socks on a sufficiently regular basis.

His correspondence had grown at an alarming rate. Now he often wrote to friends of people he had only met once. He knew that some of them were using him to improve their English, but there were also many heartfelt revelations. This had confirmed his belief that many people felt deeply ashamed about being sad and lonely. Their smiles wore them down, and the burden of apparent happiness was only alleviated when someone knew the truth.

'They tell me their secrets, you see, Ava,' he said. 'But you won't tell me yours.'

'How did you get the time to speak to all these people?' Ava asked. 'I thought you were playing in concerts.'

'They rarely let me on to the stage.' Jim lowered his head dejectedly. 'My harmonies weren't good enough, so I mainly did administrative work. I spent lots of time in cafés chatting to strangers... especially women.'

'Of course,' Ava spat. 'You've always had a wandering eye.'

'It wasn't like that,' Jim protested. 'Some of them weren't even attractive.'

'How good of you to sit with them, then,' Ava said icily. 'They must have been enormously flattered.'

Jim chose to ignore her sarcasm. Her anger gave him hope, though that hope was a bit battered. Hope did get a bit bashed up sometimes, as you grew older. You had to learn how to nourish it. This was another of the things he had learned in the shed.

'I think they liked that I was a foreigner,' he continued. 'I didn't know people they knew. They could tell me their stories – and we all need someone to tell our stories to, Ava. People even pay for it.'

'So you *charged*!' Ava leaned forwards indignantly.

'Of course I didn't. But Caddy's paying to see a therapist. She mentioned it only yesterday.' The minute Jim said it, he wished he hadn't. Maybe it was a secret, one that Dan shouldn't hear.

'Oh, dear God!' Ava gasped. The dysfunctional nature of their family was now official.

'Don't worry, dear. A lot of people are in therapy these days. It's almost as common as chiropody or...or getting spectacles.' Ava decided not to be sidetracked by maternal guilt. 'I had no one to tell my stories to.' Her glance was hard and unforgiving. 'You went into the shed and didn't even explain why. How can I believe in your compassion when you didn't show it to me – your own wife?' Her voice dipped and she stifled a sob. She didn't want him to see her crying.

'I'm sorry, Ava.' Jim was weeping instead. He wasn't making a fuss about it, but there was wetness on his cheeks. 'I should have talked more. I should have found a way to say things. I've been so terribly lonely. And…and you never want sex any more.'

Ava was suddenly aware of Dan's presence. He was standing unobtrusively near the mantelpiece and studying a bookshelf. She put a finger to her lips and pointed towards him.

'Oh, yes – sorry. I forgot we had company,' Jim muttered. Ava groaned inwardly. Why couldn't he have just taken the hint and not mentioned it? Their marriage was just a collection of such irritations – and yet… no. She didn't want to think about forgiveness just yet. It was quite possible that he was lying.

She grilled him further. She asked him to explain numerous details, including why he'd gone to Tralee to post his correspondence. She'd seen him there herself, carrying a stack of letters, that day she'd gone to the travel agent. And what about the replies? What had happened to them?

'I got a post-office box.'

'In Tralee?'

'Yes. The village is a small place, and I didn't want everyone to know my business,' he replied. Ava could understand that. Hadn't she often felt it herself?

'I'll show you some replies I got. I'll do anything I can to convince you,' Jim declared. 'I'll stop sending the letters if you want. I want you back, Ava. I wasn't sure about it for a while, but now I am.'

'Maybe I don't want to come back,' Ava snapped.

'But…but you must feel something for me, to have run away like that.'

'Of course I feel something for you. I never said I didn't.'

'You didn't say you did, either.'

'I tried to show it.'

'I know.' Jim reached out and took her hand. 'I'm sorry that I didn't notice.'

Ava didn't snatch her hand away from him. She thought of her years of intense domesticity and knew she had been speaking another language. He hadn't seen the caresses in her dusting, or the devotion in her vanilla sponge cakes; he hadn't realised that the kitchen table shone for him and that even her annoyance was usually prompted by concern. They had lost each other along the way. But then, so many people did.

His hand felt warm and tender, familiar and right and slightly moist. When they had first dated, her palms had sweated when they held hands in the cinema. She had found it embarrassing, but he had found it endearing. Sometimes your flaws could be lovable to others. Sometimes the things you tried to hide were the very things others yearned to see.

As Ava sat there, almost quivering with shock and indignation, a small ripple of hope ran between her and Jim. She realised that, for the first time in their marriage, she was unmasked. She had made it clear that she had feelings, hopes and desperations. She hadn't been able to tidy them away.

It was a very untidy situation; if it had been a room, it would have required immediate hoovering, and many things would have been carted off to Oxfam. But maybe, just maybe, they could find other ways to let go of these outworn assumptions and resentments. They were old; they couldn't waste time on lengthy reconciliations.

'I think you may be telling me the truth, Jim,' Ava said cautiously. 'I'm not entirely sure about it yet, but I think it's quite possible that you are.'

'I am. I really am!' Jim squeezed her hand encouragingly.

'I must visit the bathroom. Where is it?'

In the bathroom, Ava stared at her face in the mirror. She was trying to adjust to the fact that Jim had probably not been having numerous affairs with foreign women. She'd got so used to his guilt that his innocence seemed much more extraordinary. But he wouldn't have cried if he had been lying.

She knew that much about her husband. He didn't lie very often, and when he did it was embarrassingly obvious. His ears grew red and he started mumbling; then, when he realised his own transparency, he often feigned deafness.

Have I just been a foolish old woman? she wondered. *Have I staged a grand rebellion for no good reason?* And yet, even as she asked herself this, she knew her reasons were adequate. They might not be the ones she'd first suspected, but they were just as necessary and true.

'Ava? Ava, are you coming out of there?' Jim called. He was tapping on the door.

'I'm not ready yet.'

'What are you doing?'

She didn't reply.

'We're here when you want us.' He waited for an answer. After a minute or so, she heard him returning to the sitting-room.

If he returned to the house, she'd have to have sex again. The physical side of their relationship had always been more important to him than to her. It was one of his ways of showing he loved her, and she had often denied him it. 'Aaaah!' he always went, in a great whoosh of release; Ava had often felt she was watching fireworks in another city.

I'm not entirely without sexual desire, she thought. *I felt it for Luigi, even though we only kissed.* She thought of her husband heaving on top of her like a big ardent walrus and sighed sadly. Sex had passed her by. There was no doubt about it. It was like that time the Tour de France had come to Ireland: whole towns had waited excitedly for hours, and then the cyclists had sped by in seconds.

When Ava returned from her short exile in the bathroom, Dan and Jim were talking about film stars. This did not surprise her. When women got upset, men found comfort in facts, jokes and resignation. Their current specialised subject appeared to be American actors who had made it into Technicolor halfway through their careers.

'I prefer black-and-white films, myself,' Jim was saying.

265

'They have so much more atmosphere.' Then he noticed his wife. 'Ava!' he exclaimed ecstatically. 'Ava, you're back!'

Ava sashayed coyly over to the sofa. Her entrance had never evoked such rapture in the past.

'I think I'll go now,' Dan said.

'At least stay for some tea,' Ava said. 'You can't go home without a cup of tea.'

Dan sighed. It was very hard to contradict Ava when she was this determined. He was beginning to understand why Caddy found her rather intimidating.

'Dan has been very kind to me, Jim,' Ava beamed.

'Yes, I'm sure he has, dear. And he's very knowledgeable about American cinema.'

Ava and Jim gazed at Dan with enormous affection, and he shifted from one foot to the other in mild embarrassment.

'We would have liked to have a son, you see,' Jim mumbled.

'To go with the daughter,' Ava added quickly. 'Just the two would have been nice.'

'We tried, but…' Jim lowered his head and reached for his wife's hand. 'But it didn't happen.'

'I had some miscarriages.'

'Oh. I'm…I'm sorry to hear that.'

Ava straightened an imaginary crease. 'It's long ago now.'

'But not forgotten.' Jim gave her hand another squeeze.

Ava looked at him. It was the first time the subject had been mentioned in over twenty years.

Dan realised he couldn't leave, though the tea had been forgotten. He knew that Caddy might return at any moment, and he had a great desire to avoid meeting her, but he also knew it would be unkind to desert his post. A small but crucial drama was unfolding, and it seemed to require an audience. He folded himself into a smallish armchair and resignedly stretched out his long, denim-clad legs.

Despite himself, he was growing very fond of Jim and Ava, and he was fascinated by the fits and starts of their jerky reconciliation. He felt that he was learning something, and that

266

a French painter had known it long before him. While lingering in the background like a peacekeeping official, he had browsed through one of Caddy's art books, and a quote by Degas had jumped out at him: 'I do not paint what I see. I paint what enables others to see what I see.'

Jim and Ava seemed to be doing much the same thing with their love. They were trying to find ways to show each other its existence. Maybe they weren't even talking about the same word, but something was there – something beautiful and worth preserving.

Jim was mesmerised by Ava's jumper. He stared at it as though it might speak. Was it new? It was certainly rather flamboyant, but it suited her. He felt he should say something about it. He had so often failed to notice his wife's new hairstyles, or subtle changes in their home's interior decoration. For years she had appeared to wear much the same clothing, though she had occasionally insisted some dress had been recently acquired.

'Ava...' Jim took a deep breath. 'Ava, I believe you're wearing a new jumper.'

'Yes, I am!' She beamed. 'Do you like it?'

'I do,' he said. 'I like it very much.' There was a sharp pause, and then he added, 'Did that man you kissed give it to you?'

'Of course not! I knitted it myself.'

'Who was that man, anyway?' Jim was becoming agitated. 'And why did he kiss you?'

'We were in France, dear,' Ava declared grandly. 'You have to kiss people when you're in France. It's impolite not to. He really was just a friend.'

'Was Luigi just a friend? You said something about Luigi, too.'

'Oh, Jim, I met him years ago!' The way Ava said it implied that love and large tracts of time were completely incompatible.

As her husband stared at her suspiciously, Ava realised she would have to say something nice. 'I think it was very good of

267

you to write to those people, Jim. You're a kind man. Kinder than most.'

Jim looked at her but did not reply.

'We're very different, aren't we?' she said sadly. 'That's why you moved into the shed, isn't it? Because we're so different.'

'And it's also why I married you,' Jim said solemnly. 'Let's not forget that.'

Ava stared at him and recalled how his strangeness – the mysteries of his thoughts, the surprises of his ideas – had once excited her too. She hadn't cared that his tweed jacket had been crumpled and that its pockets had contained old sweet wrappers. She had laughed at his casualness and yearned for his freedom. She still yearned for it. She still wanted him.

She turned towards him fearfully. 'Am I *enough* for you, Jim?'

He leaned forwards and kissed her. 'Yes, my dear. And you always have been.'

'But…but then why did you move into the shed?'

It was a question she would ask him many times. And each time he would give a slightly different answer.

Chapter Thirty-Six

AS JIM TRIED TO explain something that was closer to a song than to a reason, Roz was staring at the advertisement. She'd become obsessed with it. It wasn't exactly a moving statue, but it was a sort of miracle. Harriet said that extraordinary things like this sometimes happened when the universe was trying to tell you something – she'd gone all New Age recently and was forever telling her friends to cleanse their chakras. But was she right about the photograph? It did seem like some sort of sign, but what did it mean?

Maybe it was telling Roz to persevere with her film script. She needed something in her life that came straight from her heart, and the script would be a labour of love. You couldn't look at that photograph and not know that love awoke your soul and your song. Everyone had their own song, Roz was sure of it. The photograph was all about trust. Life contained so many triumphs and so many disappointments; maybe you just had to learn to embrace them all, and that would give you some kind of faith.

Faith... God, where would she and Caddy find it again? Caddy was so numbed that she said the woman in the photo wasn't really her. Weeks ago, when Roz had said she could at least talk to a lawyer about having her image used without her permission, she had declared that she didn't care about the advertisement any more. She said that side of her was completely gone, so that girl was just a stranger. And the awful thing was that she was right. She was becoming less and less like that young girl every day. There was a dullness in her eyes, and she was tiring herself out by trying not to care about so many things. All her friends were furious about Dan's callousness, but Caddy said she didn't feel she had the right to be angry, because she hadn't been ready when he wanted her. She said she had virtually thrown him into Zia Andersson's arms and made him confused about his feelings. She also maintained that people who were involved in the 'entertainment industry' should stick together, because people like her were too uncool and unglamorous and, frankly, would just never be thin enough.

A move to the country was becoming more and more essential. Caddy sometimes rocked so hard on that rocking chair that Roz thought she was going to take off. Swimming would have helped greatly, of course, but the leisure centre was a no-go area because of Rufus, and the sea was freezing. The next best thing was to have long baths and light scented candles, which they both frequently did. If only one could claim that it firmed one's thighs!

In the country, Caddy would grow pink-cheeked and happy as she tended her organic garden. They would listen to Bach and do yoga in the sitting-room and bake their own bread and make potato-and-fennel soup. Caddy sometimes said she really didn't want to move again, since she'd just moved house already; but Roz pointed out that this meant she was in practice, and that she'd probably thrown out piles of junk so she was already incredibly organised. And, anyway, it would all be marvellously restful when they'd done it. They would wear long floaty cotton dresses and big straw hats and drift around the place collecting lavender.

Roz smiled to herself. It was the lavender that had clinched it. Caddy loved lavender, and she loved the idea of collecting it in a straw hat, carrying a big basket. She glanced at her watch. Yikes: she'd been looking at the advertisement for ten minutes, and she was supposed to be buying milk. Caddy was waiting for her back at the house.

As she walked homewards, Roz recalled the conversation they had had yesterday about the whole moving-to-the-country thing. It had suddenly seemed like a daft idea to both of them.

'We just want to run away from our lives,' Caddy had declared.

'Yes, it's terribly cowardly. We must stay here and face the grim reality,' Roz had announced with boot-faced stoicism.

'It's not what you want that matters,' Caddy had said

grandly. 'It's what you settle for.'

'Lowering one's expectations is the only true road to contentment,' Roz had agreed loftily.

But, twenty-four hours later, they thought all this was a load of bollocks.

'Dan is going to Hollywood and Samantha has gone to Nepal,' Caddy muttered as Roz reappeared with the milk. 'Even my daughter is in America. And I've only been to Greece for two weeks. It was my first decent holiday in five years.'

'I haven't stepped outside Dublin all summer.' Roz sighed expansively. 'The only exotic thing in my bathroom is a four-year-old bottle of French mosquito repellent. And any day now I may be forced to do yoga in Tunisia with Doug Mansur.'

'Of course you won't,' Caddy declared. 'You really mustn't care so much about what people think. Holidays aren't a competition.'

'They are in my office. And so are weekends. Even Wednesdays seem to have certain expectations attached to them now. It's some mid-week thing; they go off and drink cocktails.'

'You're a free woman,' Caddy said firmly.

Roz scratched her left arm. Caddy's imaginary fleas turned up at the oddest of times.

'The fact is, Roz,' Caddy continued, 'this Summer of Much Peculiarity, as you call it, has mostly been about love, hasn't it? And maybe what it's trying to tell us is that we must wise up and stop being so idealistic.'

'Absolutely!' Roz beamed. 'Has Harriet been on to you about the universe and messages?'

'Yes, she did mention them briefly.' Caddy sighed. 'But she was also trying to get rid of a set of wind chimes. She's got fifteen of them now. People keep giving them to her.'

They lashed into the almond slices. It didn't matter if they got a bit overweight, since they were moving to the country. As they munched happily, they agreed that it was the terrible

271

myth of romantic love that had brought them to this impasse. It was obvious that they had spent far too much time recovering from it, dreading it, or yearning desperately to meet 'the right man'.

'Marriage used to be a much more practical arrangement,' Roz said. 'And of course there were closer bonds within the extended family. These days people expect so much from being part of a couple.'

'Too much,' Caddy muttered, between mouthfuls of almond slice.

'It's all down to biology. Our genes just want us to reproduce. Those heady first years together are just caused by the release of certain chemicals.'

'It's all very cut and dried, when you analyse it,' Caddy agreed. 'And, anyway, it's not about *finding* the right person, it's about *being* the right person.'

'Right on, Toots!' Roz smiled.

Over two large cups of vanilla tea, they agreed that there would be great comfort in connecting more truly with nature. Modern life could be so terribly superficial. The globalisation of culture was proving absolutely unbearable. If they heard one more radio ad for horrible little technological things that put you in touch with Tokyo at the touch of a button, they would scream.

They tactfully chose not to reveal the gut-wrenching misery that sometimes assailed them. In each of their cases, it was caused by a man and was therefore severely censored.

Roz knew that Tom would always love Samantha and therefore would remain 'just a friend'. This had seemed fine at first, but now their carefree chats over coffee were burdened with longing, poignancy and rebellious toes. Roz's toes were acting up big-time. When she and Tom were together they virtually demanded to be counted. Sometimes they pined so eloquently that she had to stamp her feet on the floor. She usually grabbed the chance to remonstrate with them when Tom was off fetching their beverages. Walking barefooted through lush meadows would surely calm them down.

Caddy didn't have rebellious toes, but sometimes her whole body felt a bit twitchy. It had started three days after she heard the news about Dan and Zia moving to Hollywood. Sometimes feelings took quite a while to reach her. She had watched *How to Make an American Quilt* again. By that evening she had known that sheer willpower would make her forget him.

But she didn't want to forget him. That was what she'd decided yesterday, when she had reclaimed the painting.

Of course, she hadn't realised the implications of that choice immediately. It had remained her heart's secret until evening had fallen and a series of love songs had streamed from the radio. They were 'classic hits', and they had reminded her of barefooted summer days that glowed with the undiluted brilliance of primary colours. 'I'm Not In Love' by 10cc, 'The Power of Love' by Huey Lewis, 'Just the Two of Us'… it had been impossible not to be moved. The rainbow memories had swum round Caddy, and for a whole hour she had been so desperate she had almost gone to Dan's house and demanded to see him. She hadn't known what she would say, but it would have been something along the lines of not wanting him to leave, even though, of course, he should.

It would have been dreadfully unfair of her to ask him to stay; but ignoring him while he was in Dublin was much nicer than ignoring him while he was in Hollywood. Not phoning him or seeing him was far more satisfactory while they shared the same city. Every week she read his horoscope in his Sunday newspaper, and she often watched his favourite TV programmes. They shared the same mornings, noons and nights, and the thought of him being in a different time zone was devastating. As long as he was in Dublin, he was somehow in her life. When he was around, things just seemed to make more sense. He didn't even have to love her or live with her; Caddy just liked the idea that he might suddenly appear when she didn't expect it. The way he had in the National Gallery.

Bloody Zia Andersson… without her, Dan might have

273

come to lunch again in about five years.

At least, Caddy decided, when she and Roz were in the country there wouldn't be the constant reminders of places she and Dan had visited together. It would all seem pristine and new and unsullied by the past.

Caddy's passion for all things rural was not a recent innovation. She had always felt more at ease in the country. When she was a girl, the lush meadows, flower-laced hedgerows and deep, attentive lake had become her dearest friends. Roz, on the other hand, had the aggressive enthusiasm of a sudden convert. She was already planning a loggia and a large pond. Her study would have a stunning view, and, in such surroundings, writing about the benefits of sanitary towels with four extra flaps would surely be tolerable. She had accepted that she would never leave advertising or find true love or even fully understand her washing machine, but, amazingly, none of these things seemed quite so crucial any more. She would submit to a glorious and dramatic resignation. Inner Peace was her priority.

As a companionable silence descended, Caddy gazed contentedly at the simple glamour of Roz's patio garden. Soon they would be having picnics beside fabulously picturesque rivers. Their rural retreat would be a paradise of butterflies and buzzing bees, and, though the carrots might occasionally be crooked, their nourishing and tasty imperfection would be utterly natural.

'I'll never have to look at that stupid photograph again,' she murmured contentedly. 'That's another wonderful thing about the countryside: it's almost devoid of advertising hoardings.'

The drowsy melody of bees on Roz's honeysuckle provided a perfect accompaniment to the serenity. 'Oh, isn't it beautiful!' Roz cooed as a tortoiseshell butterfly landed with sweet fragility on the buddleia bush.

Caddy revealed that she found the iridescent glint of dragonfly wings utterly enrapturing. And Roz decided that this might be the moment to reveal that she had certain

274

reservations about cows – especially when they were standing still in a field and looking at you.

'But the countryside is *full* of cows,' Caddy exclaimed worriedly. 'You'll spend your time cowering behind hedges.'

'Of course I won't. I'll conquer my phobia through hypnotism.'

'Really?'

'Oh, yes. It's perfectly straightforward,' Roz said.

'I wish I knew more about organic gardening,' Caddy frowned. 'I've been reading about it, and it seems to require a lot of knowledge.'

'Oh, don't worry about that.' Roz beamed reassuringly. 'There's bound to be piles of invaluable information on the Internet.'

As Roz served cold elderflower tea in tall elegant glasses, Caddy said she would only request a year's leave of absence from work to start with. After all, there was just the tiniest chance that being an organic gardener might not suit her, though she also hoped to take in paying guests and sell free-range eggs.

'I'd have to go freelance,' Roz said. 'A lot of copywriters do these days. And I'd try to get on with that film script. The peace and quiet would be perfect.'

'Jemma's always wanted us to move to the country.' Caddy smiled. 'And she plans to move into a flat with friends when she goes to university. The timing is marvellous. Chump will adore it, too.'

So will Tom when he visits, Roz almost said, but she bit her tongue. She hardly dared mention him to Caddy, now that she knew the truth about his photograph.

Roz had almost fallen off the stool in José's Wine Bar when Tom had showed her the print. Her own surprise amazed her: after all, he had already sent her the perfume and spoken happily about the advertisement. She must have chosen not to hear him – and she had certainly chosen not to tell him that she knew the woman who had become his model. Sometimes the facts were the last things you needed to hear.

To distract herself from this vexing secret, Roz imagined herself writing wonderful scripts while breathing in the delicious scent of fresh country air. 'We could rent out our desirably located houses here for an exorbitant amount of money,' she said. 'And then we could come back to them if we want to. It's all so sensible!'

Caddy took a cautious sip from her glass. 'I'd need more than a year to establish an organic garden.'

'Yes, but you could learn about it. And, anyway, we'd have the paying guests.'

'And the free-range eggs,' Caddy added. 'I suppose I could do telesales or something, if I really needed to.'

'We'd rent a large cottage at first, of course. You can find incredible bargains in the country.'

'Bargains!' Caddy repeated. 'Oh, I love bargains. Especially when they're in the country.'

'I hope we find a place with a jacuzzi!'

'Yes, that would be wonderful,' Caddy agreed. Then she felt a sudden yearning to lie down on the terracotta tiles and screech, '*Oh, God, please help me!*'

This happened to her occasionally, and she was getting used to it. Sometimes pavements looked terribly tempting, too, and yesterday in the supermarket she had almost prostrated herself in the household cleaning section. The in-store music had been 'Brand New Day' by Sting, and its ebullience had been too much for her. *It isn't a brand new day*, she had thought. I*t's just the same as yesterday and tomorrow. Wherever I am, I'm in this cage. Life has passed me by.*

Luckily, life was passing her by much more pleasantly in Roz's garden. Caddy wished she didn't have to leave, but it was almost afternoon and her father would be expecting lunch.

As she was leaving, Roz looked at her firmly and said, 'There is something we must both remember.'

'What?'

'We're only feeling this free and happy because, at long last, we are learning to appreciate ourselves.'

'Oh, I hope so!'

276

'We have become the men we thought would make us happy.'

Caddy was a little less sure about that one.

'So we must strenuously avoid all romantic illusion for at least a year.'

Caddy thought of Dan and wanted to sob. 'Easy-peasy!' she said. 'Who cares about all that stuff, anyway?'

'We must be focused, and we must not allow outdated emotions to distract us from our mission.' Roz was beginning to sound like an army sergeant.

Caddy saluted her. 'Yes, Sarge.'

Roz leaned forwards and hugged her firmly. Then she marched indoors to phone some carefully selected estate agents.

Caddy normally walked home through the park, but that day she chose a less frequented route. It was longer and less pretty; its only attraction was the delicatessen at the corner by the launderette – and she didn't need anything from the delicatessen. Why was she walking this way? Her steps were quickening as though she had an assignation.

And then she realised that she did.

The advertisement was on the side wall of a car showroom. The window promised special deals on Toyotas; Caddy glimpsed the gleaming cars, waiting and still. She didn't want to look up. She didn't want to see herself unmasked. She didn't want to stare into those bright eyes, but something made her. *This must happen*, she thought. *I have to do this.*

She contemplated the photograph warily, carefully, as though seeing it for the first time. She looked at the traffic and the other pedestrians, at the pigeons, at her new yellow cotton dress. It had a motif of tiny rosebuds, pink and ready to blossom. How thrilled she had been with it. Alain had given it to her for her birthday – yes, it was her birthday! Life could feel fresh and new every birthday, if you let it, and love would always last, because that was what it did… of course she wanted to run, run towards everything, run and dance and sing! Who wouldn't?

'Oh, you poor stupid girl.' The words left Caddy's mouth before she realised she was saying them. 'I can hardly bear to look at you.'

She lowered her eyes. She shouldn't have come here. It was upsetting and silly – and yet, as she turned away, her whole body heaved with yearning.

The girl was still part of her. Caddy had been sure she had gone for ever, but now she knew that, somewhere, the girl was stored and waiting. It was she who was caged. It was she who pummelled the bars and wept. She would always want impossible things, and so she must be quietened. And yet, it was her spirit Caddy sought in every painting that she loved.

She could speak so easily to her students of passion and exuberance; she told them so gladly of lives that rebelled against restraint. Matisse collages, the deep, still wisdom of a Rembrandt portrait, the tortured bravery of Van Gogh's sculpted brush-strokes... These artists were Caddy's heroes, and it was that young girl who had brought their treasures to her.

She could believe them in art, but not in herself. It was always someone else who made the story true, someone else who found love, someone else who could believe it; someone else who was enough in herself, not just a fragment, a torn piece of patchwork left over from some dream.

Caddy's steps felt leaden as she walked away. Through living one lost so much – and, eventually, life itself. Maybe that was what you learned as you grew older: how to do without the promises – you would do this and that; you would be a certain sort of person; you would always see those first colours, perfect and untarnished; life would not diminish you... But it so often did.

She felt small and defeated as she reached Bluebell Villas. Soon, she told herself, all these things wouldn't matter so much. She would find comfort in her garden. She would remember all the things about her life that were true and good, and be grateful. She would look forward to darling Jemma's return, and she would seek solace in her own forgetfulness.

There would be nice programmes on the television and laughter with friends. And occasionally she would see a student listening, bright-eyed and lost in beauty, and smile. *Maybe*, she thought, *we always teach what we most need to learn*.

She gazed at the pink sweetpeas in a neighbour's garden. Tonight she would try to make home-made pasta for her father. But, in this moment, all she knew was that something was over before it had begun. She hadn't let it begin. She hadn't let it be new, or be what it wanted. She hadn't given it a chance, because she had been too frightened. And now she saw that she had been right.

Sometimes it was terrible being right. Caddy wished she had been wrong. She wished she hadn't always known that, somehow, Dan would leave her. In the photos of them together, he and Zia were always glowing and relaxed. Their smiles were encoded with far more than friendship. They belonged together. Anyone could see that.

Caddy thanked goodness she wouldn't be seeing him before he left for the States. She would tell all this to her occasional therapist, Melanie Swan, and cry a lake; but now she had to make lunch and comfort an old man who had his own bewilderments. She straightened her shoulders and opened the garden gate.

The statue looked particularly welcoming as she passed him. *I'm sure he'd enjoy the country life too*, she thought. *I wonder if he'd fit in the boot of Roz's car*. She patted his sculpted curls affectionately. He was her man now, and a very handsome one at that. A small smile stole on to her lips as she searched for her keys. Then she glanced into the bay window of her house.

Dan appeared to be sitting on her second-best armchair, but he couldn't be. Caddy pressed her nose against the glass. It looked like him, certainly. His hair had grown longer.

Oh, dear God, she thought, *now I'm seeing mirages. What on earth is to become of me?*

She stared at the lawn. Never had it looked so tempting.

Then she leaned against her statue's shoulders and dropped her cream linen jacket.

Chapter Thirty-Seven

'THIS IS YOURS, I think.' Dan handed the jacket to her.

Caddy stared at him. Those had been the very first words he had ever said to her. For a moment she wondered if she was back in the National Gallery.

'Are you all right?'

'Yes.' Her smile trembled. He was here. Here, in her garden. And she felt as naked as her statue.

Dan wondered if he should steer her indoors. He had emerged from the house because she was standing dazed and still by the bay window. Ava and Jim were making tea in the kitchen.

'How did you get into my house?' She looked up at him and blinked slowly.

'I'll explain later. It's a bit complicated.'

'Yes. It must be.' She looked away from him. Small details suddenly seemed magnified: she noticed that a very tiny snail was heading purposefully towards her petunias, and that a sweet wrapper was lying underneath the lavender bush. 'I thought you'd be in America by now.'

'Well, I'm not.'

'Obviously.' She frowned at him. 'Did my father let you in?'

'Yes.'

'I thought I was going to collect the CDs from the college.'

'What?'

'That's why you're here, isn't it? You've brought the CDs?'

'I've already left them with Albert.'

'Oh.'

'Do you want to go inside?'

Caddy scratched her elbow. The fleas were acting up big-time again, and they didn't even exist. It was just like the situation with Dan: every time she saw him, she felt sure there was something special between them, but there clearly wasn't. Not any more, anyway.

Somehow, now or never, she had to tell the truth.

'This is very difficult for me, Dan.'

'It's not that easy for me, either.' Dan ran a hand through his hair and frowned.

'Why did you come here, then?' She couldn't keep the annoyance from her voice. 'I wish you hadn't.'

'Why?'

'Because…' Her eyes sparked. 'Because I've got used to missing you, and now I'll have to start all over again. It's been like this ever since we met.'

Dan waited.

'One minute you're here and the next you're gone. The whole thing has had absolutely no *consistency*.'

Dan dug his hands deeper into his pockets and sighed. 'You seem to be forgetting that you're the one who didn't know what you wanted.'

'Yes, yes,' Caddy agreed impatiently. 'I know I wasn't ready when you wanted me, but it was so nice in Greece… and then you – then you…' She glared at his left eyebrow. She wasn't going to cry. She was going to be rugged and ballsy like Roz. 'Well, you know what happened. I don't have to go on about it.'

'I think your version of events is rather different from mine.'

She swung her jacket in the air and tried to look nonchalant.

'Anyway, I suppose it's kind of nice to see you before you leave… or have you decided not to go to America after all?' She tried not to look too hopeful.

'I'm still going.'

'With Zia?'

'Yes.'

Caddy clenched her teeth so hard it hurt. 'Well, then, surely you should be packing or something, shouldn't you?'

'Yes. I suppose I should be.'

282

She started to look in her bag for her keys, then realised she didn't need them: the door was already open. Why did he have to turn up to remind her of what she was losing? This was torture. 'Thanks for coming round to say goodbye, Dan, but actually I'm rather busy at the moment.'

'I didn't come to say goodbye.' Dan looked a bit impatient himself. 'I gave someone a lift.'

'Who?' She darted a cautious glance at him.

'*Cooee*!' They both jumped. 'Someone' was in the sitting-room, tapping loudly on the window. She had round, hopeful eyes, a determined nose and a generous crimson mouth that beamed at them in welcome.

'Cooee, Caddy darling,' she almost sang. 'I'm home!'

Dear God, it's my mother! Caddy almost dropped her jacket again, but Dan grabbed it in time.

The tears in her eyes felt completely inexplicable. They were gushing out of her in a great flood and she had to turn around to hide them. Ava watched wretchedly from the window. Was her daughter going to walk away? Was this going to be her welcome? Then she saw that Dan was rubbing Caddy's back and offering her a tissue. Oh, God, her daughter was crying! Was it with relief or dismay?

'She's home,' Caddy whispered to herself. 'She's come back to us.' A fresh bout of sobbing racked her shoulders.

'Yes, she has,' Dan agreed solemnly. 'And now you should go inside and have some tea.'

'I can't go in.'

'Pretend you're doing karaoke.'

'Tea...' Caddy repeated the word as though it was new and exotic. 'You'll come in and have tea too, won't you?' Her gaze was wide and imploring.

They walked slowly towards the open front door. 'What am I going to say to her?' Caddy hissed. 'Where did you meet her? Was she hitchhiking?'

Dan decided not to speak of Ava's magnificent interference, in case it sent the tea flying across the room. 'She's looking forward to seeing you.'

'Oh.' Caddy steadied herself in the hallway.

'Just say, "Welcome home",' he prompted.

But when they made their entrance Jim spoke first. 'Welcome home, dear. Did you have a nice morning?'

'Yes.' Caddy stared at Ava, who was perched on the sofa beside Jim.

'Your mother has returned from her travels.'

'So I see.'

'I've made us some tea,' Ava said cautiously. 'I hope you don't mind that I…'

'No. No, of course not.' Caddy managed a muted smile. She noticed there wasn't a mug in sight. How on earth had her mother located the china tea set? She had given it to Caddy five years ago, and it had remained in its prim white box ever since.

'I'll get another cup.' Ava fled into the kitchen. When she returned, she remarked that it looked like rain.

'At least there's been some sort of summer,' Jim commented.

'Did you have good weather when you were away?' Caddy inquired, lifting her teacup gingerly.

'Yes, but it was a little windy in London.'

'It was very hot in Greece.' Caddy looked at Dan, and then looked down.

'It's hot in Greece a lot of the time,' Jim said.

'I suppose that's partly why people go there – to be hot,' Ava suggested.

'I've started to grow organic vegetables.' Caddy threw the remark into the short but gaping silence. 'It's only a small patch at the moment, but the tomatoes were very tasty.'

'You can't beat home-grown tomatoes,' Jim said. 'Don't you agree, Dan?'

'Oh, yes.' Dan felt like giving them all a good shake. The strangest secret in the Lavelle family seemed to be that they loved one another. No wonder Caddy was so reticent with that word. Ava and Jim had loosened up for a while, but now that their daughter had arrived they were grappling for civilities.

Ava asked if there were any little mats for the teacups, and Caddy indignantly told her there weren't. In fact, Dan sensed a distinct undercurrent of rebellion. In Caddy's current mood, this interchange might prove intolerable. He knew this by the impatient glint in her eyes and the tight set of her mouth, and the way she sometimes shifted her shoulders sharply, as though trying to dislodge something.

Caddy was thinking of the photograph. Her mother would mention it at any moment, and she felt herself stiffening in preparation. How Ava would enjoy reminding everyone that she'd been right, and how she would gloat at her daughter's foolishness! But what about Ava's own foolishness? Why did it never receive the same scrutiny? Caddy studied her mother's jumper. It was wild and flamboyant. She had never seen her wearing such a jumper before.

'Would you like some sandwiches?' She had to ask it, of course. They couldn't stay here indefinitely without eating. There were human realities that needed to be attended to.

'We'd like some sandwiches very much,' Jim replied. 'That's an excellent idea.'

'Oh, isn't this grand!' Ava beamed. 'Us all together like this. It's so cosy and nice.'

In less volatile circumstances, Caddy would have ignored this, but the sudden smugness proved intolerable. 'No, it isn't grand.' The words whooshed out of her mouth in an unexpected and fiery whisper that had all the hallmarks of a geyser.

The rumblings might have abated if Jim hadn't decided to contradict her emphatically. 'It *is* grand,' he bristled. 'Of course it's grand. I think you could be more welcoming.'

'And I think she should have told us where she was,' Caddy shot back. 'Just disappearing like that – she must have known we'd be worried.'

'Don't argue with her,' Ava hissed at her husband. 'You know what she can be like.'

'What can I be like?' Caddy demanded indignantly. 'You've never known me. You've never even *tried*.'

285

'There is no call for us to have an argument.' Ava's voice rose querulously. 'And just when we were having such a lovely time.'

'Yes, what's got into you, Caddy?' Jim's voice had become steely. 'You mustn't talk to your mother like that.'

'And how should I talk to her? Not saying anything?' Caddy exploded. 'You'd all like that, wouldn't you? We could all sit here and smile and pretend it doesn't matter.'

'What doesn't matter?' Dan's voice startled them. For a moment even Caddy had forgotten he was there. She stared at the milk.

'That she has all these secrets she doesn't tell us. That she doesn't care what anybody feels.'

'I do care. I'm not like what you said.' Ava's voice was shaking, and for a moment Caddy saw the small, lost girl cowering in her eyes. She had known that little girl all her life. She had known her before she knew she was a little girl herself. Even now, her mother's sadness felt more real than her own. But it mustn't. Not today.

'If you care so much, why didn't you tell us where you were?'

'I don't know.' Ava was threading a tissue through her fingers. It was fraying and bits were falling onto the floor. 'I made a mistake. People make mistakes sometimes.'

'Yes, they do, and you make sure they know it.'

'I got you some presents.'

'I don't want them.' The words landed with a fearsome finality.

'But...' Ava looked terrified. 'But you don't even know what they are.'

'Of course you want the presents,' Jim said. 'Your mother was very kind to buy them for you.'

'And what else do I want? Tell me. Tell me what I want. You only love me when I'm pretending.'

Dan glanced at Caddy tenderly, but Ava couldn't stand to see her daughter looking so distressed. Her compassion immediately hardened into practicality. 'Don't be silly, dear,' she said briskly. 'If you don't want the presents, I'll give them to someone else.'

'This isn't about the presents!' Caddy screeched. 'Haven't you been listening? Can't you even hear me?'

'There's no need to be rude,' Ava snapped. 'I don't know where you learned such insolence. Was it in therapy?'

'How do you know I'm in therapy?'

'I told her,' Jim said sadly. 'Why are you in therapy, Caddy? You could have talked to us.'

Caddy almost hurled herself out the bay window in frustration, but Dan caught her eye and she knew that one person in the room saw her. He saw her, and he understood, and he didn't have to say a word. She might never meet anyone who could do that again. Maybe that was all anyone needed: just one person who really searched for them, and found them. Even when that person was gone, you could remember it. It had happened...

Caddy looked slowly around her and, for the brightest and briefest of moments, knew that everyone in the room shared exactly the same longing. Deep down, everybody on this earth wanted to be the woman in the photograph. And, despite their disappointments, they would keep trying to find ways to connect with one another – weird and wonderful ways, or ways that just drove you plain bonkers.

'I've just remembered I bought some lettuce yesterday,' Jim announced desperately. 'We could have it in the sandwiches. I'll help you make them if you want.'

Caddy glanced at the painting over the mantelpiece; then her gaze drifted to her father's face. It looked old and strained and sad, and she knew how torn he felt. He loved his daughter and his wife, and his dearest wish was that they should love each other. But all his hopes lay in civility and sandwiches: there would be no great homecoming, no forgiveness, no peace made with the past.

Suddenly she knew she had to leave the room. She couldn't stay here with them – not until she had gathered together all the flotsam of what she'd said. She hardly knew what she had said. It had sprung from her urgently. She had to be more careful. They were in her home and they were her guests, and they were as vulnerable as she was.

She rose from her chair. 'Excuse me for a moment,' she said carefully. 'I need to go to the corner shop to buy some mayonnaise.'

Her second entrance was much more satisfactory. Dan almost applauded, though he was also glad she had spoken her truth. Without it, this politeness would have seemed empty, but now they had all weathered something and needed the comfort of deception. There was no mention of Caddy's recent outburst; in the Lavelle family, geysers were rarely discussed after they had spouted.

Caddy's shopping bag contained a white loaf, some mayonnaise and a bag of buns. She was about to go into the kitchen when Ava asked if she would like to see her presents first.

'Oh, yes!' Caddy exclaimed, in an excellent imitation of excitement. A parade of carefully wrapped packages followed. 'I got you these drawer-liners in Le Havre. They're scented.'

'Oh, they're *lovely*.'

'And these are some linen napkins. I got them in Dieppe.'

'Oh, how very useful! Thank you so much.'

'These napkin-holders should come in handy for your dinner parties. They're hand-painted.'

'Hand-painted! You'd know it, too.' Caddy stared at the painted rabbits with pink bows round their necks.

'I'm so pleased you like them.' Ava beamed. 'I put a lot of thought into what I should buy.'

'Yes, I'm sure you did.' Caddy thought of Father Ignatius and added, 'You're a very generous person.' She gulped as soon as the words were out of her mouth. It felt like speaking Swahili.

'I'm getting rather hungry.' Jim was a direct man when it came to food.

'I should make the lunch.'

'Oh, yes, dear! That would be nice.' Ava was almost

prostrate with gratitude. 'We've been talking so much we almost forgot about eating!'

Caddy tried not to smile. Her parents didn't usually talk very much to each other, but today they were being more loquacious. From what she could gather, there had been a misunderstanding about letters to foreign women – Jim really should have mentioned this. But the speed of her parents' reconciliation was quite astonishing. She had assumed it would take months of protracted argument, if it happened at all.

Caddy went into the kitchen and Dan followed. 'I see you've put up the painting.'

'Yes.'

'It looks nice.'

'Thank you.'

'I'd better go.'

'Oh.' It was as though someone had turned out a light. Caddy blinked hard. 'When are you leaving for America?'

'Tomorrow evening.'

So soon. She tried to smile. 'Who's looking after Leonora?'

'A friend called Jake. He'll spoil her rotten.'

Caddy focused desperately on the bottle of mayonnaise. She noticed its sell-by date and the fact that part of the label in the right-hand corner was loose. Feelings were going off inside her like popcorn. Now that he was going, she might as well say it. She had to say it. It was awful to leave something unsaid and then regret it, perhaps for ever. At least it would be a comfort when he was far away: knowing that he knew the truth.

She steadied herself against the kitchen table. 'I'm sorry.'

'For what?' He moved closer.

'I'm sorry I wasn't ready when you wanted me.' She stared straight into his eyes. 'And now you've found someone else, and it's…it's… no.' She shook her head sharply. 'No, I shouldn't be talking like this.'

'Go on. Say what you want to say.' She had never heard Dan sound so commanding before.

289

'Well, it's sort of sad. For me. Not for you. I know you're happy, but...' Oh, no, she was crying again. Huge sobs were rising from her stomach. What was happening to her? She hadn't cried like this for years. 'I...I...' It was hard to speak. Her breath was coming out in gasps. 'I just wish you hadn't lied to me about Zia in Greece, because...'

She slumped down at the kitchen table. 'Because maybe my heart was sad and closed, like you said. But then it opened a bit, and it was...it was...' She clasped her hands to her stomach and bent over, as if trying to dull the pain.

Dan waited.

'It was *nice*, Dan. I liked it.'

'So did I.' It was almost a whisper.

Caddy put her elbows on the table and cupped her face in her hands. Her fingers were a kind of shield, partly hiding her misery. It was awful, having to say these things, being so exposed.

'I know I shouldn't, but I hate her.'

'Zia?'

'Yes.' Tears were streaming down her face. 'And maybe I hate you a bit, too. Because...' Her whole body felt sore with longing. 'Because you made me love you. I didn't *want* to.'

Dan sat down beside her. 'Do you still love me?'

'Probably.' She snuffled and reached into the sleeve of her jumper for a tissue.

'Well, then, it's just as well I can finally tell you something I've been wanting to tell you for weeks.'

'What is it?' She blew her nose and stared at him blankly.

He placed his hands firmly on her shoulders. 'Zia is my half-sister.'

Chapter Thirty-Eight

THE LINEN NAPKINS WERE cream, edged with crisp blue flowers. Caddy carefully placed two of them on the table, beside the cutlery, as her stomach did the rumba. She still found it hard to believe Dan's news. She sat down at regular intervals and stared into space, even though she should have been preparing a salad.

'Of course Zia isn't your half-sister!' she'd declared when he'd told her.

'She is.'

'No, she isn't.'

Dan had decided to raise the level of debate. 'My father had an affair with her mother.'

This had silenced Caddy for a moment, so he'd continued with his explanation. 'We wouldn't have found out, only her mother went apeshit when she discovered we were both in *Merrion Mansions*.'

'She isn't,' Caddy mumbled, out of pure habit.

Dan ignored her. 'She thought we were cast as lovers. Thank God we weren't.'

'Isn't.' At least the sentence was getting shorter.

'She decided to tell Zia the truth. And then Zia told me. She took her time about it, actually.'

'Truth...' Caddy repeated vaguely. 'But it can't be true.'

'Why not?'

'Because... you would have told me before now.'

'I couldn't.'

'Of course you could have!' Her eyes flashed with indignation. And then Jim had come into the kitchen and inquired about the sandwiches. Ava, apparently, was famished. Dan had said that he had to go but that he would phone her later.

'Lunch.' The word had leapt from Caddy's lips. 'You must come to lunch tomorrow. Oh, please say yes.'

Dan had hesitated. 'All right.'

'Oh, good!' She had felt almost dizzy with relief.

Dan had brushed his fingers lightly over her right arm. The unexpected caress had sent prickles of longing right through her. 'See you tomorrow, then.'

And now tomorrow was today.

The clock on the mantelpiece chimed and woke Caddy from her reveries. God, it was almost midday, and Dan would be here at one o'clock! Thank goodness her parents were in a taxi to the station. They might even be on the train by now.

She surveyed the table carefully and suddenly felt grateful for the new tablecloth and the napkins and the bone-china vase. This lunch needed all the help it could get. If Dan had been sure he wanted her he would not have kept his secret. She should have been furious with him, but she wasn't. Ambivalence was, after all, her own specialist subject.

The morning could have dissolved into a haze of self-recrimination, but Caddy didn't allow it to. She had realised that, if her happiness hung on being right, she would all too frequently be miserable. And if the only love she could find was stored and unwilling in Dan's heart, then she would always fear it, because its loss would be too great. There had to be another kind of love – the kind one didn't have to find or deserve; the kind that was just there, despite everything.

As she placed two red roses in the vase, she thought of all the blind alleys in her past, all the disillusionment and pain. If only she could wrap them into a great big ball of shadows and light and hug them to her! That was the love no one else could give. All these years, she had felt so alone that she'd forgotten she ached to give love almost more than she yearned to receive it. And now Dan might say they should just be friends. Friends… It just wouldn't be enough.

Caddy stood very still, as though already sensing a distant consolation. Then she noticed she didn't have any cheese. It was imperative that she should have cheese. Without it, this lunch would be impossible. She grabbed her bag and ran down the road to the delicatessen.

And suddenly found that she was running towards herself.

The photo was drawing nearer. It mirrored her own haste and hope. Even her own cotton dress was billowing in the breeze. Were her eyes as bright? And was her heart as joyful?

Yes! Yes, they were! And Caddy knew that, whatever happened, she would hug this moment to her. In it she was not fearful of the future, or regretful for the past. She inhabited the present, and it was enough.

'Help me!' she called out as she raced past the image.

She was smiling because she and the young girl were co-conspirators in a grand adventure: life itself, with all its unknowing and uncertainty, all its tears and joy and possibilities.

She would never feel completely ready, and maybe she didn't need to. Ready or not, life itself would guide her if she let it – if she went where she was meant to go and opened up her heart.

'I'll have some of that cheese, and those olives, and that toffee cake, and the home-made ice-cream,' she told the aproned man behind the counter.

Caddy was flushed and out of breath when she got back to her house. Dan would be arriving any minute – if he did arrive. She anxiously checked her answering machine. Oh, God, there was a message!

But it was from her mother. 'We decided to take a later train, so we're having lunch in Bewley's,' Ava announced cheerfully. 'If you look in the left-hand cabinet in the bathroom, you'll find something that might prove useful.' Caddy sighed. It would be something sturdily domestic – a new brand of furniture polish, perhaps, or the very latest thing for cleaning suede.

In the cabinet was a box swathed in soft cerise paper. She gingerly unwrapped it – and found a bottle of stupendously expensive perfume. '*At least it's not that other one,*' the handwritten note said wryly. '*Your father told me it's your favourite. Hope you have a lovely lunch.*'

Caddy stared at the small miracle that nestled in her hand.

She was the subject of research. Her mother had actually asked what she might want. So that was why Ava had bustled into a taxi, early this morning, for some last-minute shopping. Her father had also been diligent: his casual inquiries about fragrances had obviously been planned. And he must have shown Ava the photograph when they'd gone on that walk last night.

She dabbed the perfume behind her ears, then put some in her shoes and on her hair. She restrained herself from splashing it under her arms. She had become rather carried away, and she was starting to fear that Dan would reel as the delicious vapours assaulted his nose.

The doorbell rang. The sitting-room window was open, and Caddy could hear muffled voices. As she reached the hallway, she realised that Dan and her neighbour Shelagh were talking about the weather.

'Yes, it has been very changeable lately,' Dan said.

'Doesn't it make you feel odd when it suddenly gets muggy?' Shelagh inquired earnestly. 'I've been jumpy all morning.'

'Oh, it does,' Dan agreed. 'Sometimes I just feel like tearing off my clothes and going down Grafton Street in my underpants.'

Caddy opened the door quickly. Shelagh was gawping at Dan; she clearly didn't realise he was teasing her. 'I think he means his swimming costume, Shelagh.'

'Yes. Or maybe a sarong.' Dan's eyes were twinkling.

'Don't listen to him, he's an actor,' Caddy smiled.

Shelagh gazed at Dan and put her hand to her mouth. 'Oh, yes! I remember you now! You're in that ad for breakfast cereal. Cecil and I use it every morning.'

'"It keeps me light and bright, and it's so good it tastes naughty."' Dan delivered the line with jaunty authority. 'Who says that acting isn't a glamorous profession?'

'Yes!' Shelagh exclaimed ecstatically. 'That's what you say on the telly!' She turned to Caddy. 'That's what *he says*.' She seemed about to go indoors to fetch Cecil, so he could share this moment of high-fibre celebrity.

'Bye, Shelagh,' Caddy called out. 'Your dahlias look lovely.' Then she yanked Dan into the hallway, before Cecil could start talking to them about roughage and battleships.

'So here we are again,' Caddy said, as they reached the sitting-room.

'Yes.' Dan dug his hands deep into his pockets.

'I've made us a salad, and…and I got some olives, too.'

'Good.'

'We ate a lot of olives in Greece, didn't we?'

'Indeed.'

She started to fiddle with her turquoise ring, turning it around and around on her finger. It was awful, standing so close to him and feeling so awkward. She wanted to reach out. Put her arms around him before he left. But maybe he wouldn't want her to.

'Thanks for coming. I didn't know if you would or not.'

Dan smiled, then bent down as Chump solemnly proffered a paw. 'Good old Chump. He's very polite.'

'Yes, he is. If you don't shake his paw he gets really offended.'

Dan was tickling Chump's tummy. As Caddy watched, she realised she was trying to memorise his face – the curve of his long eyelashes, the strong, high cheekbones, the broad, calm forehead… What thoughts were in there? Was this another ending – or something else?

Lunch. She mustn't forget the food. It would be so easy to, in the circumstances.

'Would you like some olives?'

'Thanks, but I think I'll have them later.' Dan continued his caresses. Chump's hind legs were twitching with bliss. There were great advantages to being a dog sometimes. For a moment Caddy almost felt jealous of him.

'I think I'll have some now.' She went to the kitchen for the bowl. The olives were nice and fat, almost like the ones they'd had in Greece. She popped one into her mouth and began to suck it.

'They still have the pits in them.'

Dan straightened and studied her. 'Thanks. I'll bear that in mind.'

'Are you looking forward to going to America?'

'Yes. I suppose I am.' He took off his navy linen jacket and slung it onto the back of a chair.

'Do you want me to hang that up? Linen creases easily.' Why was she talking so quickly?

'It's fine.'

'It'll only take me a second to get a coat hanger.' She almost ran towards the stairs.

'Relax, Caddy.'

'I am relaxed.'

Dan looked at her dubiously.

'Okay, okay, maybe I am a bit antsy. That's an American expression, you know. I don't think they have one for fleas. "Fleasy" – it doesn't sound the same…' God, what was she babbling on about? She stood very still and took some deep breaths.

'So why are you antsy, then?' He was standing too close. She moved back a bit.

'I'm not a good hostess, Dan.' She looked up at him apologetically. If only he weren't so *tall*. 'Even with salad, I get a bit scared. That's why I never give dinner parties.'

'And…' He raised his eyebrows quizzically.

'Well… the whole business with my mother was pretty strange, really.' She grabbed another olive from the bowl and sucked it furiously.

Dan picked the bowl up. 'You're not having another olive until you tell me what's really on your mind.'

'That's unfair!' Caddy glared at him indignantly. Then she made a grab for the bowl. He swerved it away from her just in time.

He was grinning dangerously, and she knew the olives would not be relinquished without a confession or karate. It was high time she took up a martial art.

'Feck you, Dan MacIntyre.' She sat down on the sofa.

'Okay, maybe I am feeling a bit exposed by what I said to you yesterday.'

'You said you loved me.'

Goodness, he looked smug about it! 'I said I *probably* loved you,' she corrected.

'How do you probably love someone?' Dan was eating the olives himself.

'Well… it's sort of provisional, really. I need an explanation.'

'About what?'

'Why didn't you tell me about Zia earlier?'

'I told you, I couldn't.'

'Why not?'

'Because I promised her I wouldn't tell anyone. I keep my promises.'

'But it was unfair to me.'

Dan sat down beside her. 'I tried to reassure you. I must have said about a hundred times that we were just friends.'

'Oh, yes, you *said* it. But surely you can see why I had… doubts.' She grabbed an olive from the bowl, which was wedged between his knees.

'You've had doubts ever since we set eyes on each other.' He paused. 'And maybe I've had some doubts myself.'

Caddy paused in mid-munch.

'I was going to tell you about Zia when we got back from Greece, but then you said you didn't want to meet me.'

'Why didn't you insist?' She bristled with indignation.

'Because I don't insist on things. I'm not that kind of man.'

And then she saw how totally different he was from Alain. He would never take her choices from her. That was the only thing he would insist on – that she should be herself and face the consequences.

'That photograph affected me too, you know,' he said very softly.

'Why?'

'Because I suddenly understood why you were so frightened. And it frightened me. I couldn't bear the thought of

297

that happening to you again.'

'What do you mean?' Caddy started to pull at her tissue. Bits of it frayed on to the floor.

'If…if we decide to give it another try, who knows if it'll work out? I could break your heart, or you could break mine.'

'Yes, that's the awful thing, isn't it?' Caddy mumbled. She was now surrounded by bits of white paper. 'That's the bit I hate.' She stopped; then she looked up at him defiantly. 'But it's a risk I'm prepared to take, Dan. I'm different now. She's taught me that.'

'Who?'

'The girl in the photograph. I thought she was gone, but she's still part of me, and I can look after her. Like a daughter. Like Jemma. She only wants someone to love her, and I can do that now. I don't need someone else to do it for me.'

She stared at a feather on the sofa. Where had that come from? She picked it up and ran it gently across her forehead. 'I won't want to make you everything, Dan. I can't. I'm just not like that any more.'

Dan leaned his head against her shoulder and kissed her cheek. 'Good. I'm very glad to hear it.'

He reached for her hand and held it. Their palms were sweating, but Caddy didn't care. It was okay to be frightened. It was normal, in the circumstances. She could sit here feeling frightened, and still love him. She could want to run out the door and still run a finger along his arm, tracing the little hairs, feeling the softness, the strength.

'Maybe all the confusion about Zia suited us both, in a way,' she whispered.

'Why?' he whispered back.

'Because I know what it's like to lose you. I really thought I had. I swam in the sea and I was sad and went to the supermarket, but it was okay. I was getting over you.'

He fingered the coloured beads of her necklace.

'I'm sorry.'

'About what?'

'That it's been such a mess. It drove me mad, not being

able to tell you. The tabloids kept putting two and two together and making ten.' Dan leaned his head back and sighed. 'Zia said she couldn't stand anyone knowing the truth about us until she could handle it herself. She's been in a terrible state. She loves her father – the man she thought was her father – very much. She made me swear I wouldn't tell anyone. Not even my closest friends.' He shuddered as though trying to dislodge the memory. 'We were arguing about it that time you saw us by the pool. It's been awful.'

Caddy ran the back of her hand gently across his cheek.

'And I kept thinking that if you really loved me you'd believe me.' He turned towards her and their foreheads touched. 'But that was unfair. I'm sorry.' He kissed her fringe. 'Maybe, without knowing it, I saw it as a kind of test.'

'Which I failed abjectly.'

'Yes. *Nul points*, as they say in the Eurovision.'

Caddy slapped his knee.

'Anyway, the PR people are going to release the news to the press when we're in America. We want to be away from the fuss when it happens.'

'Oh, dear. It sounds horrible.'

'It is. Zia is the one they're interested in. I'm small fry compared to her, and that suits me just fine. Fame is a very weird business.' He pulled some dog hairs from his jeans. 'They've become obsessed with her bottom lately.'

'Well, at least you aren't.' Caddy put her head on his shoulder.

'They're still going to hound us when we're away, and Zia needs me there to support her. The only consolation is...' He looked down darkly.

'What?'

'That my mother isn't here to be hurt again.'

He looked so bereft, she almost couldn't bear it. They sat there, very still and close, and every so often she squeezed his hand gently. 'I'm sorry.'

'It's not your fault.'

'I know, but I'm still sorry.'

'We both seem to be saying that a lot today.' Dan smiled.

She traced the veins on his arms with her eyes. 'Can I kiss you?'

'Yes.'

Caddy bent forwards and her lips brushed his, as softly as a butterfly. Then she placed her hands behind his head and cradled it. How could she have been so frightened of him? Maybe she hadn't been. Maybe that was the very thing that had terrified her.

'Are you going to America for ever? I suppose I could get stand-by flights if–'

He put a finger to her lips. 'No. I'm not going for ever.' Then it was he who was kissing her, softly at first, then with a beautiful invasion. His tongue was inside her mouth, determined and dancing. The melting sensation between her legs was so strong that her knees quivered.

'Oh, Dan,' she groaned, as he wrenched up her dress and ran warm, firm hands along the insides of her thighs. 'Oh, Dan, let's go upstairs.'

He released her slowly. 'I'd like to, but I can't.'

'Why not?'

'It's almost three. I'm supposed to be at the airport at five o'clock, and I have to go home and get my cases.'

'It can't be three!' Caddy wailed. 'It was one o'clock five minutes ago.'

'Later.' Dan's warm hand gently caressed her left breast. 'We'll just have to do it later.'

'And when is later?'

'A few months.'

'Oh, good!' Caddy felt limp with relief. 'I thought it might be years.'

Dan reached for his jacket. 'I've enjoyed this lunch far more than the last one.'

'But you haven't eaten anything apart from olives!' Caddy exclaimed. 'You must have something before you go.'

Dan glanced at the table. He certainly didn't have time for a salad. 'Give me a cuddle,' he instructed. 'And then give me a

300

large slice of toffee cake. And…'

'Yes?' She looked at him expectantly.

'And when I get back, meet me at the airport in that dress.'

'Why?'

'Because I want to rip it off you as soon as we get back here.' His eyes darkened. 'But only if you're ready. Are you ready, Caddy? Do you want me to?'

Even though she was trembling, there seemed to be only one answer. And it was 'Yes'.

Chapter Thirty-Nine

EOIN KICKED A TABLE leg, and Tom grabbed his arm. He was being a total pain in the arse about the fizzy orange.

'I'll get you some fizzy orange soon.'

'I want it now.'

'They don't have it.'

'I hate it here.'

'I'll take you to McDonald's afterwards.'

'I don't want to go to McDonald's.'

'You like McDonald's.'

Eoin looked down at his new runners.

'Do you want to see the photo of your grandfather?'

Eoin pursed his mouth.

'It's over there.' Tom pointed towards it. Eoin didn't look around.

Tom took his son's hand, pulled him across the room and lifted him up. The photo was black and white. The old man was listening to the radio; he didn't look like he knew he was being photographed. His eyes were half-closed and he was wearing shabby slippers.

'I've seen it now.'

'Do you like it?'

'I don't know.'

Tom frowned. The photograph of his father meant a lot to him. It had taken courage to return home and take it – home to the wounds and gaps and disappointments, and to the bruised, silent man sitting slippered and pipe in hand by a fire that never warmed him. Not in the way he needed.

He sighed and lowered Eoin back onto the wooden floor. Eoin proffered his hand politely when he was introduced to people, but he moved closer to Tom's legs. If he moved away, his dad might go off and leave him with these people. There were some children there – not many, but a few; they were running around and weren't frightened of being forgotten.

Some of them had crisps.

Eoin tugged at Tom's sleeve. 'I want fizzy orange and crisps.'

'Okay. Okay. I'll get them for you soon.' Tom was beginning to feel guilty. He hadn't planned to bring Eoin to the opening of the *Fathers* exhibition, but Avril had rung up at the last moment. This had been happening a lot lately. Tom hadn't used his wok for a long time, because Eoin preferred takeaway chips and burgers. Without onions. If there were onions in his burger, he wouldn't eat it. Even when they were taken out, they apparently left a smell.

'I'm sorry, Eoin. This must be very boring for you.' Tom gave his son's hand a squeeze. 'They'll have fizzy orange at the newsagent's. There's one down the road from here.'

Eoin's eyes brightened.

'They'll have crisps, too.'

'I want cheese and onion.'

'But you don't like onions.'

'I like them in crisps.'

Eoin saw Roz first. She was in a shiny blue dress, looking around with a worried expression. He waved to her, and she swept across the room, gave him a pat on the head and kissed Tom's cheek. 'Sorry I'm late. The presentation went on for ages.' She was working on the launch of a new shower gel that offered instant serenity.

'I'm just about to leave, actually,' Tom muttered.

'Why?'

'Eoin wants crisps and fizzy orange.'

Roz gave Eoin a smile of solidarity. 'We'll go. You can stay here and schmooze if you need to.'

'Would that be okay with you, Eoin?' Tom inspected his son cautiously.

'Yeah.' He didn't look too displeased.

Roz took his hand. Eoin didn't really like people holding his hand, now that he was big, but Roz was nice and would let go if he asked. She liked being with him; that was the first thing he'd liked about her. He wasn't just some kid she was putting up with because she wanted to have sex with his father. Sex was one of the weirdest things he'd heard about. It was right up there with Australian marsupials and people telling you to go to bed just because they were tired.

They got the crisps and the fizzy orange. Then they sat on a park bench and talked about the best bits from films. After a while Eoin decided to ask an obvious question.

'Do you love him?'

'Who?'

'My father.'

Roz looked at the crumpled crisp packet – Eoin tended to hand her his debris. 'Let's go and see if the playground's open, shall we?' She said it a bit too brightly.

As Eoin soared on the swing, Roz thought how much he would enjoy visiting her country cottage. Tom would too. She must definitely find a place with at least two spare rooms. The only drawback was that she would have to introduce Tom to Caddy, and he would recognise her as the woman in his photograph.

In normal circumstances she would have told Tom the truth immediately, but she felt fiercely protective of his innocence. It seemed a necessary innocence, because it had helped him to contact Eoin. Would her father ever do the same thing for her? She didn't even know where he was living. The last letter had arrived ten years ago.

When Roz and Eoin returned to the exhibition, Tom's smile beamed at them across the room. They headed to MacDonald's and had burgers and chips. Eoin got a toy with his meal. It was part of a new collection, and he wanted the others. He lobbied ardently for their purchase as Tom and Roz stoically rose from their chairs.

'What would you like to do now, Eoin?' Tom asked.

Eoin hesitated. The toy-shops would be closed, and they had seen all the best films at the cinema. But he already had the treat of being up way past his usual bedtime.

After a tortuous discussion, they drove to Killiney strand. Though it was past nine o'clock, it was still light, and the breeze was almost warm. That was the great thing about summer evenings: there was such a stretch to them, such a sense of freedom. Eoin ran ahead of them and threw stones into the sea – his father had shown him how to make the flat ones skim across the water.

'He's a lovely boy,' Roz smiled.

'Yes, he is.' Tom picked up a flat white rock with specks of grey and silver.

'Does he ever get teased about…?'

'He hasn't said so. I should ask him.'

'Where does Avril come from?'

'Her parents are from the Caribbean.'

'He's so lovely and brown. I love his brownness.'

'So do I.' Tom smiled. Then, without thinking, he reached out and took her hand.

Later, when they talked about it, they said that was when they knew. Love had crept up on them silently and nestled into the space they'd made for it; when they discovered it was there, it felt so right… And it felt right that it had happened just when they'd given up on it – when they thought they were just meant to offer each other consolation and coffee, and silently understand the absence of both of their dearest dreams.

It was Eoin who had brought them together. Without him, Tom would never have seen this side of Roz. He had provided the reason for numerous outings to places they wouldn't otherwise have chosen to go to. They had queued for cartoon films and bought huge tubs of popcorn, which had remained largely uneaten. They had witnessed tears and tantrums and pleadings to remain in places long after it was reasonable. Eoin had tried their patience and distracted them from their unhappiness.

That night Roz shared Tom's bed again, but it felt entirely different. The first time, their nakedness had been spurious, for they had both been clanking with armour.

Roz snuggled her face into the curve of Tom's shoulder. They fitted together somehow – and, amazingly, she didn't hate Samantha.

'I love you more than I've loved anyone else.'

Naturally, she needed clarification. 'Why?'

'Because you're here and you love me back and you have the most amazing eyelashes.'

'Is that all?'

'You have gorgeous toes, too. In fact, I find all of you immensely desirable.'

'And…?' She looked at him bossily.

'And I can't explain it. It just feels right.'

'*Why* does it feel right?'

'Because… I'm comfortable with you. You don't make me try too hard, and you seem to understand me.'

'And are you going to try to understand me?'

'Of course.'

'You'll never love me more than Samantha.'

'I've told you, I already do.'

'But she's so…perfect.'

'No, she isn't. She kept trying to analyse me and she was nearly always late.'

'Anything else?' Roz urged hopefully.

Tom reluctantly dredged up more misdemeanours. 'She had a ruthless streak. She didn't even tell me about her new boyfriend.'

'Poor Tom.'

'And I hated shopping with her. She had this thing about shawls.'

'Yuck.'

'She wouldn't even let me watch football at her flat.'

'Oh, heinous woman!' Roz exclaimed. 'Poor Tom – thank goodness you escaped her clutches.'

Tom smiled. 'You like her. Admit it.'

'Yes,' Roz sighed, 'and you'll always love her.'

'I'll always care about her,' Tom said solemnly. 'I want her to be happy.'

'I want her to be happy too,' Roz mumbled sadly. 'Bitch! Why does she inspire this spectacularly unreasonable tolerance?' She slung an arm across Tom's chest and moaned dramatically.

'Stop thinking about her.'

'I'm not thinking about Samantha. I'm thinking about a friend who'll be furious with me.'

'Who?'

'Someone called Caddy. We had this pact about abandoning romantic illusion and moving to the country. It was all so terribly sensible.'

Tom laughed.

'Don't you laugh, Tom Armstrong. We really meant it. I might still do it if you don't behave yourself.'

'I'd follow you.'

'Thanks.' Roz kissed his shoulder and started to doze off.

Tom gazed dreamily out the open bedroom window. He felt as though he had been on a long journey – one that he hadn't even known he'd started. There were so many things he would never understand; but that seemed ordinary enough. He thought of his father and how he dreamed by the fireside.

Then he closed his eyes and let the cool moonlight bathe his tired, happy face.

Chapter Forty

IT WAS ROZ WHO brought up the cow problem first. 'I'm not sure hypnotism will completely solve it,' she said. 'It's pretty ingrained. In fact, it might take months before I could even go into a field.'

'Well, it's good you've admitted it,' Caddy replied. 'I'd hate you to spend your time quivering behind the curtains.'

Neither of them had yet mentioned the fact that they had fallen in love. It seemed so terribly disloyal.

Oh, poor Caddy, Roz thought. *How lonely she'll feel when she hears that Tom and I are going to move in together!*

Oh, poor Roz, Caddy thought. *How lonely she'll feel when she hears that Dan is my true love after all!*

There would, of course, be congratulations, and a genuine pleasure that at least one of them had found romance. But it would change so many things. They could hardly bear to think about it.

'I was staying on my uncle's farm when Dad told us he was leaving,' Roz explained. 'I ran into a field and a cow mooed at me.'

'Oh, poor Roz, how awful!' Caddy exclaimed. 'No wonder you're so frightened of them.'

They drank their cappuccinos slowly. They were sitting in José's Wine Bar.

'Still, there are *some* advantages to living in Dublin,' Roz said.

'Yes. It's so much more convenient.' Caddy nodded. 'Everything's so close at hand.'

'We must go to the theatre more often.'

'And we should visit the museums. This city is absolutely bulging with culture.'

'If only the motorcycle couriers were less aggressive,' Roz said.

They both chomped sadly on their huge slices of Black

Forest gateau. Who cared about calories? Oh, if only both of them had found Quality Men!

Roz couldn't bear it any longer. 'Let's have an adventure!'

'What kind of adventure?' Caddy eyed her warily.

'Let's go to the airport and get on the first plane, just for the weekend.'

Caddy frowned. 'I don't think I could afford that just at the moment. And, anyway, I've loads to do tomorrow. I don't know why I left it this late to prepare for next term's classes.'

'What about a train, then?'

'Oh, yes!' Caddy beamed. 'We could go to Galway.'

'We've left it a bit late, though,' Roz said. 'It's Saturday afternoon. We'd be hardly there before we had to come back.'

'College starts on Monday.' Caddy sighed desolately.

'I know!' they declared in unison. 'Let's go to *Howth*!'

So they did.

Caddy wanted to go by bus. She was a bus person. She liked the dreaminess of it. People loosened up and let their jaws go slack on buses; on trains, they didn't let themselves go to the same extent.

Roz was a train person, so they compromised: they would travel to Howth by train and return by bus. They hardly ever went to Howth. It was in north Dublin, right at the end of the DART line; if you lived in south Dublin, it was virtually another country. It might as well be a small French fishing port, really. It looked a bit like one, too.

'Oh, isn't this *foreign*!' Caddy exclaimed happily as they explored. 'Look, there's even a pizza restaurant with murals of Italian vineyards.'

'The sea looks wilder from this side,' Roz said dreamily.

'And there's a seal!' Caddy squealed. 'Oh, look! Isn't it sweet?' The seal looked up at them with soulful dark eyes, and then plunged its head lazily back into the water.

'I want to eat snails,' Caddy said.

'Why?'

'I just feel I should.'

'We must find a French restaurant,' Roz said determinedly.

309

'Then I'll be able to say I did it, in the office on Monday. I'll tell everyone I went to Howth for my holidays.'

They giggled as they walked past the yachts bobbing perkily in the marina.

'How's the parent situation?' Roz inquired.

'They're safely back in Kerry, thank goodness.'

'What an extraordinary mix-up about those letters.'

'Yes, but it's certainly spiced up their sex life.'

'How do you know?'

'I heard the mattress squeaking, and a moan that was definitely female.'

Roz thought of Tom's toe-counting. 'Caddy,' she said solemnly, 'Caddy, I have to tell you some-thing.'

'And I have to tell you something, Roz,' Caddy said. 'It's almost bursting out of me. Can I tell you now?'

'All right.'

'Oh, please don't be angry with me.' Caddy's eyes widened beseechingly.

'Why? What's happened?'

'I kissed Dan MacIntyre on my sofa. And he kissed me back.'

The Irish coffees were, of course, essential. Roz said she wouldn't listen to any news about the Dan situation until they had been ordered. They went to a pub, and Roz told the barman that the coffee part was purely descriptive – it was the whiskey that really interested them. She clattered some extra coins onto the counter and watched as the kettle boiled and the cream settled. Poor Caddy; how typical of her to hide away all these years and then fall in love with a man who was virtually married and about to emigrate, if he hadn't gone already. She would always run to the wrong people. It was tragic.

Roz carried her cargo carefully over to the small table. 'So… has Dan left for the States yet?' she asked gingerly.

'He went yesterday.'

'With Zia?'

'Yes.' Caddy took a luxurious gulp from her glass.

'It's probably best that he's gone.'

'No, it isn't; I'll miss him dreadfully.'

Roz was appalled. 'Of course you won't miss him dreadfully! I won't allow it.'

'Oh, dear.' Caddy sighed. 'I'm going to have to tell you. It's a huge secret, so you must promise you won't tell anyone.'

As Roz listened, she began to look as though she had seen a whole herd of Jersey heifers. Then she shouted, 'Oh, thank God!' and promptly burst into tears.

This time Caddy ordered the Irish coffees. The news had made Roz so jumpy and relieved that she was virtually airborne. 'It is really true?' she kept saying.

'That's my line,' Caddy smiled.

'Can I tell you my secret now?'

'What secret?'

So Roz explained that Tom Armstrong had counted her toes again and wanted to do so on a regular basis. It was wonderful and terrifying. And she was already feeling a bit wimpish.

'Oh, Caddy, should we make a break for it?' she asked, entirely seriously. 'It may not even last. We may be sobbing over our Irish coffees in a few years' time and wishing we'd gone to the country.'

'Yes, we may,' Caddy agreed. 'Then again, we may not.' She smiled bravely. 'Let's try to see it as a sort of adventure. And...'

'And what?' Roz peered at her anxiously.

'And let's not have snails for dinner.'

311

Chapter Forty-One

CADDY TUGGED DAN'S LEATHER belt. 'Let's go upstairs.'

'Now?'

'Yes.'

'But we only just–'

'I know. I'm making up for lost time.'

'I'm ironing.'

'Oh, bugger the ironing. I'll iron those shirts for you afterwards.'

'After what?'

'Stop teasing me.'

'I like teasing you.'

'Tease me upstairs.'

'Oh, all right, then.' Dan grabbed her and kissed her so hard she virtually melted onto the maple floorboards right there and then.

'I hate wanting you this much,' she moaned.

'I know – it's awful, isn't it?' His tongue hungrily explored her left ear.

'Let's see if we can stop it.'

'Okay.' He detached himself and stared at her mischievously. Caddy sat on the kitchen table. She was wearing a denim skirt, and her bare legs swung girlishly in the air.

'That table suits you.'

'Thank you. I must sit on it more often.'

Dan towered over her and pressed his groin against her quivering stomach.

'We can't do it here.'

'Why not?' He was already pulling off her jumper.

'It's hard.'

'So am I.'

She lunged at his belt buckle and prised it open with expert swiftness. His zip tore open as he wrenched off her knickers.

'Oh, please be gentle with me,' she giggled.

'I've no intention of it.' Dan did his best imitation of a growl.

It was a cold spring day, and Caddy's goose bumps weren't entirely caused by passion. 'Maybe I should turn up the heating.'

'No. I want you now,' Dan said masterfully.

'Oh, yes...yes...yes...' Caddy surrendered deliciously. Then she heard a determined knocking at the front door. 'Cooee! Anybody there?'

Oh, bugger! It was her mother. Rarely had knickers been replaced so swiftly. Dan hopped around on one leg as he pulled on his jeans. Caddy grabbed her jumper and desperately pulled down her skirt.

'Do I look as if I've...?'

'Yes.'

'Why don't you lie sometimes?'

'*Cooee!* I'm back!'

'Two hours before you were expected,' Caddy muttered mutinously. Her parents were staying with her for a few days. They had just returned from a Rhineland cruise.

'Where's Dad?' Caddy inquired, as Ava bustled happily indoors.

'Off hunting down some more harmonica music,' Ava said. She didn't notice that the house was full of pheromones. She was glowing herself, because she had located the perfect lasagne for the dinner party. She was organising the dinner party because Caddy refused to – 'I could rise to a buffet, but that's about it,' had been her exact words. All that linen simply had to be used, and Ava was determined that the new French napkin-holders should get at least one outing.

'Have you been *ironing*, dear?' she cried joyously as she saw the ironing board.

'No. Dan was.'

'Well, at least someone in this house cares about creases.' Ava smiled meaningfully. She did not add, 'Marry him,' though the words had been on the tip of her tongue ever since

313

she'd arrived. Saying that her daughter had a 'partner' was in many ways unsatisfactory – it sounded as though Caddy had started a small business… but at least Ava's magnificent interference had worked. Even if it hadn't, she wouldn't have been too upset – not after all she'd been through last summer. Who could say what was right for someone? Just trying to find out what was right for oneself was an ongoing exploration.

Maybe one day there would be wedding bells and big floaty hats, but the crucial thing was not to mention it. Her daughter was as stubborn as she was… but at least now Caddy knew about the bottle of antidepressants in Ava's handbag. And about Luigi. They'd had a surprisingly open conversation about it over a bottle of wine the night before.

'Perhaps Luigi was a dream I needed,' Ava had said. 'But it was never tested by reality.'

'We've all had a lot of that.'

'Alain gave you those scars, didn't he?' The look in her daughter's eyes had made her say it.

'Yes.' Caddy had gazed into the distance.

'I wish I'd known.'

'I wish you'd asked.'

Oh, how Ava wished it too; but she hadn't. There was no going back to that dropped stitch, the way you could with a jumper. And what was the point of these regrets? Everyone made mistakes and everyone needed to be forgiven, but it was forgiving yourself that freed you.

She began to dream happily about hors d'oeuvres.

Caddy had only agreed to the dinner party because a celebration was in order. Roz had received a letter about her film script. The script was about a girl whose father left when she was five and returned unexpectedly on her seventeenth birthday with an armful of gifts and apologies. There was a romance in it, but it was a bit half-hearted. The girl wanted to be a painter and was fond of a cow called Flora, who was bad-tempered but had hidden depths.

Roz had finished the script last November and hopefully sent it out to all sorts of people, who had sent it back, sometimes with just a compliments slip, sometimes with a scribbled note on the front page. The rewrites had been a pain in the arse, but Tom hadn't allowed her to give up on it – and now she had got this wonderful letter from a regional television company in England.

'What does it say?' Caddy had asked excitedly.

'They say it's got promise, but it needs some extra work, and they still might never use it.'

'So…so they sort of *like* it.'

'Yes. I suppose they do.'

'Oh, how encouraging!' Caddy had exclaimed. A morale-boosting celebration was clearly called for.

Harriet was invited, and so was Zia. Jemma had rung to say she would be late and would be bringing her laundry, which had to be washed in phosphate-free detergent. She was working in a pizzeria and was doing Environmental Studies at university. She was also sharing a flat with a boy called Ethan. She had her own room – Caddy had visited to verify this fact. And during the visit, they'd had a disturbingly revealing conversation.

'You could live at home with me, dear,' Caddy had said.

'I don't want to. I need my own space. We're too close. I…I need to establish my own boundaries.'

Oh, goodness, Caddy had thought, she's already reading self-help books.

'You weren't there when I was small and needed you. I was a latchkey child,' Jemma had suddenly added.

'No, you weren't, Jemma,' Caddy had contradicted her calmly. 'Mrs O'Driscoll collected you from school when I couldn't. As far as I remember, she spoiled you rotten with biscuits and Coke.'

'You never listen to me.'

'Yes, I do.'

'No, you don't. I've told you hundreds of times that I want to visit Dad, but you never let me. But I visited him in Canada anyway. Brad and Cheryl gave me his address.'

Caddy had sunk down onto her daughter's bed, and Jemma

had put an arm around her shoulders. 'It's okay, Mum. He's not like he was.'

'How do you know what he was like?' Caddy had narrowed her eyes. 'You were a baby when I left him.'

'He told me what he was like, and he's sorry. He's different now. He's with a woman who's nothing like as pretty as you are, but they love each other.' She had handed Caddy a small parcel. 'He wanted me to give you this.'

Caddy opened it. It was a brooch shaped like a big blue butterfly.

'He made it for you. He said you always liked butterflies.'

Tears sprang to Caddy's eyes. 'Yes. I used to... I mean, I do.'

They'd hugged each other wordlessly. Mothers and daughters... there would always be so much to forgive and to be grateful for – and so much more mystery than one had expected.

The sound of saucepans clanking in the kitchen broke Caddy's reverie. Ava was scurrying around, preparing her feast. She was clearly enjoying herself, so Caddy didn't interrupt her. Instead she stared guiltily at Leonora, who was shading her eyes with a paw as she dozed fitfully on a cushion. The move to Bluebell Villas had been a terrible wrench for her. Caddy had visited her with titbits when Dan was in America, but it hadn't won her over. Chump had thought he could boss Leonora around, but she was quick on the draw with her paws. It would be many months before their arguments became happier and they enjoyed the warmth of each other's fur. For the moment, it was enough that they weren't tearing chunks of fur out of each other. It was a delicate truce; it reminded Caddy of her feelings towards the woman who was now asking her if she had a heated trolley.

'No, Mum, I don't have a heated trolley.'

'They're very useful.'

'I'm sure they are, but I don't need one.'

'I could get it for you for your birthday.'

'I'd never use it.'

'Oh, and we still have that electric blanket – are you *sure* you don't want it?'

Caddy felt herself relenting. 'I suppose Jemma might like it.'

'Yes, of course!' Ava beamed. 'I must post it to her as soon as I get home.'

Ava was about to go back to the kitchen when the painting over the mantelpiece caught her eye.

'What's it called?'

'The painting?'

'Yes.'

Caddy hesitated. 'It's by an artist called Murillo.'

'But what's it *called*, dear?'

'The Return of the Prodigal Son.'

'The Prodigal Son,' Ava repeated uncertainly, as Caddy gazed at her. 'They forgave him, didn't they? They forgave him. I should remember. I've read it so many times.'

Caddy looked at her mother's old, bewildered face. There was such cautious, fearful hope in her eyes.

'Yes. They forgave him.'

Ava's lower lip quivered. 'Well, I…I suppose I'd better get on with the cooking.'

'*Thank you*.' Caddy hadn't planned to say it. How soft and overdue the words sounded!

'For what, dear?'

'For making the meal.' Oh, God, her eyes were misting over! 'And for… the other things.'

'What other things?'

'All the other things I didn't notice.'

Ava stood very still. Her own eyes were shiny, and she was blinking hard with joy and embarrassment.

'I know about Father Ignatius.'

Ava looked down guiltily. 'I'm sorry. I should have told you.'

'There's no need to be sorry. You helped me when I needed it.'

'But–'

'And I know you brought Dan here that day. I was furious when he told me, and then I thought – what if you hadn't? We needed a matchmaker. We needed you.'

Ava fumbled at her sleeve for a handkerchief. Oh, how those words restored her heart's arrears! Her eyes brimmed and she gulped with surprise. 'Oh, Caddy,' she whispered. 'It means so much to me that you've said these things.'

'I know.'

Ava began to sob gently. 'I'm not good at saying things.'

'But you say them in other ways, don't you?'

'Yes.' Ava looked at her daughter tenderly and dabbed her eyes. Then she glanced at the clock on the dresser. 'Dear God, it can't be that time!' she cried. 'I haven't made the puff pastry yet. I need it for the hors d'oeuvres.'

'We don't have to have hors d'oeuvres.'

'Yes, we do. Of course we do. The dinner would be absolutely nothing without them.'

Caddy rubbed her back and realised that it was possible to love and resist and despair of someone all at the same time. Then she volunteered to make the dessert and to iron the tablecloth.

The guests started to arrive at seven. Harriet arrived first. She was usually fashionably late, but tonight she was buzzing with excitement about meeting Zia Andersson. She cornered Caddy in the utilities room. 'Do you think she'd open the Friends of Georgian Dublin garden fête?' she hissed excitedly.

'I doubt it. She's going back to the States tomorrow.'

'Oh.' Harriet lit a long brown cigarette and tilted forwards. 'What's she like?'

'Very nice. And she's said lovely things about my vegetables.'

'What are you talking about?' Harriet's eyes narrowed disapprovingly.

'I'm growing organic vegetables in the back garden, as a hobby. There's still some lawn, but most of it's under cultivation now. I even have a wormery.'

'A *what*?' Harriet recoiled.

'A thing for making compost. You need lots of worms. It's great for the soil.'

'Yes… well…' Harriet straightened a stray strand of hair. 'Quite. But surely you won't be staying in this place for long.'

'Why wouldn't we?' Caddy frowned.

'When Dan makes huge films in Hollywood, you'll have to move to a mansion in Killiney. I know you'd probably prefer slopping around here in your sandals' – Harriet smiled indulgently – 'but it simply wouldn't look right in *Celebrity Ireland*. They run a big feature about VIP houses every month.'

'I don't think Dan will be going back to Hollywood,' Caddy said. 'He's decided he wants to spend more time teaching drama. And he's been asked to direct a play. He's very excited about it.'

'Oh.' Harriet was obviously crestfallen. 'So we won't be seeing any more of him in those delightful breeches.'

'Perhaps occasionally.'

Harriet brightened slightly. 'I saw the photo of you both at that play.'

'And it was on page ten, thank goodness. All that fuss about Zia being his half-sister seems to have died down.'

'But it was wonderful publicity,' Harriet purred.

Caddy glowered, but Harriet didn't notice. She was thinking she must get Dan to open the fête before he sank into obscurity and pesticide-free parsnips. It was the very least he could do. After all, if she hadn't taken charge of his holiday arrangements he would still be living *à deux* with that bloody cat.

She began to teeter determinedly towards him on pencil-high gold sandals.

The doorbell rang. It was Roz and Tom. They had brought a huge bunch of flowers and a bottle of champagne. Tom still felt guilty about the photograph. When Roz had told him the truth, he had been appalled.

'But she *likes* it now,' Roz had reassured him.

Jemma arrived just as they were about to eat. Her hair was

319

magenta and she was wearing one of Caddy's favourite jackets. So that was where it had got to. Caddy remarked that it would be nice if at least some of her best clothes remained in her wardrobe, and Jemma smiled her beautifully innocent smile and handed her a huge bag of washing.

The meal was delicious. Rarely had food contained such nourishment, Ava thought; and a number of the guests had admired the hand-painted napkin-holders.

'Tom's becoming an expert at photographing food,' Roz said. 'We use him a lot at the agency. It's quite a specialised area.'

'A friend showed me the basics,' Tom explained, 'and then I experimented.'

'But your first love is still faces, isn't it?' Roz looked at him tenderly.

'Yes. I'm building up a portfolio for an exhibition. I suppose you could say the food thing is my bread and butter.'

Roz groaned tolerantly. She'd heard that comment at least ten times already.

Ava beamed as Caddy and Dan served the coffee and liqueurs. And she almost fell off her seat in ecstasy when they handed her a box of table-mats featuring antique prints of Dublin landmarks. 'To thank you for your culinary expertise,' Caddy said as she kissed her. The guests clapped enthusiastically, and Ava blushed with pleasure.

She was so dumbfounded by this unexpected present that she didn't speak for at least a minute. Then she had a wonderful idea. 'Jim, dear,' she said softly, 'why don't you play the harmonica for us?'

'*No!*' Caddy almost screamed. Had the woman gone completely bonkers?

Sadly, no one else at the table was aware of the full horror of this suggestion. 'Oh, do play the harmonica for us, Jim,' Harriet coaxed – an after-dinner recital would be wonderfully Victorian.

'It's such a soulful instrument,' Zia said sweetly. And Tom mentioned relevant LPs from his jazz collection. There was no getting out of it: a concert would be staged.

Jim was protesting wildly, but Ava wasn't listening. She shoved him to the top of the table. 'He's improved beyond belief lately,' she whispered to her daughter.

The first honk betrayed the awful truth. The guests sat bolt upright like passengers beside a learner driver. After a few minutes a rebellious restiveness was evident, and the smiles were so rigid they were almost grimaces.

Oh, poor Dad, Caddy moaned inwardly. She longed to grab the harmonica from him, but he was becoming more and more determined. He puffed and squeaked, and Ava hummed loudly.

Somehow her humming made a difference. Suddenly, amazingly, Jim found that the melody no longer completely eluded him. It was vague, but getting clearer. He sucked and blew – and soared straight into its centre.

Once he was there, it guided him. Its embrace was beautiful, and startled tears flowed freely down his face. All his life he had wanted to express the beauty stored inside him. And now, at long last, he had found his way.

He can play the harmonica, Caddy thought. *My father can almost play the harmonica!* In the front row, Ava dabbed her eyes and felt an exquisite tenderness.

'Oh, Dad, well done!' Caddy was the first to embrace him.

'Yes, darling, you were magnificent!' Ava exclaimed. 'I have rarely heard "Moon River" played more beautifully.'

The others looked on bemusedly at these extravagant compliments. The man clearly hadn't a note in his head. There had been a substantial improvement halfway through the recital, but it certainly hadn't merited this praise. Were they simply lying to cheer him up? But it was clear that mother and daughter were entirely sincere.

'I know. You don't have to tell me,' Caddy murmured that night, when she and Dan were in bed. 'I heard what you heard, but I heard something else too.'

'What?'

'I heard the attempt. I heard the hope.'

'And the love?'

'Yes. I – we – heard that most of all.'

'I'm afraid none of the rest of us did.'

'I know.' Caddy sighed. 'But he has improved immensely. I'll have to tell him that his style isn't to everybody's taste.'

'Tell him he has an incredibly loyal following of two.'

'I think that might be enough.'

She smiled and gazed out the window. As the sky darkened, the stars were getting brighter. She watched them and felt as though she had been on a long journey. Some things were ending, and some were just beginning, and they joined in an invisible ocean where all things remain.

She nestled her head deeper into the pillow. There had been so many secrets – too many. But maybe the biggest secret was that all our secrets are the same.

Dan was lying still, lost in his own thoughts. As Caddy turned and studied him, she felt a strange urge to tell him to go.

Go, she wanted to say. *Go while this is still beautiful, because it may turn into something else. I may start to hide behind you. I may try to turn you into something you don't want to be. I may run towards you and find you've gone.*

But she didn't say these things, because he was looking at her. And, as they watched each other, she forgot her fears and hopes. He called feelings out of her – feelings that, when she had been with other people, had seemed so alone. But if he left, the world would still keep turning.

She pulled up the duvet to cover his arms. (They talked a lot about arms when they were in bed together.

'I'm lying on your arm.'

'Don't worry.'

'I could move.'

'It's not uncomfortable.'

'Actually, now that you mention it, my arm does want to move…')

'I love you.'

'I love you too, Dan. But please don't allow me to make

322

you everything.'

His hands were moving downwards. She was wet already, and his finger was pushing at the spot that made her moan. It was probably the G-spot, but it was the E that made all the difference.

'Do you want to?'

She didn't have to answer. He slid inside her. He felt hard and male and urgent. Her hands tightened on his back as he moved within her. He was staring into her eyes in a way that left no place to hide, but she didn't want to hide – not from him. She moved her hips and felt his fullness. He was groaning, and his eyes closed.

She arched her back as he deepened his thrusting. It was like a beautiful dance, a symphony of touches.

The melting, when it came, was long and sweet. As her muscles clenched and released, she felt his climax. They shuddered, and in the sweet stillness that followed she listened to his heart.

He brushed the hair from her forehead. 'I'm sorry he did that to you.'

'So am I. I think he is too.'

'I have this feeling I should have been there. To protect you.'

'We didn't even know each other then.'

'I wish I'd met you earlier. I wish you'd run to me instead.'

'But then I wouldn't have Jemma.'

'I'm glad you have Jemma.'

'So am I.'

Dan smiled at her. When he smiled like that, he seemed very old and wise. He was a patient man – and it was just as well: he wouldn't have been there if he wasn't. Caddy knew most men wouldn't have waited this long for her. And she wouldn't have wanted them to. She stared into his beloved eyes. She wanted to comfort him, too – to offer what he needed.

She watched as he lowered his face towards her own, and felt him run a finger searchingly between her lips. His hand touched her cheek gently, so very gently. Then he kissed each scar so carefully that she laughed and cried.